"Dance?" ... *large, long* ...

Placing her drink on a side table near the fireplace, Brynne let Devin ease her into his arms and along his powerful length. She involuntarily shivered as her body came into contact with his. Her head barely reached the middle of his chest as she slid her arms around his taut waist.

Everything about him was familiar, even the clean smell of his dark skin. His full, mustache-framed lips were bare inches from her temple. She swallowed down a whimper of awareness while fighting against bittersweet memories and the pain lodged in her heart. It was all she could do to hang on and pray the love song would end soon. Why did it have to be Natalie Cole's "This Will Be an Everlasting Love"? Anything but that song . . . *their* song.

His voice was deep, vibrant against her temple when he inquired, "Why, Brynne? Why did you leave without an explanation? Wasn't I entitled to that much?"

Brynne heard the anger in his voice, but she also recognized the hurt. She bit back a sob, barely managing to say, "It doesn't matter anymore. It's over. All of it. Excuse me." She pushed against his chest.

Devin dropped his hands to his sides. "Running again?"

She snapped, "Too bad, Devin, that everyone can't be perfect like you. You've never had to run away from anything in your life, have you?"

By Betty Ford

AN EVERLASTING LOVE
UNFORGETTABLE

ATTENTION: ORGANIZATIONS AND CORPORATIONS
Most HarperTorch paperbacks are available at special quantity discounts for bulk purchases for sales promotions, premiums, or fund-raising. For information, please call or write:

Special Markets Department, HarperCollins Publishers, Inc.,
10 East 53rd Street, New York, N.Y. 10022–5299.
Telephone: (212) 207–7528. Fax: (212) 207-7222.

BETTE FORD

AN EVERLASTING LOVE

HarperTorch
An Imprint of HarperCollinsPublishers

❦

HARPERTORCH
An Imprint of HarperCollins*Publishers*
10 East 53rd Street
New York, New York 10022-5299

Copyright © 2005 by Bette Ford
ISBN: 0-06-053308-0

First HarperTorch paperback printing: March 2005

HarperCollins ®, HarperTorch™, and ❦™ are trademarks of Harper-Collins Publishers Inc.

Printed in the United States of America

Visit HarperTorch on the World Wide Web at www.harpercollins.com

10 9 8 7 6 5 4 3 2 1

To God goes the glory.

To Rosena Ford,
love you, Mom.
I couldn't do it without you.

To my cousins,
Vinson and Jonathan Carter,
your help has proven to be invaluable.

To my editor, Selina McLemore,
you have no idea how much your patience
and encouragement mean to me.

To the ladies of romance,
Francis Ray, Carla Fredd, Anita Williams,
Beverly Jenkins and Cindi Louis.
Thanks for your continued love and support.

One

≡

Brynne Armstrong looked up at the sound of the knock on the open door. Her office, like most of the offices in the Sheppard Women's Crisis Center, was cramped, barely able to hold the oak desk, visitor chair, file cabinet, and sofa beneath the window. The center was housed on the third floor of an older building near the Wayne State University campus, on Cass Avenue in downtown Detroit, Michigan.

"Brynne, you just have to say yes." Laura Murdock, a social worker at the women's center, was also a friend and fellow member of the Elegant Five Book Club. "I'm begging you to—"

Brynne interrupted, "Hold on a second. Let me get this down." She went back to typing the summary of her notes of the last session with Joyce Lewis into her laptop. Brynne was a counselor at the center, who specialized in helping rape victims.

Laura made herself comfortable in the chair in front of the desk. The instant Brynne looked up from the computer screen, Laura started in on her. "I really need you to come with me tonight. I don't want to go alone. It's not every day that a gorgeous, ex-NBA player throws himself a birthday party and invites us." She laughed, "Didn't I tell you I was going to get Ralph Prescott to notice me?"

"Yes, you did." Brynne tried not to wince at the familiar last name.

It brought back painful memories. She leaned back in her chair with an indulgent smile on her pale brown face. Prescott was a common name, and she had no business getting upset because of it. Hadn't she made a point of not asking a single question about the possible connection? Asking that particular question was the same as giving in to the despair that never quite went away. She refused to look backward. She had kept her feet firmly planted forward since she left St. Louis years ago.

"Well?"

"Well what? Laura, he invited you to the party, not me. He doesn't know me from a hole in the wall." Brynne's beautiful face, with its small African features, was framed by stylishly cut, short, dark brown curly hair. "Believe me, I won't be missed. Besides, it's a week night. Did you forget I'm a single mother with a three-year-old to consider? At twenty-six, I'm old enough to know better than to try and dump my child on one of my friends."

"That sweet baby girl goes to bed at eight o'clock. She isn't going to know you aren't home."

Brynne shook her finger at the other woman. "Spoken like a single woman without a care in the world. Won't know I'm gone? Hardly."

"You know what I mean. Both Vanessa and Trenna will be happy to keep her, and you know it. I, on the other hand, can't go to that man's house alone. What will he think?"

"That you're there for the party? That you're a grown-up?"

Laura was right, their mutual friends, Vanessa Grant and Trenna McAdams, dearly loved her daughter, Shanna. The two other women, along with Maureen Sheppard, were all single and members of the Elegant Five.

"Just because they're willing does not mean I'm willing to impose. I'd like to keep the friends I do have. And believe me, that isn't how you go about it."

"I don't see the problem. So what if it's a week night? Your group session at the center is on Thursday evenings. Pl-e-e-a-se. You aren't doing anything but going home and put your feet up and spend the evening in front of the television pigging out on popcorn."

"Honestly, Laura, when are you going to give up? You've been badgering me since you got that invitation. Call one of your other girlfriends. Believe me, you won't hurt my feelings if you go without me."

"You have to be kidding. Every one of those women is on the prowl. This one is too fine to let get away. At least with you, I don't have to worry about you going after my man. You are immune! What's up with that?"

Brynne quirked a perfectly arched brow. "If you want me to come, you're taking the wrong approach."

"I take it back. Honestly, Brynne, you've had days to find a babysitter."

"Doesn't that tell you something? I don't want to go. I'd rather stay home with my little girl and do nothing more exciting than watch a Barney tape."

Laura shot back with, "Sad! You are pitiful, Brynne Armstrong. You should be out there trying to find a daddy for that pretty little cupcake. Heaven knows, you could use some backup."

Brynne compressed her lips. Her child's father was beyond a touchy subject with her. It was something she didn't discuss with anyone, even her close friends.

Laura stopped suddenly, recognizing what she'd said. "Honey, I'm sorry. I didn't mean to upset you. I'd forget my head if it weren't attached. I'm truly sorry if—"

"Forget it. It's okay. I don't see why you need me to go with you. You're a beautiful, confident professional woman."

Laura smiled, letting out a small sigh of relief. Like

Brynne, she was petite, but her skin was a dark rich caramel and her shoulder-length black hair was braided. "Yeah, yeah. I know, but I plan to look good. I'm wearing my green leather pantsuit. I really want to impress this man."

"Why? You don't know the guy."

"What I know, I like. He's rich and can afford me." She giggled.

Brynne joined in. She waved a pointed finger at her friend. "You're so wrong. The trouble is, you're serious, but I'm not about to get into a rich man, poor man argument with you. It will be just your luck to fall in love with a gorgeous brother without a dime to his name."

The other woman scoffed, "Not in this lifetime. Believe me, I grew up poor and I don't like it. Well?" she prompted, as she watched Brynne straighten her desk and place her laptop in the top drawer of her file cabinet and lock it. "I'm not leaving until you say yes."

Throwing up her hands, Brynne said, "Enough already. I'll go!"

Laura jumped up and hugged her while Brynne laughed.

"If you don't let me go, I'm going to be late picking up Shanna from nursery school."

"Who's going to watch her? Boring Vanessa?" Laura asked. "She never dates."

"Vanessa is not boring," Brynne said with a frown. "I will call and see if she's free."

Vanessa had worked for a short time at the center before she got her current job as secretary to Gavin Mathis, the professional football player. Vanessa had been raising a teenage sister and five-year-old twins, brother and sister, since their mother died. Even though Vanessa's modest home was on the opposite side of town, Brynne tried to help her in any way she could. The extra baby-sitting money would certainly be put to good use. Besides which, Shanna adored the twins.

"Vanessa has no life. Has she ever had a boyfriend?" Laura asked.

"Get off her case. She has a great job but she still has a sister ready to graduate from high school in another year. And yes, she has had a tough time of it since her mother died in childbirth, but she managed, all on her own."

Laura said, "I'm not criticizing. I love Ms. Vanessa. Honey, you have to admit she is painfully shy."

"Why can't you believe some women are actually happy without men in their lives?" Brynne grabbed her black leather hobo bag from the bottom desk drawer and black leather coat off the coat rack behind the door. She didn't wait for a response. "I'll meet you at the party at nine. And I am warning you now, I'm leaving before eleven."

"Wait. You're forgetting the address." Laura grabbed a notepad from the desk top and hastily wrote it down.

"Thanks," she said before she tossed back as she hurried out, "No later than eleven."

"Thank you!" Laura called after her.

Brynne was stopped twice before she reached the elevator and made it down to the lobby of the Valerie Hale Sheppard women's center. Brynne had been impressed by the founder, Francine Coleman Hale, and her devotion to helping women in painful, often times abusive situations. The center was named after Mrs. Hale's late daughter, and was run by her granddaughter, Maureen. Both affluent African-American women believed that regardless of ethnicity, age, or income, the center was there to aid and support the women of Wayne County.

After a glance at her watch, Brynne was practically running by the time she reached the parking lot. Pulling her collar up against the late February chill, she hurried to her late model SUV. It was after five, and the cloudy daylight was waning. Once inside, she quickly turned the key in the ignition and snapped her seat belt into place.

Shanna would worry herself sick if her mother wasn't there when she expected her. And Brynne understood. Except for a few close friends, they had no one else.

Brynne's parents had been killed in a car accident four

years earlier on their way home from her college graduation in St. Louis. Quite naturally, she had been devastated. Both her parents, like her, were only children, and had lost their own parents before Brynne was out of elementary school.

Brynne took her responsibility as a sole parent seriously. She worked hard to make certain her daughter didn't lack love or confidence because she didn't have a father. She knew how fortunate she was that money hadn't been an issue for them. Her parents had both been doctors and had made sure she was well provided for. She'd been able to finish graduate school and have her baby without worrying about money.

Unfortunately, nothing could make up for the loss of the only two people in the world who had loved Brynne unconditionally. And she believed her parents would have understood her decision to have her baby and raise her alone.

After quickly calling Vanessa, Brynne eased her SUV into the busy downtown traffic. She forced herself not to give so much as a passing thought to Laura's offhand comment about the lack of a man in her life.

At one time Brynne had wanted nothing more than to share an everlasting love, just as her parents once had. In fact, she had fallen in love and looked forward to having a family and home of her own someday. All too soon, she learned that dreams don't always come true. It had taken years, but she had grown up and put that fantasy behind her. Now she concentrated on what was important, raising her daughter to be a strong young woman while helping women who had been physically and emotionally violated recover and lead productive, happy lives.

Laura had never understood why she was so close-mouthed about her baby's father. Brynne had never bothered to explain. How could she when she'd worked so hard to put it behind her?

Little Hearts Nursery School was only a mile from

Brynne's office. It was located on the main floor of Morgan Corporate Law Offices.

Shanna Marie Armstrong raced to hug her mother's legs the moment she walked through the double doors. "I didn't think you was ever going to come, Mommy." She tugged until her mother squatted down for a hug. "A hard squeeze, Mommy!"

Brynne gently complied. Kissing Shanna's plump cheeks, she said, "I missed you today. How was your day? Were you a good girl?"

Shanna bobbed her head, ribbons and barrettes dancing from her shoulder-length ponytails. She was a miniature version of her mother from her large, dark brown eyes and thick, dark brown, curly hair, to her pale almond brown skin tone and small African features. While Brynne was petite, Shanna was tiny and a ball of energy.

Brynne had always considered it a huge blessing that her baby girl looked just like her. There were no painful reminders when she looked at her child. From the moment she held her daughter for the first time, all Brynne felt was love and pure joy.

"Come on. Let's get you ready to leave. Do you need any help with your coat?"

"No, I can do it myself, Mommy. I'm a big girl," Shanna insisted as she ran over to the row of child-size oak coat racks along the far wall.

"Hi, Brynne. I didn't see you come in," Trenna McAdams, the owner and director of the school, said as she hurried over.

The two had met when Trenna came by to welcome Brynne into the exclusive, gated Southfield neighborhood that provided the high level of security that Brynne desperately needed back then. From that first meeting, the two women had become fast friends.

Trenna smiled, giving Brynne a hug. "Glad you made it on time. Shanna starts to worry around four-thirty. Nothing

I say or do seems to help. Her eyes don't light up again until you walk through the door."

"I know. The child has a memory like an elephant." Brynne sighed. "I was late once in six months, and she hasn't let me forget it. Evidently it must have scared her more than I thought at the time."

She didn't add that it was around the time her little girl began to recognize she wasn't like the other children. She only had a mommy but no daddy. Nor did she have the added assurance of grandparents or aunts and uncles. There was just the two of them, although having friends like Trenna, Vanessa, Laura, and Maureen helped considerably. And Brynne had never taken their love and support for granted.

Brynne asked, "How was she today? Did she give you any trouble?"

"Not a bit. She's smart and happy and beautiful, of course." Trenna laughed.

"She can also be bossy and stubborn. But thanks. I'd better get her moving. I don't know how I let Laura talk me into going with her tonight to some guy's birthday party," Brynne ended, with a sigh.

"It will do you good to get out and have a little fun. Do you need a babysitter? I can come by and stay with her."

"Thanks, Trenna, but no. Although it's more convenient for me to bother you, I've already talked to Vanessa, and she has agreed to watch her for me. I can't impose on you whenever I need a sitter. You keep Shanna with you on Thursday evenings as it is."

"It's not an imposition and I love that little girl, but I do understand."

"I'm only going to give Laura a little moral support. I've got to run. See you tomorrow."

"We'll talk in the morning when you drop Shanna off. I want to hear about the men at this party," Trenna teased.

"I'm ready!" Shanna chimed at her mother's approach.

The school was crowded as parents collected their chil-

dren and their belongings. Brynne, exchanging greetings
with the other mothers and kids, had to bite her cheek to
keep from laughing. Her daughter's current favorite color
was red, and her bright red coat was unbuttoned, her tiny
red boots were on the wrong feet, and her red and white
hat, fringed scarf, and mittens were all on inside-out.

"You did a good job. Here, let's get those boots
changed." Brynne soon had Shanna redressed, and then
hurried her out the door.

Brynne couldn't share Laura's interest in the men. As far
as she was concerned, the men at the party or anywhere
else didn't matter. She had enough problems without looking for more. A man was the reason she didn't even know
the name of her baby's father. And she was destined to continue to be haunted because of it.

Even though he was surrounded by friends and family,
Devin Prescott was trying not to show that he was bored.
At thirty, he was one of the select African-American star
quarterbacks playing in the NFL. The St. Louis Rams' sea-
soned player was used to a certain amount of play from the
ladies, but after years of being in the limelight, the attention had gotten old.

"What's the matter, big brother?" Anna Prescott Mathis
said as she linked her arm through his. "You're supposed to
be smiling, not frowning. This is a party, remember?"

Devin's smile was indulgent as he looked down at his
baby sister. He was genuinely pleased by the love and happiness she'd gained from her recent marriage to Gavin
Mathis.

The Prescotts were a tight-knit family. Devin, like their
oldest brother, Wesley, and their cousin, Ralph, had had his
doubts about the lovebirds. It stemmed from the fact that
Gavin, like them, was a professional jock and long-time
friend. They knew Gavin's reputation with the ladies as
well as they knew their own, and because of that, they
weren't about to make it easy for him to take advantage of

Anna. An experienced ladies' man wasn't what any of them wanted for their beloved sister and cousin, but once Gavin had popped the question, the objections slipped away.

Devin had flown home to Detroit for the Valentine's Day wedding and wound up staying. Used to coming and going as he pleased, he had impulsively dropped a bundle on a three-bedroom condominium. He told himself it was a good investment and that he could either rent the place out during the football season or let it stand. It wouldn't be a problem, considering he had plenty of family to check on it after he flew back to St. Louis at the beginning of the football season. The move allowed him to train with Wesley and Gavin during their off-season, something that would keep all three of them in top shape for the upcoming season.

"Where is your husband? Shouldn't you be annoying him?" Out of habit, Devin added gruffness to his deep voice. Although he'd perfected a rough exterior, effective during the NFL season, when it came to his family he was pure marshmallow, and they knew it.

Their parents, Lester and Donna Prescott, had raised them in a home filled with love. There was never any doubt that if Devin needed anything, his family would be there for him. Of the four siblings, Wayne, at fifteen, was the youngest. Their cousin, Ralph, had been raised with them after his parents died.

"My husband doesn't need me to follow him around like a lost sheep. I'm waiting," Anna persisted. She was a professional chef, and her catering company was supplying the food for the evening.

"For what? You think I need a babysitter?"

At six-three, Devin was a tall, broad-shouldered man. His skin was a deep mocha brown, his eyes were dark gray, and he kept his black hair cut close. He was the most reserved and tight-lipped of the men in the family.

"You need something, big brother. You've been scowling ever since you arrived. This is Ralph's birthday party, loosen up. Try smiling once in a while. You're scaring the ladies," she said as she took a sip from his drink. "It's sparkling water," she complained of the clear liquid with a lime floating in the squat tumbler.

Devin chuckled. "What did you expect? You know I'm in training, as are your husband and older brother. And I'm not scowling. But I do get a bit tired of some of these lovely sharks circling in here. Where does Ralph find them all? Too many of the beautiful ladies here are after what they can get and not bothering to hide it. The instant they realize that a man has a couple dimes to rub together, they get that sparkle in their eyes . . . dollar signs. You'd think Ralph would be sick of it," he ended in disgust.

Even though he and Ralph were cousins, best friends, and business partners, Devin didn't share his taste in women.

Anna laughed. "You know our cousin. He doesn't care as long as the lady in question is young and pretty. He's too busy having fun to even consider settling down any time soon. You, on the other hand, care too deeply. When are you going to talk about her?"

Two

Devin stiffened and moved back as if he'd just realized he'd stepped into something decidedly unpleasant. "Her? Who?"

"The woman who hurt you." At his look of shock, she whispered, "What? You think I haven't noticed? Something has changed you since you moved to St. Louis. And unlike Ralph, you don't talk about your feelings, but that doesn't mean you don't have any."

His scowl was back. "Look, just because I don't wear my feelings on my sleeve doesn't mean there's a problem. If there was something or rather someone to talk about, you all would have known about it. I'm not that closemouthed."

Anna laughed up at him. "Yes, you are, but I love you anyway."

He sighed. "Why are you getting so serious on me tonight, sis? You expecting or something?"

She laughed. "This isn't about raging female hormones. This is about you. All I want is for you to be happy. There's nothing wrong with that, is there?"

"Uh-oh. Sounds serious," Gavin Mathis, Anna's husband, wide receiver for the Detroit Lions, said. Gavin was accompanied by teammate and brother-in-law Wesley, as well as Kelli Warner-Prescott, Wesley's wife.

"Looks like she nailed you, little bro," Wesley added with a wide grin, his arm around Kelli's waist.

"I'm admitting nothing. My daddy didn't raise any fools," Devin said, grateful for the diversion. "I think what I need is a real drink. Excuse me."

Devin walked out of the crowded living room, and wove his way through the packed hallway toward the kitchen, where a temporary bar had been set up. He waved at Janet Raye Matthews, Anna's friend and business partner, who along with two assistants was busy refilling buffet items in the dining room.

He grabbed a beer, wondering where he could go to get a little peace, but knew it was a wasted effort. It was too early for him to duck out. He frowned as he took a drag from the bottle, knowing his baby sister had come too close to the truth. Hell, he had almost asked her how she knew, before he thought better of it.

There was no way his sister could have known that he'd done just that, fallen in love too quickly and lived to regret it. That mistake had cost him emotionally, and he'd been careful not to repeat it. Anna couldn't know because he had kept the information to himself, not even Ralph, his confidant, knew. Anna was wrong about one thing. Talking about it wouldn't change what happened. In handling it his way, he hadn't burdened his family with his broken heart and wounded pride.

He hadn't set out to keep Brynne a secret, especially not from his family. He'd intended to wait until he had something to tell. Yet he'd lost his head early on in the relationship, and before he knew it, he'd picked out the ring, planned the candlelit dinner that he would prepare himself. As it turned out, it had all been for nothing. She'd walked out of his life and never bothered to look back.

Afterward he congratulated himself on keeping his mouth closed. It had been so much easier to go on as if it had never happened. His pride, not the depth of his feelings, had been the only thing that kept him from going after her like a lovesick fool. It was all he had left.

"Fool," he mumbled aloud.

"Did you say something, handsome?" An attractive woman paused to look up at him as he slowly threaded his way back through the crowded central hallway.

He stopped, forcing a smile. "Nothing that matters."

"You're Ralph's cousin, aren't you. The professional football player." She stepped into his path. "All you Prescott men are tall, dark, and athletic. What did your mothers put into your formula?"

Devin suppressed a frustrated groan as he wondered why he even bothered to come. He was not fit company for anyone. Just then the front door opened and there were more new arrivals, mostly women, all friends of Ralph. Music poured from the sophisticated sound system.

"Well?"

"As far as I know, only a few baby vitamins." He waited for her to ask if he was as rich as his older brother and cousin, but evidently good manners finally won the day. He asked, "Enjoying yourself?"

"Very much. And it's Shirley." She offered her hand.

"Devin." He shook her hand.

"So how long have you been playing pro ball?"

"A few years."

"Are you with the Lions'?"

"St. Louis Rams."

The doorbell sounded yet again, and Devin absently watched Ralph move to answer it. He noticed two more ladies walk inside. "Football runs in the family. Our dad coaches high school football. I wouldn't—" He stopped suddenly.

Devin's gaze was on one of the women at the door. Even though she offered only a profile, he would have recognized her anywhere. She barely stood above five-two, yet her small body was shapely, with sweet curves above and below her tiny waist. Her soft brown curls had been cut short, a decided difference that in no way detracted from her feminine appeal. She wore a dark red pant suit and her trademark four-inch-high heels. He almost laughed, recalling she never wore flats if she could help it. He doubted she even owned a pair of sneakers.

He didn't need to approach to know that her voice was warm and husky, or that she preferred chocolate ice cream with almonds to cheesecake. No, he didn't need to get close to know her pale brown skin smelled like crushed gardenias . . . her signature scent. It was a deeply feminine scent that suited her to perfection.

Her African features were small, her mouth lush and incredibly sweet, while her skin was as soft as raw silk. How could any man forget the feel of her in his arms, her delectable body moist, open, and accepting his? She satisfied him in ways no other woman had even come close to doing and kept him coming back for more of the same.

She used to say that he took life much too seriously, and she'd tried to loosen him up a bit. They'd laughed, they'd played, but most important, they'd loved. Four years later, he hadn't forgotten a single thing about her, including the fact that she had turned down his marriage proposal as if he and what they'd shared meant nothing to her.

"Devin, would you care—"

He nearly jumped, having forgotten the woman at his side. With considerable effort, he forced his eyes away from the foyer and asked, "Sorry. What did you say?"

She pouted prettily, but it didn't capture his interest. "I asked if you'd like to dance."

"Maybe later. Excuse me." Devin walked away and reached the arched entrance into the living room a few paces behind the late arrivals. He placed a restraining hand on his cousin's shoulder. "How well do you know her?"

Ralph, who topped his cousin by three inches, looked genuinely perplexed. "Who?"

"Brynne Armstrong," was all he could get past the constriction in his throat. His heart was still hammering as he watched her talking to the woman she'd arrived with.

"Brynne? I don't know a Brynne." Ralph looked at him sharply as he handed their coats to one of the maids hired for the night.

Devin snapped impatiently, "I'm talking about the petite lady in red."

"Oh yeah. Laura's friend. I just met her a moment ago, but obviously you know her. She's a knockout, if you like them in small packages." Ralph asked, "Where'd you meet her?"

"St. Louis, a few years back." When Devin would have walked away, Ralph stopped him by placing a hand on his arm.

"What's wrong?"

Devin said offhandedly, "Not a thing. She's an old friend."

"Yeah? Then why do I get the feeling you aren't pleased to see her?"

Devin tried without success to look away, but his hungry gaze missed nothing as his eyes traveled over her shapely figure. How could it be? She was even more beautiful than he remembered. Suddenly he was bombarded with emotions he hadn't felt in years, not since the day Brynne disappeared from his life. The most recognizable were a combination of hurt, anger, and desire. The anger prevailed as he took note of the looks she was getting from every other man in the room. He told himself he should leave before he said or did something he'd regret.

"Dev?"

Devin looked his cousin in the eyes as he said, "Because I'm not. Excuse me."

Taking a deep, calming breath, he moved forward, determined to conceal his emotions. Knowledge was power, and he was not about to give her any control over him, not ever again.

* * *

"I think I'll check out the food. Coming?" Laura asked.

"You go ahead. I'm not hungry," Brynne said absently, amazed by the sheer number of people.

Laura nodded before she walked away.

Brynne sensed someone was standing behind her. When she glanced over her shoulder, she instantly froze as she stared up at the man she had once loved with all her heart. She took a deep breath, as if filling her lungs could clear her head and eliminate the panic.

"Devin . . ." she finally said with equal measures of disbelief and apprehension. "What are you doing here? I mean, I didn't expect to—"

"See me here? Or see me, ever again?" he asked evenly, although a muscle jumped in his jaw as if he were grinding his teeth.

"I have no expectations where you are concerned." She angled her chin upward, trying not to notice the way his dark gray eyes followed the lines of her body or the heat that look generated so deep inside. He was every bit as good-looking as he had been when she ran from him. He hadn't changed, but she had . . . big time. "So you've moved back to Detroit?"

"Yes, for the time being. I'm still with the Rams, but when I came home for my sister's wedding, I decided to stay through the off season. How about you? Are you living in the area?"

"I moved back home and finished my master's at Wayne State. I work at a women's crisis center in the city." She took care to keep her explanation to a minimum.

"Good for you. We both know how much those degrees mean to you, only one more to go. No sacrifice too great."

Brynne's eyes went wide, but she said nothing. It was the reason she'd given him for turning down his marriage proposal. At the time, while it had sounded like an excuse to him, it had been the simple truth. The last promise she'd made her mother before her death was that she would not let anyone or anything stop her from completing her education.

Devin stood with his arms folded over his wide, deep chest. "What brought you out on such a cold, bitter night? My cousin tells me you came with a friend."

"Cousin? Who?"

"Ralph Prescott, our host for the evening."

"I didn't realize. Yes, I came with a coworker." She berated herself for not asking instead of preferring to believe the familiar last name was a coincidence. She rushed on to say, "If I'd known, I wouldn't have—" then stopped abruptly.

"Wouldn't have come?" he finished for her. "Yeah, I guessed that much."

"I wouldn't have wanted to intrude."

"There isn't a problem, Brynne. It's always good to see an old friend."

"Friendship" was a woefully inadequate word to describe what they'd once shared, but she chose not to make an issue of it. They'd first met at a mutual friend's home while attending a dinner party and hit it off instantly. Their attraction was very much in evidence that first night. Soon they were quickly drawn into an intense love affair—an affair that ended badly.

"You're not wearing a ring on that left finger. Are you here looking?"

Brynne managed a smile, recalling that there were no secrets or subterfuge with this man. It was simply not a part of his makeup. He was the most straightforward, honest, and serious man she'd ever met. He was also private and didn't care to talk about his personal life. Back in St. Louis his openness had been a refreshing change. Now it felt intrusive, but now she was the one with the secrets.

"How have you been, Devin? You are looking well. No injuries?" As her eyes followed his long, lean, muscular length, a tingle of awareness raced along her spine. He still took excellent care of himself, but then he was a professional athlete.

He was indeed a very handsome, wealthy man. Women

found him attractive, but he had never been on the make. Collecting women like trophies, as some of his teammates did, wasn't an option for him. It was simply not part of his makeup.

From the first, he let her know he wanted her and he went after her, determined to make her his. She didn't stand a chance against his formidable personality and intense masculine appeal. Back then she wasn't trying to get away from him. She enjoyed the attention, and she adored him. He had been an unselfish lover who made sure she knew that she mattered to him.

Even though it had bothered her that there were plenty of women willing to do just about anything to gain his interest, it had never fazed him. The women had tried everything, but it hadn't worked, not with Devin. He hadn't hesitated to let anyone who got in his way know he was with Brynne. She'd never had a reason to doubt his devotion or commitment to their relationship. Devin Prescott was a man of conviction and courage. He'd never run from a fight.

The problems were hers alone. She was the coward, not he. She wasn't foolish enough to think he'd ever understand her overwhelming fears or shame. She hadn't been able to face him. She took the easy way out . . . she ran.

He said, "I'm well . . . busy. I took a hard hit two years back. Had some shoulder surgery to repair the damage last year, but the arm's fine now. Would you care for something to eat? Drink?"

What she wanted was to leave, to pretend that she hadn't seen him, to pretend that it didn't still hurt just to look at him. She didn't need this, would never be ready for it.

What they shared was in the past. None of it mattered anymore. Taking a deep, fortifying breath, she reminded herself that they had both moved on with their lives. Revisiting the past would serve no useful purpose.

"Brynne?"

"I'm not hungry. I ate with—" She stopped, then hastily

added, "I had dinner before I came, but I could use something to drink. A Pepsi?" She looked up at him expectantly.

She breathed a quick sigh of relief, for if he noticed the slip he didn't comment. Her plan was pitifully simple, just as soon as he went one way, she intended to go in the other. There was too much he didn't know, too much she could never tell him. She was not the same woman who had fallen in love with him four years ago.

Instead of walking off, he cupped her elbow and urged her along with him through the crush of people toward the kitchen. When they passed Laura, in conversation with some guy, Brynne tried and failed to catch her eye.

"Your cousin has quite a crowd here tonight."

"Mmm, too many people, if you ask me."

Brynne noticed when Devin nodded to another man, but didn't stop to talk or make introductions. Once she had her drink in hand, he urged her along with him.

"Where are we going?" She stopped suddenly, almost running into his broad back.

"To the den, where we can hopefully hear ourselves talking."

Brynne nodded her agreement, even though the last thing she wanted was to have a conversation with this man. The den was toward the back of the large house and was only a little less crowded. Taking a long sip of her soft drink, she looked around, all the while wishing that she hadn't let Laura talk her into coming tonight. She didn't ask for this, didn't need it. She had worked so hard to get her life back on track . . . now this!

"Dance?" Devin held out a large, long-fingered hand.

Placing her drink on a side table near the fireplace, where a fire burned in the screen covered grate, Brynne let Devin ease her into his arms and along his powerful length. She involuntarily shivered as her body came into contact with his. Her head barely reached the middle of his chest as she slid her arms around his taut waist.

Everything about him was familiar, even the clean smell

of his dark skin. His full mustache-framed lips were bare inches from her temple. She swallowed down a whimper of awareness while fighting against bittersweet memories and the pain lodged in her heart. It was all she could do to hang on and pray the love song would end soon. Why did it have to be Natalie Cole's "This Will Be (An Everlasting Love)"? Anything but that song . . . their song.

His voice was deep, vibrant against her temple when he inquired, "Why, Brynne? Why did you leave without an explanation? Wasn't I entitled to that much?"

Brynne heard the anger in his voice, but she also recognized the hurt. She bit back a sob, barely managing to say, "It doesn't matter anymore. It's over. All of it. Excuse me." She pushed against his chest.

Devin dropped his hands to his sides. "Running again?"

She snapped, "Too bad, Devin, that everyone can't be perfect like you. You've never had to run from anything in your life, have you? Excuse me. I need to find the restroom."

Three

It took three tries before she found the correct door. She didn't breathe easy until she locked it behind her. As she stared into the mirror without seeing her image, Brynne's eyes filled with tears.

Devin had never backed down from anything in his life. It was not part of his makeup. That was the reason she'd feared his response. His involvement would not only exacerbate the situation, but could also put his career in jeopardy if he became embroiled in controversy. She had done the right thing . . . done the only thing she could do at the time to keep herself sane. She had come home to Detroit.

Unfortunately, things weren't the same. Her parents hadn't been there to welcome her back. They'd been killed in an accident the previous summer. The house she'd grown up in hadn't felt the same without them. But then she wasn't the same either. She no longer saw the world as a challenging place filled with possibilities. She knew the horrors that were out there.

No, she wasn't the same woman Devin had once loved. Their dreams for a shared future were shattered. No matter what he believed her reasons for leaving had been, they didn't compare with the truth.

Wiping at the tears, she sank down on the lid of the commode, grateful for the support because her legs were shaking. In fact, she was trembling all over. What she was, was a mess. Her life had fallen apart once. She wouldn't let it happen again. As long as she remembered that Devin was no threat to her, she was safe.

She almost laughed aloud when she realized that she was still capable of feeling desire. Unfortunately, it was desire for the man who hated her. He had once touched her heart as no other man could, but that didn't matter anymore. Desire and vulnerability went hand and hand, and they were the last things she needed in her life.

She had to get out of here and as far away from Devin as humanly possible. She wasn't up to facing the hurt she had created in his beautiful dark gray eyes. He hadn't deserved it. She'd never meant to cause him pain. The fact that she was also suffering was not an excuse. She'd left without explanation, because she knew he'd never accept her reason for going.

"Oh Devin," she whispered aloud as she tried to rub away the goose pimples on her arms.

Seeing him again had only opened old wounds. It was a waste of both their time, pretending there were anything left to discuss. What happened, happened, and there was nothing she could say or do to change that.

The knock on the bathroom door caused her to jump, and her heart raced with dread. "Yes?"

"Can you hurry it up? A line is forming out here," an impatient female voice said through the closed door.

"Sorry. I'll be right out."

Brynne was weak with relief that it was not Devin. She washed her hands, then searched her bag for a compact to repair the damage. Cautiously opening the door, she mumbled a hasty apology, then began to make her way through the crowd. She concentrated on the front of the house in her search for Laura. Her anxiety returned in spades as she looked around, feeling an urgent need to hurry.

Laura was in the dining room, talking to a handsome man. Brynne grabbed her arm and whispered, "I'm leaving. Good night."

"But it's only a little after ten."

"I've got a headache." Brynne gave the other woman's hand a squeeze. "Sorry about this. I'll see you in the morning."

"Do you need me to drive you home?"

Brynne's heart raced with fear as she glanced quickly over her shoulder. "No. I'll be fine. Just tired. See you."

She found her coat in the front hall closet before hurrying out the door. She was practically running by the time she reached her car parked toward the end of the long curved drive. She sank gratefully into the soft upholstery. She didn't breathe easily until she maneuvered between two parked cars and was able to pull out onto the road.

"It's over," she whispered again and again. Yet her hands had not stopped shaking, even when she was miles from Ralph Prescott's home. Her churning stomach and aching heart reminded her that it wasn't over. How could it be? Devin was in Detroit with plans to stay until the football season began.

"That's not your concern," she mumbled aloud. She had her life and he had his. They both had moved on. Every sigh, every kiss they had once shared was in the past. Unfortunately she hadn't been able to forget. Oh, she had done her level best to put it all behind her. However, seeing him again had brought it all back.

Their last night together had started out so beautifully, filled with romance—candlelight, flowers, champagne, and him. Devin had thought of everything. He had prepared an exceptional meal, rack of lamb, creamy sweet potatoes, mixed green salad, and her personal favorite, lemon pound cake. They'd danced, and then he'd made love to her with an unexpected urgency and tenderness.

Cradling her against his heart, Devin had asked her to be his wife. That was when it all had begun to unravel. He hadn't understood that her hesitation wasn't a refusal. He wouldn't listen when she told him she loved him every bit as much as he loved her. He had his mind made up and wouldn't consider waiting until she finished her doctorate. He claimed it had taken him years to find her. He wanted her promise that very night and would accept nothing less. To do that she would have to break the final promise she'd made to her mother.

Brynne sighed aloud, wondering if she should have tried harder to make him see her point. Two years wasn't that long. She shook her head, knowing she had done her best to make him understand.

No matter what she said, she couldn't make him see that accepting his proposal would mean breaking the last promise she had given her mother. She couldn't do it. How could he expect it of her? Their evening ended with a terrible argument. She had dressed and left without saying goodbye, refusing to let him see her tears.

Brynne eased to a stop in Vanessa's drive. She sat staring at the small brick home as she took a few calming breaths. Eventually she felt strong enough to approach the well-lit porch. The residential street was quiet, but there was enough bite in the air to cause her to shove her hands into her pockets after ringing the doorbell.

"Hi. Back so soon?" Vanessa Grant said with a welcoming smile.

Although the two women were vastly different in appearance, they both believed in putting family first. At six feet tall, Vanessa towered over her friend. She was painfully shy around men and never bothered with makeup or fussed with her appearance. Her engaging smile lit her flawless, toffee-toned skin.

"I didn't expect you until after eleven. Didn't go well?" Vanessa asked as she closed the door.

"It was too crowded and noisy. Gave me a headache. I'm not use to weekday parties. What am I talking about? I can't remember the last time I went to a party without balloons and clowns," Brynne managed to joke. "Did Shanna give you any trouble?"

"Your little sweetheart is never any trouble. She dropped off as soon as I put the twins in bed."

Brynne nodded. "That's not surprising. She loves you and the kids."

Vanessa was a dear friend, and Brynne genuinely admired the way Vanessa hadn't hesitated to take over the care of her younger siblings after their mother's death.

Following her into her bedroom, Brynne smiled when she saw her little girl curled up in the center of her friend's bed, a quilt covering her. "Thanks, Vanessa. I appreciate you taking her on such short notice."

"It's not a problem, and you know it." She touched Brynne's arm before she could wake her daughter. She asked softly, "What's wrong?"

Brynne busied herself by stuffing her daughter's things into her backpack. "What makes you think something is wrong? It's late and I want to get her settled in bed for the night or I'll never be able to get her up in the morning."

Vanessa nodded but didn't look convinced. "I'm surprised you were able to get Laura to leave so early."

"She stayed. There were too many good looking men at the party. It's a good thing I insisted on driving myself."

"Men? You're kidding. I'm surprised that Ralph didn't invite wall-to-wall women. From what I hear, they flock to him like bees to honey." Vanessa frowned.

"That's right, you know him." Bynne nearly asked why Vanessa hadn't warned her that Ralph was one of those Prescotts. But then, why would she? None of Brynne's friends knew about her involvement with Devin.

"Yes. Gavin married Ralph's cousin, Anna."

Brynne frowned. "You should have gone to the party with Laura and left me here with the kids."

Vanessa laughed. "I wasn't invited, remember? But even if I had been, I wouldn't want to go near that man. Ralph has half the women in Detroit running after his gorgeous behind, including Laura. No, thank you. I have better things to do, like wash clothes. You tell me, what woman in her right mind would try to go up against those kinds of odds?"

Only half listening, Brynne was too busy berating herself for not using her head. Vanessa was Gavin Mathis's secretary and had more than likely met all the Prescotts at one time or another, including Devin. Brynne was the one who hadn't made the connections. And because of that she had come face-to-face with the man she'd walked out on four years ago.

None of her friends knew the circumstances surrounding Shanna's birth or the events of the fateful night that nearly destroyed her. Brynne hadn't been able to talk about it. It wasn't that she'd planned to be secretive. Yet, even years later, it was still too painful to examine. And a single look into Devin's gray eyes had brought it all back.

"Brynne, honey, something has upset you," Vanessa insisted. "I can't remember seeing you like this. Please let me help."

"It's nothing. I'm just tired and have a headache." It was the excuse she had given Laura. Unfortunately, it was also true. Her neck and shoulders were taut from the beginnings of a tension headache. She leaned over and gently kissed her daughter's cheeks. "Wake up, sweet pea. It's time to get you home."

"Sleepy, Mommy," Shanna complained. Her lashes fluttered, but her eyes were closed.

"I know but we have to get home." Brynne quickly set her up and began putting on her shoes, then coat and hat.

"Thanks, Vanessa, for looking after her."

Brynne rose with Shanna in her arms, her small face

tucked beneath her mother's chin. She kissed her daughter's forehead, saying, "You're getting heavy, baby."

"Big girl," Shanna mumbled around the thumb in her mouth.

"I enjoyed having her. I'll get the door." Vanessa hurried ahead with Shanna's backpack in her hand.

"Talk to you tomorrow," Brynne said as she walked out onto the porch.

Despite the cold, Vanessa hurried down the porch stairs to pull the side door of the van open for them. "Are you sure nothing is wrong?"

"Nothing a little rest can't fix." Brynne quickly settled Shanna into her car seat and then buckled her in. Pulling the door closed, she turned and gave Vanessa a hug and slipped a check in her hand. "I don't know what I'd do without you."

"You don't have to," Vanessa smiled, then glanced down at the check. "I can't take this. It's too much."

"Nonsense. Use the extra to buy yourself something pretty. When is the last time you bought a new dress?"

"I don't need anything new."

"Sure you do." Brynne accepted the backpack before she kissed Vanessa's cheek. "You'd better hurry inside before you freeze," she said as she slid behind the wheel and started the engine.

"Night." Vanessa waved before she raced for her front door.

After tucking Shanna into bed, instead of going to her own room and getting some much-needed rest, Brynne sat on the side of the bed, watching her baby sleep. It was some time later that she realized what she was doing, studying her little girl's features for any sign of Devin.

"You've really lost it," she muttered to herself as she left the room. She made the routine round of the house, double checking all the locks and windows, as well as making sure the alarm was activated before she went into her bedroom.

"Forget you saw him," she mumbled aloud as she undressed.

She was overreacting. Shanna was a miniature copy of herself, right down to her tiny toes. There was no resemblance to the man she'd once loved and believed would someday father her children. It was too late now for regrets.

After creaming her skin free of makeup, she brushed her teeth, then decided to postpone her shower until the morning. She changed into a silk nightshirt before climbing into her queen-size bed. After turning off the light, she pressed her cheek into the pillow, releasing an anguish-filled moan.

The worst was over, she reminded herself. She had proven that by building a new life for herself. Seeing Devin again couldn't take away what she had done on her own. She was a survivor. And she reminded herself that she wasn't the same woman Devin had fallen in love with. She hadn't been for a very long time.

It had been a mistake from the very beginning. They'd fallen in love too quickly. They hadn't given themselves time to really get to know each other. The sexual need and passion had gotten in the way—big time. They had both wanted marriage but their timing was way off.

Maybe if he had met her parents he would have understood. Her father was an obstetrician/gynecologist and her mother a neurosurgeon. From a young age, they had stressed the importance of education. They had been proud of her, pleased by her decision to continue on toward a Ph.D.

The accident had occurred when her parents had been on their way home from her college graduation ceremony. Their car had been hit by a semi-truck. Her father had been killed at the scene while her mother lingered, only to die later at the hospital. Brynne managed to see her before she passed. The last promise she had made to her mother was that she wouldn't let anything keep her from finishing her education.

It had been a painful summer. Brynne had been forced to

grow up quickly. After burying her parents and closing up
their home, she'd gone back to her apartment in St. Louis.
It had taken all her resolve to pull herself together and go
on with her life. Her career goals were firmly in place
when she registered for her grad school classes in the fall.
She met Devin shortly after the semester started.

"Devin . . ."

He was as big, handsome, and dangerous to her peace of
mind as he had been the day she left for good. And the
question of whether he had fathered her child would remain unanswered.

"Shanna, we don't have time for you play around with your
food this morning. Will you please eat that oatmeal so we
can get out of here?"

Brynne said as she put her own empty cereal bowl into
the dishwasher.

"I don't like it," her daughter complained.

Brynne sighed. Her sunny little girl was as tired and out
of sorts as her mother. What they both needed was a few
more hours of sleep.

"Yes, you do." She stopped when she realized she was
arguing with a three-year-old. "Finish your toast and drink
that milk, please."

Dumping the cereal down the garbage disposal, Brynne
rinsed the bowl and placed it into the dishwasher in record
time. The morning was going from bad to worse. Nothing
she said or did could please her daughter. Shanna hated her
green outfit her mother had picked out. She didn't want her
hair braided, but wanted ponytails. She even complained
about her tights. By the time they were both dressed,
Brynne was strongly considering going back to bed and
pulling the covers over her head.

"Come on, sweet pea. Get your coat and backpack while
I finish up here."

"Don't want to, Mommy."

Brynne scolded, "Not another word from you, Shanna Marie Armstrong. You get moving, and I mean now."

Shanna pouted, but she ran to get her things.

When Brynne had dropped her daughter off, she warned Trenna that Shanna was grumpy and to call if she acted up, then she headed to her office. She had barely gotten her coat off before Laura rushed in.

"You missed all the fun," Laura boasted. "I not only met Gavin Mathis and Wesley Prescott, but some of their teammates from the Lions. Girl, that place was crawling with millionaires. Ralph's gorgeous cousin, Devin, asked about you after you left."

Brynne, proud of the fact that she managed not to scream that she didn't want to hear, said with false cheer, "Sounds like you had a great time."

"So did you, girlfriend. I saw you dancing with Devin. I don't know what you did but you sure got that man's attention." Laura grinned, waiting to hear all the juicy details.

Well, she was bound to be disappointed, Brynne decided as she booted her computer, then picked up the telephone. "Megan, will you please send my first appointment in. Thanks."

"Brynne!" Laura complained. "I want to know what you said to get that multimillionaire quarterback's attention."

"Nothing worth repeating. I'm glad one of us had a good time. I should have followed my instincts and stayed home. My little girl and I are both cranky from lack of sleep. I won't be surprised if her teacher calls and demands I come get her before the day is out." She asked with a smile, "Well? Did you manage to get more than a smile out of Ralph?"

Laura complained, "Not even a dinner invitation. The man has too many women chasing him. I turned my sights to Jeff Bancroft. Another one of those gorgeous football players."

"I am glad to see your heart wasn't broken," Brynne teased.

"Please. My feelings weren't even hurt."

There was a timid knock on the door.

Brynne rose to her feet, smiling. "Good morning, Miss Graham. Please come in."

Laura said hello to the other woman, before she said to Brynne on her way out, "See you later."

Indicating the chair in front of her desk, Brynne said to Miss Graham, "Please have a seat." She went over to the small side table. "May I get you something to drink before we get started?"

Brynne focused on the problems of the recent rape victim, pushing aside her own concerns. She could handle Laura's curiosity. What she didn't want to consider was the possibility that Devin might come looking for answers she could never give.

Four

≡

Each day without hearing from Devin eased Brynne's fears a bit more. It verified that he, like she, realized they had nothing to say to each other. She was finally able to relax on Friday evening when she tucked her daughter in for the night.

"Story time, Mommy." Shanna yawned tiredly.

"Would you like to read the new book Aunt Trenna gave you?" Brynne asked as she walked over to the child-size shelves that ran along the wall. Shanna's bookshelf was crammed with picture books.

"Three Bears, Mommy," she said around another yawn, barely able to keep her eyes open.

Brynne swallowed a groan as she found her daughter's current favorite, and then settled beside her on the pale maple wood double bed. "Ready, baby?"

"I'm not a baby. I'm a big girl," Shanna insisted as she snuggled with her head on her mother's shoulder.

"I know, but you're still my baby girl."

Brynne had read the story so many times that she could have recited it without the book, but she read it slowly, hoping Shanna would drop off before the end of the story, thus avoiding the father question.

"Mommy, I want a daddy like baby bear," Shanna mumbled tiredly.

"I know. But it's time to close those pretty brown eyes, sweet pea."

"Mommy, guess what."

"What?" Brynne kissed her cheek.

"Jackie's going to have a new daddy, 'cause her mommy is getting married."

"That's nice."

"Mommy, she got two daddies. I want a daddy, too!" she complained. "Can we go to the mall to get him?"

"The mall?"

Shanna nodded. "Jackie's mommy found him at the mall."

"Found him at the mall?"

"Can we go tomorrow?"

Baffled, Brynne repeated, "At the mall? Don't you mean, Jackie's mommy met him at the mall, while shopping?"

Shanna shrugged her tiny shoulders. "Can we go?"

Brynne frowned. Once her little girl got something in her head, she could be downright stubborn. Brynne had no idea how a three-year-old could be so muleheaded.

"Mommy?"

Brynne kissed her cheek before she said, "Mommy can't just go shopping and pick out a daddy for you. Mommies and daddies meet and fall in love and then get married. And they can meet anywhere, not just at the mall. Okay?"

"Okay . . ." Shanna rubbed her eyes with small balled fists.

"Come here. Let me rock you to sleep. My big girl is so tired. Mommy is tired too. I'm going to sleep really hard and have happy dreams. How about you?"

Shanna nodded, her head on her mother's breast.

Brynne rocked her daughter until she dropped off. Then she tiptoed out, leaving a night light on in both the bedroom and connecting bath. She went into the family room, but rather than settling in front of the television housed in the entertainment armoire, she paced across the Oriental carpet done in shades of gold, cream, and crimson that covered the maple wood flooring. Both the sofa and club chairs with ottomans were covered in dark gold leather. The chenille throws and the pillows that lined the sofa were crimson.

Find a man at the mall. Brynne shook her head in disbelief. To say it had been an eventful week would be putting it mildly. After straightening the family photos on the mantel, she stared down into the fire burning behind the screen in the red brick fireplace. The drapes were closed, shutting out the cold, snowy night.

She sighed, shaking her head at her daughter's request. If only it were that simple to find the answers. Curling up in one of the armchairs, she tucked her legs beneath her. But then, she shouldn't be surprised. Shanna had never even seen her with a man. Brynne didn't date.

During the last six months, Shanna had recognized that she wasn't like her little classmates because she didn't have a father. She was still too young to understand that, indeed, she had a father.

Someday Shanna would demand to know her father's name, which was her right, and Brynne wouldn't have an answer. For years she'd pushed the thought away, unable to deal with the painful truth. How could she possibly explain to her sweet child that her mother had made love to the man she loved, and later that same night had been raped by another man?

Either man could have fathered her precious little girl. For so long, Brynne had told herself it was better not to know. Because she was afraid of the answer, she had pushed the thought away, time and time again. She would rather her daughter thought she was a slut than believe she was conceived due to something as hateful and horrific as rape.

Brynne had been too afraid to even hope that Devin

might be her baby girl's father. Yet, over the years, that tiny wish had remained in her heart. Seeing him again had caused her to wonder if the possibility was more than wishful thinking on her part. But what if Devin was Shanna's father? What then?

If it were true, Brynne didn't have a doubt in her mind that Devin would despise her for keeping his baby from him. She covered her face with her hands, refusing to give in to bitter tears. She couldn't quite believe that she would ever find herself in such an unenviable situation. She had loved only one man . . . made love only with him.

Brynne wrapped her arms around herself as the unhappy memories filled her thoughts. On their last night together they had made slow, sweet love, but the evening had ended with a bitter argument. Rather than stay the night, she had insisted on going home alone. Her so-called friend and classmate had been waiting for her. She had invited him inside her apartment, and he had taken advantage of her . . . taken what was hers alone to give.

Nine months later, Shanna had been born. Brynne never regretted her decision to have her baby. How could she? From the instant she gazed into her baby's eyes, she'd fallen in love. From her birth to this day, Brynne had done everything in her power to protect her child and keep her safe from the ugliness of the world.

Now suddenly Brynne faced a new dilemma. Shouldn't she at least try to find out the truth? Would Devin agree to take a paternity test? Did she have the nerve to ask? Brynne almost screamed no at the mere thought.

Was there another option? Just imagining Devin's reaction to the request had her shuddering with dread. He already resented her for leaving the way she did. How could she tell him about rape when she had been unable to talk about it to anyone, not even her closest girlfriends? Because of her schooling, Brynne was convinced she didn't need rape counseling and had never sought outside help.

Brynne was just beginning to recognize how tired she was of carrying this burden inside her. Years of not knowing who had fathered her child had taken their toll. Just knowing one way or the other was bound to be a relief.

But this wasn't about her or even Devin for that matter. This was for her baby girl. The sooner Brynne knew the truth, the better prepared she would be to help her daughter face the pitfalls that lay ahead. For Shanna, she would dare anything. She would find a way to contact Devin and ask him to take the paternity test.

Devin sat brooding as he waited in the lobby of the Sheppard Women's Crisis Center. The waiting area was filled with women from various age ranges, income levels, and ethnic backgrounds. Many had small children with them while others were alone. He shifted, rotating his broad shoulders, uncomfortable with the number of hostile glances sent his way. This was clearly no-man's-land.

After a long weekend of calling himself every kind of fool while enduring several restless days and sleepless nights, he had convinced himself he was doing the right thing. Brynne had made her point when she left Ralph's without a word to him. Even though he knew she didn't want anything to do with him, he had come anyway. He had to know what had gone wrong between them. All he wanted was some answers.

He thought he had put it all behind him and moved on. That was until he had taken Brynne into his arms. The dance had been a mistake. He should never have touched her. The instant he had felt her soft curves against him, the memories had come flooding back. If he lived to be a hundred, he could never forget what it was like to be inside her, surrounded by her moist heat. The longing had started all over again.

At first he'd assured himself that it was because he had gone so long without sex. That was the reason his hormones had taken over, but he knew better. He'd wanted

Brynne from the instant he'd laid eyes on her back in St. Louis. Years apart hadn't changed the truth.

Despite the fact Brynne had hurt him as no other woman could, he still wanted her. Although time, distance, hurt, and anger had changed him emotionally, physically he reacted to her as if she were still his alone.

He swore beneath his breath. So what if he desired her. He wasn't stupid enough to beg her for another chance. It didn't matter that she was every bit as lovely and downright sexy as he remembered. Not for an instant had he forgotten that she'd walked away without an explanation. He'd held the pain deep inside for too damn long. It was time to let it go. He needed answers. And Brynne was the only one who could supply them. His instincts told him there had to have been more than an argument to end their relationship.

He had gone over their disagreement hundreds of times. Naturally, he had been upset because she refused his proposal. He had too much pride to do what he wanted to do, which was to beg her to stay.

He had been scheduled for an out-of-town game. And because he was still angry, he'd left the next morning without calling her. He'd been certain that once they'd both had time to cool off, they could work it out. What he hadn't expected, had not even suspected, was that she would pack up and leave town without so much as a word to him. Four years later, he still had no idea what had gone wrong.

Quite frankly, he resented that she still maintained a measure of power over him. Evidently the Prescott ego was alive and well. It had kept him going after her departure. Yet after seeing her the other night, he had shamelessly questioned his cousin. He had even gone so far as to question her friend.

"Mr. Prescott." The receptionist came over and said with a smile, "Can I get anything for you? More coffee?"

"No, but thank you." He glanced at the Rolex watch on his wrist. "Do you know how much longer she will be?"

"No, but it shouldn't be much longer."

He nodded. He could well imagine Brynne's reaction when she learned he'd come to her place of business. He wouldn't put it past her to keep him cooling his heels indefinitely. He wasn't expecting a warm welcome.

Just then, he glanced up as a young woman left Brynne's office. The receptionist smiled at him before she hurried inside.

She was making notes on her laptop when Megan Martin came inside her office. "Brynne, there is a gorgeous man out here waiting to see you. Devin Prescott. Should I send him in?"

Brynne's heart skipped a beat. She took a quick breath before she said, "Yes, please." Smoothing unsteady hands down the straight skirt of her cream silk suit, which she'd teamed with a bronze silk blouse, she rose to her feet.

Devin's large, hard-muscled frame momentarily filled the doorway. He was every bit as devastatingly handsome as he had been the other night. He wore a beige leather jacket, cream turtleneck sweater, and dark brown trousers. His dark gray eyes studied hers as he came inside and closed the door.

"Devin, what a surprise. Please, won't you have a seat." Her lips trembled as she forced a smile. She sank gratefully down into her chair once he'd taken the visitor's chair.

"I won't keep you long," he said evenly.

"It's okay. I don't have another appointment until eleven. A whole half hour." She was babbling but couldn't seem to help it. "How was your weekend?"

"My weekend?" He cocked a brow. "Let's not pretend, okay? I came for some answers." He paused before he went on to say, "You ran from me four years ago. You're still running. I'd like to know why."

Struggling not to show how uneasy she was, Brynne said, "Why does it even matter after all this time?"

"It matters to me."

When Brynne dropped her lids, her eyes touched the photograph of Shanna facing her on her desk. A reminder of what needed to be done. She resisted the urge to place the photo facedown. Instead she tried and failed to meet his gaze. Her eyes settled on a space just past his left shoulder.

She didn't need to be told that she had hurt him. But he wasn't the only one who had suffered. She took a fortifying breath before she said, "Devin, this is my workplace. It's not the right place for a personal discussion."

"Where is the right place, Brynne? You tell me. The way you took off the other night, I'm beginning to think there will never be a right place or time."

Swallowing to dislodge the lump in her throat, she said, "You're right. We do need to talk. Can I meet you for lunch at the restaurant down the block? Around twelve-thirty? Bailey's is nothing fancy, just good down-home food. It's only a few doors down on Second."

If he was surprised by the invitation, he didn't show it. Other than a tightening of a muscle in his lean cheek, his expression didn't change. Devin stood, towering over her. "That will be fine. I'll see you then." He looked at her a moment before he walked out.

Brynne slumped heavily against the back of her chair as if she were exhausted. Her hands as well as her knees were shaking. She reached for her Shanna's picture. She silently assured herself that she could do this. She would ask him to take the paternity test, for Shanna's sake.

Brynne, a few minutes late, found that her lateness only seemed to add to her anxiety. She hurried into the restaurant, crowded with lunchtime diners, when she'd rather turn around and head for the relative safety of her office. Recalling her little girl's request that they go to the mall to find her a daddy was what kept Brynne moving toward Devin's table, which was in a corner, somewhat away from the other diners.

"You made it." He rose to his full height and held her chair.

She managed a smile as she sat down. Her stomach tightened with nerves, and she wondered if she would be able to eat. "Hi. Sorry, I'm late. I had to take a last-minute telephone call." She rushed on to say, "As you can see, the menu is simple, but the food is excellent. I recommend the club sandwich, but the spaghetti is exceptional. I know it isn't—"

Devin reached across the small table, covering her tightly clasped fingers. "What's wrong?"

"Nothing." She nearly jerked her hand away but thought better of it. "It's just—" she stopped abruptly, wondering how in the world she could find the words to tell him why she had packed her bags and left St. Louis.

"Just what?" he quizzed, his eyes gazing into hers.

"It's been a long time since—"

"What? Since we shared a meal? Or a bed?" His eyes moved slowly over her small features, her full red-tinted lips, to linger at the pulse point in her slender throat.

Both, she nearly shouted. She had no trouble recalling every minute of their last time together. Yes, they'd shared a meal and made love. If only her evening had ended there.

"You're not making this easy for me," she admitted.

"Easy? Nothing has been easy between us for a long time. I thought we meant something to each other. Was I wrong?"

She dropped her lids, unable to bear the sparks of need and the hurt she thought she saw smoldering in his dark gray eyes. "If you're here to start another argument . . ." Her voice trailed off.

He shook his head, yet a muscle jumped in his cheek, betraying his tension. "Sorry. I had hoped for a meal and conversation. Surely we can both handle that." He didn't wait for a response before he said, "You're looking well, Brynne. Have you started working on that doctorate now that you apparently finished your master's?"

She nearly choked, as she'd just taken a sip of water. "My master's is in counseling. And no, I haven't started on the doctorate." Her priorities had changed since she had her daughter. She was waiting until Shanna was older.

"May I ask why?" Although he smiled, his gaze held no trace of humor.

"I decided to work a few years before going back," she hedged.

He surprised her when he said, "You've cut your hair. I liked it long, but it's beautiful, just as you are. But then you don't need me to tell you that, do you? You've always been an exceptionally lovely woman."

Brynne swallowed a gasp as shivers of awareness ran up and down her spine. Devin's full, mustache-framed lips and good looks had always captured her attention. His powerful shoulders and upper torso bulged with well-defined muscles. His long-fingered hands were strong, yet gentle. She only had to close her eyes to recall the time they had been lovers. She had never been able to tell him no.

But then Devin did everything well. He was an accomplished athlete who used his body to earn his living. He was one of the highest-paid quarterbacks in the NFL, plus he was an intelligent man. She knew he'd have no trouble replacing her. After all, women flocked to him in droves. Only for a time she had been his woman.

Lost in thought, she nearly jumped when he said, "You came to Ralph's party with a girlfriend, which made me assume you weren't involved with a man. You don't have a ring on that left hand. Did I assume wrong? Are you available? Or are you living with some guy?"

She bristled. "Living together isn't my style. Besides, that isn't why I agreed we need to talk."

"We both know you're not here for old times' sake. You made that clear the other night when you skipped out on me without so much as a goodbye. But then you're not big on those, are you, Brynne?"

She couldn't fail to note the stubborn angle of his jaw.

The man had muleheadedness down to a science. He was an expert. Nothing he said had caused her stomach to ease or gave her reason to let down her guard, not even for a moment.

"Are you ready to order?" The gum-popping waitress stopped at their table. She barely glanced at Brynne, but her eyes lingered on Devin's strong features.

"Coffee, please," they both said at the same time, then laughed at the memory. They were both avid coffee drinkers and used to frequent coffee bars.

While the waitress filled their mugs, Brynne was relieved to focus on something other than Devin. She looked at the menu.

"What can I get you?"

"Brynne?" he prompted.

"Club sandwich on toasted wheat, please. And a side salad with honey-mustard dressing, please," she ordered.

"I'll have the same but make that two sandwiches." Devin handed back the menus.

"Someone's hungry." The waitress beamed at him.

"Always." Devin didn't notice because his gaze was on Brynne. As soon as they were alone, he said softly, "You didn't answer my question. What do you want to discuss?"

Five

═══

"*You were right when you said we needed to* talk. This is relatively private, so we can't be overheard."

He learned back in his chair. "Now I'm curious." He reached for the cream, pouring a single drop into the center of his coffee.

Brynne had been so busy watching him that she forgot her own drink. She stirred in a spoonful of sugar.

"I see you still take it with a little sugar," he commented, his deep voice soft, almost velvety.

Silently she chanted, *I can do this . . . I can do this,* while taking a cautious sip of her coffee in hopes of settling her nerves and loosening her tongue.

"Why private?" he asked tightly. "You haven't wanted to be alone with me since the condom broke when we last made love."

A quick swallow kept her from spewing coffee all over the table but left her coughing to clear her windpipe.

"Are you all right?" He leaned forward.

Brynne shook her head as she fought for breath. When she could speak again, she said, "I'm fine. Or at least I will be once I get my breath back." She took a cautious sip from her water glass, and then went on to say, "I'm here because you need to know that I have a three-year-old daughter." She told him the day of her birth, then paused before she went on to say, "I've put this off long enough, but now it's time I know if you're her father."

"What?" He was the one who nearly choked. "What do you mean you don't know?"

"Will you please lower your voice? Do you have to tell everyone in this restaurant?"

Devin's eyes narrowed as he said in a harsh whisper, "Why don't you know who her father is? You've had years to figure it out, damn it."

Brynne stiffened, surprised that he'd sworn at her. It was something he'd never done. She forced herself to ask, "Will you take a paternity test?"

Devin's features had gone as cold as stone. "How can you calmly sit there and tell me you were sleeping with another man while you claimed to be in love with me?"

"Believe me, I'm not calm. You have no idea how difficult it is for me to come to you this way." Hands tightly clasped in her lap, she whispered, "In fact, I was sure I couldn't do it. I'm not doing this for me or you. I'm doing it for my daughter's sake. As for the other man . . ." Brynne bit her lips to keep from screaming out a denial. "It isn't what—"

"Stop! I don't want to hear about the bastard." His voice shook with fury. "I don't want the details of you in bed with some other guy." He swore beneath his breath.

"I need to tell you while—"

He sneered, "Damn it, I told you I don't want to know. All I want is to understand why. Why did you decide to drop this on me nearly four years after the fact?"

Unable to meet his gaze, she said unhappily, "I've raised her alone, but she is getting older now. She's going to want to know about her father."

"What about the other guy? Did you have him take this test? Or are there other men?"

"No!" she nearly shouted, then caught herself. "I'm asking you because I don't know where he is . . . nor do I care." She shuddered at the thought. Seeing the hurt and disappointment in Devin's eyes upset her more than she expected. She had to explain, yet somehow the words wouldn't come. She swallowed with difficulty before she said, "If you'd let me explain about him, I—"

"Hell, no!" A muscle jumped in his cheek as if he were grinding his teeth. "Why now? At least back then I loved you. It's not like you haven't known how to reach me."

Brynne struggled for control, to hold back the tears that burned her lids. "Shanna looks like me. Recently she noticed that unlike the other children, she doesn't have a daddy. She will someday want to know who fathered her. It's her right to know. Devin, please! It's a simple test. It won't take long."

Suddenly he stood up and without explanation walked out of the restaurant.

Brynne stared after him in horror. Disheartened, she slumped in the chair. Biting her bottom lip to keep from sobbing, she didn't say a word when the waitress put their plates on the table. Too upset to leave, she stared down at her plate. She had failed not only herself, but her baby girl as well. In all honesty, she couldn't entirely blame him. If the situation where reversed she would have done the same.

She had tried to explain, but he preferred to believe the worst . . . that she had cheated on him. Why had he cut her off repeatedly? Evidently he wasn't interested in what really happened that night.

She consoled herself with the thought that it was no doubt best this way. After all, she hadn't been sure she could tell him about the rape. It was bad enough that she knew what a coward she had been. Rather than face her attacker and see him punished, she had run. She didn't need to be told that it was something Devin would have never done. He had never run from a fight in his life. And no doubt he would never understand her overwhelming fears and her shame.

She looked up at the sound of Devin sinking back down into his seat. His eyes were cold and his mouth was tight with anger, but he was there.

"I thought—" she began, and then stopped abruptly.

"That I walked out on you? The way you did me? No, I needed some air." He hissed, "I would be lying if I didn't admit I'm more angry than I can ever remember being. You lied to me. Hell. You've been lying to me for four damn years. You left me wondering what I'd done wrong, while you were in the wrong this whole time."

He paused to take a breath before he snapped, "But the worst part of it, you had a child that could be mine and kept her from me. That I can't forgive or forget . . . not ever. Yes, I'll take your damn paternity test." He took a pen from the inside pocket of his jacket. Using the paper napkin, he wrote down his cell and home telephone numbers. He carefully placed it beside her plate but looked as if he'd rather throw it in her face.

"You make the arrangements, and then let me know where and when. I'll be there." He paused before he said tightly, "But understand this, if she turns out to be mine, get ready for a custody fight. My child deserves better than a mother who doesn't even know the name of her father . . . a hell of lot better."

Devin pulled out an engraved gold money clip. He dropped a large bill on the table. "Lunch is on me. I hope you choke on it. Goodbye." He walked out again, only this time he didn't return.

"For a man who recently signed a three-year contract for seventy million and with a ten million signing bonus, you are in one hell of lousy mood," Wesley protested. "What is eating at you, little bro? You've hardly said two words to either Gavin or me since you walked in the door."

The three men, with the help of their personal trainer, had worked out in Gavin's home gym and had just finished laps in the pool.

Using powerful arm muscles to pull himself out of the water and onto the tile flooring surrounding the Olympic-style pool, Devin grumbled, "Leave it alone."

"Does it have something to do with the petite woman you were dancing with at Ralph's party?" Gavin asked as he made use of one of the bath sheets stacked on the built-in shelf.

Devin swore heatedly. "Next time I see Ralph, remind me to pop him in his big mouth."

"He's concerned about you. We all are. Something is eating at you," Wesley persisted. "Who is she?"

"I said to leave it alone." Devin didn't look back as he walked into one of the changing rooms where he'd left his clothes. He knew he wasn't fit to be around, but he'd hoped the workout would rid him of some of the anguish eating away at him.

Hell no. He didn't want to talk. What would it change? Not a damn thing. On the drive over, he'd been furious, so much so that he couldn't remember how he got there. He hadn't remembered much beyond Brynne's admission that she didn't know the name of her baby's father.

Why had he gone looking for answers in the first place? He should have let well enough alone. He was the one left feeling as if his heart had been ripped out of his chest. How could he have been so wrong about her? How could he have been so blind not to know the kind of woman she was? How could he have been fool enough to trust her with his heart? If anything, he should be celebrating the fact she turned down his proposal. If not for that, he'd be married to that beautiful little whore.

He swore as he shoved his damp trunks into his leather duffel bag, and then left without a word to anyone. As he passed his sister, Anna, in the kitchen, she asked if he could stay for dinner. He shook his head and continued on his way out the side door. He didn't stop until he reached his Jaguar parked in front of the four-car garage.

It took all his concentration just to drive to the condominium he had recently purchased in downtown Detroit. Its sole purpose was to give him the privacy he sorely needed.

Devin couldn't breathe easy until he'd shut his front door behind him. He collected a bottle of Scotch and a glass from the built-in bar in the corner of the den, and then collapsed into the deep cushion of the brown leather chair.

Tears he didn't dare let fall stung the back of his throat along with the fiery liquid he swallowed. As he emptied his glass, he tried not to think, not to remember. He focused on nothing more than filling and emptying his glass.

He must have dropped off because he woke when he heard the doorbell. "Go away!" he shouted. Judging by the level of liquor in the bottle on the coffee table and the churning in his stomach, he should be good and drunk. So why did it still hurt?

The bell chimed again and again, and then the pounding started. It sent him clumsily to his feet. He reached the door and yanked it opened.

"What the hell is wrong with you? Go bother someone else!" he yelled as he swung the door closed.

Ralph caught it before it slammed in his face. He eyed his cousin before he said, "I am not leaving. Not until you tell me what in the hell happened to you."

The two had been best friends since childhood. During their early years in pro sports the cousins had invested in a floundering private airline. With the help of a mutual friend to manage the day-to-day operations, they had turned the small business into a multimillion-dollar fleet of private planes, catering to the very wealthy. Their clientele included the well-known in both show business and professional sports.

Devin snarled, "Go home. I'm not in the mood for entertaining."

"Gavin and Wes were worried about you. What in the hell happened?"

Devin turned so fast he nearly fell on his face. He used the side table in the hall for support. "There is the door. Use it." He gestured wildly.

"Yeah, sure." Ralph caught him before he sprawled on the floor. "Let me help you." He caught Devin under an armpit and steadied him. "How much did you have?"

"Not nearly enough. I haven't been able to forget one word she said to me at lunch." He laughed, nearly sending them both to the hardwood flooring. "Not that I ate any lunch, mind you. That cheating little slut has been playing me all this time." Pulling away, he retraced his steps.

"Cheating? It was that serious between you two?"

Realizing what he had let slip, he dropped his head. "I don't need you. I don't need anyone," he grumbled as he sank into the large leather armchair he'd recently vacated. "Go home."

"When was the last time you ate?" Ralph scowled.

"Which one of them sent you here? Gavin? Or Wes? Why don't all of you mind your own damn business?"

"Uh-huh." Ralph crossed from the den into the kitchen.

Devin picked up his glass and swallowed. "I told you—"

Ralph called, "Yeah. I also know which side my bread is buttered on. Aunt Donna would chew me up one side and down the other if I left you like this." He filled the coffeemaker and switched it on before looking into the refrigerator. He began to pull out the fixings for sandwiches. The Prescott men knew their way around a kitchen, thanks to Donna. She had insisted on it.

Ralph returned with a tray of sandwiches and two coffee mugs. "Eat."

Devin complained, but he ate the food and drank a mug of strong black coffee. When he finished he heaved a sigh, leaning back in his chair, unaware of the sorrow in his dark eyes.

"Well?" his cousin prompted from where he'd made himself comfortable on the sofa.

"Brynne asked me to take a paternity test. It seems I might have a daughter."

"What the hell!"

"Yeah. My thoughts exactly," Devin grumbled bitterly.

"How long have you known this woman? How much did she mean to you?"

"Everything. She meant everything." He ran an impatient hand over his close-cut natural. "The last night we were together was four years ago, I asked her to marry me. I was in love with her, and I thought I knew her. Hell, I thought she loved me. Evidently I was wrong on all accounts."

"Back up. Start from the beginning," Ralph insisted, reaching for the Scotch bottle and pouring a portion into his coffee.

Devin told him how they met, how quickly they fell in love, and about their last night together.

"You say she left you?"

"Packed up and left town. Apparently the idea of marrying me sent her running all the way back home to Detroit. When we met, we thought it was such a great coincidence that we were both from Michigan." He scowled. "She wanted to get away from me so bad that she left before the semester was over."

"That doesn't make any sense, especially since she said no because she wanted to finish her education." Ralph frowned. "None of this is making too much sense. Women. I sure can't figure them out."

"Tell me about it. I went to her office today, hoping for an explanation. I never expected to be hit with this."

"She plans to sue you for child support?"

"Don't think so. She wants to know who fathered her child." Devin pushed out of the chair and began pacing in front of the unlit fireplace. "How could I have been so wrong about her? I still can't quite believe she cheated on me."

"Did she tell you anything about the other guy?"

Devin rubbed his unshaven jaw before he admitted, "She tried but I cut her off. The last thing I wanted was to hear about her and some other man. It was bad enough knowing she lied to me from day one. Well, maybe not the first day." He stopped, unable to reveal even to his cousin that Brynne had been a virgin back then. He had been her first man.

Ralph scowled. "Yeah, I wouldn't've wanted to hear the details either. And you don't think she wants money? Why did she wait so long to ask for this test?"

"I wish I knew. It wasn't like she didn't know where I was."

"So you're going to take this test?"

Devin's hands were balled at his sides. "I have to know. Have to know if I have a daughter."

"Why the hell didn't you use protection? What? Did she fry your brain or something?"

"I did! But the damn condom broke. I told her that night I'd stand by her if she got pregnant. Hell, I was secretly hoping she would get pregnant with my baby. I wanted her that bad. It took her four years to tell me she had a baby. Four damn years!"

Ralph shook his head. "I can't believe she's not after the money. Gavin and Wesley are the only proathletes I know who were lucky enough to find women who genuinely loved them and not their income."

"She doesn't need money. She came from a wealthy family." He rubbed his stubbled cheek. "How could she have kept my baby from me? The kid is three years old."

"It might not be yours."

"Yeah, I know. I told her straight out, she better hope the baby isn't mine, because I'll fight her for custody. I don't want a child of mine raised by a slut."

"Aren't you moving a little fast? This little girl could just as easily be the other man's."

"Or men. Who knows how many men she's slept with."

Devin scowled, not sure whom he was more disgusted with. He had wanted her even after she left him. He hadn't stopped wanting her, not until the moment she revealed her duplicity. "I don't know, but I imagine it shouldn't take long to have the test done and find out the results. I left it up to her to make the arrangements."

"You think that was a good idea? Maybe you should call your lawyer, let him take care of it?"

Devin shook his head. "I don't think there will be a problem. I keep telling you it isn't about money. Brynne is an only child. Her parents were both very successful doctors. They left her everything when they were killed in a car accident. Plus she has a trust fund from her grandparents, who were also well off."

Devin hesitated before he admitted, "I'm under no illusions that she's after me. If she wanted to put this on me, she could have done it years ago. I'm the one who wanted a commitment, not the other way around. Obviously, she was never in love with me."

"When are you going to tell the folks about this?"

"No need at this point. I don't want the family knowing about any of it. Even Gavin and Wesley." He looked pointedly at his cousin. "Did I make myself clear?"

"Crystal clear. They won't hear it from me, cuz. I know how to keep my mouth shut."

Six

"Mommy, I don't want to go to the doctor!

I don't want no shot!" Shanna complained as Brynne released her from the restraints of her car seat in the back of the SUV.

"I've already told you, young lady," Brynne said as Shanna scrambled out of the car. "We aren't going to Dr. Brad. No shots. This is Mommy's doctor. And he isn't going to do anything that hurts. Promise. Now give me your hand."

Brynne anxiously glanced around the parking lot. The last thing she wanted was to run into Devin while she was with her daughter. She still hadn't gotten over his fury when they'd talked in the restaurant. That had been upsetting enough. Other than a brief informative call to tell him about the test and give him her home telephone and cell phone numbers, she hadn't spoken to him.

She thought it best that Devin and her daughter did not meet. What good would it serve when he could just as easily not be her father? Wishing didn't make it true. Yet Brynne would be lying to herself if she didn't admit how relieved she would be to know her daughter hadn't been fathered by a rapist. No mother wanted that for her child. And her precious little girl deserved so much better.

"Why do I got to go? I want to go to school, Mommy. My teacher needs me to help pass out the puzzles. She always lets me." A frown creased her small brow as she hurried to keep up as they approached the building. Her mitten-covered hand was firmly held in her mother's hand. "Mommy! You go too fast."

"Sorry, baby girl," Brynne slowed. "Don't worry. I'm sure Aunt Trenna can find something else for you to do when you get to school." She forced a smile as she held the glass door open for her daughter to pass through.

"Good morning, Ms. Armstrong," the receptionist said as they approached the counter in the small lobby.

"Morning, Mrs. Stewart."

"The doctor will be with you shortly. And who is this pretty young lady?" She smiled. "Surely this is not Shanna? She's so big."

Shanna beamed. "I'm a big girl. Almost as big as Cindy Moore in my school."

"Yes, you are. I might have a lollipop for you when you leave, Miss Shanna."

Shanna's eyes sparkled. "Please."

"Shanna?" Brynne prompted, as she gazed around the waiting room. "What do you say?"

"Thank you." Then Shanna said, in a loud whisper, "But Mommy, she didn't give me nothin' yet."

"Shush. Now come sit down."

Brynne nearly jumped out of her skin when a tall man walked out of the doctor's office. She couldn't catch her breath until she realized it wasn't Devin. As long as she lived she would never forget the look of betrayal in his eyes when she blurted out the request. If only she could do it all over again. She suddenly sobered. It really wouldn't have mattered what she said because it would not change the past. She still had no idea who fathered her child.

The DNA test was quick and painless. Shanna had her lollipop, and Brynne was able to get her out of there without running into Devin. Unfortunately, Brynne knew she wouldn't be able to relax until she knew if Devin Prescott or Connor Helm had fathered her child. She had requested an independent lab because she didn't want there to be any doubts about the validity of the test results.

She had to make sure that there was nothing Devin and his team of high-priced lawyers could later take apart in court if Shanna was his. She refused to dwell on his threat to seek custody if Shanna turned out to be his. She knew she was a good mother.

"Ring . . . please," Brynne whispered aloud. "Put me out of my misery." She stared at her silent cell phone. She could have stayed home, for all the good she had been at work. It had been a rough week.

For the first time in memory, her own problems overshadowed those of the women seeking her help. She didn't have any appointments that morning, however, and was supposed to be catching up on her paperwork. Her office door was closed, and she had asked not to be interrupted. Even Shanna had noticed something was wrong. As they were eating breakfast that morning, she had asked if Brynne had a tummy ache.

"Ring," Brynne mumbled aloud. She jumped when the cell phone finally rang, and then nearly fell out of her chair as she made a grab for it. "Hello?"

"Hello, Brynne. It's Dr. Jackson."

"How are you?" she forced herself to ask.

"I'm well, thanks. I have those test results."

Her stomach instantly filled with nerves. Holding the receiver so tightly her fingers ached, she urged, "Tell me."

"With ninety-nine point nine percent accuracy, Devin Prescott is your daughter's father."

"Oh!" Brynne gasped, covering her mouth with a trembling hand as her eyes filled with tears of heartfelt relief. She took a few deep breaths before she was calm enough to ask, "There is no mistake?"

"None. Mr. Prescott fathered your daughter."

"Thank you, Doctor. I appreciate your letting me know so quickly."

"You're welcome. Shall I fax you a copy of the results?"

"Yes, please. I have the machine set up at home." She quickly gave him her number. Then she said, "I know it's up to me to give Mr. Prescott the news, since I requested the test, but, Doctor, would you please . . ."

"You'd like me to contact Mr. Prescott?"

"Yes, please. And would you also fax him a copy of the results?"

Brynne knew it was wrong but she just wasn't up to talking to Devin . . . not yet. She needed time to calm down, time to let it sink in. She didn't want to say anything she might regret later. Things were strained enough between them.

"Of course. I have his number here."

"Thanks again, Doctor. Goodbye."

She was still shaking after she returned the small phone to her purse. She had no idea how long she sat trying to absorb the news. There was no question that it was good news for her baby girl. Shanna would finally have what she'd been longing for most—a father. There was also no question that this news would place Devin not only into her daughter's life, but also into her own.

Knowing Devin, he wouldn't hesitate to exercise his parental rights. There was no question that he was furious and believed she had betrayed him. He was a powerful man with a team of skilled lawyers at his disposal. Even though she expected the worst, she felt so blessed that Devin was her baby's father and not Connor.

She should have tried harder to tell Devin the truth. Now that she hadn't, she was wondering if it was best to leave it unsaid. All that mattered now was that Shanna wouldn't have to grow up with the stigma that her father was a rapist.

The truth had been worth the embarrassment and shame it had cost her in asking him to take the paternity test. Finally the worrying and wondering were behind her. Nothing could take away the deep sense of relief and gratitude she felt at this moment, not even Devin's threats.

When the knock sounded on the door she called out, "Come in."

"Mrs. Cummings asked if she could see you."

"Okay, Megan, but give me a couple of minutes before you send her in."

Brynne grabbed a tissue and her compact out of her purse. As she quickly touched up her makeup, she couldn't help speculating on how Devin was taking the news.

Devin knew he was in a bad way when he turned into his parents' drive without memory of where he had been. He had been driving aimlessly for hours. He realized that he should have called Brynne, but he didn't trust himself even to speak to her—not until he cooled down.

His folks and younger brother Wayne were at the kitchen table eating dinner when he let himself in through the back door.

"Hey, son," Lester Prescott said with a wide grin. "Just in time for your mama's baked ham and sweet potatoes."

Donna jumped up, opening her arms for a hug. If she was surprised by the length of time he hung on to her before he kissed her cheek, she didn't show it.

"Hi, Mama, Dad, Wayne," he mumbled.

"Go wash up, son. I'll get your place setting."

"Don't bother."

"Hey, Dev. I'm glad you came over. I need your help talking Mom and Dad into getting me a car for my birthday. Both you and Wes had cars when you were teenagers."

"Yeah, but not until we'd graduated from high school and were heading to college. You still have three years."

"You are not helping," Wayne complained, then grinned. "Ma must have known you were coming. She made apple crumb cake."

Devin managed a smile. "Nothing for me." He shrugged out of his leather jacket and dropped it on the back of one of the bar stools around the center island.

Lester said, "Something's wrong?"

"Yeah. I need to talk to you and Mama. It can wait until after dinner," he said as he walked over to the counter, pulled out a mug from a cabinet, and filled it with coffee from the machine on the counter. He took a seat at the table and began asking his brother about the track team. He caught the look of worry his parents exchanged.

After thirty-five years of marriage, they were still very much in love. They had so much love to share that they hadn't hesitated to take in Lester's nephew, Ralph, and raise him as one of their own after his parents were killed.

"Wayne, why don't you load the dishwasher and put the food away while your father and I talk with Devin? And don't forget, no video games or telephone calls until your homework is done," Donna cautioned as she took her place setting over to the sink.

"Okay," Wayne said, sending his brother a look filled with questions.

It wasn't until his parents were seated side by side on the sofa in the sitting room of their bedroom suite with the door closed that Devin began pacing.

"What is it, son? Surely it can't be that serious? If it's money, your mother and I have put away most of the money, you, Wesley, and Ralph have thrown at us whenever you fellows have gotten a signing bonus."

Devin stopped and stared at his father in dismay. "That's money for you and Mama's retirement. And Wayne's education."

"You are also our son. Whatever you need, we are glad

to help," Donna quietly insisted with a worried frown on her soft brown features.

"Thank you, but no. It's not about money. I have more than I'll ever need, even without the majority of it invested. And the business is doing exceptionally well. Hell, I wish it was that simple."

"Son," Lester warned. He'd raised the boys to respect women, starting with their mother and sister. Swearing in front of either one was a decided no-no in Lester's opinion.

"Sorry, Mama. I don't know how I can say this without letting it rip. Here." He held out a legal-size envelope. He handed it over, then propped a shoulder against the mantel.

"Son, these are the results of a paternity test. According to this you have a child," Lester said incredulously.

"Yes, a little girl. Shanna Marie Armstrong. She's three. Until a week ago, I didn't know she existed," Devin said tightly, his voice laced with bitterness.

"What in the hell were you thinking, boy? And why didn't you use a damn rubber? You know better than to be caught up in some—" Lester stopped, suddenly realizing what he had let fly, his face creased in a scowl. "Honey, I—"

"Forget it, Lester. Well?" Donna demanded. "Answer your father! What's wrong with you, having unprotected sex with all these diseases out there?"

Devin felt as if he was fourteen again, when he had a crush on the girl down the block. "I always use protection. Only in this case the condom broke."

"Who is this woman? Why did it take her all this time to tell you about this child? What is she? Some kind of hoochie after your money?"

Devin laughed, he couldn't help it. That word wasn't something he expected to hear coming out of his very classy and demure mother's mouth. "I wish it were that simple." He sighed wearily, dropping down into an armchair adjacent to the sofa. "Her name is Brynne Armstrong. And she's not after money. She's from a very prominent family. You probably heard of them. The family is from Detroit, even though I met Brynne in St. Louis.

"Armstrong, you say?" Lester said thoughtfully.

Donna insisted, "I don't care about her family. I want to know why she kept our grandbaby and your little girl a secret all this time."

"After an argument she left St. Louis without a word to me. Just disappeared. I figured she'd gone back home to Detroit. I was so torn up about it, I refused to go after her. I didn't even try to look her up when I was in town. I didn't take kindly to her turning down my marriage proposal." A muscle jumped in his jaw as if he were grinding his teeth.

"You were in love with her," his father said in stunned disbelief.

"Yeah."

"Why did you keep this from us? No one loves you more than we do," Donna said. "You're a part of us."

Devin lowered his head before he looked directly into his mother's eyes, dark gray like his own. "I never intended to keep her a secret, Mama. We fell in love so quickly, and then she turned down my proposal. I couldn't talk about it," he confessed, with difficulty. "It hurt too much. It still does."

He didn't see the look his parents exchanged while he stared broodingly into the unlit log-filled grate.

Donna asked, "How do you feel about her now?"

"It doesn't matter how he feels about her now, honey. What matters is our grandbaby. You say they live in the Detroit area?" Lester quizzed.

"Yes." Devin frowned. "My little girl doesn't even know she has a father. And she knows nothing about me." His voice revealed his keen disappointment. "Brynne has kept her to herself all these years."

"If you loved her, then Brynne must have some redeeming qualities. Although I'm hard pressed trying to understand why she kept Shanna from you." Donna snapped furiously, "It wasn't as if she didn't know how to get in touch with you. There is no excuse for it."

"Evidently I was the only one in love because she was sleeping with some other man at the same time." Devin swore furiously.

"Devin, watch your—"

"Hush, Lester. Let the boy say what he has to say," Donna interrupted. "If you want to help, then get us all a brandy. We could use something."

"Dad's right. I shouldn't let my anger and frustrations get the better of me." He was unaware of the scowl marring his handsome features. All he was aware of was the unmistakable resentment and bitterness eating away at him. "I ran into Brynne at Ralph's birthday party. She was there with a friend. I saw her again when I went by her office. She works as a rape counselor downtown at the Sheppard Women's Crisis Center."

Absently he smoothed his mustache before he continued, "She claimed her reason for turning me down was because she didn't want to marry until after she got her Ph.D. A promise she gave her mother before she died. Brynne didn't say a thing about another man, that's for sure. I thought she loved me."

He paused before he went on to say, "I stopped by her office wanting answers as to why she left town. She surprised me by inviting me to lunch. That was when she asked if I'd take the paternity test. I can't ever remember being so angry." His voice shook when he grudgingly confessed, "I didn't trust myself to even speak to her after her doctor called with the news. I was scared of what I might do if I went to see to her."

"Nonsense!" His mother snapped. "You're my child and you'd never raise your hand to a woman. Even when you were little, when Anna followed you around like a puppy, you never hit her. The worst you did was flush her Barbie doll down the toilet."

"Your mother is right. You know how to handle your temper."

Donna, clearly outraged, came to her feet, hissing, "But

that doesn't mean I don't feel like slapping her. How dare she keep your baby away from you? I could see it if you were the kind of man unwilling to accept responsibility. But that isn't your way."

Devin was surprised by an unexpected urge to defend Brynne to his parents. He reminded himself that she deserved their anger. He had evidently been wrong about her. She was not the woman he'd thought he'd fallen in love with.

"Did she ask the other man to take this test?" Donna wanted to know.

"No. She claimed she didn't know how to reach him." His fists were clenched at his sides when he said, "The last thing I wanted was to hear about were the details of her with some other guy. If I could get my hands on the bastard—"

"Devin, you and your mother both need to settle down. No one is going to hit anyone. Donna, come sit down and drink this." Lester patted the sofa cushion beside him. Once she was seated, he handed her a brandy snifter and passed a snifter to his son. "Enough of this crazy talk. We aren't a violent family. With our faith we will get through this."

"This is my son she hurt. And I don't like it." Donna's eyes filled with tears.

"Mama, please don't." Devin had to blink back his own unexpected tears.

"Sorry, son." She wiped her eyes and then patted his hand. "I'm fine, really. I'm worried about you. I want you to be okay too."

"All I want is my daughter. I won't rest until she knows she's a Prescott and that I'm her father. And she is loved."

His parents nodded their agreement. Devin, unable to sit a moment longer, moved restlessly around the room.

His voice was edged with impatience when he asked, "How am I supposed to get back those first few years? Where do I even begin?"

"You begin by calmly talking this out with your mother

and me. You're not alone in this. We have your back."

"Your father is right, son. We can't change the past. We can only go forward from this point."

Devin nodded. "I know. When Brynne told me all this, I told her that she'd better pray that Shanna wasn't mine, because I plan to seek sole custody. No child deserves to grow up with a mother who is so promiscuous that she can't name the father of her child. I meant it. I intend to get my lawyer working on this right away."

Lester came over and placed a hand on his shoulder. "Hold on, son. You have to be careful here. You just found out you're a father. You have no idea what kind of mother this young woman has been to your little girl."

"Your father is right, Devin. You can't let your anger with the mother interfere with the bond you want to form with your little girl."

"I can't help it. Mama, Dad, she kept my baby from me for three years . . . three years I can't get back."

"You had better help it," Lester cautioned. "This isn't about wounded pride, but what is best for your daughter. How can you care for a little girl when you're on the road so much of the football season?"

"That's right. You have to calm down and examine your heart. What you want is what is best for Shanna. And that baby girl needs both a mother and a father," Donna insisted.

Devin flopped down in the chair he'd recently vacated. Thoughtfully, he said, "Yeah. I know this isn't about getting even, but I can't help how I feel." He sighed heavily, swearing beneath his breath. Eventually he said, "I know you're right. Shanna is all that matters now . . . not me or Brynne."

"You're going to have to find a way to meet with her mother and work this problem out. If you need to wait until you can talk to her without your anger getting in the way, then give yourself more time," his father advised.

Seven

Brynne was reading in bed when the call she'd been expecting finally came. "Hello?"

"It's Devin." His deep voice was taut, almost gruff.

"Did you—"

"Yeah. I spoke to your doctor."

"Oh" was all she could get out.

"Now there is no doubt that Shanna is mine. It would have been nice if you had called with the news, but it doesn't matter now. All that matters is Shanna and what is best for her." He took a deep breath before he said, "I want to see her, Brynne. There are also some legal arrangements we need to discuss."

"Okay, but it would be best if we talked before you meet Shanna."

"You can't keep her away from me. Not now that we both know the truth."

"Devin, I'm not trying to keep her away from you. Shanna needs to have her father in her life. There is no denying that, but you and I have things to settle between us before that can happen."

"Okay. When?"

"Tomorrow, after work. Crammer's?"

"Yes, I know it. Six?"

"I'll see you then."

Brynne held on to the telephone even after he'd hung up. As she returned the receiver to its proper place, she wished she'd had the nerve to tell him how blessed she felt because he was her baby's father. Not that her feelings mattered to him.

All that should be important was that Devin would do well by their child. At last Shanna was going to get her fondest wish. She would have a daddy. That in itself made Brynne happy.

However, life was about to become even more complicated. There was no doubt that establishing any connection between her and Devin was going to be an uphill battle. For her daughter's sake, she hoped they could at least be on friendly terms. How to go about accomplishing such a goal was a true challenge.

Devin was furious with her. Clearly he blamed her because she'd kept Shanna a secret. And he was right. It was her fault. She should have had the courage to have gone to him after the baby was born, to establish paternity. Her cowardliness had kept father and daughter apart.

Brushing away self-pitying tears, she accepted there was nothing she could do to change the past. From this moment on she must concentrate on smoothing the way between father and daughter. She couldn't help speculating if easing the way would entail explaining her reasons for leaving St. Louis. Or was she simply looking for a way to alter his decidedly low opinion of her?

Until recently, Brynne had thought she had done a good job of putting her life back together. Unfortunately, her child had suffered, having to grow up without her father. Devin had also paid a high price due to Brynne's silence and had missed out on their daughter's first years of life.

"Our daughter," she whispered aloud.

It was going to take some getting used to. For Shanna's

sake, she and Devin would have to find a way to get along. Divorced couples faced this kind of challenge and managed to stay on friendly terms, regardless of how badly they'd once hurt each other. What she and Devin had once shared had to be less painful than a failed marriage, didn't it?

Blame lay heavy on Brynne's slim shoulders. She had to find a way to make this right for her baby girl. Somehow she also had to find a way to tell Devin about the rape. Until that day came, she would focus on what was important—her child's happiness.

Although the restaurant was crowded for a weekday evening, Brynne had no difficulty finding Devin at the bar. He was surrounded by mostly females. Perhaps it was his superior height, his unbelievably wide shoulders and deep chest? Or maybe it was his dark brown skin and intense dark gray eyes that drew people to him like a magnet? He looked good in a black sweater, gray tweed sports coat, and black dress trousers. Judging by the way the women were smiling up at him, they evidently liked what they saw.

Brynne, unaware of the way she lifted her chin a notch and squared her slim shoulders, threaded her way through the crowd toward him.

"Hello, Devin. Sorry I'm late." She smiled, determined to ignore the butterflies in her stomach. She had taken special care with her appearance, deciding on a dark teal silk dress and teal leather blazer trimmed in black. Her black four-inch heels and short-handled purse completed the look of confidence and sophistication she attempted to achieve.

"No problem." His deep voice was clipped. "Excuse me," he said to the others before he stepped away from the bar. He cupped Brynne's elbow. "This way. I believe our table is ready."

Determined to ignore the way her skin tingled from his mere touch and the scent of his aftershave, Brynne allowed him to guide her to the hostess station. She stood silently while he gave his name and watched the attractive hostess beam up at him as if she'd just won the lottery. Brynne was relieved when they were finally seated in a corner booth that offered a degree of privacy.

"I thought we were only having coffee."

He said, "I don't know about you, but I'm hungry. Might as well order dinner."

She folded her hands, ignoring her menu. She wasn't sure she could manage food.

"Where is Shanna?"

Her eyes locked with his for a long moment. She tried to decipher what she saw in his dark gaze. The anger was evident, but could there also be pain? She dropped her lashes.

"She's with Trenna McAdams, a good friend and neighbor. Trenna owns the nursery school where Shanna has been going since she was two months old. She'd only spend a few hours there on the days I had classes while finishing my master's degree. She's only been enrolled fulltime since I started at the women's center."

Devin nodded. "Does Shanna like school?"

Brynne flashed a brilliant smile. "She loves it. She's an active, outgoing little girl."

"What's the name of the nursery school?"

At Brynne's surprised look, he lifted a brow. "I have years to catch up on."

As she answered, she fully accepted that her sole responsibility for Shanna was over. From now on, they would share parental concerns. The paternity test had changed the lives of all three of them.

"How much did she weigh when she was born?" he asked.

"Six pounds, two ounces. She was a beautiful baby."

"And she was healthy?" he quizzed.

"Very, thank God. She has always been tiny."

"Did you bring any pictures?"

"Yes." Brynne dug into her purse and pulled out her wallet. "This was taken at her birthday party. We had it at one of the local pizza restaurants."

Devin quietly studied the photograph before he looked at Brynne. "She's beautiful."

"Thank you." Warmed by his sincerity, she dropped her lids. "You can keep that."

He moved his finger over the surface of the photograph before he tucked it into his wallet. "Thanks. I want to meet my daughter. How soon can you arrange it?"

"Of course. But we have some things to settle."

The waiter chose that moment to interrupt. "Good evening." After taking their drink order, he rattled off the evening's specials before he asked, "Are you ready to order?"

Devin, clearly annoyed by the interruption, deferred to her, asking, "Should I order for you?" It reminded them both of a happier time when they took turns ordering for each other.

Brynne shook her head and then said, "I'd like a cup of clam chowder and the Caesar salad with pecan-crusted chicken, please."

"And you, sir?"

"I'll have steak, rare, a baked potato with no sour cream or butter, and a large salad."

Once they were alone she hastily said, before she lost her nerve, "Devin, I'm sorry I kept her a secret from you. I honestly believed I was doing what was best for Shanna. You see, the other man was—"

"I thought I made myself clear," he said in a harsh whisper. "I don't want to know a damn thing about him or why you did what you did. The only subject we're here to discuss is our daughter."

Brynne bit her bottom lip to hold back the tremor. She took a fortifying breath before she said, "You don't understand. It's not what you think."

A muscle flexed in his jaw as he interjected, "I've spoken to my lawyer, and he is drawing up the papers for you to sign."

Frustrated, she frowned. "Papers? What kind of papers?"

"Since Shanna is mine, I will support her. I owe you a considerable amount for her care, going back to the day she was conceived." He proceeded to name a more than generous lump-sum payment that would be followed by a monthly allotment that would be deposited in Brynne's account.

"There is no need."

"Believe me, there is a need. We Prescotts take care of our own. If you prefer, the lump sum can be put into a trust fund that she can draw on when she reaches twenty-two. Naturally, her college fund will also be taken care of."

Brynne could see by the angle of his jaw that he wasn't going to budge on the matter. Releasing a sigh, she gave in. "The trust fund will be fine and also the college fund. Monthly child support payments aren't necessary. Devin, this isn't about money."

"I'm not backing down on this. Nothing we do here can restore the time I've lost with my daughter. I suggest you accept the money so we can move on to more important issues."

Brown eyes momentarily locked with dark gray ones. Brynne dropped her gaze, knowing that there was no earthly way she could make up for the loss. The blame rested squarely on her. Father and daughter had suffered because of her, and the knowledge weighed heavily on her heart.

Just then their waiter returned with a glass of wine for her and a large mug of imported beer for Devin.

She sighed unhappily, toying with her glass. Evidently it was too late for explanations. He'd made his point. He was no longer interested in her or her reason for leaving St. Louis. What was worse, she could not hold it against him. She had been the coward, not he.

Brynne forced herself to say, "I thank you on Shanna's behalf."

He nodded, taking a sip of his beer. "About her last name. I want her to have mine. I also want my name on her birth certificate."

Suddenly angry, she hissed, "Is all of this part of your campaign to take her away from me? Because if this is what this is about, I want you to know I will fight you until my last breath before I will let that happen. You're going to have to prove I'm an unfit mother. And that's simply not true."

He said coldly, "This is not about you. This is about establishing my legal rights as Shanna's father. Now about my visitation rights."

"There is no need for a formal agreement. I won't keep her from you. I've had her all to myself for all this time. I want her to get to know you."

"I don't believe you. I'm not trying to be cruel, but I no longer trust you. I'd be more comfortable with a legal document with every detail spelled out in black and white."

Brynne was frankly relieved that the waiter chose that moment to bring their first course. She dropped her eyes, hiding the tears that threatened to spill down her cheeks. Devin couldn't have wounded her more if he'd hauled off and slapped her. The knowledge that he no longer trusted her hurt.

Unfortunately, she understood it too well. She had given him more than enough reason to doubt her. She tasted her soup in hopes of concealing her vulnerability. They were not lovers, nor were they friends.

She swallowed before she said, "I think it's best if we give Shanna a chance to get to know you before telling her that you're her father."

Devin finished chewing before he said, "What are you suggesting? That I not see her until—"

"That's not what I am saying. You may see her tomorrow evening, if you're free. In fact, you are welcome to come for dinner."

He put down his fork. "Just like that?"

"Yes." Brynne couldn't look into his eyes when she reluctantly said, "I don't date. I'm only telling you this because I've never brought a man home to meet Shanna. It will be enough of an adjustment for her to be around a man, even casually."

"Would you care for something more?" their waiter asked after placing their entrée in front of them.

Devin waited for Brynne's response, but when she remained silent, he said, "No thank you." If he was shocked by her disclosure, he didn't show it. He waited until they were alone before he said, "Well, Shanna will have an adjustment. She has four uncles, counting Gavin Mathis, my sister's husband, and my cousin Ralph, plus grandparents, all anxious to meet her."

"Devin, can we please start out slowly? You're coming to dinner tomorrow evening. Hopefully, if you can come over twice a week in the beginning, it should give her a chance to get to know you . . . to get used to you."

"Brynne, we're going to have to tell her something."

"I know. But for now I planned to tell her that you're an old friend of mine, who I knew in St. Louis. Then later, when she is comfortable with you, I'll tell her the truth." Using her fork to pierce a bite of chicken, Brynne said, "I should be the one to eventually tell her that you're her dad."

He frowned, evidently deep in thought while absently drumming his fingers on the edge of the table. He said, "Okay." And then he resumed eating.

"Just okay?"

"Yeah. You're her mother, and you know her better than I do. I don't want her traumatized because the two of us couldn't make it work. We'll do it your way. Take it slow and give her time to get to know me."

Brynne stared at him, lost in his strong, dark features. It had been so long since she'd been able to just look at him. Even longer since she'd seen him relaxed, even happy. At one time his happiness meant the world to her. She had altered the course of their relationship when she turned down his marriage proposal.

Often she thought if she had stayed with him that night, how different her life might have been. But she hadn't stayed and things between them had spiraled downward, ending with her being alone and raising their child on her own. The one good thing that had come from their love affair was Shanna. She had no doubt that Devin was a good man and would make an excellent father. Already he was putting their child's need ahead of his own.

"Thank you for understanding. I'm—" She stopped abruptly. She'd nearly told him how relieved she was that he was Shanna's father. Recognizing that she was emotional and that now wasn't the time to indulge in self-pity or regrets, she stared down at her plate rather than look at him.

"You what?"

She carefully placed her napkin beside her place. "I think I'd better leave while we're still on speaking terms. I don't want Shanna to sense our estrangement."

Devin reached into his inside jacket pocket and dropped a large bill on the table.

"Please, stay and finish your meal. You don't have to escort me out."

He rose to his feet. Holding her chair, he said, "Yes, I do. For one thing, I don't have your address. Besides, my mother raised me to always escort a lady to her door, if possible. At the very least, to her car."

She grabbed her purse, recalling that he'd seldom talked about his family during the time they were involved. Yet he had mentioned them several times this evening. She would be the first to admit that there was so much she didn't know about him.

What difference did it make now? What they had once shared should have no bearing on their ability to parent Shanna. She had no business being upset that he was no longer interested in her reasons for leaving him or that he preferred to believe she hadn't valued what they'd once shared and had cheated on him. In fact it was better this way, certainly safer. Safer? Where had that thought come from?

She hadn't sought counseling because she had been certain she could handle being raped on her own. It was only recently that she was starting to question that decision, wondering if perhaps she'd been wrong in not seeking professional help.

There was nothing to be alarmed about, she assured herself. She simply wasn't comfortable around men, actually preferred her female-dominated work environment. All her friends were single and women. Brynne frowned as the word "safe" popped into her head yet again.

"Did you say something?" Devin asked as he held her coat for her.

Sliding her arms inside, she shook her head and took a quick step away. She was overreacting to the entire evening, from the privacy of a meal with a man to the mere courtesy of being helped with her coat.

Outside the March wind was brisk with no hint of spring in the air.

Brynne searched her purse for one of her business cards. On the back she quickly wrote her address while they waited for their cars to be brought around.

"Thanks." He put the card into his coat pocket before he said, "I'll let you know when the papers are drawn up, and then you and I can go over them with our lawyers."

"Fine," she said tightly. It had been an emotionally draining evening, and the last thing she wanted was to get into yet another argument.

Relieved when her car finally arrived, Brynne thanked the parking lot attendant and then slid inside. To Devin she said, "We'll expect you at six-thirty."

"I'll be there. Good night." Devin closed her door and then waited until she engaged her locks before he moved to his own car.

Eight

"Mommy, can I help now?" Shanna tugged on Brynne's apron.

"Shanna Marie, you know not to pull on me while I'm working at the stove."

"But I want to help," Shanna pouted.

"No buts, young lady. If Mommy stepped back and didn't know you were there, you could have gotten a burn. Do you understand me?"

Shanna nodded, moving away while her bottom lip jutted.

"I didn't hear you."

"Yes, Mommy," she whispered, then complained, "I never get to help."

Brynne sighed, suspecting her daughter must be sensing her own anxiety. Shanna had been clinging to her ever since they'd gotten home. Brynne managed a smile as she turned off the double boiler beneath the creamed potatoes on the stovetop.

"Who helped me set the table?"

"I did!"

"Weren't you the little girl who helped put her toys away in the family room? Or was that another little girl?"

"It was me, Mommy." Shanna giggled.

"Then I don't have to go over to Lisa's house to get her to add the raisins and walnuts to the salad?"

Shanna said eagerly, "I can do it."

"Good. You go wash those hands, and I will get everything ready."

As her daughter raced to the half bath off the family room to wash, Brynne wondered how she was going to get through the evening without a major meltdown. Her stomach felt as if it was in knots, and she also felt the beginning of a tension headache. She told herself it was only because she had never had a male guest in her home. But she knew better. It wasn't as simple as that.

Devin Prescott wasn't just any man. He was not only her daughter's father, but also her ex-lover whom she had once loved with all her heart. She'd been convinced they would someday share their lives, and she would carry his children close to her heart. Only a part of that particular fairy tale had come true. Their single connection was their little girl. No doubt they would be fighting over what was best for her for years to come.

Although Devin had it under control, his brooding anger and resentment simmered just beneath the surface. Why was she still letting it bother her? Didn't she have enough to deal with just getting through this ordeal without a major mishap? After all, this was not about the two of them. The evening was about Shanna getting to know her father surrounded by the comforts of home.

"I'm ready," Shanna announced.

Brynne laughed. Shanna looked as if she had taken a bath with her clothes on. "I think somebody needs dry clothes. Come on, sweet pea." She turned her daughter around and steered her toward the bedrooms. "We have to hurry. We want everything ready when my friend comes."

Full of questions, Shanna asked, as Brynne pulled the

damp top over her head and motioned for her to pull off her damp slacks, "Is Mister Man your boyfriend? Julie's mommy has a boyfriend. Is he going to be my daddy?"

Brynne, having been searching through her daughter's bureau, stopped. She took a deep breath before she pulled out a red turtleneck and a red corduroy jumper trimmed with a blue floral border.

Determined to keep it simple, Brynne explained, "His name is Devin Prescott. Mr. Prescott is an old friend of Mommy's. He isn't my boyfriend. We knew each other when Mommy lived in St. Louis, a long time ago."

"Where was I?"

Brynne smiled. "It was before you were born."

"Can I wear my blue dress, Mommy? I want to look pretty like you."

Brynne knew a con when she heard one. Shanna was one determined little girl. That explained the wet clothes. A glance at the clock confirmed Brynne didn't have time to get into an argument.

"Mommy, pl-e-e-a-se."

"Yes, but you have to hurry."

Once Shanna was dressed in her navy blue dress with the white ruffled hem and white tights, Brynne tied blue ribbons on her braids. As Brynne buckled the tiny straps of her black patent leather Mary Jane shoes, Shanna asked, "Will he be my friend too?"

Brynne kissed her cheek. "Yes. Now let's get dinner finished. Mr. Prescott should be here soon."

As Brynne quickly straightened the room she wondered what Shanna should call Devin. It didn't seem right for her to call him by his last name. It was much too formal, but she shouldn't call him by his first name either. She couldn't call him Uncle Devin because that would really confuse her when she learned his true identity.

They were in the kitchen finishing up the Waldorf salad when the buzzer at the front gate sounded.

"Hurry, Mommy," Shanna called as she raced for the front door.

"Don't open that door," Brynne warned as she put the salad bowl in the refrigerator.

"I won't. But hurry, Mommy. I want to see my new friend."

"Just a minute." Brynne's hands were trembling so, she had trouble pushing the intercom button. She told Daniel, the security guard at the gated entrance, that Mr. Prescott was expected. She glanced in the hall mirror, checking the soft curls framing her face, and smoothed the navy tailored dress she'd worn to work that day.

She knew she was taking a huge risk by trusting Devin. He could easily break his promise that he would leave it up to her to decide when the time was right to tell their daughter the truth. Despite the passage of time and the strain between them, deep inside, she still believed he was an honorable man.

After switching on the porch light, Brynne watched Shanna excitedly bounce from one small foot to the other. At the sound of the doorbell she jumped, and Shanna giggled. Taking a deep breath in hopes of calming her nerves, she unlocked and opened both the front and storm doors.

She managed a smile. "Hi. I see you didn't have any trouble finding us."

"None." Devin surprised her when he leaned down and kissed her cheek, then handed her a box of chocolates.

"Thank you. Please come inside."

His large, powerful frame seemed to fill the small foyer. How had she forgotten how big he was, how he towered over her? Unconsciously she inhaled, filling her lungs with his clean male scent and the citrus aftershave he preferred. The years had been good to him, adding to his dark good looks.

Moving back, she nearly stepped on Shanna, who had been hiding behind her. Brynne reached back and put her hand on her little girl's shoulder, urging her forward.

"Devin, this is Shanna Marie Armstrong. Shanna, this is mommy's friend, Mr. Prescott."

Shanna peeked up at him through her dark lashes.

"Shanna?" Brynne prompted. She was surprised that her outgoing daughter had suddenly turned shy. And the normally outspoken Devin was silently studying his little girl.

Devin made the first overture. Squatting down, he said, "Hello, Shanna. You are as pretty as your mother."

Brynne encouraged, "What do you say?"

"Thank you," Shanna whispered shyly.

"You are welcome. This is for you." He handed Shanna a miniature version of the expensive chocolates he'd given Brynne.

"Thank you," Shanna whispered, hiding a big smile behind her hand as she clenched the box to her tiny chest.

After hanging his cashmere coat in the closet, Brynne said, "She's not normally shy, but for some reason she is tonight. Please come on back to the family room. Shanna was just helping me with dinner, weren't you, sweet pea?"

Shanna nodded, her thumb in her mouth.

Brynne smiled, pulling that thumb out. She didn't have to worry about losing her daughter, Shanna hung on to her skirt as they walked past the elegantly furnished cream and gold formal living and dining rooms. They followed the hall until it opened into the large family room directly across from the roomy kitchen.

A fire burned in the brick fireplace, behind the glass-covered screen in the family room. An oil painting of Brynne with Shanna in her lap hung behind the deep-cushioned, leather sofa, which was flanked by matching armchairs.

"Your home is very nice," he said quietly. "The painting is beautiful."

"Thank you. It was painted when Shanna was two."

She noticed that Devin hadn't taken his eyes off Shanna. In fact, he looked as if he were in shock, almost as if he'd been hit by a runaway train.

"Please, have a seat." Once he was seated in one of the armchairs near the fireplace, Brynne asked, "Would you care for something to drink? We have soft drinks, coffee, and tea, unless you want something stronger."

"Nothing for me, thanks. May I help?"

"We're almost ready. Shanna will bring in the appetizers," Brynne said as she crossed to the kitchen with pale maple cabinets and stainless steel appliances. She picked up the small tray of sliced cheeses and whole wheat crackers, handing it to her daughter. "Got it?"

Shanna nodded, then she slowly walked to the family room, taking care not to drop the tray. Devin was smiling as he thanked her for the offering and helped her set it down on the wide ottoman. Brynne hid a smile as she watched Shanna sit down in her child-size leather rocking chair with her cheese and cracker. She was too shy to speak to him, but nodded and then shook her head when he asked about her favorite toy.

Brynne turned away, blinking back unexpected tears at the sight of father and daughter together. She busied herself by filling serving bowls with creamed potatoes, green beans, and Waldorf salad. Once she'd placed the roast and warm dinner rolls on the table, she said, "Shanna, would you please show our guest to his seat at the table?"

Brynne had decided on the more relaxed atmosphere of the kitchen alcove rather than the formality of the dining room. She suppressed a laugh as Shanna grabbed Devin's hand and tried to pull him out of his chair and along with her to the round oak table in front of the curved picture window that overlooked the covered deck and backyard beyond.

Devin's eyes twinkled. Evidently he was trying not to laugh. Shanna pointed to his seat before she took her own place with the booster seat in the chair across from Brynne.

"Mommy, can I help?"

"Yes, you can ask Devin what he would like to drink

with his meal," Brynne said as she filled their water glasses.

Shanna shyly asked what he'd like. She giggled when he said he'd like apple juice.

"Did I say something funny?" he smiled.

"Apple juice is Shanna's favorite drink." She filled her daughter's water glass with milk and then the wineglasses with juice.

Once Devin had said grace, Shanna seemed to relax. She smiled when he asked her what she liked best about school. She began telling him her friends' names and that she loved to finger paint. She even offered to show him her scrapbook with all her drawings and paintings. Brynne suggested it could wait until after dinner. When Devin complimented Brynne's cooking, she laughed.

"What funny, Mommy?"

"Devin knew Mommy before I could cook much of anything. He was always cooking for us back then."

Shanna, busy eating the apples and walnuts in her salad while avoiding the green beans on her plate, said, "In Saints . . . What is it called, Mommy?"

"St. Louis," Brynne said automatically, glancing away from Devin. As the memory of the last meal he cooked for her the night of their argument flooded her thoughts, she shuddered.

"Where was I, Mommy?"

The question brought her back to the present. "That was before you were born. Remember, I told you."

Devin began telling Shanna about the things he, his brothers, and his cousin got into when they were kids. Shanna giggled, wanting to hear more. After dinner when Devin insisted on washing the dishes and Shanna volunteered to help, Brynne knew he'd gained her little girl's approval. While Brynne stored the leftovers in plastic containers, Shanna carefully placed the rinsed dish he handed her into the dishwasher.

She looked up at him saying, "Mister Man, Mommy said you are her friend." She paused before she seriously stated, "Mommy said you would be my friend too. Will you?"

Devin dropped down to her level. "Would you like me to?"

Shanna bobbed her head up and down vigorously.

"I'd like that too. But you have to call me Devin, like your mommy."

Her eyes went wide. She grinned before she turned to Brynne to ask, "Can I, Mommy?"

"Yes." Suddenly emotional, Brynne had to blink back tears. It was so gratifying to see them together. It finally hit her that Shanna was as much his as hers. At the same time, she again felt incredibly guilty for keeping them apart. It weighed on her conscience how her cowardly delay in seeking him out had robbed both Shanna and Devin of precious time together—time they could never regain.

Once the three of them were settled in the family room, Shanna begged to show Devin her favorite video, *Corduroy*. She raced to get it from one of the lower shelves in the entertainment armoire opposite the fireplace. She popped it into the VCR/DVD player before she jumped up on the sofa between Devin and Brynne.

Brynne didn't even try to hold back a giggle at Devin's confusion when he realized that Corduroy was actually a teddy bear who had been left on the toy shelf in a big department store because his overalls were missing a button. By the time they sat through two viewings of the video, Shanna was curled up on Brynne's lap, her head on her mother's breasts, nearly asleep.

"Will she wake up if I turn it off?" Devin said as he tenderly traced their daughter's soft cheek.

"Probably, but it's her bedtime."

"Let me carry her. Please?"

"Of course." She watched as he carefully lifted their daughter into his arms while trying not to react when he mumbled an apology as he accidentally brushed against her highly sensitive nipple. He handled Shanna as if she were as delicate as spun glass.

"This way." Brynne hurried ahead to show him Shanna's bedroom, which was next to her own.

He placed her down on her double bed, which was covered in a white comforter printed with bright red apples. He paused to lightly brush his lips against Shanna's forehead before he moved away to lean a shoulder against the door jamb. His gaze moved around the colorful room, taking in the child-size shelves lining the walls, filled with books, dolls, teddy bears, and toys. There was a child-size toy chest, chair and table with a roll of craft paper mounted underneath, as well as a tray of crayons and markers waiting to be used.

Brynne ignored her own tension as she undressed her daughter down to her panties and undershirt.

"Aren't you concerned she will wake up, and you can't get her back to sleep?"

"No. She's like you. She a sound sleeper, and if she does wake she will go right back to sleep, even after a bath. She's also stubborn, like you." Brynne candidly admitted, "Unfortunately, I only noticed those things after the paternity test."

They exchanged a long look before he said, "I'm glad she has a few of my traits. It's amazing how much she looks like you."

"Be right back." Brynne gathered pajamas and then carried Shanna into the bathroom. She sat her on the counter while she washed her face and hands.

"No, Mommy," Shanna protested sleepily.

"Yes, sweet pea." Once Brynne had her changed, she tucked her into bed. She was surprised to find Devin hadn't moved.

Shanna snuggled down with her favorite teddy bear tucked in one arm. As tired as she was, she mumbled, "Story, Mommy."

"Not tonight."

"Pl-e-e-a-se," she said around a yawn.

Brynne whispered to Devin, "It's a waste of time to argue. She loves picture books." Then she asked Shanna, "What would you like to hear?"

"Three Bears."

Brynne nearly groaned aloud. It was Shanna's current favorite and always ended with her daughter asking for a father of her very own. Brynne looked through the collection of picture books until she found what she was looking for. Following their nightly ritual, she kicked off her shoes and settled in the double bed with her daughter's head on her shoulder and began reading. Devin made himself comfortable in the cushioned, adult-size rocker in the corner.

Brynne had to force herself to focus on the printed words. When she finished, Shanna told Devin that she didn't have a daddy, but her mommy promised to go to the mall and get her one. Devin nodded, without voicing the question in his dark gaze, while Brynne blushed, knowing that she should be grateful that Shanna hadn't asked Devin to be her daddy.

"Time to close those pretty eyes, sweet pea," Brynne said as she kissed her daughter's cheek and gave her a hug. She switched off the bedside lamp but left night lights on in the bedroom and connecting bath.

Devin was a few steps behind her. He didn't speak until they entered the family room. "I owe you."

"I don't understand."

He surprised her when he walked over to her and cupped her small shoulders. His voice was hoarse with emotion when he said, "Our daughter is beautiful, both inside and out. She is a sweet, loving, and happy little girl. That is your doing."

He surprised her even more when he lightly brushed his mouth against hers before he stepped back. "I thank you for the love and excellent care you've given her. Words aren't adequate to express what I feel." His voice deepened when he said, "I owe you an apology. I was wrong to accuse you of not being a good mother. You've done it all. And you've done it alone. It couldn't have been easy for you. I will forever be in your debt because I know you didn't have to have her."

Deeply touched, it was all she could do not to break down and cry. She hadn't expected his understanding, certainly not his thanks. Her legs were far from steady as she sank down onto the sofa.

When she recovered her voice, Brynne said, "You don't owe me anything. I loved her even before she was born." She managed a smile. "I think we both could use something stronger than juice. I have a bottle of wine. Excuse me." She made a hasty retreat into the kitchen.

Needing to collect her scattered wits, she was careful to keep her back to him as she collected the wine, glasses, and corkscrew. She placed them on a small tray along with a small plate of shortbread cookies.

Neither her heart nor her breathing had returned to normal. They were both still racing. She had not frozen in his arms, but then he had taken her by surprise. She'd never expected to feel his arms around her, not ever again. She certainly hadn't been prepared for his thoughtfulness. But she should have been. Devin had always been fair in all his dealing. And she would be lying to herself if she failed to acknowledge how much his praise meant to her. After the painful things she'd endured, choosing to keep and raise her baby was the one thing she'd never regretted.

He stood staring down at the flames dancing in the grate. He didn't look up until she said his name. She handed him the corkscrew for the bottle of wine on the tray she placed on the coffee table. "Would you?"

"Nice," he said, as he examined the label before he opened the bottle of Cabernet Sauvignon and filled their glasses with the lush, dark berry, fruity wine.

"Thanks." She took a sip before she said, "I should thank you for not telling her the truth. I'm sure you were tempted, especially when she told you about wanting a father."

"Yeah, I was tempted, but I gave you my word." His mouth had gone taut as if he were angry, yet his voice was even when he asked, "Why does she think you can get her a father from the mall?"

Upset with herself for even bringing up the promise, Brynne explained how one of her classmates' mothers had met her fiancé at the mall. She finished with, "No matter how hard I've tired to explain, she still thinks the mall is the solution."

"Why didn't you tell her the truth? She clearly wants her father."

Brynne shook her head. "It's much too soon. It seems to me that you should want her to get to know you."

Devin took a sip from his glass, then placed it on the mantel. He began to pace in front of the French doors. "What I want is to claim her as mine. She's a Prescott. She has a whole family who already love her and are eager to meet her. She even has the Prescott gap between her front teeth. It's tiny, but it's there."

"I didn't realize," Brynne whispered.

"How could you, when you were focused on forgetting everything about me and what we shared?" His deep voice was tinged with bitterness. "Forget I said that. This isn't about our failure. I still don't understand why you didn't tell her tonight."

"I told you. I'm trying to do what I think is best for her. She's only three. She needs time to adjust to just having you here in our home." Her eyes were troubled when she said, "I'm not trying to deny that you've missed her first three years. And I accept full responsibility for that," she said quietly. "You have no idea how much I wish that I had told you when I realized I was carrying her. But I can't change what happened."

"Hindsight is perfect every time. The point is you didn't

come to me then, and there is nothing either one of us can do about it now." Devin glanced at his watch. "I should go before we get into an argument."

Surprisingly, Brynne realized that she didn't want him to leave, not just yet. "Would you care to see Shanna's baby pictures before you leave?"

He smiled. "Yeah, I would."

"I'll be right back."

Nine

She hurried into her bedroom, not willing to explore her motives. She should have been glad he was leaving. Somehow they had managed to get through the evening without getting into a shouting match. She should have just let him leave. Maybe she was just trying to ease her guilt by making it up to him in some small way? There was no point in recalling how overwhelmed she had been by his thoughtful words, especially when she had expected nothing beyond his brooding anger.

Tonight he had shown Shanna the side of his personality Brynne remembered from long ago. He'd been playful, warm, even loving with their little daughter, and for that she had been thankful.

Brynne found what she was looking for on a shelf in her walk-in closet. She refused to even glance at herself in the mirror as she passed it. Her hair and makeup weren't important. Nor did she speculate on the brief kiss he'd given her. Instead she quickly returned to the family room, sat on the sofa, and handed him the first of the photo albums.

She laughed. "As you can see I took lots of pictures.

This first album is from the day she was born to her first birthday, from then to the next birthday, and so on."

Devin grinned at the newborn picture of Shanna on the outside cover. "She's beautiful." He began to slowly turn the pages. "Did she come early?"

"No. She was born on my due date."

"Did you have a difficult labor?" he asked as he turned another page.

"No, everything was normal. I was in labor seven and half hours, relatively short for a first baby. Or at least that's what my doctor claimed."

"Were you alone?"

She wanted to ask why it mattered, but memories of him telling her how much he loved her, how much he longed to see her heavy with his child, came rushing back.

"Brynne?"

"No. Vanessa Grant and Trenna McAdams, my two best friends, were with me."

Devin nodded but didn't comment. As he studied each photograph, she studied him from beneath her lashes.

He chuckled. "How old was she here? Was this when she started walking?"

Brynne smiled. "She stared walking at ten months. She was about nine months in that picture. She was such a good baby . . . so happy."

"She looks so much like you. Right from the first."

She offered quietly, "Take out the ones you want, and I can make copies for you."

Devin's dark gray eyes locked briefly with brown ones. "Thank you."

Brynne looked quickly away. "You're welcome."

When he closed the final album, he stood up. "I really appreciate you sharing these with me."

Brynne silently walked with him to the front door. Although shaken, she remembered her manners and retrieved his coat from the front closet. The last thing she wanted was for him to detest her. That brief kiss had been his way of thanking her for her care of Shanna. As long as she kept that in mind, they wouldn't have a problem. Grateful or not, she must not forget that he wasn't about to back down on what he believed was best for Shanna.

"Which day in the next week is convenient for us to meet with our lawyers to go over the child support and my visitation rights?"

Annoyed, she snapped, "I thought we agreed on a trust fund and visitation rights?"

"I want it in writing so there won't be any cause for mis-understanding later. And yes, we agreed she is to have a trust fund, a college fund, and monthly child support payments. What we haven't done is hammered out the specifics."

Suddenly exhausted, Brynne didn't have strength to get into a shouting match with him over money or anything else for that matter. "Fine. I'll speak to my attorney and get back to you."

She didn't want to analyze the memories that had returned. Little details about him and their time together that she'd been certain were buried in the past. There was no point in looking backward. So what if they had once believed they couldn't get enough of each other, or that they hated the things that kept them apart, such as the demands of his career and, in her case, graduate school.

Devin asked pointedly, "When can I see her again?"

"Friday evening. Dinner again?"

"Today is Wednesday. Why the delay? I thought—"

Disheartened by his lack of trust, she insisted, "Devin, I'm not putting you off."

"Are you sure this is about Shanna and not yourself?"

"What's that supposed to mean?" She crossed her arms beneath her breasts, glaring up at him.

"You tell me. All I want to do is see my little girl. What?" He sneered, "Does that inconvenience you and your man? Is that the problem? He doesn't like another man hanging around your place?"

"What makes you think that? I told you I don't date," she practically shouted at him.

"You're reluctant for some reason. You told me you don't bring men around Shanna. That doesn't necessarily mean you don't have a man stay overnight while she's asleep. What else am I suppose to think?"

"You're supposed to believe me." Brynne poked a finger into his wide chest. "I haven't asked about your sex life, so kindly keep your nose out of mine."

"More secrets, Brynne?"

Glaring up into his dark eyes, she had to tilt her head back in order to meet his challenging gaze. "Your sex life is no longer my concern. That ended a long time ago."

"It's not a secret, Brynne. I'm not involved with anyone right now. The only female in my life that matters is my daughter. For once in your life, be honest."

"Why is this important?" she demanded, one hand on a shapely hip.

"Once Shanna gets to know me, she will be spending time with me, my family, and my friends. Then she will no doubt tell you who I'm seeing and vice versa. Get used to it, darling. We have a child. We will be in each other's lives for at least fifteen years. Probably more. We have to get along, for Shanna's sake."

Even though she knew he was right, she didn't like his answer. She didn't want to stand back and watch him fall in love, marry, and possibly have children with another woman.

Deciding a change in topic was called for, she said, "Friday evening is best for me. I oversee a group therapy session on Thursday evenings."

"Friday it is." He ran his hand over his close cut natural. "I know it seems as if I'm trying to pressure you, but I'm really not. It's just that I've missed so much. And I have a lot to make up to her."

"I'm sorry—"

"I didn't say that to place blame on you. I have only known she's mine for a few days, but already I love her."

Brynne's throat filled with the tears that she was determined not to let fall. Eventually she said, "She will know that one day soon."

"I hope so. Would you prefer going out to dinner on Friday?"

"Why don't we leave well enough alone? Having dinner here went well tonight."

"Okay. If she needs anything or is sick at any time, please give me a call. It doesn't matter if it's the middle of the night."

"I promise." She placed her hand on his arm. "Now, I'd like a promise from you."

He said nothing, but waited for her explanation.

"You know the location of her school, and she knows you. I would like you to promise that you won't take her without my knowledge."

"What are you suggesting?" Devin snapped. "That I might kidnap her?"

"No, I never said that."

Devin hissed through clenched teeth, "I'd never do anything to hurt her. Even trying to see her without your approval would jeopardize the trust that I'm trying to build between my daughter and myself. But for you to suggest such a thing demonstrates how far apart we are. Evidently neither one of us trusts the other one." He paused before he went on to say, "There is one major difference between the two of us. I've never done anything to violate your trust in me. Can you say the same?" With that he walked out.

That Friday, Devin sat in his car a block away from the Armstrongs' home, drumming his fingers on the steering wheel. He was giving himself time . . . time to collect himself . . . time to make certain his defenses were firmly in place. He wasn't about to make the same mistakes he had made the other night.

He'd loved his tiny little daughter from the instant he'd seen her. Without question, Shanna had a place of her very own in his heart. She was bright, funny, beautiful, and perfect in every way. Despite her initial shyness, his little girl had gradually warmed up to him. Perhaps she sensed his love? She was precious from her shy smiles, to her little-girl giggles, to her playfulness. And there was no doubt in his mind that she adored her mother.

When it was time for him to go, he hadn't wanted to leave. He had wanted to take Shanna home with him. He probably wouldn't have been able to leave if he had doubts about her mother's care. He wanted to protect his little girl from all the ugliness in this world. He had no idea what it meant to be a father until he looked into his child's eyes. Shanna in her own way told him how much she wanted a daddy. He wanted nothing more than to be the best father he possibly could.

Until that night he'd placed the blame squarely on Brynne's shoulders for keeping Shanna a secret. He was so caught up in his own selfish needs to claim his child that he hadn't considered the loving and secure home that Brynne had given their daughter. In his zeal, he'd failed to put Shanna and what was best for her first. Evidently he still had a lot to learn about being a parent. Things Brynne already knew.

He'd been caught up in the past, consumed with jealousy that Brynne had deceived him and hadn't loved him as deeply as he'd loved her. He'd been unable to get beyond her leaving him.

Finally Devin accepted a basic truth. Because of the complications of Shanna's conception, Brynne could have just as easily decided not to have the baby. It had been her choice. And she had made the decision alone.

He would be eternally grateful that she had had Shanna. He would be less than a man if he hadn't thanked her. What he hadn't planned was the kiss. He'd pulled Brynne close until her soft breasts were pressed against his chest as he inhaled her unique feminine scent. That had been a huge mistake.

He might have been able to keep the sensual memories at bay if he hadn't gotten a taste of her full, lush lips. And he'd been paying for that lapse with restless nights and persistent hard-on.

What in the hell was wrong with him? So what if he was still attracted to her? Or that he'd wanted to make love to her from the moment he had first laid eyes on her again? Evidently he was suffering from selective memory loss. The Brynne Armstrong who had kept his child a secret from him was nothing like the woman he'd fallen in love with back in St. Louis.

Brynne was the very last person he would have expected to sleep around. She had been a virgin the first time they'd made love. He'd gone over their last night together, again and again, but it didn't add up.

Maybe he should have listened to her explanation about the other guy? But how could he, when just the thought of her with another man sent him into a rage? There was no doubt in his mind that even at this late date, if he knew the man's name, he would go after him with his fists.

Brynne was different these days. She was uneasy around him. Although she tried to conceal it, nonetheless, he sensed her apprehension. Sure, he'd been angry with her, even resentful, since learning that she had made a fool of him as well as kept their child a secret. But that didn't mean he would harm her. He'd never given her reason to fear him. Yet he'd be the first to admit that it had taken a great deal of effort on his part to keep his temper under control. But harm her physically? Never. He'd walk away first. Why did she think he was less than a man?

Well, he couldn't sit out here all evening. With a resolute sigh, he drove to the gated entrance and gave his name. Within minutes he'd parked in her driveway, pocketed his keys, and grabbed the oversize black teddy bear with a kente cloth vest and hat. With long, purposeful strides, he approached the front door and rang the bell.

He heard Brynne remind Shanna that she was not to touch the door, and then Brynne disengaged the lock and swung the storm and front doors open. He tried to ignore the way his breath caught in his throat as his gaze moved over her petite frame. Why did she have to be so blasted lovely?

"Good evening," Devin said formally, and then grinned when he caught sight of Shanna peeking at him from behind her mother. Like her mother, she was dressed in red. She wore corduroy jeans and a long-sleeved Pooh Bear tee-shirt. "Hi, princess."

"Hi." Shanna smiled, shifting from one sneaker-clad foot to the other. "I like your bear. Is that for me or Mommy?"

"Shanna Marie, mind your manners," Brynne said quietly.

"Sorry," she mumbled, but her brown eyes sparkled with curiosity. "Is it for Mommy?"

"We'll have to wait and see," Brynne cautioned. "Devin, won't you please come inside?"

"Thanks."

Closing the door behind him, he had to force his gaze away from Brynne's pretty dark eyes, creamy pale brown skin, and those lush, red-tinted lips. She had tucked the mandarin-collar, red silk blouse with its black trim into the waist of her black slacks, drawing his eye to the shapely curves of her petite figure. She also wore a pair of her trademark high-heel shoes. Did she have to look so damn good?

Devin dropped down until he was eye level with Shanna. Smiling, he asked, "How's the little princess tonight? You look pretty."

Shanna grinned shyly at him. "I really like your teddy bear."

Devin nodded solemnly. "I'm glad you like him. I

bought him for you. I thought you might have a place for him in your room. Do you?"

Shanna clapped her hands, jumped up and down. "Yes!"

"You promise to take good care of him?"

She nodded so vigorously, her entire body shook with her enthusiasm. "He's the biggest bear I ever saw." She reached up, wrapped her small arms around Devin's neck, and gave him a hug. "Thank you, Devin."

"You're very welcome." He brushed a kiss against her soft hair, enjoying her little-girl baby powder scent. He had to force himself to let her go. His eyes burned as he longed for the day she would call him Daddy. There was nothing he wanted more than to be there to watch her grow up.

"That was very thoughtful of you, Devin. Let me take your coat and we can go into the family room."

He shrugged out of the dark gray leather coat, revealing pale gray slacks and a charcoal sports jacket over a turtle-neck sweater. He chuckled as he watched his daughter struggling to carry the bear. "Need any help with that?" he asked, trying not to laugh out loud.

Shanna shook her head, determined to hang on to her prize.

"I didn't forget you," he told Brynne. He reached into the inside jacket pocket and handed her a miniature black bear in a tiny kente cloth vest and hat.

Brynne laughed. "Thank you. Look, sweet pea. Look what Devin brought me."

Shanna giggled. "He is just like mine, Mommy, only little."

After hanging his coat in the hall closet, Brynne said, "Shanna has a surprise for you."

"Yes!" His daughter grabbed his large hand and began trying to pull him along with her while hanging on to her toy.

"Need some help?"

Shanna shook her head firmly. Finally grabbing the bear

by one huge paw, she urged, "Hurry, Devin." She didn't stop until they reached the large combination kitchen and family room.

Devin noted the table in the kitchen was set for three and a big salad was on the counter. "What kind of surprise, princess?"

"It's a—" She blinked in surprise when her mother playfully put her hand over her mouth and then placed a finger over her own full lips.

"It's a surprise, remember?"

Shanna nodded eagerly.

"Devin, will you sit in the armchair, and Shanna will go get your surprise." Brynne laughed indulgently as the little girl took off like a shot, bear in tow. Avoiding his gaze, she said quietly, "The bear was a wonderful surprise, but you shouldn't have."

"Why not?" he asked as made himself comfortable in the armchair, resting his hands on his thighs.

"Because I—"

"Here it is!" Shanna called as she raced to Devin's side. She plopped the box in his lap, then climbed up on the ottoman to watch. "Open it."

"A present for me?" He teased her.

"Mmm-hmm. I helped stick the—"

"Shanna," her mother said.

She giggled, covering her mouth. "I forgot I wasn't 'pose to tell. You have to open it."

"I'm afraid Shanna isn't good at keeping secrets. As you can see, she can hardly stand the excitement."

"Hurry, Devin."

"Okay." He grinned as he broke the ribbon holding the box closed and lifted the lid. "A photo album?"

"A scrapbook of me!" Shanna announced. She helped him open the cover. "All me. This is me when I was a little baby. I help Mommy stick on the pictures and the borders. Lots of pictures."

Devin swallowed back the lump in his throat as he slowly turned the pages. There were pictures of every stage of Shanna's development from the day she was born.

"Do you like it?" Shanna asked her brown eyes sparkling.

"I love it," Devin answered, his voice thick with emotion. "Thank you, Shanna . . . Brynne. When did you have time?"

Brynne said, not quite meeting his gaze, "You're welcome. I worked on it after Shanna was in bed, and she helped me finish while I cooked dinner. Hope you're hungry. We're having steak, and Shanna is having a hamburger."

"You don't like steaks, pumpkin?"

Shanna giggled at the name. "I like cheeseburgers and French fries."

Devin fired up the grill on the patio. They were soon sharing steaks along with baked potatoes and salad at the kitchen table. After they ate and cleaned up the kitchen, they roasted marshmallows in the fireplace.

"Somebody is getting sleepy," Brynne stroked the little girl's cheek.

"No, Mommy. Not yet."

"Yes, Shanna Marie." Brynne got her on her feet and turned Shanna to face Devin. "Say good night."

With her thumb in her mouth, Shanna whined, "Can Devin stay and read my story?"

"Will you?" Brynne asked softly as she stared at the place just past his shoulder.

Feeling as if he'd been handed a priceless treasure, he nodded. "I'd like that."

"I'll call as soon as I have her settled," Brynne said as she led Shanna toward the bedrooms.

Moving restlessly around the room, Devin paused to study the photographs on the mantel. Pictures of Brynne and Shanna, a few of Brynne and Shanna with women— her girlfriends, he assumed. There were no photos of Brynne with a man. The only photo with a man was one of a much younger Brynne with her parents. He remembered it being in her apartment in St. Louis.

He also recalled how happy and carefree Brynne had been back then. She was reluctant to sleep with him, unsure of him and herself. After a few weeks of dating, she was finally ready. He'd never forgotten the night they had become lovers. It was also the night she told him that she loved him.

And he'd believed her. Perhaps it was because of the way he felt about her. She wasn't like the women who chased after the pro ball players. She hadn't been interested in him for his fame or for his money. She took her time getting to know him. He believed Brynne was special. And he didn't want her to get away. All too soon, he was asking her to be his wife.

If only he understood what had made her change. Maybe then it would all make sense. She had once trusted him enough to give her body. And she had given herself wholeheartedly, holding nothing back. He had done the same, without fully realizing that by doing so, he'd allowed her to hold his heart in the palm of her small hand for safekeeping.

If only he knew what had caused her to stop loving him. Maybe then he could accept her reasons for turning to someone else. And it would stop hurting so damn much.

He swore beneath his breath. Past hurts and mistakes no longer mattered. He would be fine as long as he kept his hands and lips to himself. He was here for one reason, to get to know his little daughter and for her to get to know him. Until his baby girl became comfortable with him, there was no way for him to see her without also seeing her mother.

"Ready," she called.

Ten

As they left their daughter sleeping, Brynne asked Devin, "Would you like some coffee?"

"None for me. What I would like to know is why you canceled the appointment with the lawyers and did not reschedule another one."

She'd been dreading that question all evening. And she still had not come up with an answer. She couldn't very well tell him the truth that she hadn't recovered from Wednesday evening.

Everything about that evening had shaken her. She had been prepared for a continuation of his brooding anger and resentment, but hadn't expected his sincere gratitude for her having the baby and her loving care of their daughter. When he took her into his arms, and held her against his deep chest, instead of pushing him away as she should have, she had leaned into him and accepted his warmth.

Over the past few years she'd become an expert at keeping men at arm's length, never letting them get too close. The mere thought of intimacy was disturbing, but participating was downright frightening!

With Devin, however, it felt different . . . she was different. Yes, she had been afraid, but not of his hurting her. Despite his belief that she had been unfaithful to him, he would not lay an angry hand on her. She knew it wasn't his way. She had been so shaken by her response to him that she'd not called her attorney or set up the meeting with him and their lawyers. She hadn't wanted to face him this evening.

"Brynne?"

"I'd like a cup. Excuse me." Hoping for a few minutes alone, she walked away.

She could handle pouring out the leftover coffee and starting a fresh pot. He was another matter all together. Unfortunately, he'd followed her into the kitchen and leaned against the counter. His powerful arms were crossed over his deep chest.

She needed something to occupy her hands, but thanks to Devin the kitchen was spotless, so she busied herself by preparing a tray, including a plate of freshly baked gingerbread cookies.

"Well?" he prompted.

She snapped, "Well what?"

Devin's eyebrows shot up. "Why are you upset?"

"I'm not!"

"Sure you're not," he jeered. "Did you speak to your lawyer?"

"You're trying to pick a fight and believe me, we're already on shaky ground. It's my understanding that we were going to try to be civil for our daughter's sake."

"Shanna is asleep," he said. "About your attorney . . ."

"She has ears! It will upset her if she wakes up and hears us arguing. Have you forgotten she's just beginning to be comfortable around you?"

"Sorry. I know. I'm pushing. Being a father is new to me. I'd like to have the financial aspects of our agreement settled, as well as the visitation rights."

"I'm aware of that," She sighed. "I'll contact my lawyer on Monday. Hopefully, it will be taken care of in a few weeks."

Devin nodded. His dark gaze moved over her. "I appreciate the scrapbook. It means a lot."

"You're welcome. Shanna enjoyed helping."

"She didn't suspect anything?"

"Why would she? She's still so young that it seems perfectly normal to her that mommy's friend would like her baby pictures."

"Have you decided when you're going to tell her about me?"

Their eyes locked for a long moment. Brynne was the first to look away.

"No. She's only seen you twice. It's too soon." Brynne paused, then said, "Give her time, Devin. She likes you. That's why she asked you to read her bedtime story."

He smiled, unwittingly drawing her eyes to his full, masculine lips. "That's good to know."

Brynne dropped her lids, balling her hands into small fists at her sides.

He surprised her when he said, "I know this isn't easy for you, having me in your home. But—"

"We are both doing what we have to do. Let's leave it at that."

"My parents are anxious to meet their granddaughter. I know it's too soon for me to take her on her own, but you are more than welcome to join us for dinner on any Sunday. It's the perfect way for Shanna to meet my family."

Brynne felt as if her stomach had done a somersault. "I seriously doubt your family is interested in meeting the woman responsible for keeping you away from your daughter for so long."

"No one will say anything, if that's what you're worried about."

"Perhaps not. But, Devin, that doesn't mean I won't be uncomfortable, as will your family. Shanna is a sensitive child. She'll sense something is wrong. I think its best if you wait until she knows you better and then you can take her to meet your family on your own."

"Okay," he said impatiently. "But Shanna has the entire family that love her and want to get to know her."

As Brynne reached for the glass coffee carafe, she wondered why she wasn't relieved. She'd won that round. Maybe it was because she knew the next battle was just around the corner. Would they always be at odds with each other?

She said nothing as Devin carried the tray into the family room and placed it on the ottoman in front of the sofa. The fire was still burning in the grate. Brynne followed with napkins and dessert plates. Once she'd poured the coffee, she settled back on the sofa, careful to keep a cushion between them.

"It was kind of you to bring the bear. She loves it."

He chuckled. "She looked so cute trying to carry that thing. Now that was a picture."

Brynne sipped from her mug. "You're going to have to stop bringing her things."

"Why? I've already missed three birthdays and three Christmases. I plan to make up for lost time."

"If you bring her a present every time you come, she is going to expect it."

"What's wrong with that?" Devin asked as he cradled his mug.

"Plenty. She is only three years old. She's too young to understand what you're trying to do. She's going to start expecting gifts from you, as if you're Santa Claus. You want her to love you and respect you for the man you are, not because of what you can give her."

Placing his mug on the side table, he rose and began to move restlessly around the room. Deep in thought, he eventually stopped, resting one hand on a lean hip. "I haven't thought of it that way. I want to be a good parent." Reluctantly he admitted, "Evidently I have a lot to learn."

"It takes time. You're pushing too hard. When Shanna was born, I didn't know how to change a diaper. I had to learn, and quickly. It will be the same for you. You can't expect to get it right all at once."

She stiffened when he came over and sat down beside her. "Brynne, our baby girl deserves the best. I have so much catching up to do."

"What you have to do is let her learn the kind of man you are. She's going to love you and look up to you. And she's going to be proud that you're her dad." Brynne surprised herself when she reached out to squeeze his hand. "Give her and yourself some time."

Looking into her eyes, he nodded his agreement. "Okay. No more gifts and pushing you to tell her about me or rushing the meeting with my folks."

"Good." She blushed and quickly dropped her lids when she realized she'd been staring at his mouth.

Suddenly realizing where she'd left her hand, she jerked it away and balled it at her side. Embarrassed, she did her best not to take note of the frown creasing his brow. The last thing she needed was for him to think she was interested in rekindling their love affair. No, that wasn't quite true. The last thing she needed was for him to suspect that she was uncomfortable around him. It wasn't that she actually feared he would harm her. Perhaps it was his size and strength that she found so intimidating?

Brynne shook her head as if trying to clear it. After the way she had hurt him, she didn't need to be reminded that Devin had no interest in her. All she needed to remember about him was that he was a good man and he would do right by their daughter. Her concern should be solely centered on whether his exuberance might get the best of him, causing him to spoil Shanna rotten.

Devin came to his feet, stretching his long, muscular body. "I'd better get going. I can see myself out, but I know you need to lock up and set the alarm."

Brynne wrapped the cookies into a napkin. "We made

the cookies last weekend. I'm sure she'd like you to take some."

"Thanks."

"When will we see you again?" she found herself asking.

"I'm flying back to St. Louis this weekend. Is next Tuesday evening okay for you?"

She nodded. "Fine."

"Don't bother with cooking. I'll bring dinner."

"You don't have to do that," she said, hurrying to keep up with his long powerful strides.

He sent her a cocky grin from over one broad shoulder. The grin was familiar, and brought back memories of a happier time. It also caused her heart to race.

"Yes, I do. Enjoy your weekend. Night."

The weekend passed slowly. Brynne couldn't believe the number of times Shanna asked about Devin. He seemed to be her favorite topic, much to her mother's discomfort. Time and time again Brynne was forced to remind herself that it was a good thing that her little girl took an instant liking to him. It was bound to make things easier.

Yet she was sick of explaining that Devin had gone out of town and couldn't go with them to the cleaners' and grocery store on Saturday morning or to a movie that afternoon. On Sunday Shanna hadn't given up and wanted to know why he hadn't come with them to the church.

Despite the excuses Brynne was forced to make, she didn't have a clue why he'd gone away. It could as easily have been due to business as to personal reasons. For all she knew he was spending the weekend in bed with his current lady. And if that was the case, it had nothing to do with her.

On Monday Brynne was frankly relieved when she could take Shanna to nursery school and she could go to work and not hear the man's name for a few hours. Unfortunately, Devin had never been far from her thoughts. She couldn't help but smile while recalling his face when

Shanna handed him the scrapbook filled with her photos. He'd been as excited as their little girl.

Memories of the good times seemed to creep into her thoughts at odd times during the day. The worst was when she went to bed because her thoughts of him were so clear, she often dreamed about him. The most disturbing dreams were the erotic ones in which she actually relived their lovemaking. She had no idea why. Perhaps it was because they had loved deeply and shared so much?

Devin had been an exceptional lover. He was generous in the care and attention he devoted toward her pleasure. The man had a slow and tender hand and often brought her to climax again and again before he sought his release.

Brynne hated to admit it, but she believed whomever he was with now was indeed a lucky woman. It was an effort not to hate the woman's guts. Brynne needed no reminder that she was the one who had given him away, or that she was no longer woman enough to give him what he needed sexually.

At her office, she called her lawyer to discuss the arrangements for the settlement and visitation.

As promised, Devin brought their dinner on Tuesday evening, Chinese take out. Shanna was thrilled to see him and full of girlish chatter and giggles. The evening passed pleasantly, both Brynne and Devin sticking to safe topics.

During the weekly staff meeting on Wednesday, held in the office of the director of the center, Maureen Hale Sheppard, it was a struggle for Brynne to keep her mind on business.

Maureen asked as she looked up from her notes, "Anything more on the Carter case that we should be aware of, Laura?" Maureen was seated at the conference table in the corner of the beautifully furnished room. The sofa and every available chair were taken by staff members. Despite the beauty of the costly oil painting behind Maureen's desk, the expensive Oriental rug underfoot, the chenille sofa, and the framed plaques and degrees on the wall, or even the fact that she came from one of the most wealthy and influential African-American families in the country, Maureen had also been touched by the harshness of rape. Her mother had been a victim, and Maureen's biological father had been her rapist.

Laura, munching on a cracker, said, "Yes. Mr. Carter not only abused his wife but also sexually violated his teenaged daughter. As you know, I'm working with protective services to get her out of the home. Unfortunately, I still can't convince Mrs. Carter to press charges against him."

Maureen sighed. "At least she continues to come here for counseling. For that we have to be grateful."

"I would have been even more grateful if we could convince her to nail the bastard," Andrea Jones, one of the counselors, snapped.

Everyone laughed in total agreement.

"Brynne, how is the newest member of your therapy group doing?" Maureen asked.

"Ms. Martinez is doing well." Brynne didn't need to glance at her notes. "She has been able to talk about the details of the rape. Even though she still won't identify her attacker, she's making progress."

"Good. If we can get the other two women to talk to the prosecutor, we could be assured of convicting this Andre Smitt," Maureen said thoughtfully.

"I'll give it another try," Laura volunteered, "but I'm not making any promises. All three ladies are afraid. And I don't blame them. This guy is brutal."

"None of us blame them." Maureen glanced at the crystal clock on the wall, adjacent to the elegant glass and mahogany desk. "If no one has anything to add, we can get back to work."

While the others collected their empty plates and cups, Brynne held back. As was her custom, Maureen had ordered deli, cheese, and fruit trays. The staff took turns bringing in dessert. Today had been Brynne's turn.

"The lemon squares were delicious, Brynne. You have

to give me the recipe." Maureen teased, "Can I borrow Shanna to help?"

Maureen was not just the founder's granddaughter. She had degrees in psychology and counseling, but she was also a friend and an Elegant Five Book Club member.

"Glad you enjoyed them. I'm sure Shanna would love to volunteer her help." Brynne realized her hands were shaking as she tucked the remaining bars into a plastic container.

"Have you ladies finished our new book?" Laura asked with a grin.

Both Brynne and Maureen shook their heads. Brynne admitted, "I haven't started."

Laura teased, "Now I don't feel so guilty. At least I've started."

"We still have a few weeks." Maureen laughed.

Brynne busied herself, cleaning the conference table.

"You don't have to do that," Maureen said as she cleared away what remained of the trays.

"I don't mind." Brynne asked, "Do you have a few minutes?"

Maureen smiled. "Sure. Just let me check with Janine to see how many calls have come in." She stepped out to speak to her secretary.

Although Maureen's grandmother, Francine Coleman Hale, had her own office in the executive wing, she left the day-to-day operation of the women's crisis center to her granddaughter.

"Is something wrong, Brynne?" Laura, having collected her notes in her leather portfolio, hesitated.

"There are just a few things I have to talk over with Maureen." Brynne felt guilty about the evasion, but then if she could talk about what happened, she wouldn't need help.

Laura nodded. "I have some calls to make. Tell Shanna how much I enjoyed the lemon squares. I'll see you later." She hurried out.

On trembling limbs, Brynne sank down into her chair, hoping to display a calm she didn't feel.

When Maureen returned, they were alone. She lifted her brow in surprise when Brynne requested that she close the door. She came over and took the chair next to Brynne's. "What's the problem? One of our clients?"

"No. This is personal. And it is something I thought I'd handled on my own years ago. Recently I realized that I was wrong."

"Sounds serious."

"It is." Brynne took a deep breath, then blurted out before she lost the nerve, "You see, four years ago, I was raped."

Eleven

—

"Oh, Brynne, I'm so sorry." Maureen reached over and squeezed her hand. "I had no idea."

"No one does. It's my deep, dark secret." Brynne brushed impatiently at the tears suddenly flooding her vision. "I can't keep it inside anymore. It's beginning to eat at me, and I am not going to let it claim any more of my life. It has certainly destroyed any thought of intimacy with a man." She cringed at the thought of taking a man inside her body.

"Are you telling me you didn't get counseling?"

Brynne nodded.

"But why? You're a rape counselor, for heaven's sake. And a damn good one at that." Maureen's disbelief was written all over her strikingly beautiful face.

Dropping her gaze, Brynne clasped trembling hands tightly in her lap. "I didn't think I needed counseling. After all, it was my field. I know the procedure. I was certain I could handle it on my own." Her laugh held no humor. She went on to add, "What I did was push it as far away as I could. I buried it so I could get on with my life. It wasn't until my pregnancy that I knew I had a problem. I had no idea whose child I carried . . . my lover or my rapist." She paused before she admitted, "I was so determined to move forward that I refused to look back. I had my baby and got on with my life."

Maureen nodded her understanding. Her own life had been negatively affected by being the child of a rapist. "Well, we can't change the past. What can I do to help you now?"

"It wasn't until recently that I knew I needed help. I'd like you to take me on as a client."

"Me?"

"Yes, you're the best." Brynne reminded her, "You're not the director of this center because of your looks or family connections."

"I'm flattered, but we are friends. What if I can't be completely objective?"

"I'm not worried. Why should you be? Please, Maureen. Do this for me. I don't think I can talk about this with anyone else."

"I'd like to help, but my schedule is crazy." She walked over to her desk and picked up her planner. "What about Dana? She's our most experienced counselor."

"Do you have any idea how difficult it was for me to come to you with this?" Brynne shook her head. "If I'm going to do this, then it has to be with you."

Maureen frowned, "Did you say 'if'?"

Brynne nodded. "You're the only one I know I will be able to talk to about this. I trust you."

"You know how straightforward I am. Some people have problems with my approach, but it works for me. Are you willing to deal with that?"

"Yes. I don't need you to hold my hand or to coddle me. I value your honesty."

"Okay, then. We're going to have to work through our lunch hour. It's the only way I can fit you in. Two sessions a week, Monday and Thursday."

"That's fine. Thank you. I can't tell you how much this means to me."

"Don't thank me. I'm not going to be easy on you." Maureen smiled. "I imagine you want this kept between the two of us."

Brynne nodded.

"Okay. We tell the others we're working on a special project."

"I appreciate that." Brynne gathered her things. "I'd better get out of here. I have a client coming in at one. And your next appointment is probably waiting. Maureen, thanks again. Bye."

"Just be on time. And don't forget to bring your lunch."

The two women were seated on the sofa in Maureen's office with their lunch spread on the low coffee table in front of them.

Maureen said, "Okay, Brynne. I want you to start at the beginning. You said the rape happened four years ago."

"Yes, while I lived in St. Louis." Brynne hesitated and then swallowed nervously. "I'm sorry. I thought I could do this."

"You can. This happened while you were in grad school?"

Brynne nodded, twisting the pearl and diamond ring on her right hand, a gift from her parents.

"Why did you decide to study so far away from home?"

"I did my undergraduate work at Rucker University. It's a small, private college. And their graduate program is one of the best in the country. After my parents passed, I saw no reason not to go back and finish there. I had friends and an apartment. I felt comfortable there."

"Did you know your attacker?"

Brynne stiffened, but she nodded. "He had been in several of my classes. In fact, we often studied together. I thought of him as a friend." She bit her bottom lip to hold back a tremor. "I couldn't have been more wrong."

"Is that why you left St. Louis? Because of the rape?"

"Yes, I closed up my apartment and left. I left without

finishing the semester. I was so scared, I just started my car and didn't stop going until I reached Detroit and home."

"Tell me about the man in your life."

"Back then?"

"Yes," Maureen said, quietly.

"I was in love with Devin Prescott. Shanna's father. We hadn't known each other very long."

"Did you tell him about the rape?"

Brynne shook her head. "I couldn't. Afterward, nothing was the same, especially me. I was no longer the woman Devin fell in love with. I didn't even recognize myself."

"Who raped you, Brynne?"

"Connor Helm. We were in the same psychology class. He came by my apartment, said he had missed class, and asked if he could see my notes."

Maureen nodded as she took notes. "Tell me about the rape. Was it at night?"

"Yes. That evening started so perfectly. Devin and I shared a romantic dinner at his place. He prepared a wonderful meal for me. Later we danced and then made love." She explained, "Devin plays professional football. He's from Detroit, but he plays for the St. Louis Rams. We had only been seeing each other a couple of months. And he surprised me when he asked me to marry him that night."

Brynne reached for her bottled water. She took a sip before she went on so say, "I turned him down, not because I didn't love him, but because I wanted to finish my education before I married. I tried, but I couldn't make him see that I wanted to be his wife, just not any time soon. I wanted to keep the promise I made to my parents, especially my mother. It was her dying wish that I not let anything keep me from finishing my education.

"I couldn't make Devin understand." Brynne sighed. "We got into an argument and were both angry when I left his place and drove back to my apartment."

Brynne ignored her container of chef's salad. Restless, she rose and began to move aimlessly about the office.

"Connor was waiting outside my door. He asked if he could copy my notes." She covered her face as if she could block out the painful memory. "I invited him into my apartment. I didn't even give it a second thought."

She dropped down on the sofa again, uncertain if her legs would hold her. "It wasn't until he was inside that I realized he was very angry. He'd heard the rumors that I was dating Devin, the wealthy NFL star quarterback. He wanted to know if it was true." She shook her head. "I was so stupid. I was surprised at his interest, but not alarmed. I told him that I'd been dating Devin for some time. Instantly, Connor's whole demeanor changed. He was no longer that easygoing man that I thought I knew. Furious, he demanded to know if I was sleeping with Devin.

"That was when I got scared and asked him to leave. He started talking nonsense. Like, how could I let another man touch me when I knew I belonged to him? And that I knew I was his, and that he loved me."

Brynne shook her head vehemently. "Maureen, we had never been more than friends. Sharing an occasional meal or studying together. I didn't know what he was talking about, but I knew better than to argue with him." Rubbing her hands up and down her arms to take away the sudden chill, she forced herself to say, "He began following me. When I tried to get to the telephone, he grabbed me and tossed the phone across the room. I was so scared, but I demanded to know what he thought he was doing. He insisted it was time we made love . . . that it was what we both wanted. That was when I started screaming no, fighting him, and trying to get away. I couldn't believe how strong he was. He kept insisting that I wanted him . . . only him. Saying he could prove it.

"By this time I was really scared. I kept trying to make him understand that he was wrong, but he wouldn't listen. When he started taking off his clothes, I managed to break free and run toward the door. He caught me and dragged me into the bedroom."

Brynne shuddered. "He stood between me and the door. I was screaming at him, demanding that he leave, telling him no over and over. He grabbed me by the hair and started kissing me. Telling me he loved me. The more I fought him, the tighter he held me down. We were on the bed and he was forcing his tongue in my mouth. I bit him hard and he slapped me. He grabbed my blouse and ripped the buttons off and tore it from my body."

Tears rushed down her cheeks, and she shook so badly, even her voice quivered. She spoke quietly, determined to force the words out. "I hit and scratched him, but he was too strong for me. He held me d—"

"Do you need a break?" Maureen asked.

Brynne shook her head. "If I don't tell you now, I never will. And I can't keep it inside any longer."

Maureen nodded as she passed the box of tissues. "What happened then?"

"I fought him, but the harder I fought, the stronger he seemed." Brynne sobbed.

"We can stop."

"No! I have to tell you. I have to . . ." She dried her eyes and blew her nose as she tried to stop the flow of tears that ran down her cheeks. "I scratched his face and he slapped me before he held my hands over my head. I screamed and he covered my mouth with his so no one could hear my screams. I tried to keep my legs together but he forced them apart. I couldn't get him off me. I couldn't make him stop.

"He had no right to come inside me. No right! I'd just made love with Devin." Brynne's hands were balled into fists. "I have never hated anyone until then. At that moment, I wanted him dead. I tried everything I could think of, but it didn't stop him. He forced his way inside me, making what had been beautiful with Devin into something so ugly . . . hateful. I hated it! I hated him! I must have passed out because when I came back to myself, it was over. He had finished. I remember rolling into a tight ball.

"I couldn't stop crying. He tried to comfort me, saying

he knew I really loved him and wanted him . . . that I'd always wanted him."

Maureen gently squeezed her hand. "What did you say?"

"Nothing. There was nothing left to say. He'd already taken what he wanted. When he tried to hold me, stroke my hair, I screamed at him to get away from me. I pushed at him. He must not have expected it because I got away. I ran to the kitchen and grabbed a butcher knife. He followed me. I screamed at him to get out. I kept on screaming until he left.

"But before he left, he warned me to keep it between the two of us. He told me no one would believe me. He reminded me that his grandfather was the head of the university. That no one would take my word over his. And he told me, if I told Devin, he would make sure that Devin knew that I cheated on him. We both knew I'd invited him into my apartment, and that was proof that I wanted him there. I remember shaking my head and screaming at him to get out until he finally left." Brynne slumped against the sofa cushion, exhausted.

Maureen beamed. "You did it. You got it out." She went on to say, "I know it doesn't feel like it helped right now. Trust me, it will, given time."

Brynne nodded. "I know. I've seen the results in others." She sat quietly, taking deep breaths, leaning back with her eyes closed. Eventually she opened her eyes and said, "It's entirely different when it happens to you. Maureen, I managed to push it away, keep it buried inside of me. If I hadn't run into Devin at that party I went to with Laura, I probably wouldn't have dealt with it at all."

Maureen glanced at the clock. "Our time is up. You did very well, my friend."

Brynne accepted her comforting hug. "Thank you. Already it feels as if a weight has been lifted from my shoulders." She reached for her purse and searched for her compact. "I must look a mess. I didn't mean to fall apart like that."

"Don't apologize. Remember you did nothing wrong." Maureen offered, "You're welcome to use my powder room to freshen up."

"Thank you. I won't be more than a minute."

It took longer than she expected to bathe her swollen lids with a cold washcloth before she could repair the damage to her makeup. Unfortunately, it would take a great deal more than cold water to restore her shattered nerves. Brynne recognized she felt something she hadn't felt before, a tiny seed of hope that she could someday overcome this despair. She was so tired of feeling like a victim.

"Feeling better?" Maureen looked up from the notes she was typing into her laptop computer. Her concern was evident on her pretty features.

"Yes. Almost like a person." She walked over and hugged the other woman. "I'm sorry I fell apart on you."

"Don't apologize. Just keep in mind, it's going to take time but it will get better. You've helped so many others. Now it's your turn to be helped," Maureen soothed.

"I'm hopeful. We both know we don't always succeed."

"This time it is personal. You've come to me for help, not the other way around. Together we're going to get you through this. You did well today. Keep that in mind, sister girl."

"I will. I have to go. I gave you my word that this wouldn't interfere with your work or mine. Bye." Brynne collected her uneaten lunch and then hurried out the door.

Brynne kept her appointment with her lawyer to review the papers Devin's lawyer had sent over. If her lawyer was surprised about how quickly she accepted Devin's generous offer, she didn't indicate it. Everything they discussed was clearly spelled out. The document included the amount of the trust fund, child support payments, and visitation agreement that Shanna spend two weekends a month with her father. The final requests were that Prescott be added to

Shanna's name and that Devin's name be placed on her birth certificate. There were no surprises.

Brynne left the office with a substantial check in her purse. A check she didn't need or want, but one that would be deposited in a new joint account for Shanna. The experience left her feeling sad, wondering if her daughter would someday blame her for keeping her and her father apart.

Money couldn't make up for Devin not being there when their daughter was born or his not seeing her first smile or her first steps. There was no doubt about it. He had missed so much and put the blame squarely where it belonged, on Brynne's shoulders.

During the next few weeks, Brynne was amazed at the relative ease with which Shanna accepted Devin into her life. Shanna was more comfortable with him after each visit. She talked nonstop about him, eager to see him again.

Brynne acknowledged to herself that it was nearing the time when she should tell her daughter the truth about Devin. She debated whether she should tell her while he was in their home or if it would be better for her and Shanna to have a mother-daughter talk. She didn't want to rush her child, nor did she want to drag it out longer than necessary. There was no doubt that both father and daughter had suffered enough because of the secrecy.

Unfortunately, the tension between Brynne and Devin hadn't eased, although they were both on their best behavior in front of Shanna. They worked to make sure there was not even a hint of discord between them.

The only one disturbed by his ongoing presence in their home was Brynne. She was forced to see him several times a week, and their conversations were limited to a single topic, Shanna. Brynne knew she had no choice but to adjust. Her daughter's well-being was at stake.

"Mommy, hurry! Devin will be here any minute!"

Devin had invited them both to the circus for the Saturday matinee. Shanna was so excited she could hardly sleep the night before.

Brynne, who had been cleaning up their breakfast dishes, said, "I'm almost done. We have lots of time."

"Mommy, I don't want to be late. We might miss the clowns."

"We have plenty of time, sweet pea. Come here. Mommy wants to talk to you."

Shanna pouted, shaking her head. "No! I'm going to be a big girl at the circus. I won't cry, even if I get scared."

"I know you're a big girl. You're not in trouble, sweet pea." Brynne took a seat at the kitchen table and pulled Shanna onto her lap. She hugged her tight. "We can talk without you being in trouble, you know. I have a surprise for you."

"A present?" Shanna perked up with her brown eyes sparkling expectantly.

"No, honey, not a present." Brynne kissed her cheek. "I know you like it when Devin comes over to visit."

Shanna nodded. "He's lots of fun. He gives me piggy-back rides."

Brynne laughed, "I remember. You giggled so hard your stomach hurt."

"Devin is your friend and my best friend too. Right?"

Brynne cupped her daughter's chin. "That's right. But he's more than your best friend, honey. Devin is your daddy."

Shanna's eyes went wide. "My pretend daddy?"

"No, sweetheart. Devin is your real daddy."

Shanna was all eyes as she watched her mother. "For real?"

"Yes. And you can get to see him and go places with him."

Shanna squealed and hugged her mother's neck. "That makes me happy!"

Brynne knew the news made her little girl very happy. Devin was the father she'd been wishing for. Brynne had wondered and worried when was the best time to tell Shanna. She had even discussed it with Maureen. Last night she had realized that Shanna already loved and trusted him, which made her finally accept it was time.

Brynne kissed her daughter's cheek. "You're going to have both Mommy's and Devin's last name."

Shanna wrinkled her nose. "New name?"

"Mmm-hmm. Your name is Shanna Marie Armstrong Prescott. Think you'll like that?"

Shanna with her thumb in her mouth was thoughtful for a moment. Then she asked, "Do I get to call Devin Daddy?"

"I don't know. That's up to you and Devin. Why don't you ask him when he gets here? Now, young lady. Let's go look in your closet and see if we can find something special to wear to the circus."

Shanna gave her mother another tight hug. "Squeeze, Mommy. Hard," she insisted. Satisfied, she jumped down and ran into her bedroom.

Twelve

"*How much longer am I going to have to* put up with your foul moods?" Anna Prescott Mathis demanded.

Devin took his eyes off the road to glance at his baby sister. "What? I haven't done a thing. Did you have a fight with that knuckleheaded husband of yours?"

"Leave Gavin out of this. He's not the one who dragged me out of bed on a Saturday morning. This is about you. Do you have any idea what a royal pain you've been since you learned you're a father?"

"I haven't been taking it out on you."

"Really? What do you call all this brooding you've been doing? You can barely string three words together while dragging me in and out of department stores for two solid weeks, looking for furniture for Shanna's room. Don't get me wrong. I don't mind helping. What I mind is your attitude, big brother." She sent him an impatient glare. "When am I going to meet my niece anyway?"

"I wish I knew," Devin snapped, returning his eyes to the road.

"Is that the reason for this mood?"

"You haven't heard a word of complaint from me. I don't know what you're talking about, Short Stuff."

Anna rolled her eyes at the familiar nickname her brothers and cousin were so fond of calling her, since they were all well over six feet. "Dev, you're angry. You have been for weeks. You can't keep it locked inside forever. Talk to me! You're bound to feel better."

"And you have that on whose authority?" he quipped as he pulled into the Somerset Mall.

"Don't even try it. I put up with you butting into my business when I fell in love with Gavin. If I'd listened to you, Ralph, and Wes, I never would have gotten married. Well, now it's your turn to be on the receiving end. So start talking."

"That was different."

"It's not different. We're family. And you know I can keep my mouth shut if I have to."

"It's not that." He concentrated on finding a parking space. Once he'd parked, he turned the engine off. Anna caught his arm before he could get out of the car.

"Tell me about Brynne. What is she like? We all know this is not about your baby girl, but her beautiful mother."

"How do you know she's beautiful?"

"Ralph, who else?" She laughed. "The first thing he notices about a woman is her looks. Poor thing doesn't know any better."

Devin chuckled, and then he sobered. "He's right. Brynne is beautiful. I can't seem to get her out of my head."

"You're still angry with her for keeping Shanna a secret? Don't you think you need to talk this out with her?"

"Talk about what? Why she couldn't keep her legs closed? I don't want to hear what she has to say."

"How are the two of you going to be on good terms if you can't stand to be in the same room with her? I think your baby girl is going to notice. Or are you so angry, you no longer care?"

Devin snorted. "You're not pulling your punches, are you, sis?"

Anna insisted, "That's not an answer."

Devin stared out of the window for a time. Eventually he said, "There isn't one damn thing I can do to change the past. Yet I can't let it go." He rubbed a hand over his close-cut natural before he reluctantly admitted, "I was in love with her, Anna. I wanted her to be my wife. And I thought she loved me. Then she left me without one word. Now after four years, I discover that she was sleeping with someone else while I was busy picking out a ring and planning the perfect evening for my proposal." His voice was filled with frustration when he added, "I've tried to forget, but I can't! How could I have been so wrong about her?"

Anna reached across the console and squeezed his hand. "You don't believe she ever really loved you, do you?"

"How can I? She turned to another man. I was happy. I thought she was too."

"Was she dating lots of guys when you met? Maybe you were so caught up in her looks that you didn't realize she was sort of 'out there.'"

Devin shook his head. "Brynne was nothing like the experienced women I used to date. She was in grad school, focused on getting her degree. That was all she ever talked about. Her parents were killed in a car accident a few months before we met. She was still grieving."

"How did you meet?"

"At a dinner party at a mutual friend's home. Brynne wasn't impressed with my looks or my career. She came from a wealthy, well-educated family. Both of her parents were doctors. My being a millionaire didn't faze her. My having a college degree interested her.

"Hell, she wasn't even dating when we met." He paused. "Sorry, I don't mean to swear, but it is so frustrating." He went on to say, "Like her parents, she was interested in helping others. She was working toward a master's in counseling. It was all she ever talked about."

Anna suggested, "Maybe she just broke up with some-one else and didn't want you to know?"

"I doubt it. If she was in love, she hadn't slept with him. She certainly didn't hop into bed with me right away. When we made love for the first time, I knew she cared deeply for me. She was a virgin."

"What?"

"Yeah. Brynne wasn't promiscuous. So you see why this doesn't make sense?"

"How did she explain the other man? What did she say?"

"Not much, I wouldn't listen." He pounded his hand on the steering wheel. "I couldn't take it. When I even think about her with another man, I see red."

"Don't you think it's time you got some answers? From what you said about her, something isn't quite right."

"I can't talk to her about the bastard," he growled impa-tiently. "I don't trust myself to hold on to my temper."

"You may not have a choice but to talk it out. That is, if you're going to have any peace at all. Because it is pretty obvious to me that you still have feelings for her. Love just doesn't evaporate into thin air."

Devin knew he wasn't ready to examine his feelings for Brynne. "Forget I said anything. Let's go." He stepped out of the car and made his way around to open her door.

"I can, but can you, Dev?"

Devin didn't answer, but began walking toward the main entrance. They were inside the mall when he finally said, "Brynne has moved on with her life, and so have I. My only concern is my little girl."

If only it were that simple. He'd spent the last few weeks trying to get over his hurt and overwhelming sense of be-trayal. Nothing helped. If only he could hate her and be done with it. He found he didn't have it in him to hate his child's mother. Yet the anger and resentment continued to eat away at him. He was at a standstill, unable to move for-ward or backward.

* * *

When Devin rang Brynne's doorbell, he knew he was in trouble. He should have never walked into the bookstore. He had intended to purchase books for Shanna's new room, not buy out the prekindergarten section of the children's department. Brynne would have his head if she knew what he had done. All he wanted was for his baby girl to have all the comforts of home while at his place. When the time came, he wanted everything in place.

Even Anna had laughed at his enthusiasm when they'd hit the toy department. At least he wasn't fool enough to bring all the picture books with him, but he'd tucked a few of the circus books into a shopping bag, along with a stuffed clown.

He had to admit he was a bit nervous. This would be their first outing as a family. Only they weren't exactly a family. For the time being, he had no choice but to accept that Shanna would be more comfortable with her mother along.

When he thought of a family, naturally his parents came to mind. They'd been married thirty-five years and were still very much in love. Over the years they'd shared everything and raised five kids together. He'd always imagined it would be the same for him and his siblings.

What he never expected was to have a child outside of marriage. Or to be so estranged from the mother of his child that he couldn't consider marrying her. No matter how much he didn't like the idea of Shanna growing up in a home without him, there was nothing he could do about it.

He was a Prescott, no different from his father or his older brother, Wesley. He also wanted what was best for his child. Unfortunately, he didn't have a clue as to how to change the situation or himself. He couldn't ask Brynne to marry him while knowing that she had been unfaithful to him, not even for his baby's sake.

In the meantime, he thought he was doing a credible job of keeping his mouth closed and his thoughts to himself. He and Brynne hadn't had an argument since she signed the child support and visitation agreement.

"Sorry to keep you waiting." Brynne said somewhat breathlessly as she opened the storm door. "We were running a bit late."

Devin refused to let his gaze wander below her chin. He knew better than to let his eyes caress the soft swells of her beautiful breasts, her tiny waist, or her sweetly rounded hips.

"I'm early." He closed the door before following her down the hall, determined not to notice the swing of her hips in the tight jeans. Some things hadn't changed. Although petite, the girl never lacked curves. Hell, she could have any man she wanted. So why had she stopped dating? He was not fool enough to believe the men in Detroit had lost their eyesight. Another piece of the blasted puzzle that didn't fit.

Damn, he had no business noticing the way she filled out those jeans. Unfortunately his hormones weren't cooperating. He knew exactly how sensitive her breasts were, but also how she liked to be caressed. Hell, if he lived to be a hundred, he'd never forget how sweet she tasted. His sex ached with need as he recalled how exquisitely her tight sheath felt along his hard length. He swore silently.

Even though she had nearly ripped his heart out of his chest, he still wanted her. He hadn't been near another woman since Brynne reentered his life. He hungered for her alone. He sure as hell hadn't told his sister that whenever he was within reaching distance, his shaft lengthened and his senses went wild. He spent too many nights dreaming about her. Knowing she was also celibate wasn't helping either.

"Shanna! Devin's here," she called as they entered the family room. That was when she spotted the bag. "Dev, what's that? More presents?"

"Just a few books and a stuffed clown." He lifted a brow. "You got a problem with that?"

"Hi!" Shanna called as she raced into the room. Instead

of coming over to him, she darted behind her mother and peeked at him.

Devin grinned. Like her mother, she was dressed in jeans and a pink turtleneck sweater. "Hey, little princess. All ready for the circus?"

Shanna nodded her head vigorously.

"Shanna?" Brynne prompted.

"I'm ready." She giggled from behind her mother.

"So you've gone all shy on me, today? I thought we were friends."

Shanna looked up at her mother, pulling on her sweater until she came down to her level. She whispered loudly in Brynne's ear, "Can I ask him?"

"Go ahead."

She nodded before she slowly made her way over to Devin. She stared up at him for a time, and then she tugged on his hand.

Devin squatted. "What is it?"

Shanna asked shyly, "Are you my daddy?"

Devin's eyes went wide as he stared into his baby girl's pretty brown eyes. His heart raced as his questioning gaze flew to Brynne. He saw her nod.

"Are you?" Shanna persisted.

"Yes," Devin said in a husky whisper. He swallowed the emotion that was ready to steal his control. "I'm your dad."

"Good," Shanna clapped her hands, then threw her little arms around his neck and kissed his cheek. "Can I call you Daddy?"

Careful not to crush her, he concentrated on inhaling her scent. She smelled like Ivory soap and baby powder. "Yes, Shanna. I'd like that a lot." Devin whispered, "thank you" to Brynne, but he couldn't see her because his eyes were filled with tears. He blinked hard.

Rising to his full height and lifting Shanna with him, he gave her a spin all the time keeping protective arms around her. He laughed when he heard her giggles. As he carefully set her down on her feet, he realized just how much he truly loved her.

She grinned. "What's in the bag?"

Devin chuckled, handing it over.

"Look, Mommy," Shanna said excitedly. "Storybooks and a clown. Thank you, Dev—I mean, Daddy."

Grinning, Devin had to clear his throat before he said, "You're welcome. You can't read them until we get back, though. Why don't you take them into your room and get your shoes, so we can get going?"

"Okay!" She gave him a big smile and then dashed off.

He walked over to Brynne and pulled her against his chest. He said, close to her ear, "Thank you. You have no idea how much this means to me."

She wiped at her own tears, smiling up at him as she took a step back. "It was time."

"My heart nearly stopped when she asked if I was her daddy." He sighed in relief. "She's happy about it. And that's because of you."

"Don't thank me. I did what I should have done a long time ago. I should never have kept you two apart. I'm sorry."

Devin surprised them both when he cradled her face in a wide palm. "Stop beating yourself up. I know I've said some harsh things. But it's in the past. All of it. What you did today makes up for everything. If I forget that for a second, you have my permission to smack me."

With her head tilted back, Brynne looked up at him as if in disbelief. As if she doubted he meant what he said, and as if she wondered if he could forgive and forget. Devin stared down at her, marveling how much their little daughter looked like her. He waited to see if she would pull away. When she didn't, he slowly covered her mouth with his.

What started out as a mere brush of the lips to demonstrate his gratitude quickly turned into much more. He groaned low in his throat as he traced the seductive curve of her pink-tinted lips with his tongue. His movements were unhurried. Brynne trembled. He had no idea if it was anticipation or dismay that caused the tremors. Yet those tremors didn't stop him from taking her plump bottom lip into his mouth to suckle. He moaned, savoring her sweetness, before he moved into her mouth to do the same to her tongue.

Gathering her close, Devin closed his eyes as he inhaled her ultra feminine, unique scent while enjoying the heat of her mouth. It had been so long . . . too long since he'd been free to hold her like this . . . caress her like this . . . taste her.

They both jumped and then pulled apart when Shanna called, "Mommy! I can't find the pink sneakers. Mommy!"

Both of them took a step back, but it was Brynne who dropped her thick lashes, concealing her eyes.

"Excuse me," she mumbled before she nearly ran out.

Devin sank into the nearest armchair. His legs felt as if they could no longer support his weight. Absently he smoothed a hand over his hair as he struggled to accept what had happened.

He'd been blindsided by his daughter's asking if he was her daddy. That alone was enough to knock him off his feet. Next he'd meant to offer a simple thank-you to Brynne and ended up taking her sweet mouth in a kiss, brimming with unexpected longing. And then he hadn't wanted to stop . . . holding her . . . kissing her . . . tasting her.

Hell, if it hadn't been for Shanna calling her mother, he wouldn't have been able to stop. What the hell had happened to his self-control? Even now he was breathing as if he'd been flattened by a three-hundred-and-fifty pound linebacker.

And to make matters worse, he was as hard as a rock. Past mistakes had been pushed aside while his sexual need eroded his common sense. This kind of thing never happened to him. He knew his limits.

He swore beneath his breath. What had happened to him? He sighed heavily. Brynne was what happened. One taste of her sweet mouth and he'd forgotten everything.

"Daddy!" Shanna ran over to him. "Me and Mommy is ready to go to the circus."

With a wide grin, Devin swung her up to his shoulder. "Then we'd better get moving."

Thirteen

The circus, with its predominantly African-American performers, was held at Cobo Hall in downtown Detroit. Children, young and old, were bubbling with anticipation.

Brynne was amazed at how close they were to the action. She felt as if she could reach out and touch the animals as they paraded past. Shanna was so excited, she bounced up and down in her seat. She never stopped talking as she munched on a hot dog, popcorn, and cotton candy.

Shanna was not the only one enjoying herself. Devin seemed to be having as much fun as their daughter. He chuckled at the clowns, gasped at the daring high wire acrobats, and clapped at the tricks by the animals.

Brynne found herself wondering if this was what their life would have been like, if she'd accepted his proposal years ago. They would have been a family, raising their child together, and when the day was over, she wouldn't be spending the night alone in her home while he was miles away in his condo.

"Mommy, look! Aren't they cute?" Shanna, now on

Devin's lap, pointed to the tiny dogs jumping through hoops.

Brought back to the present, Brynne firmly pushed away sad thoughts of what couldn't be. "Yes, they are."

"Can I have a puppy?"

"When you're old enough to take care of one," Brynne said quietly.

Shanna made a face, clearly not liking the answer, but she was soon distracted by a long-legged clown riding on a small pony. She giggled. "Look, Daddy!"

Brynne listened as Devin told Shanna about the time he went to the circus with his brothers and sister when he was a boy. She found she was able to relax and not feel as if she had to be on her guard every minute they were together. It had been so long since she'd been comfortable in a man's company. Suddenly she recognized that, for the first time in four years, she truly felt safe.

Despite his size, Devin had always been gentle with her, even tender when they made love. There once was a time when they had no secrets and had hopes for a shared future. She shivered at the bittersweetness of the memory.

"Cold?" Devin asked as he helped Brynne into her coat before helping Shanna.

"A little," she said as she zipped Shanna's coat.

"Do we have to go?" Shanna complained.

"It's all over, sweet pea. Time for all the animals and sleepy little girls to have their naps," Brynne said with a smile.

Devin picked Shanna up, so she wouldn't be jostled or lost in the boisterous crowd, while Brynne carried the tote bag full of all the goodies Devin had bought for Shanna. For once she hadn't scolded him for spoiling her.

When they'd reached the parking lot, Brynne noted the temperature had dropped considerably. Although the ground was dry, the March day had been cold and sunny, with no hint of spring. A cool breeze off the Detroit River made Brynne glad she had insisted that Shanna wear her hooded parka and gloves. Her own cream leather jacket, colorful scarf wrapped around her neck, and pink wool tam kept her warm. Devin didn't seem to be bothered by the cold. He wore a black leather jacket and gloves, but his head was bare.

"Watch it." He caught Brynne around the waist, to prevent her from being run over by a crowd of exuberant teenagers, shifting her in front of him.

"Thanks."

He asked, "Did you have a good time?"

Surprised by the question, she smiled. "Yes, I did. How about you?"

"Yeah. I especially enjoyed watching Shanna's reactions. As for me, I can't remember the last time I've been to the circus. Probably not since I was a kid with my family." He glanced down at their tired daughter, who rested with her head on his shoulder. "How about you, little princess? Did you have fun?"

Shanna nodded, clearly worn out.

Brynne said, "She went to the circus with her nursery school last year, but she was so little, she doesn't remember much."

"Did you go with her?" he asked.

"I could never let her go without me. It's not that I don't trust the teachers, but it was easier for me to come, rather than spend the day worrying myself sick, wondering if she'd get lost or was afraid or even sick from eating too much." Then Brynne said with a teasing glint in her eyes, "Her class is going to the petting farm in a few weeks. Would you like to go with her?"

"I'd love to." He chuckled. "What? Did you expect me to turn tail and run at the thought of a busload of three-year-olds?"

Brynne laughed. "I did. Don't tell Shanna you're going, or you'd never hear the end of it."

"I've got a lot to learn," he said as they approached Brynne's SUV. They'd taken her van instead of his Jaguar.

"I can't believe I forgot she would need a car seat or that she should sit in the backseat because of the front air bags. Don't worry, Brynne. I will get it all taken care of, including buying an SUV."

Brynne put her hand on his sleeve. "I'm not worried. It's an adjustment."

Once he got Shanna settled in her car seat, he came around and held Brynne's door open. He teased, "Need a boost?"

"Very funny. Just watch your mouth, Mister Man." She couldn't suppress a smile, recalling the way he used to tease her about her preference for high heels. She missed the laughter and long talks they once shared. They had had fun together.

The evening traffic on Interstate 696 was busy. A fender bender ahead of them had slowed the traffic almost to a crawl.

Brynne glanced back at her daughter. "You're awfully quiet back there, sweet pea. You okay?"

"Sleepy, Mommy."

"Too much of a good thing, huh," Devin said.

"I'd say. She's exhausted, but if she goes to sleep this early, she'll be awake at dawn, ready to play."

Devin laughed.

"Keep laughing and I will teach her how to punch in your telephone number." It was Brynne's turn to laugh at his incredulous look. "Let her call you at four in the morning to chat."

"I think I walked into that one." He glanced at her. "Hungry? Shall I stop and pick up pizza for dinner?"

Brynne smiled. "Yes, pizza might keep her awake, at least long enough to eat a slice. Oh and order a large antipasto salad, please."

"Okay." Devin took the Twelve Mile Road exit to Southfield Road. He was less than a mile from her place when he spotted a popular pizza restaurant. He squeezed into a space between two cars. "Be right out."

At the sound of the door closing, Shanna roused herself enough to ask, "Where's my daddy going, Mommy?"

"To get some pizza. He'll be right back, baby girl."

"I'm a big girl," she said, pulling a toy flashlight from the tote bag and beginning to play with it.

"I know you are," Brynne said tiredly. It had been an eventful day for all of them. Shanna wasn't the only one running out of steam. As she leaned back against the headrest, Brynne was pleased by Shanna's reaction to learning that Devin was her father. It had gone better than she even dared hope. But then Shanna was still too young to realize that she had always had a father.

It was Devin's response that had thrown her off balance. Overwhelmed with emotion and love for Shanna, he'd taken Brynne into his arms and kissed her as if the mistakes of the past were just that—in the past.

What she found more shocking was her response to him. She hadn't frozen. She'd let him hold her and kiss her as if they had not been apart for four years and she hadn't been raped. And if she were honest with herself, she'd admit that it felt good . . . too good for her peace of mind.

For the first time, she hadn't panicked at the mere thought of being held by a man. Why? And why with Devin? For so long she had avoided men and any form of intimacy. She had firmly pushed all hopes of romance and marriage out of her life. She had never been tempted to alter that decision. Why had she responded? Was it because Devin had surprised her? Hadn't given her time to stiffen up, to fear him?

Brynne sighed wearily. One kiss and a hug were a long way from true intimacy. And she was a very long way from forgetting the personal mountain that she had lost hope of climbing beyond. The lessening of Devin's anger didn't mean he'd forgiven her for leaving him and not telling him about Shanna. She honestly couldn't blame him for being bitter and resentful. He had good reason for wanting to keep her at a distance. Their temporary truce was probably just that—temporary.

But there was another nagging worry. What if the kiss meant he still sexually desired her? If that was the case, how on earth was she supposed to handle it?

"Didn't go to sleep on me, did you?" Devin said as he slid behind the wheel. He passed her two large flat pizza boxes and a plastic container of salad.

"Two large pizzas? Are we expecting company?"

He chuckled. "I can eat one without help. I thought you and Shanna might also like a slice."

"Gee, thanks." She forced a laugh, suddenly scared by the possibility that he might want to have sex with her.

Brynne was jumping to conclusions and letting her imagination get the better of her. She and Devin were working at being good parents, and if they were extremely lucky, becoming friends. She had almost convinced herself by the time they waved at the guard and drove past the gate. Devin parked in her garage.

He asked, "Can you handle the food while I get the baby?"

A sleepy Shanna took exception to the remark and insisted, "I'm not a baby, Daddy. I am a big girl."

Devin and Brynne exchanged a smile before he released his seat belt and went to get Shanna.

"Big girl, huh?" he said, kissing her forehead. "You can hardly keep those pretty brown eyes open."

Shanna trustingly wrapped her arms around his neck as he lifted her. Brynne had unlocked the back door and disengaged the alarm. She held the door open as Devin carried Shanna inside, then placed the food on the kitchen counter.

"What do you think?" Devin asked softly.

Brynne smiled, "I think I'd better get her ready for bed. Will you please take her into her room?"

"Sure." Once he had her on the bed and taken off her parka and gloves, Brynne finished undressing her. He said, "Don't you think she should eat something?"

Brynne laughed, "She had more than enough to eat.

Devin, will you please hand me the blue pajamas in the top bureau drawer?"

"No problem." When he handed her the pajamas she had Shanna down to her underwear. "How can you do that without waking her?"

"Practice. Thanks."

"Need any more help?"

"No, I can handle it from here."

Devin leaned down and kissed Shanna's cheek before he left the room.

When Brynne walked in, she saw that the coffee table in the family room had been piled with a salad bowl, plates, napkins, and silverware while the pizza was heating in the microwave. He had also opened a bottle of Chardonnay.

"You've been busy."

"Have a seat. It's almost ready." Devin handed her a glass of wine before going into the kitchen. When he joined Brynne, he carried in the bubbling hot pizza.

"Looks good." After spreading a napkin on her lap, she helped herself to a slice of pizza and salad, while hoping he didn't notice the slight tremor in her hands. The instant he'd joined her on the sofa, her heart started to race. Brynne tried to relax and focus on nothing more than enjoying the meal.

When he finished, he leaned back against the sofa, patting his flat stomach. "A perfect ending to a perfect day. I enjoyed watching Shanna. She was so excited, she could hardly sit still."

Brynne glanced over at him to find his dark eyes moving over her features, down the slope of her neck to linger on the swell of her breasts. Decidedly uncomfortable, she immediately looked away, nearly dropping a forkful of salad in her lap.

He was smiling when he said, "I've said it before, but it needs to be repeated. Brynne, you've done an exceptional job with Shanna. She's happy, smart, and well adjusted."

"Thank you." She placed her empty plate on the coffee

table, and then picked up her wineglass. "You're good with her. She loves you."

"And I love her. More than I can express." He surprised her when he picked up her hand that had been resting in her lap and toyed with her slender fingers. "She gave me quite a jolt, when she asked if I was her dad. And to have her call me Daddy. Wow! For a moment, I felt as if I'd been tackled from behind. Bam! I think my heart stopped." He gently squeezed her hand. "Brynne, I wish I—"

"If you thank me for being a good mother one more time, I will deck you."

Incredulous, he shook his head as if trying to clear it. "What's going on with you? Why are you so jumpy?"

"Nothing is going on. I did what needed to be done. That's all. You don't have to keep throwing my past mistakes in my face every time I turn around." She hopped up and began clearing the table.

"I'll do that."

"No, this is my home. If you want to do something, go home." Refusing to look at him, she hurried off into the kitchen.

Devin was right behind her. He caught her shoulders and gently turned her to face him. "Are you going to tell me what has you so upset?"

"Nothing is wrong. The day is over and it's time for you to leave. That's all you need to know, Devin Prescott. Why don't men know how to take no for an answer?" She pushed past him but was shaking so badly she nearly broke the plates she dropped in the sink.

Devin shook his head, holding his palms up as if in need of self-defense. "Since I don't know what's going on here, why don't you break it down for me, and then we'll both be on the same page."

Fighting back tears, she folded her arms beneath her breasts. "I've already told you, nothing is wrong."

"Brynne, please. Can't you trust me? Maybe I can help."

"My problems don't concern you," she shouted at him.

"Keep it up and you'll wake up the baby." A muscle jumped in his jaw as if he were grinding his strong white teeth. "All I'm doing is trying to make things better between us. I don't want us to continue to be at odds with each other. We have a little girl whom we both love very much. If we let it, the past can keep a rift between us for the next thirty years. I don't want Shanna growing up thinking her parents hate each other."

"Are you telling me you've forgotten why I had to ask you to take a paternity test? That I don't believe. Devin, you've been angry with me for weeks. Let's not pretend, okay? You said on more than one occasion that you don't trust me as far as you can throw me."

"Brynne, please. I'm trying—"

She glared at him. "Stop trying to fix something that's broken beyond repair. The past is right where it has always been . . . right in our faces. There isn't a thing either one of us can do to change what happened. I left you and I took your child with me. I didn't tell you about her for four years."

"Look, I'm bending over backward here to—"

"Who asked you to? Certainly not me! Shanna's asleep. So you can take your pizza and leave. Do me a favor? Go bother someone else and leave me alone!"

Brynne took off down the short hall toward the bedrooms. She slammed her bedroom door behind her. Dropping down on the bed, she didn't even bother brushing away the tears that trickled down her cheeks.

She didn't need him feeling sorry for her. He couldn't change what had happened to her. He couldn't make the fear go away. He had no right to look at her as if he still desired her. She had enough to contend with.

When she finally calmed down she started thinking rationally. She couldn't believe that she had been so upset that she hadn't seen Devin out. It wasn't like her to be so careless. Instead of washing off her makeup and changing into her nightclothes, she raced to lock the doors and set the alarm. She didn't have the luxury of pretending nothing bad could happen because she lived in a gated community. Bad things happened to good people every day. She wasn't willing to risk her daughter's or her own safety.

She looked in on her daughter, then walked into the kitchen; she was surprised to find that Devin had cleared away what remained of their meal, and had even washed the few dishes that had been left in the sink.

As she curled up on one end of the sofa in the family room, she refused to dwell on what had sent her into a tailspin. Just the possibility that Devin wanted more than friendship scared her. When she caught him looking at her with sexual desire in his beautiful gray eyes, it had caused her to panic. She would rather deal with his anger and resentment than have his masculine charm aimed her way. He was too virile, too male, and simply dangerous to her peace of mind.

She had to stop him, before he asked for what she could no longer give. Just the thought of a man inside her had her quaking with fear. She could not go down that road ever again. Kissing would never be enough to satisfy highly sexed, virile man.

Maintaining a certain measure of distance would be best for all of them. Shanna had her dad. Devin had his little girl. Weeks of therapy had allowed Brynne to be able to talk freely to Maureen about her rape. It was enough for Brynne.

On Tuesday morning, after kissing Shanna goodbye, Brynne was on her way out of the nursery school when Trenna stopped her.

"Hi, you got a minute?"

"Good morning." Brynne glanced at her watch before she nodded, "That's about all I have. My first appointment is at nine. What's up? Did you finish Connie Briscoe's new book?"

"This isn't about the book club. Come on into my office so we can talk privately." Trenna led the way down a short hallway to her office.

"Sounds serious." Brynne closed the door behind her. "Did Shanna have a problem in school yesterday? She didn't mention it. Why didn't you call me at home last night?"

"I didn't get in until late." Trenna motioned to one of the visitors' chairs while she sat on the edge of her cluttered desk.

Brynne teased. "Have a date? Who is he?"

"No date. Laura and I went to a movie. You're the one who has been holding out on us. Shanna told me and anyone who would stand still long enough to listen that she has a new daddy. And that he took her and her mommy to the circus. What's going on, Brynne?"

Brynne dropped her lids, trying to conceal her embarrassment. What had she been thinking? She should have been the one to tell Trenna, first thing on Monday. She been so caught up in her worries about Devin that she had completely forgotten.

She said softly, "It's true. Her father will be in town for a few months. I finally told her the truth about him. That's all. There was nothing much to tell."

"Nothing much to tell? As long as I've known you, you've never mentioned a word about the man. I didn't know if he was a one night stand or someone from the past who hurt you badly."

Brynne sighed tiredly. "It has never been easy for me to talk about my past. No, he was certainly not a one-night stand. I hadn't been in touch with him since I left St. Louis. I didn't know I was pregnant until I was back in Michigan." She paused, uncertain what she could say comfortably. Finally, she admitted, "I ran into him at that party Laura dragged me to, a few weeks ago. I'm sorry. I can't talk about him or what went wrong between us without getting upset."

Trenna nodded. "I don't mean to pressure you. But I have some concerns. I love you and Shanna. But I need to know what I'm to do if he shows up here. Am I supposed to release her to him?"

It was difficult for Brynne to say. "Yes, his name is on her new birth certificate. He's going to be picking Shanna up from school on Tuesdays and Thursdays. He mentioned that he wants to go with her on the field trip to the petting farm. Oh, and he might want to volunteer in her classroom, if that is okay?"

Trenna nodded. "This is so sudden, Brynne. Are you sure about this?"

Gathering her purse, Brynne said, "Yes. I'm sorry, but I have to go."

"Not so fast. You haven't told me the man's name. And you need to add his name to her release card."

"Sorry." As she took the blank information card and a pen, she said, "Shanna's father is Devin Prescott."

Brynne couldn't help feeling guilty because she couldn't tell Trenna the entire story. It wasn't that she didn't value their friendship, or that she didn't trust Trenna. What Brynne didn't trust were her emotions. She couldn't talk about why she left Devin and St. Louis without breaking down.

"Any relation to the Wesley Prescott who plays with the Lions?"

"His younger brother."

"The brother that's one of the highest-paid quarterbacks in the NFL?" Trenna asked incredulously.

"I suppose. I didn't realize you followed football."

"And I didn't know you knew a gorgeous multimillionaire. So Devin Prescott is Shanna's father," Trenna repeated, as if she couldn't quite believe it.

"Yes. And it has been over for a long time. The only

good that came from our relationship was Shanna. I will bring in her new certificate as soon as I get it from Lansing. I've had Prescott added to her last name." Brynne hesitated before she added, "I know I've been secretive, but I just couldn't talk about him. It still hurts. Please, don't be angry with me."

Trenna gave Brynne what she needed most, a reassuring hug. "We'll talk when you're ready."

"Thank you for understanding." A glance at her watch had Brynne on her feet and calling, "I've got to run. I will see you later."

Brynne's heart felt heavy as she hurried toward her SUV in the school's parking lot. Vanessa, Trenna, Laura, and Maureen were more than book club members. They were good friends. Out of necessity, only Maureen knew about the rape.

She hadn't meant to keep her past hidden. The rape and unexpected pregnancy had been hard enough to deal with alone, but a discussion about it had been out of the question.

Her argument with Devin the other night and her talk with Trenna this morning had proven that even after weeks of therapy she wasn't as far along as she would like. She consoled herself with the knowledge that at least Shanna was happy.

Brynne was the weak link in this new arrangement. She didn't need to be told that she was not handling the changes in their lives well. She'd been a nervous wreck since Devin had left on Saturday. When he'd called on Monday about dinner on Tuesday and Thursday evenings, she suggested that it was time he picked up Shanna at school, and just the two of them should go out to dinner.

Devin hesitated, asking if they weren't rushing things. He mentioned that Shanna had so many adjustments to make in a relatively short period of time. Even though Brynne knew this, she insisted that he and Shanna had a relationship to build. Now that he had gone along with her suggestion, she felt guilty. She couldn't help wondering if she had been thinking about herself rather than what was best for her little girl. Life had never been easy, but, good grief, it was getting more complicated by the second.

As Brynne drove to her office, she tried to convince herself that her baby wouldn't be permanently damaged by having dinner alone with her father. And that she wasn't really a bad mother.

Fourteen

"**Okay, Brynne, you've been here for ten** minutes and haven't said one word," Maureen said. "What's going on? What's got you so upset you can't sit down for longer than a second?"

Brynne dropped down onto the sofa. The chicken salad sandwich she'd brought from home no longer held any appeal. Instead of pacing, she stared at her French manicured nails. Eventually she said, "I don't know where to start."

"What set you off? Does this have anything to do with Shanna's father? Did you two have an argument?"

During a previous session Brynne had told her about the paternity test and Devin being back in their lives.

Brynne nodded. "On Saturday Devin took us to the matinee at the circus. The day ended badly and I practically threw him out of my home that evening. I was so upset."

"Did he do something to make you feel threatened?"

"Devin? No, unless you call looking at me with desire threatening. It was all me. I panicked. I know I'm not making any sense. Let me start at the beginning." Brynne took a deep breath before she said, "I told Shanna that Devin was her father."

"How did that go?"

"Beautifully. I couldn't have asked for more. Shanna was thrilled because in the few weeks he has been coming over she has come to love him. Devin was overjoyed by her acceptance. While she was out of the room, getting ready, he hugged me, thanking me for telling her the truth. I might have been okay if it had stopped there. He said he was ready to forgive and forget what happened in the past. I was so surprised that I didn't protest when he kissed me. A kiss that quickly got out of hand."

"Did you push him away?"

"No," Brynne blushed, unable to met Maureen's eyes.

"Did you slap him? Scream?"

"No, I let him kiss me. I'm embarrassed to admit that it was Shanna who interrupted us."

Maureen's eyes went wide. "She walked in on you?"

Shaking her head, Brynne said, "She was in her room and called for my help." Her hands were clenched in her lap when she confessed, "I responded to him, just as I did when we were in love. Maureen, it got me wondering if he still found me desirable. What did I do that for? The next thing I knew I was in a panic even before we got back to the house.

"It didn't help that Shanna fell asleep in the car. I was so upset, I hardly tasted the food we brought back with us. He acted as if all were forgotten, and we could be friends. I don't know. I wasn't ready to hear that. I felt so vulnerable. And then when I thought I saw desire in his eyes, I lost it. I picked a fight with him. Threw everything I had done to him back in his face, trying to make him angry."

"How did he take that?"

"He knew something was wrong with me . . . he just couldn't figure out what." Brynne blinked back tears, refusing to let them fall. "I was such a mess that I told him to get out and ran into my bedroom and shut the door."

Maureen, busy taking notes, smiled. "Well, you certainly are not afraid of the man. No, dear heart. You ran away from the way he made you feel, not him. If you were afraid of him, you would have never left him alone in your house. You would have walked the man to the front door and waited until he left, and then locked the door behind him and set the alarm."

"But—"

"No, Brynne. This is about you. Did you consider that you were upset because he reminded you of something you've forgotten? You are still a woman . . . an attractive woman at that. Accept it."

Brynne frowned, "Was that the counselor talking or the friend?"

"Both. It sounds to me that Devin is getting over his anger and resentment, which was only due to what you allowed the poor man to believe. Don't you think it's time you corrected that mistake and told him the truth? There was no other man. What there was, was a rapist."

Brynne frowned. "I know. Logically, I realize I should have made him listen a long time ago, but that scared me silly. Deep in my gut a part of me won't let me do it." She jumped to her feet, moving restlessly about the room. She turned back to Maureen, saying, "Every time I try to explain the words get stuck in my throat. I can't get them out."

"So you're telling me you're going to continue letting the fear control you?"

"Did you hear with I said? I've tried. On the day I asked him to take the paternity test, and then several times later, but he always stopped me." Her legs were so unsteady that she sank back down to the sofa she shared with the other woman. She finally whispered, "He didn't want to hear . . . I didn't want to tell."

"Brynne, admit it. You left it so long because you're ashamed." Maureen paused, and then asked, "Why? You have no reason to blame yourself. You're in no way responsible for that hateful act. You were the victim."

"I know that!" Brynne shouted, then said, "Sorry. It's just that I don't want Devin to look at me differently."

"Do you? Then why are you still blaming yourself for letting the man inside your apartment?"

Brynne's laughter held no humor. "Because I should have known better." When Maureen would have interrupted, Brynne shook her head, "I know we have been over and over this. But I have to accept my part in all of it. I did let him into my home."

"Tell me why you think Devin will 'look at you differently,' as you put it? I don't think he will, but you won't know unless you tell him what really happened. What are you afraid of, Brynne? That he won't want you? Or that he hasn't ever stopped wanting you?"

Brynne jerked her head up as if the other woman had slapped her, and she was reeling from the impact. "I'm not afraid of anything. He simply took me by surprise and I overreacted to his kiss."

"Then you have nothing to lose by being honest with him."

Brynne stared at her hands. "You're wrong. I lost it all the day I packed my car and left St. Louis. I promised myself I would never look back."

"But you have looked back. And you did it for your daughter's sake. Because of you, she has her father. That is something to be proud of." Maureen reached over and gave Brynne's hand a reassuring squeeze. She surprised Brynne when she asked, "How long do you think it's going to be before Shanna realizes all is not well between her parents? Shanna is a smart little girl. She going to sense something is not quite right. If you're cool and standoffish with her father, then she could very well withhold her trust and her love from him. Is that what you want?"

"You know it isn't! I want her to have the same kind of relationship I had with my dad, close and loving. I feel guilty enough for the time they've already lost." Her eyes filled with tears. "What kind of mother would I be, if I tried to come between them?"

"I'm not saying you'd do it deliberately. But deliberate

or not, the results are the same." Maureen was thoughtful for a moment before she said, "There couldn't be a better time to tell him, especially since Devin is at the point where he is willing to forgive and forget."

She shook her head. "You expect too much."

Maureen didn't push. She glanced at her watch. "Our time is almost over for today. Just think about it. I will help in any way I can."

Sighing heavily, Brynne whispered, "Am I making any progress?"

"Absolutely. But you don't need me to tell you that. You've completely opened up with me, and you've told Shanna that Devin is her dad. That leaves only two key people you have to be honest with."

"Vanessa and Trenna?"

Maureen corrected her, "Devin and you. You've been able to accept that he's a decent and caring man, who deserves a chance to be father to Shanna. You still have to face your fears. You have to find out if you still have feelings for him. And what if anything you're going to do about them."

"Maureen, have you heard anything I said to you today? Devin hates me. He's being kind because he's grateful for the care I've given Shanna. Believe me, he won't respect the weak woman who invited her rapist into her apartment. The same pitiful, weak fool who in the end couldn't report the rape or face Devin afterward."

Brynne was sobbing when she went on to say, "It doesn't matter how I feel about him. I don't deserve his love or his forgiveness." She raced for the door, oblivious of the tears blinding her. Maureen got there ahead of her, blocking the exit.

"Running didn't solve anything four years ago. It isn't going to solve anything now. You listen to me, Brynne Armstrong. What you did was invite a friend into your home. You didn't rape yourself. So stop punishing yourself. You did nothing wrong." Maureen's cool demeanor was gone. "Did you fight him? Or did you lay down and take your clothes off for him?"

"You know I fought him. I broke my nails scratching him and bruised my hands hitting him. I tried to kick him in his groin, but he was too strong for me. He held me down. And he was so strong, I couldn't get away."

"Are you ashamed of that?"

"No!"

"Exactly!" Maureen put her arm around her friend and gave her a comforting hug. "You have nothing to be ashamed of. No one deserves to be raped. You know that when it comes to the women you work with here. It's time you applied it to yourself. Brynne, you are one of the best, dedicated, tireless counselors we have. It's not just something you studied in a textbook. You understand because you've lived it. You're a survivor. You know firsthand the pain of being violated . . . what it's like for someone to take what is yours alone to give. Don't let me ever hear you say you're ashamed again."

Brynne smiled at the scolding. "You won't. I'm going to get past this."

"Good. You've come a long way from that woman who fled St. Louis. You've made a home for yourself and your baby while you earned your degree. It takes courage to do any one of those things, but you, dear heart, have done them all. So don't tell me you can't confront one misguided man. Devin deserves the truth every bit as much as Shanna deserved to have her father in her life." Maureen smiled. "What he does with that truth is up to him, not you."

Brynne sighed heavily. "You're right. I owe him the truth."

Despite her promise to Maureen, on the days that Devin picked up Shanna from school and took her out to eat before bringing her home, Brynne was relieved that she didn't need to do more than speak to the man. Even though she barely saw him, she heard more than she cared to from Shanna. Devin was their daughter's favorite topic of discussion, and she never seemed to run out of things to say about her daddy.

Every morning Brynne reminded herself what needed to be done, and every evening she scolded herself because she hadn't done anything about it.

"I need to take care of this and get it over with," Brynne muttered to herself as she collected her briefcase and purse from the passenger seat. She slammed the car door as if to relieve pent up frustration before she turned off the alarm and unlocked the back door.

Her evening group session at the center had gone well, and she was tired. She absently flicked on lights and sorted through the mail. She'd just hung her coat in the hall closet when she heard the front doorbell.

"Hi," she said as she swung the door open.

"Hi Mommy." Shanna raced in, a wide grin on her small face. She hugged Brynne's legs before she tugged on her mother's hand until she sank down and gave her a kiss and hug.

"Hi, sweet pea. Did you have fun?" Although her eyes were on her child, her awareness was with the large man who quietly shut and locked the door.

"Daddy took me to Chuck E. Cheese. We played video games, Mommy."

"He did?" Brynne forced a smile.

"Uh-huh," she nodded vigorously, her braids bouncing, "We had pizza."

Straightening, Brynne shot Devin a look. "Seems like you two had a good time."

"Hi. How was your day?"

"Busy. Yours?" Brynne, aware of his dark gaze moving over her petite frame, avoided making eye contact, keeping her gaze on their daughter.

"My day was fine. Did you eat?"

Brynne nodded, leading the way toward the back of the house, wondering why she could not seem to say what she needed to say and get it over with. Why did it have to be so difficult?

When they reached the family room, Brynne said, caressing Shanna's cheek, "You have a good day at school?"

Shanna grinned. "I had fun. I got to be it for duck-duck-goose, and they didn't catch me. I was so fast."

Devin and Brynne both laughed.

"Good for you. Why don't you put your things away in your room? Time for your bath and then bed. You can get undressed all by yourself, right?"

"Yeah. Can I turn the water on, Mommy?"

"Yes, I'll be right in. Not too hot. Give your dad a kiss before you go."

Shanna ran to him, then squealed when he swung her up into his arms. She was all giggles, patting his lean cheeks and then kissing his jaw. He tickled her tummy, sending her into another fit of giggles, before he put her back on her feet. She took off for her room.

He asked, "Long day?"

"Yeah." Brynne was so tired of the strain between them. She found herself wishing she had the right to walk into his arms and absorb his quiet strength. "Did she give you a hard time?"

"Not at all. Any time I spend with my daughter is good. If you don't mind, I'd like to tuck her in tonight."

"Of course. Excuse me while I check on her." She found Shanna sitting on the rug in her bathroom playing with her tub toys.

"It's ready, Mommy."

Brynne bent down to test the water temperature. She smiled. "Ready for a polar bear." She let out some of the cold water and added warm water.

"I don't like hot."

"I know, sweet pea. Okay, you can climb in."

Brynne knelt on the rug to bathe her. When she glanced

over her shoulder she saw Devin leaning in the door. "You scared me," she complained

"Sorry. How can you find her with all those toys?" He grinned.

"All done, sweet pea." She thanked Devin for the bath towel he handed her. "You can stand up, Shanna."

"I can't, Mommy. Daddy will see." She shook her head. "He's a boy!"

"Sorry. I'll wait in her room."

Brynne explained, "Devin, she is just not used to—"

"It's not a problem. I'll wait in here."

"Okay, sweet pea, stand up." Brynne quickly wrapped her into a thick towel.

"Mommy, I didn't mean to hurt Daddy's feelings," Shanna whispered, tears in her large brown eyes. "Is Daddy mad at me?"

"No, honey. Daddy isn't mad. He loves you very much. When you stay overnight at Daddy's house, he's going to help you with your bath and to get you dressed when you need help. Okay?"

"Okay."

"Let's get you into those pajamas. It's time for sleepy girls to be in bed."

"I can do it myself, Mommy. I'm a big girl." Shanna insisted as she struggled to pull on her pajamas.

Brynne walked out of the bathroom, saying to Devin. "Your turn. She still has to brush her teeth and say her prayers. Are you up to it?"

"Yeah." He grinned.

Brynne, ignoring the way her heart suddenly raced from the familiar smile, left father and daughter to finish up. When he entered the family room, Brynne was on the sofa with her book propped in her lap, sipping a glass of root beer.

"All done. She's tucked into bed, already asleep." He reached for his jacket, draped on the back of an armchair.

"Good." Brynne frowned at the same page she had read

three times without comphrension. She said, "Devin, I think—"

At the same time, he said, "Sunday is Easter. And—"

They both said, "Sorry," then laughed.

"Ladies first," he urged.

"No, you go ahead." Her stomach knotted with nerves. She silently assured herself she could do this.

He nodded. "Sunday is Easter Sunday. I think it would be a good time for Shanna to meet my family. But I don't know if she is ready to do that on her own. Would you, both of you, have Easter dinner with my family at my parents' home?"

"Are you sure that's a good idea? I mean for your family meeting me? They must blame me for keeping Shanna—"

"This is not about blame. It's a simple holiday dinner. My parents are anxious to meet their grandbaby. My entire family is ready. I'd take her on my own, but I don't want her to be frightened with the whole family there."

Brynne's own nerves were none too steady at the prospect. But then this was not about her. "I understand. It might be a bit overwhelming for her. Yes, we will come."

Devin smiled in relief. "Good. I'll pick you up around one-thirty, after church?"

"We'll be ready."

"What were you going to say, before I interrupted?"

Fifteen

≡

As Devin studied Brynne's pale brown features, he noticed the way she repeatedly opened and then closed her small hands into tight fists. He couldn't help wondering what brought on her anxiety. She was uncomfortable and had been avoiding him since the day they took Shanna to the circus. The same day he told her he wanted them to start again and put their past mistakes behind them.

Evidently she wasn't interested in a truce, because things had been strained between them since that day. In fact, they'd exchanged no more than a few words in the past couple of weeks. She had made it clear that she wanted nothing from him beyond him being a good father to their child. That knowledge didn't even come close to sitting well with him.

"Brynne?"

"Nothing important," she began, and then stopped. "Yes, it is important," she contradicted herself. "I've been trying to talk to you about this for a while, but every time I start, I can't seem to find the words." She carefully placed her drink on the side table and closed her book, putting it aside.

"A lot of things that should not have been said have been said. Mainly from me," Devin said. "Going back to the way I handled your request for the paternity test, I—"

"This isn't about you, Devin. It's about me. It would help if you took your coat off and sat down." Once he had done both, she asked uneasily, "Can you just listen and not interrupt, until I get it all said? Please?"

Intrigued, he said without hesitation, "If that's the way you want it."

She looked everywhere but at him when she said, "Recently I started getting counseling. Something I should have done years ago. I don't know, but maybe if I had, my baby wouldn't have had to go so long without her father." Brynne was practically wringing her hands when she blurted out, "I was raped. That was the reason I left St. Louis the way I did."

"What the hell? Raped!" Devin felt as if he'd been sucker-punched. He jumped to his feet, his entire body suddenly taut with outrage and tension.

"It happened the last night we were together, after I left your place."

Wrapping her arms protectively around her middle, she revealed, "We'd argued. I was upset, and you wanted me to stay and settle it. I refused when you offered to drive me home, because I had my own car. I said something about how we needed time apart. Do you remember?"

"How could I forget? You'd just turned down my proposal. I was furious, but how did—"

"Devin, please. Sit down. Let me do this my way, or I'll never get it out. As it is, it's taken me four years to even tell you this much." Her eyes were focused on something beyond his right shoulder.

He nodded and seated himself again, folding his arms over his chest, unaware of the way he held his mouth tight or how his brows were creased in a scowl.

Brynne rose from the sofa, moving to stand in front of the French doors, even though she couldn't see much of the dark backyard. She said softly, "When I got back to my place, he was waiting for me. He was someone I thought of as a friend. We had several of the same classes. We'd studied together, had lunch together.

"He explained he'd missed class that day and asked if I would let him see my notes. I didn't even hesitate to invite him inside. It wasn't until he was inside that I realized he was angry. He said he'd heard the rumors that I was dating you. He wanted to know if it was true."

Tears slowly fell from her pretty brown eyes, and Devin had no trouble seeing her anguish. He ached to touch her, comfort her, but didn't dare touch her for fear of frightening her.

"I was surprised, but not alarmed. Suddenly he was furious, demanding to know if I was sleeping with you. I got scared then and asked him to leave. He started asking how I could let another man touch me when I knew I belonged to him, that he loved me. I didn't know what he was talking about. We were never more than friends.

"He started following me, and when I tried to reach the telephone, he grabbed me and tossed the phone across the room. He insisted it was time we made love . . . that we both wanted it. I was screaming no, fighting him, trying to get away, but I couldn't. He was so strong. He kept saying I wanted him . . . saying he could prove it. I tried and tried to make him see that he was wrong but he wouldn't listen. That was when he started taking his clothes off and I managed to get away and ran for the door. He caught me and dragged me into the bedroom."

Devin wasn't even aware of moving, but he paced in front of the fireplace. It was all he could do not to approach her, but he kept silent so she could say what she needed to say.

He saw her shudder as she told him the rest, how the other man held her down and raped her. She told how she tried to defend herself, that she bit him and he slapped her, that she kicked him and he hit her again and again. She explained how she tried everything she could think of but she couldn't stop him.

Having moved to stand directly behind her, he could only imagine her anguish as he studied her reflection mirrored in the glass panes of the French door. Afraid to touch her, but desperate to hold her and assure himself she was at least physically okay, he gently turned her to face him. Ignoring his own pain and rage, he whispered, "I'm so sorry. . . . so very sorry."

She nodded and then said, "I kept it inside so long. Not even my girlfriends know. Only recently I realized I needed help and I was able to talk my boss, Maureen Sheppard, into counseling me. It has been slow going, but I'm getting better." She looked at him and softly said, "I'm sorry I kept it from you. Even though I knew I should have told you . . . I just couldn't."

"Shush. Come sit down. You're shaking so badly, I'm afraid you're going to fall."

She allowed him to help her back to the sofa. Once they were seated, her hand in his, she said as if in a daze, "I really tried to get away, but he held me down. I fought him . . . honest I did."

"I know you did." He tenderly kissed her cheek.

She was trembling badly when she whispered, "He kept saying you had no right to touch me. That I was his. He kept saying that I needed a real man like him, the entire time he was forcing himself inside of me. I begged him to stop . . . begged him to use a condom . . . he refused. When he finished, he warned me that I better not tell anyone. He laughed, claiming no one would believe me anyway since I invited him inside. That was proof I wanted him there, and it would be my word against his. He swore that if I told you, and you came after him, he would see to it that you lived to regret it."

"What?" Devin was so furious he could barely get the word out. "He threatened you by using me?"

She nodded. "He said he could ruin you. I knew he

meant it. Besides, he said what I already felt. That I was not the same anymore."

"Sweetheart, that's not true."

"Let me finish." When he nodded, she said, "I felt so dirty . . . shamed. He tried to stroke my hair. I screamed at him to get away from me. I finally managed to get away. I ran to the kitchen and grabbed a knife. He followed. I kept screaming at him to get out. I was not about to let him get near me ever again. I think I would have stabbed him if he had tried. All I wanted was for him to leave . . . to leave me alone. And when he finally left, I ran and locked my door."

She said around a sob, "I did all the wrong things. All I knew was I hurt inside and out. I couldn't stand it. I had to get clean. So I got into the shower and I stayed there until the water went cold and my teeth were chattering. I was so scared that I kept the knife with me. I was exhausted, but I wouldn't get back into that bed. I tried to sleep on the couch, but every time I closed my eyes I saw his face.

"The next morning before I could decide what to do, he called and warned me to keep my mouth shut. I hung up on him and took the phone off the hook. I kept telling myself to go on as if nothing was different, as if I were the same. It didn't take long for me to learn I wasn't all right. I put the knife in my purse, and then I got ready. I put on makeup to cover the bruises and went to my first hour class. He was there waiting for me. I warned him to stay away from me, and then I ran to my car and drove back to my apartment and locked myself inside."

Unable to contain his fury, Devin swore beneath his breath as he began pacing the room. With his hands balled into fists, he asked in a deceptively quiet tone, "Who is he?"

"It doesn't matter now."

"I want to know his name," he nearly shouted.

"No!" She tilted her chin stubbornly while her hands were clasped in her lap.

Devin swore beneath his breath. He said, "Why didn't you call me? I would have taken care of him for you."

Brynne shook her head as she blinked away tears. She wrapped her arms around her small frame. "I couldn't. I couldn't take the chance. Devin, there was not a doubt in my mind that you would go after him, and it could have ruined your career. I didn't want you to be hurt by him. He'd already done enough harm. Besides, it was over and done with."

Devin swore heatedly. When he realized she was cringing, he stopped abruptly. "I'm sorry. I didn't mean to blame you or make this any harder on you."

"Please let me get the rest of it out." She took a deep breath before she said, "I was a mess. I was scared to go to the door, scared to answer the telephone. I stayed locked inside for the rest of the day. He came by that evening, but I wouldn't let him inside. I knew then I couldn't stay in St. Louis. If I was to survive, I had to leave. I started packing. I left about five in the morning, and I kept on driving until I got back to Detroit . . . home."

"There never was another man, was there?" he asked tightly, recalling all the nasty accusations he'd laid at her feet.

"No." She lifted her chin.

Devin's hands were braced on his hips, his normally loose-limbed body was tight. When he approached her, she stiffened, and her pretty dark eyes went wide with apprehension. He swiftly realized that his volatile temper was scaring her. He shoved his hands into his pockets and took deep calming breaths in the hopes of regaining control of his emotions. She'd been through enough. He wouldn't add to her distress.

"You faced it all alone, but you didn't have to. I was in love with you. I would have done anything for you . . . anything. Damn my career! I would have protected you with my life." He tried not to let his own hurt show. "How could you forget I wanted you to be my wife?"

* * *

Brynne saw his anguish in his dark gray eyes. She felt as if her own heart was breaking all over again. "I told you!"

"Because we had that fight that night?"

"No! I was not the same. I knew you wouldn't want me anymore."

"How could you even think that?"

"Because I knew how much my being untouched meant to you. You were my first. And you were proud to have a woman who had never known another man. I was no longer that woman."

Devin stared at her, looking as if she'd slapped him. He finally said, "How could any man who called himself a man blame his woman for another man's abuse? The bastard raped you! He took something precious from you. It wasn't your fault."

"I know he raped me, but I didn't feel the same afterward. I've taken the courses, so I know what I should have done." She sighed wearily. "Maybe that was why I was so determined to help other rape victims. The problem was that while I was good at helping others, I couldn't help myself."

Her laughter held no humor. "You see, I thought I had handled it, put it all behind me. I didn't realize what I'd done was bury it deep inside. That way I didn't have to deal with it. I honestly thought I was over it, until Shanna started wanting a father. It made me really face the fact that someday I would have to tell her the truth. I would have to tell my baby that I didn't know who her father was. I was petrified that her father might be my rapist. And then I ran into you at that party."

Devin came and sat in the armchair close to where she was seated on the sofa. He said softly, "If there is anything I could do or say to make it up to you for the blame I heaped on your head when you asked me to take that paternity test, I'd do it in a heartbeat. I can't even tell you how angry I am for what happened to you or how sorry I am that you were hurt. I wish I could have been there for you."

Brynne nodded as she ran her hands restlessly up and down her arms. "You didn't know. I didn't want you to know. When I finally tried to tell you about the rape, you didn't want to hear about the other man. And deep down, I was relieved you didn't want to hear. I'm not sure I could have told you even then."

"I should have listened, but I was so damn jealous. That's not important now. All I'm asking is for one thing. I want the bastard's name."

Alarmed, Brynne was on her feet. "Why?"

Devin said through clenched teeth as he loomed over her. "He's not getting away with this. If it takes the rest of my life, I promise I will hunt him down and make him pay. Who the hell is he?"

Brynne pressed both hands against his chest and pushed as hard as she could. "I don't plan to ever tell you. My baby finally has her daddy. She isn't going to lose him due to some crazy vendetta." She flung her arm out as if she could push the thought away. "It happened a long time ago. It's over. There's nothing either one of us can do to change what happened."

"He has never been punished. Never even arrested," Devin snarled in outrage.

"That's my fault. And it's too late to do anything about it. Every bit of evidence I had against him was destroyed long ago. I didn't save my clothes, the sheets . . . anything. I didn't take pictures of the bruises. I didn't even go to the police or the hospital. The only thing I did was have regular HIV tests, but that was only later, after I realized I was pregnant. And I thank God, they've all been negative." She glared at him. "I don't need to be reminded that I made one mistake after another. I accept that, but I refuse to go on punishing myself any more because of it."

"Brynne—"

"No, Devin. No more. It's late, and I'm exhausted. Go home."

2004

He clearly wasn't ready to drop it or leave, yet he said, "Okay. Walk me to the door."

Brynne nodded, watching as he shrugged into his heavy suede jacket.

At the door, he asked, "Are we still on for Easter Sunday?"

"Of course."

He surprised her when he asked, "Can I have a hug?"

Brynne hesitated, and then she moved to encircle his taut waist. She closed her eyes as she rested her cheek against his wide chest while fighting back an unexpected rush of fresh tears. She blinked hard, allowing herself just a moment more.

Devin held her gently before he eventually said, "Good night, babe." He brushed his lips against her temple, and he stepped back.

"Night," she whispered.

Devin was in a bad way, so filled with anguish that he was physically ill. Unable to continue driving, he was forced to pull over to the side of road, where he lost the contents of his stomach. Wiping away the tears that momentarily blinded him, he climbed back in the car and rested against the seat until his stomach settled. Shaking with rage, he was unaware of the way his hands were balled into fists. He wanted the bastard's name. He swore, then sighed his frustration. He didn't dare give in to the fury, to go out and punch something or someone that got in his way.

Even though he knew he wasn't fit company, he eventually had himself under control enough to drive over to his brother and sister-in-law's home. They'd offered to feed the two bachelors in the family. He'd already missed dinner, but food was the last thing on his mind.

Ralph's car was parked in the wide curved drive. Devin hoped that for once his cousin hadn't brought a date because he needed to talk and get some sound advice.

"Hey, little bro. I thought you were busy playing daddy tonight," Wesley said with a wide grin as he took a step back from the open front door. "Get in here. It's cold out there."

"Who is there, honey?" Kelli called from behind her husband.

"It's me," Devin said, moving past his brother and placing a kiss on Kelli's cheek. "Sorry I missed dinner. Save me any dessert?"

"Of course. Thanks for the pictures. How's that pretty little girl of yours?"

Devin managed a smile. "She's fine. Getting prettier and smarter every day."

Wesley slapped him on the back. "When are we going to meet her?" he asked as they walked toward the large family room in the spacious, luxuriously appointed house.

"Yeah," Ralph added, looking up from a generous slice of coconut cake he'd been enjoying.

"Easter Sunday dinner," Devin said absently.

His family, all smiles, congratulated him.

"It's about time. Mama and Dad have been champing at the bit, eager to meet their new grandbaby," Wesley said.

"I don't blame them. I can't wait to see that little sweetheart." Kelli grinned, pointing to the newly framed photograph of Shanna that graced their mantel along with photographs of the entire family, including their baby, Kaleea. "This deserves a big piece of cake," she teased as she headed for the kitchen.

"Where's my niece?" Devin asked.

"Asleep. I put her down over an hour ago. Want a peek?" Wesley asked.

"Yeah."

"I heard that," Kelli called. "If you two wake her up, both of you are in trouble."

Wesley chuckled. "We won't." He led the way into the pink and cream bedroom next to the master suite. A night light softly illuminated the crib.

Devin resisted the urge to lean down and kiss the baby's soft brown cheeks. She slept on her back with her stuffed bunny in her arms. He gently caressed her soft black curls. "She's beautiful. I missed seeing Shanna at this age. I missed so much."

Wesley squeezed his shoulder. "Still riled up about that? It's time to let it go, don't you think? Come on before we wake her." He pulled the door nearly closed behind them.

Devin admitted as they retraced their steps, "I'm past the anger and resentment, but the disappointment lingers. The album Brynne gave me helped a lot to ease that ache. The rest of the anger died tonight."

Wesley looked at him for a moment. "I don't believe it! You can hold a grudge longer than anyone I know." They'd entered the family room. He said, "You haven't forgotten the time I borrowed your football. Remember?"

"Hell yeah, I do. That football was signed by Jim Brown. You had no business touching it. You had one signed by Walter Payton."

"Not that again." Ralph grinned from where he relaxed in an easy chair. A cheerful fire burned in the fireplace. "Let it go, Dev. That happened twenty years ago."

"So." Devin sat down on one end of the sofa, taking note of the dessert plate and coffee on the side table. "Thanks, Kelli."

"What did you mean, the anger died tonight?" Wesley questioned as he pulled his wife out of one of the leather armchairs, took the seat himself, and pulled her onto his lap. "You expect us to believe you aren't still upset that Brynne kept your baby girl a secret for four years?"

Realizing that he was hungry, he dug into his cake. He swallowed before saying, "My anger had been gradually dissipating as I got to know my little princess and saw what a wonderful mother Brynne is." He frowned as he recalled the painful details of Brynne's rape. Pushing the plate aside, he said. "Everything changed when Brynne told me the truth."

The anger, frustration, and anguish were all evident in his face when he revealed to his family, "I was so wrong about Brynne. She didn't ask me to take the paternity test because she'd been with another man. She'd been raped. She was terrified when she came back home to Detroit. And she didn't trust me enough to tell me about the rape."

"Oh no!" Kelli gasped. "That's horrible. That poor woman." Her face reflected her sympathy. "Has she dealt with this alone all this time?"

"Yeah. She buried it," Devin ground out. His emotions were still raw and close to the surface. As of yet, he hadn't even come close to sorting them all out.

Ralph and Wesley were much slower to respond. They stared at Devin in combination of shock and fury.

"Some bastard went after your woman," Ralph said in outrage.

"No wonder you walked in looking as if you could take someone's head off," Wesley growled. "She told you tonight?"

"Yeah." Devin ran an unsteady hand over his close cut natural. "I don't know how she did it, keeping this inside all these years. She didn't tell anyone, not even her girlfriends."

He moved restlessly over to the fireplace, coffee mug cradled in his big hands. "She had been terrified that the rapist was Shanna's father. And it wasn't until Shanna started telling her she wanted a daddy that Brynne faced the fact she would eventually have to tell her she didn't know who her father was. When she saw me at the party, she decided I was her only way of finding out the truth."

"I don't even want to imagine carrying a rapist's child." Kelli shuddered at the mere thought. "Poor thing. I'm so glad Shanna turned out to be yours. That baby deserves better than to grow up knowing she was conceived from hate and not love."

Devin nodded. "Yeah. Me, too."

"You say she kept this inside all this time?" Ralph questioned. "That had to be rough. No woman deserves that. Is that why she became a rape counselor?"

"Yeah, to help others. She was in graduate school working on a degree in counseling when we met. Because she knew all the answers she felt she didn't need counseling. It was a mistake that cost her years of suffering."

"I hope she is getting help now," Kelli said optimistically.

"Yes, finally."

Wesley said, "What happened to cause her to tell you this now?"

Devin shrugged. "I don't know, but I do know she has been trying to tell me about the bastard from the beginning. I stopped her cold, every time she brought up the subject of the other man. All I wanted to know was if Shanna was mine."

"Why?" Ralph demanded.

"We can tell you've never been in love, cuz," Devin quipped. "The last thing any man wants to hear about is the guy messing around with his woman, while his back was turned. Am I right, Wes?"

"Damn straight." His brother backed him up. "That is, not unless you're interested in doing a life sentence."

"No woman is worth that. What is with this love thing? It started with Wes, then Gavin, and now you, Dev. What? Is it in the water? Tell me, so I'll know what to give up now. I want no part of it. I like my life just the way it is, thank you very much."

Kelli glared at him. "What's wrong with falling in love, Ralph Prescott?"

Sixteen

"Everything. Your life is no longer your own. Look at Devin. He's about ready to go after that lowlife with his fists."

"Devin has a good reason to be furious. There's nothing remotely normal about this situation," Kelli snapped. "Besides, I haven't met a Prescott male who isn't protective of his lady. Like father, like sons. And you are no different than the others. Just wait until it's your turn." She went on to predict, "Personally, I can't wait to meet the lady who wraps you around her little finger. The way I hear it, the bigger they are, the harder they fall."

"Uh-oh." Wesley roared with laughter, a twinkle in his dark eyes. Of the Prescott men, Ralph was the tallest. "I guess we all heard that."

Ralph shook his head. "Hear my words. This love mess stops with Devin. I'm not going down. I'm not saying that I don't appreciate women, as much as the next man, but love . . . no way."

Kelli quirked one perfectly shaped brow. "That's your problem, big guy. You appreciate too many women. If you aren't careful, you're going to end up a lonely old man, with no family of your own."

Both Wesley and Devin shook with laughter.

"Aw, honey. Don't get mad. He can't help himself." Wesley nuzzled her cheek.

Kelli braced her hand on his shoulder as she rose from Wesley's lap. "I think I'll say good night before I say something I'll regret." She walked over and gave Devin a hug. "I'm looking forward to meeting both Brynne and Shanna on Sunday. She sounds like a very courageous lady. She is coming, isn't she?"

Devin smiled, "Yes, she is."

"Good." Kelli went over to Ralph, then leaned down and kissed his cheek. "I love you, even if you are a knuckle-head."

Ralph grinned, "I love you too, cuz. Too bad you're taken."

"Well, she is, so let go." Wesley growled at Ralph, who'd held on to her hand. To his wife, he said, "See you later, sweetheart." He didn't take his eyes off his wife until she disappeared from view, then he joked, "You lucked out, cuz. She didn't tell you what she was really thinking."

Ralph shrugged, taking a drag of his beer. "Believe me, I've heard worse from Aunt Donna. The lady doesn't mince words." His gaze was on Devin when he said, "I take it you are still in love with her?"

Neither man seemed surprised when Devin said, "Yes. I thought I'd stopped when she walked out on me without so much as a goodbye. I was angry when I saw her again, sure I hated her, especially when I learned about Shanna. Yet I wanted her, even though I believed she'd been unfaithful."

"Love doesn't just stop, you know. You can't turn it off and on like a water faucet," his older brother said. "When we love, we go all the way. Must be in the genes."

Deciding a change of topic was in order, Ralph asked, "Am I right in assuming the bastard was never prosecuted?"

"She didn't report it. He threatened her . . . terrified her. So much so, she just ran until she felt safe. This happened during the football season, and I was out of town for an away game when she left St. Louis. She never even tried to contact me."

"A woman with a lot of guts," Wesley surmised. "You better hang on to her, bro."

"I plan to, that is, if I can convince her to give us another shot. There's no doubt that she didn't trust me enough to tell me about the rape back then. And due to my jealousy and resentment, I've given her no reason to believe in me now."

He swore in frustration. "Early on, I had a feeling that something wasn't right with her. Believe me when I say I tried, but I couldn't quite make myself believe she'd slept with someone else while claiming she was in love with me. It didn't fit, considering I was her first."

"You're too hard on yourself," Wesley said.

Ralph said, "Wes is right. You had no way of knowing she'd been raped."

"That doesn't change the hell she's been through and is still going through."

"Dev, have you thought this through? From what I've heard, it takes a long time for a woman to recover from rape. And some women never do. She might not ever want to be with a man again." It was a well-known fact that once a Prescott male made a commitment, he stuck to it. "Are you willing to go without sex for the next forty or so years?" Ralph's voice reflected his doubts.

"If necessary," Devin said without hesitation.

"Would you do the same?" Ralph looked pointedly at Wesley.

"For Kelli, I'd do whatever it took to make her happy and whole again," Wesley said emphatically.

Ralph shook his head incredulously. "No woman is worth that kind of living hell."

"The right one is," Devin insisted.

"That's right," Wesley echoed. "What are you going to do about this guy? I know you're not about to let him get away with this."

"Although I believe it's too late to prosecute him—after all, it's her word against his—I'd like to track him down and make him pay." Grudgingly, he admitted, "Brynne doesn't trust me to deal with him without getting myself into legal trouble. I can't go after him unless she changes her mind and gives me the bastard's name."

"Mommy, do you think my new granny will like my Easter dress?" Shanna asked from her car seat in the back of Devin's Lincoln Navigator.

Brynne, busy wishing she'd refused his invitation to have dinner with his family, was reluctant to meet his mother. The woman had to resent her for keeping Shanna a secret for so many years. How could she not? Unfortunately, Brynne hadn't slept the night before, worrying about it. She jumped when Devin said her name.

"What?"

"Shanna asked you a question."

"Sorry, sweet pea. What did you say?" She glanced over her shoulder at her daughter.

"Will my new granny like my Easter dress?" Her small face was creased in a frown.

Brynne smiled reassuringly. "She's going to love your dress and you too. Your daddy likes your dress, remember? Don't forget, you're going to meet lots of family today."

Shanna nodded, causing her pigtails to bounce around her small shoulders. "Daddy told me all the names. Didn't you, Daddy?"

"That's right, princess."

"Will my new auntie be there?"

"Yes, your Aunt Anna is coming. She's my baby sister." Glancing in the rearview mirror, he said, "She's helping me get your room ready for when you come to visit at my house."

Shanna clapped her hands. "Really?"

"Really!" Glancing at Brynne, he said softly, "You're kinda quiet. Not nervous are you?"

She whispered, "Doesn't matter. This is for Shanna, not me."

"Brynne, it's going to be fine. Honest."

"Mmm-hmm," she mumbled, not convinced.

If Devin didn't like her response, he didn't show it. He concentrated on his driving. When he pulled into the wide driveway of a large colonial home that was already crowded with cars, he parked behind Wesley's Mercedes-Benz.

"Looks like everyone is here." After turning off the engine, Devin smiled at his passengers. "You ladies ready?"

Shanna nodded eagerly, trying to release her safety belt.

"Hold still, Shanna. Let your dad get that." Brynne ignored her trembling hands as she fumbled with her own safety belt. It took two tries before she was free.

Devin opened Shanna's door and swung her up into his arms before he came around to open Brynne's door. "All set?"

Brynne nodded, but she didn't take the hand he held out to her. Instead she slid unaided from the van. She nervously smoothed the skirt of her dark green suit. The last thing she wanted was for his family to get the wrong idea about them. They were working at being friends, nothing more.

He placed a hand at the small of her back as he ushered them toward a side door, explaining. "We hardly ever use the front door." He held the door for Brynne and led them into the large, sunny, and fragrant kitchen that seemed to be filled with people.

"Mommy." Shanna reached for her.

"It's all right, princess." Devin smiled as he set her down.

"Lester, look who's here." The pretty, petite older woman came forward with a wide smile. A tall, older man was right behind her.

Brynne didn't need to be told that they were his parents. The family resemblance was unmistakable. Devin had inherited his tiny mother's dark gray eyes and smooth complexion, but his height, muscular build, and mocha brown skin tone came from his handsome father.

"Mama, Daddy, this is Brynne Armstrong. And this little princess is Shanna Marie, your granddaughter."

Brynne offered her hand. "It's a pleasure to meet you both."

"No, sweetheart. We're the ones who are pleased." Donna surprised Brynne by enfolding her in a warm hug. The two women were nearly the same height. "You're every bit as beautiful as Devin told us. And so is this little one."

Brynne smiled. "Thank you." Then she offered her hand to Devin's father. "Mr. Prescott."

Lester was just as warm and informal as his wife. "None of that mister stuff. Call me Lester. You're the mother of our grandbaby." He also gave her a gentle hug. "She is beautiful, Dev."

Brynne smiled as she urged her daughter forward. "Shanna, say hello to your grandfather and grandmother."

Shanna smiled shyly. "Hi, I'm Shanna. I'm three years old." She proudly held up three fingers.

"Hi, sweetheart. I'm your daddy's mommy. You can call me Granny. Would you like to see the cookie Easter basket Granny made for you?"

Shanna clapped her hands excitedly, thrilled at the pink, cellophane-covered basket filled with colored eggs and cookies and a plush Cookie Monster toy inside.

"What do you say, Shanna?" Brynne prompted.

"Thank you!" She beamed.

"I made chocolate chip cookies. They were your daddy's favorite when he was little."

Shanna giggled. "My daddy's not little. He is real big." Everyone laughed.

Brynne watched as a young woman with long dreadlocks approached. "Hello, Brynne. I'm Anna, Devin's sister. That big guy over there by the counter is my husband, Gavin. Our oldest brother, Wesley, is the one holding his baby daughter, Kaleea. And at the stove, stirring a pot of collard greens, is his wife, Kelli."

As they slowly made their way around the room, Anna introduced Brynne to her teenaged brother, Wayne, and her teenaged brother-in-law, Kyle. Brynne was also reintroduced to Ralph and his date, Lisa.

Brynne was surprised that she was able to relax in the warm, friendly atmosphere. The house was lovely, but more important, the love and closeness the family shared was evident. There was plenty of good-natured teasing all around.

Shanna was chattering with her grandparents, telling them about her school. She was shy with her uncles, but instantly fell in love with her little cousin, ten month old Kaleea, who was all smiles and giggles. Shanna begged to help Kelli change the baby's diaper and was disappointed when the baby was put down for a nap.

The women put the finishing touches on the Easter meal while the men settled in the family room to watch the basketball game. When Brynne asked what she could do to help, Donna put her to work making the salad dressing for the green salad. Devin was called to carry the glazed ham and Ralph the rib roast into the dining room.

Kelli pulled out the bubbling macaroni and cheese from the oven while Anna filled a large serving dish with candied yams. Donna filled the bread basket with her homemade rolls. The sideboard in the dining room was already brimming with homemade cakes, fruit pies, and sweet potato pies.

Once everyone was seated, Lester said grace, offering special thanks for having Shanna and Brynne with them. Brynne couldn't remember seeing Devin more relaxed or happy. Shanna sat between her parents. She giggled when her granddaddy told her a story about her dad and Uncle Wesley when they were little.

After the meal, the men took over the kitchen clean-up and the ladies relaxed in the living room. While Wayne and

Kyle entertained Shanna with a video game, Donna asked Brynne if the two of them could talk privately. Donna showed Brynne into the cozy sitting room of the master suite.

When they were seated side by side on the sofa, Donna said, "I'm sure being here with all of us wasn't exactly easy for you. I hope you're not finding it too much of a strain."

"Not at all. Everyone has made us feel welcome," Brynne said candidly. "Shanna is having a wonderful time. Mrs. Prescott, you and your husband have a warm and loving family."

"Please call me Donna. I imagine you're wondering why I asked to speak to you privately. I just wanted you to know how much my husband and I appreciate your care of our grandbaby. Naturally Devin raves about her. And he is right. Shanna is a loving, well-adjusted little girl. We owe that to you."

"Thank you, but you don't have to say that."

"Yes, I do. I'm sorry things didn't work out for you and Devin back in St. Louis. I want you to know, regardless of what the future holds for you two, Brynne, you are always welcome in our home."

"Thank you." Brynne was genuinely touched.

"I also hope that once you get to know us, you will allow Shanna to spend time with us. Lester and I already love her."

Brynne smiled. "I'm not concerned. Shanna is lucky to be a part of such a loving family." She hesitated before she revealed, "I will always regret that due to my circumstances, I kept Devin and Shanna apart. He's such a good father, so patient with her. I couldn't have wished for more. And she adores him."

Donna was equally candid when she said, "Make no mistake, we were very upset that Devin didn't know about Shanna for so long. But now we understand and accept that you did the best you could under the circumstances."

Devin's mother reached out and squeezed her hand. "Brynne, you've been through a tough time, and there is nothing any of us can do to change the past. Devin told Lester and me what you've been through. And I'm so sorry. I imagine your parents would have been proud of how you've handled yourself and raised Shanna. You've proven yourself to be a remarkable woman and mother."

When Brynne's eyes filled with tears, Donna gave her a hug. "I didn't mean to upset you."

Brynne closed her eyes, relishing the other woman's kindness. "You didn't. You remind me of my mother. I miss her." Wiping away her tears, she admitted, "It has taken me a long time to talk about the rape."

"I know we're just getting to know each other, but if you ever feel like talking, please call me. I'd be honored if I can help in any way. Because you're Shanna's mother, that makes you family."

"Thank you. You have no idea how much that means to me."

Donna teased, "I suppose we should get back before my beautiful granddaughter starts looking for you."

Brynne smiled, "I'm glad we talked. You and Lester are welcome to come and visit Shanna any time. I'd like her to get to know her new family."

"Thank you so much. I hope you and I can be friends."

"I hope so."

Getting Shanna settled for the night after meeting Devin's family wasn't an easy task. Shanna couldn't stop talking about her little cousin Kaleea.

When Devin entered the family room with a glass of Chardonnay in each hand, Brynne blurted out, "You told them what I told you in confidence."

After giving her a glass, he made himself comfortable in one of the leather chairs. He hedged, "What do you mean?"

"Please, you know exactly what I mean."

"If you are asking if I told my family that you were raped, yes I did. I wanted them to understand why you didn't tell me about Shanna."

"I didn't give you permission to tell anyone. It's not your secret."

"And I didn't realize that you felt that way. Babe, I thought it was important that my family understood what you'd gone through. What is wrong with that?"

"To you, nothing!" Looking away, she abruptly changed the subject. "Your mother was extremely kind. Like the rest of your family, she evidently felt sorry for me."

"That's not true. I never meant to hurt your feelings," Devin persisted. "My family naturally took my side in this, and I didn't want them resenting you. You've been through enough."

Brynne ignored the comment. "I really like your mom. Like I said, she was very understanding."

Apparently Devin decided not to push because he said, "My mother is a kind woman, but she's also protective of her family. I'm not sure what she said to you privately, but whatever it was, she said what was in her heart. Did she say something to upset you?"

"Don't pretend you don't know," she said as she took a sip of wine.

"I don't. All she told me was that she liked you. So tell me."

Brynne, busy smoothing her skirt, didn't see the way his dark eyes stroked her pale brown features and slender throat.

"Well?" he prompted.

"Nothing earth-shattering or upsetting, for that matter. Like I said, she was kind. She wanted me to know how much she and your father appreciated my care of Shanna. And that I'm always welcome in their home, no matter what happens between us. She acknowledged that I had a difficult time, and if I ever need to talk, that I'm welcome to call her. She hoped we can be friends." Brynne paused before she said, "Your mother was very generous, considering."

"Considering what?"

"Oh, please. Like you don't know."

He leaned back in his chair, casually propping his right leg on his left knee. "Indulge me."

She folded her arms beneath her full breasts, unwittingly drawing his eyes to their softness. "I kept your daughter away from you and your family. Nothing can make up for that. You're part of a close, loving family, and Shanna is included in that love because she's yours."

"Are you done, Brynne Armstrong? Because I've heard about as much of this blame thing you insist on carrying on your shoulders as I can stomach. When are you going to stop beating yourself up about the past? Baby, you did what you felt you had to do to survive. I accept that without question. My family and I aren't heartless enough to hold you responsible for the situation that bastard forced you into."

"You're forgetting something." She was determined to ignore the endearment he'd let slip. "Yes, I was raped, but I made it worse by running. If I had stayed and reported what happened and told you what happened . . ." She hesitated, shaking her head. "Never mind. It doesn't matter anymore. Hindsight won't change one single thing."

Apparently frustrated, Devin snapped, "In no way was it your fault. Don't you dare even think it. If you must discuss blame, I accept my share. Evidently I wasn't the man I should have been, because you couldn't come to me with this." He pounded his chest for emphasis. "That's something I have no choice but to live with."

"No! Devin, you weren't to blame. I deliberately kept it from you." She wrung her hands out impatiently. "Why are we even discussing this? It's late. Shouldn't you be going?"

Taking a deep breath, he said, "No, I'm where I want to be. And I wish with all my heart that I could have been there for you when you needed me the most. I hate that you had to go through it alone."

He leaned forward as he said in a deceptively quiet tone,

"I know you've decided it's too late to have this guy prosecuted, but I want him, Brynne. I want to give him a taste of the hurt he caused you. He had no right to touch you! Excuse my language, but he's nothing but a weak son-of-a-bitch, not even fit to be called a man. Damn it! It's time he had to answer to another man!"

"Not you!"

Standing with his hands balled into fists, he hissed, "Why not me? You were mine at the time. We belonged to each other. He destroyed what we shared. If not for him, we would be married today."

"You don't know that."

"I believe it. And I can't forgive or forget what he did to you." In a harsh whisper, he said, "Give me a name, Brynne."

"I'll never tell you that. I don't trust you. You would go after him in a heartbeat, even though at this point, it's my word against his. Devin, you have too much to lose."

He threw his hands up in a helpless gesture. His voice was raw with emotion when he said, "I lost it all, four years ago . . . the day I lost you."

"Will you use your head? You have a wonderful career. You also have a daughter who needs her daddy in her life and not in a jail cell. My life has been destroyed. Your going after him won't alter what happened to me. All it will do is destroy your life too. And I'm not about to let that happen."

Devin was beside her so fast, she blinked in shock. He cupped her shoulders in his large hands. "Oh hell, no. He hasn't destroyed your life. We're not going to let that happen. Do you hear me?"

"Yes, I hear you. I'm sure Shanna heard you too, the way you're shouting. Let go, Devin. You're hurting me."

"I'm sorry." He dropped his hands immediately. "When you said your life was destroyed, I guess I lost it. If you believe that, then you're letting him control not only your past but also the future."

She sighed tiredly. "It's late. Let's postpone this discussion to another night."

"Like we've postponed our relationship for four damn years?" he growled. "No, Brynne. You've had your say. Now it's my turn."

Brynne thrust her chin upward. "Not tonight. I have work in the morning, even if you don't."

Staring down into her dark eyes, he insisted, "I've kept this inside for too long. I need to say this. And damn it, you need to hear it."

"Don't . . . please," she whispered, suddenly afraid of what he might say.

Devin cradled Brynne's face. "A lot has changed between us. At one time we did have hopes and dreams of a shared future. I want it back, baby. I want—"

She pressed her fingertips against his mustache-framed full lips. "Please don't say this. Don't even think it."

He kissed her fingertips. "I want you back, Brynne. The simple truth is, I've never stopped wanting you."

"That's not true." She stood up, determined to put some space between them. Nonetheless, she couldn't stop the shivers of awareness that raced over her. "You can't mean that."

"It's true." He shoved his hands into his trouser pockets. "Why else was I angry when we met again? I hadn't gotten over you walking out on me. I also made matters worse when I found out about Shanna because I blamed you for keeping her a secret and the years we lost." He closed the distance between them, but he didn't touch her. "Despite all that, it didn't stop me from wanting you. Some things haven't changed. Baby, you have no idea how badly I want you. I've been fighting my body, denying my hunger for you. You felt my arousal when we danced at Ralph's party. Whenever I'm close to you, I'm aroused."

Brynne glared up at him, her arms folded protectively over her breasts. "You're talking about sex. I don't do that anymore," she announced.

"No, babe. I'm talking about making love. I'm also talking about love and caring. I feel all those things for you. I never stopped."

Unable to bear his closeness an instant longer, she knew that somehow she had to make him see that she wasn't the same woman he'd once loved. She hissed, "Get over it! I don't do sex anymore. And I don't like to be touched."

Devin stiffened, and then he asked softly, "Are you saying you no longer have any feelings for me?"

"Of course I have feelings for you. You fathered my baby girl," she hedged, not about to take on that subject.

"We're not talking about our daughter. And you know it." He frowned. "I'm afraid you're right. This isn't the best time for this discussion. I didn't mean to pressure you. For now would you just consider giving us another chance?"

Emotionally drained and frightened, Brynne knew she wasn't thinking clearly. What they once felt for each other seemed like another lifetime. Her entire world had changed.

"Devin, I can't—"

He interrupted, "I don't expect your answer tonight. It has been a long day. I'm sure meeting my entire family at once wasn't a piece of cake. We're a loud and noisy bunch, and we do take some getting used to. Come on, walk me to the door."

Relieved, she followed him. "You have a great family. I enjoyed myself and so did Shanna."

"Good." When they reached the foyer, he pulled on his overcoat. "I'm glad because there was no doubt everyone liked you." He grinned. "They already love Shanna."

She smiled. "Your parents have volunteered to babysit."

"They mean it," he said as he smoothed on leather gloves. Glancing out the glass front door, he shook his head. "The snow is really coming down. Hard to believe it's spring."

"Devin, about the two of us. Please, try to understand—"

"Think about it. Maybe on Tuesday the three of us can go out to dinner?" When he leaned toward her, she took a hasty step back. "Just a hug, babe. Okay?"

Brynne hesitated, but then reluctantly nodded her agreement. Devin opened his arms and waited for her to make the first move. When she slipped her arms around his waist, he held her briefly against his chest.

"Good night," she whispered, shaken when she automatically inhaled the clean, familiar scent of his dark skin.

Devin ever so briefly brushed his lips against her temple. "Sleep well. Don't forget to lock up and set the alarm."

She nodded. "Drive carefully."

"I will," he said as he stepped out into the elements, closing the door quietly behind him.

As Brynne made her way back to her bedroom, she realized she was shaking. She didn't want to even acknowledge his request. Why didn't he realize that he was asking too much of her? Give them another chance? How could she? There was no two ways about it, she wasn't the same person he fell in love with. The sooner he accepted it, the better off they would all be.

Seventeen

During her session with Maureen, Brynne confessed to being upset that Devin had broken her confidence by telling his family about the rape.

"So?"

"What do you mean, so? It was very difficult for me to even share it with him. I don't appreciate him telling his family. I understood why he felt he had to tell his parents, but the others? No! He had no business blabbing my personal business to the world."

"Why are you surprised? According to you, they're a close-knit family. That's what families do. Besides, it should not matter who knows. The rape has nothing to do with who you are today. It had everything to do with a pathetic, sick, twisted man who couldn't have you any other way than to force himself on you. Brynne, you didn't cause that hateful act, and it's not yours to claim."

Silent for a time, Brynne admitted, "I never thought of it that way. I've always considered it a part of me because it happened to me. But you're right."

"Yes, I am right. Let Devin tell whomever he wants to

tell. It doesn't change who you are. You did nothing wrong. It's time you stopped blaming yourself."

"I'm not anymore."

"Then why haven't you told your friends? Vanessa, Trenna, and Laura all love you and Shanna."

Unable to find the words to explain the unexplainable, Brynne remained silent.

"You've made a start toward recovery, but there is still more that needs to be done. Have you considered participating in your counseling group, not as the supervisor, but as a member of the group?"

"Absolutely not! I don't even know if I can tell Vanessa, Laura, and Trenna about the rape. The other is out of the question. I can't do it."

Maureen persisted, "Think about it."

"The women in my counseling group are my clients. I've been working with some of them for months. I don't want to risk losing their respect or my credibility."

"You might gain their trust once they realize you know what you're talking about, because you've lived it. You have a lot to be proud of. You've made a new life for yourself and your child."

Brynne worried her lip. Was Maureen right? Had she been holding on to the blame and guilt by keeping the rape a secret from her friends? Out of necessity, Trenna knew that Devin was Shanna's father since he had taken on his share of parental responsibility by volunteering at the nursery school and picking Shanna up from school twice a week.

"I don't know," Brynne whispered.

"Give it some thought. We have to stop now." Maureen reached out and hugged her friend. "I'm proud of you. You've made a great deal of progress in only a few short weeks."

"Thank you, but it's not enough."

"Brynne, we've just started talking about your therapy group."

"No. It's Devin. He says he still wants me and wants us to start over."

"And?"

"What do you mean, and? I can't. Maureen, I can't stand to be touched."

"You told me that he has kissed you and held you."

"That was different. For one thing, I wasn't expecting it. I didn't have time to freeze up."

"Do you have feelings for him?"

"Of course I do. Without him I wouldn't have Shanna. And he's an excellent father. I couldn't have wished for more."

"That isn't what I mean and you know it, Brynne Armstrong."

"All I know is that I'm not the woman he fell in love with all those years ago. She no longer exists."

Maureen said, "Then maybe it's time you both got to know this new woman you've become, huh?"

"It's too late for us. Devin is a sexy, virile man. How long is he going to be satisfied with a sexless relationship? Believe me, not long. What's more, Maureen, I don't blame him. He deserves the best."

"What about what you deserve? Brynne, I've got eyes. I can see you still have feelings for him. You are forgetting that you know what he's like. You were once lovers."

"Yes, but—"

Maureen interrupted, "Wait before you say no. Hear me out. And I'm saying this as your friend, not your counselor. You'll never know what it could be like with Devin, unless you're willing to take a risk. Give yourself another chance to see if the two of you can make it work."

Brynne's petite frame shook with anger when she said, "It's easier said than done."

"Maybe. Nothing has to be decided today. You've got time, but while you're at it, decide if you plan on being a rape survivor who's willing to do the work necessary to become a whole woman again. Or are you going to continue being a rape victim, afraid to live your life to the fullest? The choice is yours, my friend."

Brynne complained, "At the moment, I'm about ready to say forget the whole thing. You're not offering me a bit of sympathy."

"And why is that? If you want someone to hold your hand and cry with you, then that's not me. I told you from the first, I wouldn't go easy on you. I don't believe in putting a pretty hat on a pig. Anyway, you look at it, it's still a hog."

Instead of venting her frustration, Brynne found herself laughing along with Maureen.

On Thursday evening, Brynne had just gotten home from her group session when Devin brought Shanna home.

"What happened to my baby?" Brynne cried.

There were Band-Aids on Shanna's cheek and chin, and another on her elbow. Her hands and face were clean, but her jeans were caked with mud, her hair ribbons were gone, several of her braids had come undone, and her hair was full of dirt. Brynne ran her hands over her daughter's extremities to assure herself that Shanna had not suffered an injury.

"I had fun, Mommy," Shanna said, wiggling out of her mother's embrace. "Daddy and me and Uncle Wayne played football. I got a touchdown! All by myself, didn't I, Daddy?"

Brynne sent Devin a disbelieving glare. "You played football with her? She's only a baby."

Devin smiled sheepishly. "She's fine, babe. Wayne and I were tossing around the football before dinner at my folks. Shanna wanted to play. It's my fault she fell and scraped her chin, elbow and knees."

"Want to kiss my boo-boo, Mommy?"

"Of course, sweet pea." Brynne bent down and kissed her cheek and chin. "I'm just glad you're not hurt. Daddy evidently forgot you're a girl."

"Girls play football. Aunt Anna told me she played with Uncle Wes and my daddy," Shanna insisted.

"You're right. Girls can do anything they want to do." Brynne smiled. "It looks like you not only need a bath but a shampoo. Kiss your daddy good night."

Shanna ran to hug his knees. "Night, Daddy."

Devin laughed, dropping down for a hug and wet little-girl kisses on his cheek. "Night, princess."

"Come on. It's going to take me an hour to get the tangles out. Night, Devin. Close the door behind you." Brynne didn't wait for a response, but urged their daughter along with her.

When Brynne emerged from tucking Shanna in for the night, instead of going into her room to change out of her damp clothes, she headed down the hall toward the foyer to check the lock and set the alarm.

"Going somewhere?" Devin said from the shadowed depths of one of the armchairs in the family room.

"Devin!" She jumped, pressing a hand against her breasts. "You scared me. I didn't realize you were still here. I thought you had left."

"I'm not going anywhere until we've talked. Besides, I don't like the idea of the house being open. You shouldn't be comfortable with it."

"I'm not. The doors lock automatically, but I do set the deadbolts and the alarm before I go to bed. Besides, you're the only one that I—" She stopped when she realized what she almost let slip. She trusted him to let himself out. "Is this talk going to take long? I'm wet from your little girl's bath."

Devin smiled. "Go change. I'll wait." He stretched out his long legs as if he had all the time in the world.

"Okay, I won't be long."

Brynne hurried into her bedroom and walk-in closet. After taking off the pant suit she'd worn to work that day, she reached for an ivory and gold-trimmed cashmere robe. She was tightening the sash around her waist when she changed her mind. She took off the robe and changed into a pair of faded jeans and coral long sleeve tee-shirt.

She freshened her lipstick and ran her fingers through her short curls, then stopped, suddenly annoyed with herself. What was she doing? This was no date. Purposely turning her back on the mirror, she walked out of her room.

Devin stood in front of the open doors of the armoire where the CD player, television and video/DVD player where housed. He was sorting through Brynne's collection of CDS.

"What is it?"

If he was surprised by her blunt question he didn't show it. He placed a CD into the player before he turned to face her. "If you have no objections, I would like for Shanna to spend the weekend at my place. Her room is ready, and I think she's ready."

With a hand on her hip, Brynne said, "Tomorrow is Friday. Why did you wait until the last minute to tell me this?"

"If this weekend isn't convenient, then we can try the following weekend. I'll only be in town until the end of June. I have training camp, remember? I'd like to spend as much time as I can with my little girl."

The soft, bluesy tones of Aaron Neville flowed from the speakers as Brynne made herself comfortable on one end of the sofa. She didn't breathe easy until Devin was also seated, but in the armchair.

"I take it you have plans for her this weekend?"

Rather than answer, she said, "This weekend will be fine. I'll get her things ready and you can pick her up on Saturday. One night should be enough for the first time."

He asked, "Are you sure?"

"Yes. What time do you want to pick her up?"

"Around twelve? I'd like to take her to the zoo." Devin grinned when he said, "You're welcome to come."

"No thanks." Brynne folded her hands beneath her breasts, unknowingly drawing his eyes to her lush curves.

"How did I know you were going to say that? It's hardly surprising. You've done everything you can to avoid me."

She dropped her lids. "You know why."

"No, babe, I don't. If you'd just talk to me, then maybe I could understand why you won't give us a chance. But you won't even do that, will you? It's been several days, yet you still haven't given me an answer. Or is your silence my answer?"

Exasperation was reflected in her voice when she said, "Why are you forcing the issue? I've changed. I'm not the woman that you fell in love with four years ago. That woman doesn't exist anymore. Devin, why can't you accept *that* Brynne is gone and is never coming back."

He leaned forward in the chair, his hands clasped between wide-spread knees. "No, babe. You might want her gone, but I have seen glimpses of her. I see her when she takes such loving care of our daughter. I heard her when she laughed at my father's stupid jokes and relaxed with my family around the dining room table. The only time I don't see her is when we're alone. That's when her defenses are firmly in place."

His dark gray eyes bored into her brown ones. "Brynne, don't you know I would never do anything to hurt you? Some things haven't changed. And I want you back in my life. I want the three of us to be a real family."

She stared at him in disbelief. "You can't be serious?"

"I assure you that I'm very serious."

She shook her head. "But why, Devin? You are a healthy, virile man. How happy are you going to be with a woman who can't have sex with you? How long are you going to put up with that?"

"Baby, you don't know that. Hell, we haven't tried."

Brynne blinked back unexpected tears, her small frame stiff and her hands clenched in her lap. "I know, Devin. Believe me, I know I'm not the same on the inside where it counts."

"I can't accept that. You responded to my kisses. I felt your responses."

"You surprised me. I wasn't expecting you to kiss me. That doesn't mean that I want to sleep with you," she persisted.

"Like I said, how do you know? You haven't tried."

"I told you—"

"You told me that you've changed. We've both changed. I'm not some horny teenaged kid. If it's going to take time, then I'm willing to wait." He slid from the chair onto the cushion beside hers. "Don't you know? You, Brynne Armstrong, are worth the wait." He took her small hands into his large one.

Pulling free, she rose as she snapped, "I can't! Why can't you accept that?"

"Answer me this. Did you mean what you said when you told me you were in love with me back in St. Louis?"

Incredulous, Brynne insisted, "Of course I meant it. I couldn't lie about something that important."

"Well, I meant it too. I still love you." He also rose, shoving his hands into his pockets as if he didn't trust himself not to touch her. "Why can't you give yourself a chance to just see if you still have feelings for me? If for no other reason, do it for our daughter."

Frustrated, she could barely hold back a scream. Instead she hissed, "That's not fair, and you know it."

"Yeah, I know." He grinned. "But hey, I'm fighting for our family here."

"That's just it. Devin, we are not a family. And we never will be. How can we when I can't let you near me?" She sighed deeply. "You're a good man. You certainly deserve so much more than the pittance I have to offer . . . so much more."

Devin moved to the fireplace and stared down into the unlit grate. Eventually he turned, crossing his arms over his deep chest. "So you're going to let him win?"

"What?"

"You're letting the bastard who raped you win." He ran a hand over his close-cut natural, resting one large hand on a lean hip. "He wanted you for himself. And four years later, he's still manipulating you."

"This isn't a contest we're talking about." She walked over to glare up at him. Pushing a finger into the center of his chest, she said, "No one won! I'm the one who lost it all."

"No, baby. You didn't lose yourself. He couldn't take your femininity away from you, not unless you let him. Don't you see, by denying your sexuality, he's still exercising power over your life. He meant to destroy what we had. And that's exactly what happened."

Her dark eyes were filled with anguish. "You don't understand what it was like . . . you can't."

"Then explain it to me. Make me understand," he said gently.

She dropped her head so he couldn't see the tears blinding her. She shook her head. "Devin, please, just go. It's late, and I have a full day ahead of me."

"There you go, closing down on me." He growled impatiently, "What you want is for me to shut up and pretend nothing is wrong. I won't do that, Brynne. I can't."

"I want you to leave . . . now."

"Okay. I'll go, but we're not finished with this discussion, not by a long shot. Baby, I know this is hard for you. And I'm willing to wait for as long as it takes for you to trust me again." Suddenly he smiled as he pulled on his jacket. "Come on. Walk me to the door."

Brynne followed along while struggling to collect her defenses. They were moving past the living room when she took a big breath, forcing herself to say, "Devin, I'm not trying to be difficult. I'm only being honest with you. I don't want you thinking that it's all going to just go away, because it isn't. There is no quick fix."

He didn't respond until they were in the foyer, and then he turned to face her. Tenderly caressing her cheek with a lean finger, he said, "I didn't mean to upset you and I didn't mean to make you cry. My intent is not to make this difficult for you. But, baby, you might as well get used to having me around. I'm not going anywhere. Nor am I giving up on us."

"Devin—"

He interrupted. "See you on Saturday."

"Okay." She wrapped her arms around herself.

He surprised her when he requested, "May I have a hug?"

"No."

"Pretty please with whipped cream and cherry on top," he teased.

Not for a moment did she think he would force the issue, but he was also born stubborn. If she wanted him to leave anytime soon, then she had to give a little.

She moved forward, enclosing his trim waist. For only a moment, she cautioned herself as her eyes closed and concentrated on nothing more than inhaling his clean male scent as she rested her cheek against his chest. Brynne found herself relaxing enough to enjoy his strength and warmth. She was the first one to pull back.

Dropping his arms, Devin said quietly. "Thank you."

Shivering, she ran her hands up and down her arms. "It maybe a bit tricky on Saturday. Shanna and I have never spent an entire night apart."

"I'll keep that in mind. Night, Brynne. Sleep well."

"Vanessa, I can't remember being this restless." Brynne frowned as she helped herself to a handful of popcorn from the huge bowl on the coffee table. "I've been wandering around the house going from room to room. It was kind of you to let me come over here and impose on you for a few hours."

"Stop it. You know you are always welcome." Vanessa relaxed on the opposite end of the sofa.

"I didn't know what to do with myself with Shanna at Devin's place. I suppose I have no choice but to get used to it. Shanna's going to be spending every other weekend with him, until he goes back to St. Louis."

"Brynne, it's going to be okay. Give yourself a little time

to get used to the idea." Vanessa reassured her before she confessed, "You could have knocked me over with a feather when you told me that Devin Prescott was Shanna's father."

Vanessa's twin brother and sister were watching a movie on the television in her bedroom and her teenaged sister had gone to a slumber party at her girlfriend's home.

"You have been such a good friend. I'm sorry I didn't tell you sooner. You not only know his older brother and sister, but you also work for his brother-in-law."

"Honey, you don't have to explain. It's hard to talk about a relationship after the breakup. I, for one, am glad you decided to come back to settle in Michigan."

Brynne admitted, "While we were involved, Devin and I never really talked about our families. We fell in love so quickly." She hesitated, then reluctantly said, "And it ended badly." She still hadn't been able to tell her friend about the rape. It had been hard enough to discuss her failed relationship with Devin.

"It's a good thing you decided to go with Laura to that birthday party. If you hadn't gone, you wouldn't have known Devin was in the city."

"Shanna has blossomed since she's been spending time with her father and his family. Her grandparents adore her." Brynne frowned as she revealed, "I'm the only one having trouble adjusting to the changes. Next I will have to get used to the idea of my baby flying to St. Louis to see her dad. I just know he's going to insist on it."

Vanessa frowned. "That's right. Are you going to let her fly alone?"

"No. I won't send my baby on an airplane alone." Brynne was adamant.

"I don't blame you. I'm sure you and Devin will work something out. The important thing is that Shanna is finally getting to know her dad."

Brynne nodded. "I know I'm borrowing trouble, Vanessa, but I just hope that she doesn't one day blame me for him not being in her life for the first three years. I was wrong not to tell him." She sighed unhappily.

"Blaming yourself isn't going to change the mistake. You weren't out to hurt anyone."

"But I am to blame because of how I ended it. There is something I need to tell you, but I don't want to get into it tonight. I have a difficult time talking about it."

"You don't have to, not until you're ready. Just remember, I'm not only a good listener, but I love you."

Brynne smiled, blinking back tears. "I love you too. I don't know what I would have done without you these past few years. Remember the night Shanna had the awful bloody nose? I was ready to rush her to the hospital until you told me how to stop it. And the time she got the chicken pox? I was a mess."

Vanessa laughed. "You did fine. Besides, the twins had already been through it.

"You've been such a good friend."

"So have you."

"But—"

"Stop or you will have both of us crying. What makes you so melancholy tonight?"

"I have no idea." Deciding a change of topic was needed, Brynne said, "Tell me about you. What have you been up to?"

The other woman shrugged. "Other than taking care of the kids and work, not much."

"But why, Vanessa? You're a beautiful woman. It's time you take some time for yourself. When is the last time you even had your hair done? You never go out with Laura, Trenna, or Maureen. Why? I'd be glad to watch the kids for you."

Vanessa wrinkled her nose. "Don't you start on me. You sound like Laura. All that girl talks about is men. She doesn't think a woman can call herself female unless there's some guy in her life. Well, I don't want, or need a man in my life, especially a player like Ralph Prescott."

Brynne laughed. "It might do you good to go out once in a while. Have an adult conversation. I meant it when I said I'd be thrilled to keep the kids for you."

Vanessa shook her head. "You know how I am. I'm not going to go looking for a man. For what? I'm not tiny like you or beautiful like Maureen and Trenna."

"Stop it. You are beautiful. But I'm not talking about men or looks. All I'm talking about is you getting out and having fun."

"I'm not comfortable in social situations. I'm aware of being too everything . . . tall, heavy, and awkward. I learned a long time ago not to worry about what I can't have."

"Vanessa, that's ridiculous. You are not too anything. You're just shy because you'd spent so many years caring for your little brother and sisters. You never do a thing about yourself."

"Brynne, I am fine. Really."

"You are not fine. You work all day for Gavin Mathis and the rest of the time you're looking after kids."

"That's about to change." Vanessa grinned.

"What? Tell me."

Vanessa laughed. "I don't know for sure, but I've applied for a college scholarship. I might be going back to college in the fall."

Brynne hugged her. "That would be wonderful. You've been wanting to go back and finish that degree for a long time."

Vanessa grinned. "Nothing is certain. It depends on me getting that scholarship. I can't afford to take loans or grants. I still have my sister to think of. She will be starting her senior year in the fall. And she wants to go to college. Her education must come first."

"I understand. You've been talking about going back to college since the day I met you. What about your job? Will your boss allow you some flexibility in your schedule?"

"Yes." She shook her head. "Who am I kidding? I can't do it if it's too much of a hardship on my family."

Brynne insisted, "Don't worry now. It's going to all work out. I just know it is."

At the sound of her cell phone, Brynne said, "Sorry, I have to get it." She searched through her purse. "Hello? Devin, what's wrong?" Brynne listened, and then said. "No. It's not a problem. I'll be there within the hour. Goodbye."

Vanessa asked anxiously, "Is Shanna sick?"

Brynne laughed as she hung up and dropped the phone into her bag. "Shanna is giving her dad a hard time. She's crying. I could hear her in the background. She claims she can't go to bed unless I kiss her good night and tuck her in."

Vanessa laughed. "So you are going?"

"Yes, I have to. If he brings her home, she'll think all she has to do is cry to get her way. But I don't want her crying herself to sleep either. I have to do something. She's just not used to being away from me."

"Poor baby."

"She's acting like a little brat, but I understand. This is the first night we've ever slept apart." Brynne laughed. "Devin also just realized he has no idea what to do with her hair. They're going with his family to church in the morning."

"Looks like you will be spending the night, girlfriend."

"No, I'll braid her hair and stay until she falls asleep. This is her sleepover, not mine." Brynne paused to give Vanessa a hug. "I will see you tomorrow at my place for our book discussion and brunch."

"I can hardly wait. That book was something else."

"I'll see you around twelve."

Brynne was buttoning her coat when Vanessa said, "Take my advice and go home and pack an overnight bag. Just in case you can't get her to settle down."

Eighteen

―――

"It's all right, princess. Your mommy will be here soon," Devin soothed as he cuddled a pajama-clad Shanna. Her damp cheek was on his shoulder and her thumb was firmly anchored in her mouth.

When the doorbell sounded, Devin raced to answer it, forgetting his sock-clad feet. Every light in the house was on, and he had no idea how to settle her down. It was nine-thirty, past his daughter's bedtime.

"Hi, glad you could make it." Devin pushed the storm door wide. He recognized the sparkling humor in her beautiful dark eyes as she looked from him to their daughter.

"Hi. Well, young lady. I see you've been giving your dad a hard time."

Shanna blinked big, sad eyes at her mother.

Brynne asked, "Were you scared because Mommy wasn't here?"

Shanna shook her head. "Daddy doesn't have monsters under the bed. He's big."

When Devin moved to hand her over, Brynne shook her head. "If she's big enough to act up, then she's big enough to walk."

Once she was on her feet, Shanna wrapped her small arms around her mother's waist.

Brynne asked, "Well, young lady, what's wrong? You should have been in bed more than an hour ago."

Shanna said in a loud whisper, "I missed you, Mommy. My daddy doesn't know how to tuck little girls in bed."

Brynne nearly laughed out loud at the look of shock on Devin's face. "I missed you too, sweet pea. You told me you were going to be a big girl. How come you didn't show Daddy how to tuck you in?"

She hung her head. "Sorry, Mommy."

"Don't you have something to tell your dad?"

Shanna nodded. She took his hand and tugged until he dropped down to her level. She wrapped her arms around his neck. "Sorry, Daddy. I love you."

Devin swallowed as he hugged her, saying, "I love you too, princess."

Brynne smiled. "Did you two have a good time at the zoo today?"

Shanna, all smiles now, began telling her mother about the animals and her new coloring book filled with zoo animals.

He looked sheepishly at Brynne. "Sorry about this. She got so upset I didn't know what to do. I was afraid she was going to make herself sick."

"It's not a problem. She can be stubborn." She teased, "Wonder where she got that from?"

He grinned. "Still, I took you away from something."

"It's not a problem. I was visiting with my friend Vanessa."

Brynne gave Devin her jacket before she looked around the spacious living room with its plush, oversize charcoal gray sofa, love seat, and armchair. "Very nice." Brynne sank onto the sofa. Before Shanna could climb into her lap, Brynne sent her to get her comb and brush.

Devin waited until after Shanna disappeared up the carpeted staircase in the hallway. "I can't believe I let her play me like that."

Brynne giggled. "She loves you dearly, but she is used to her nightly routine. Give her time, Devin. She will adjust to being here with you."

"If we were in St. Louis, I would have had to find a way to cope."

"Here, Mommy." Shanna climbed into her lap.

Brynne quickly took down her ponytails and brushed out her soft curly hair. She explained, "I'm going to braid it, so your dad can take the braids out in the morning. You can wear it down, with your pink headband for church."

Shanna nodded her understanding while Devin looked on, baffled.

"Me?" he gasped.

"You. It's easy. All you have to do is take down each braid and run your finger through the waves. Nothing to it." Brynne hid a laugh at the doubt in his dark eyes. "Did you enjoy your day, Devin?"

"Yeah. She liked my chili." He leaned back in his chair with a wide smile, noticing that Shanna's lids had gotten heavy as she rested against Brynne. By the time she finished, Shanna was nearly asleep. "Poor baby. She's worn out." He rose to his feet. "I'll carry her. She is getting too big for you."

"Yeah, she is." Brynne followed them upstairs to Shanna's new bedroom.

"Devin, it's lovely."

Brynne looked at the delightful mural painted on the wall, depicting a cherry tree filled with ripe fruit, birds, and squirrels. The dark cherrywood double bed was covered with a white plush comforter embroidered with cherries and trimmed in red piping. The room was filled with stuffed bears, toys, a child-size table and chair, and a built-in bookshelf filled with books. There was also an adult-size rocking chair. It was nearly a duplicate of Shanna's bedroom at home.

"You've gone to a lot of expense to make her feel at home. Thank you," Brynne whispered.

Devin smiled. "I'm glad you like it. I wanted her to be comfortable. I plan to have her room in St Louis done just like this one."

Brynne's heart sank at the mention of St Louis. "I'd better take her into the bathroom before she gets in bed. We don't want any accidents." When they returned, Devin had the comforter and blankets pulled back. Brynne tucked Shanna in and kissed both her daughter's cheeks. Shanna was sound asleep before they walked out of the room.

Devin left the nightlights on in both the bedroom and the connecting bath. As they walked down the stairs, he shook his head and said, "I can't believe I let her pull my strings." They had reached the foyer. "I should have just waited her out. She was bound to fall asleep sooner or later."

Brynne laughed. "Don't worry about it. You did fine. Besides, she will do better next time. And she will probably sleep until morning."

He motioned to the sofa. "Have a seat. Can I get you something?"

"No, but I'd like to see the rest of the house."

The house was lovely. Brynne admired the den with its built-in bookshelves. She had forgotten how much Devin enjoyed reading. He had all of Walter Mosley's books. Love of reading was an interest they shared. He showed her the formal dining room and cozy kitchen.

"Devin, it's a great house, large for a condominium."

"Yeah, I like it. If nothing else, it's a good investment. Why don't you have a seat in the living room? Be right back." He returned with a tray on which were two tall mugs of root beer filled with French vanilla ice cream and a large bowl of nachos chips and salsa.

"You remembered." Brynne laughed as he passed her one of the floats, a treat they used to enjoy while watching old movies in front of the fire. One of Natalie Cole's CDs played softly in the background. "Hope you don't mind." She gestured toward the CD player.

"Not at all."

Brynne sat on one end the sofa with her legs tucked under her. She confessed, "Vanessa and I were talking about when the time comes for Shanna to visit you in St. Louis. Devin, I must admit I have a few concerns. I can't stand the idea of my baby flying without one of us with her. We're going to have to work something out. Either you're going to have to come for her, or I'll have to take her to you."

Settling on the opposite end of the sofa, he propped his feet on the coffee table. "Babe, that's months away. Why are you worrying about that now?"

"I didn't say I was worried, I said I was concerned. It started with me missing her tonight and knowing she isn't safely tucked in her bedroom down the hall. I kept thinking what if she needed me during the night." She hastily assured him, "It has nothing to do with you. I know you'll take excellent care of her." She laughed, smoothing a curl away from her brow. "I wasn't surprised when you called. In fact, I was expecting it. I knew she would have a difficult time of it and would probably need a kiss good night, as much as I needed to kiss her. She's still only a baby."

Devin took her hand in his, rubbed his thumb against her knuckles. "You don't have to be apart from her . . . unless you want to."

"What do you mean?"

"Babe, you know what I mean. I'd like nothing better than for us to be a family. Marry me, Brynne. Let's get on with our lives."

She tugged her hand from beneath his. "Devin, I'm being serious, and you're playing around."

"I'm serious about this." He took a swallow of his drink, studying her features. "I want us to be a family. I want both you and Shanna to be with me every single day. What's wrong with that?"

"Nothing, if we had parted because of a simple disagreement. It's so more than that and you know it. I'm not Shanna. You can't chase the monsters from under the bed by saying boo. It's much more complicated than that."

She bit her lip as she looked at him anxiously. Choking back a sob, she whispered, "I don't understand why you even want to get involved with me again. You have no idea how much I wish I was the same woman you fell in love with back in St. Louis."

"You're wrong, Brynne. It işn't that complicated." His voice was brimming with emotion as he said, "Baby, I want you now, just as much as I wanted you the day we met. I'm in love with you. That hasn't changed."

"No, you can't be." She wanted to demand that he take it back. She couldn't bear the thought of it, not after what happened.

"Yes, I am."

She shook her head, aware that his baritone voice had been deeper than normal, an indication of his mood. He had seduction on his mind. She felt the heat of his need in his gaze. She didn't have to look to know that his eyes had darkened, like smoldering charcoals burning with sexual desire.

He'd had the exact look in his eyes their last night together . . . the night their daughter had been conceived. She didn't have to touch him to know that his dark skin was hot or that his pulse raced. She had no difficulty recalling his taut midsection or his large nude frame. When he came to her, his shaft had been thick, heavy with desire, and she had gladly opened her heart and her body to him, never once considering holding any part of herself back. He had been her love . . . her man.

Clenching her hands in her lap, she worried her bottom lip. How could she have forgotten that? Devin had a keen sexual drive. Once was never enough. She would be lying if she didn't admit that she had wanted him that night, just as much as he'd wanted her.

Yet, despite his six-three frame, he'd never used his size to take advantage of her in any way. Devin had always been a generous lover. He had taken his time, never rushing her toward completion. He had been both tender yet thorough.

She closed her eyes, having no trouble recalling that he was all male . . . too much man for her peace of mind.

Frightened by the mere thought of him in bed, she wondered how long he would put up with hugs and kisses, but no sex. There was nothing wrong with him. He wanted what she couldn't possibly give. Unfortunately, there were no guarantees that she would ever be whole and able to give him the lovemaking he'd craved. No . . . marriage was bound to leave them both miserable.

Brynne's eyes burned from unshed tears, because she knew what she was about to say would hurt him, yet she must say it regardless. "Devin, I've tried to be as honest with you as I know how. If we had it to do all over again, and I hadn't been raped, then it could be different between us. But"—she hesitated, holding back an endearment at the last second, before she said—"we can't change the past. We have no choice but to move forward and raise our daughter as best we can."

He caressed her cheek, cupped her nape as he tilted her chin until her gaze locked with his. "The one thing you haven't told me is how you feel about me now. Were you in love with me back in St. Louis?"

"You know I was," she blurted out.

"Did those feelings stop the day you left?"

"Of course not. I still have feelings for you, but you want more than I can give. Devin, I don't blame you. You're a normal healthy man. But—"

He didn't let her finish. He leaned forward until he could press his mouth against the side of her throat. "Yes, I want you. I can't help that. Babe, that doesn't mean that I would ever hurt you. I'm not about to try and force you to do something you don't want to do . . . not ever."

She shivered uncontrollably as she felt his soft lips moving down the length of her throat to the sensitive base. He kissed her there before he laved the scented hollow with the heat of his tongue.

"Devin," she gasped as her hand pressed against his

chest while at the same time she arched back, exposing more of her soft throat to him.

"Yes . . ." He stopped, studying her full lips.

Brynne stared at him, mesmerized by the way his gray eyes had darkened even more. He kissed her cheek, the bridge of her nose, and then he brushed her forehead so softly she barely felt it. When he kissed her lids closed, she sighed, leaning against his chest. Her breathing quickened as he dropped his head. She waited expectantly, but he didn't cover her mouth with his. Instead he gently worried her lips with the tips of his blunt fingers.

Brynne quivered when Devin replaced his fingers with his tongue. He traced the shape of her lush mouth, pausing in the corner where her lips met, to tease the soft skin. She wasn't aware of holding her breath or even parting her lips as she unwittingly opened for him. Her heart seemed to hammer in her chest, racing with delicious expectation. Yet he didn't take her mouth, didn't suckle her bottom lip, and simply teased the sweet corner again and again.

"Devin . . ." she whimpered with impatience as she gasped for breath. Her head was spinning and her nipples were hard and aching. "Please."

He groaned as he slowly sponged her plump bottom lip repeatedly, yet still he held back. He didn't enter her mouth to give her the full, hot strokes of his tongue that she could not forget. Leaning back, his hands resting on his muscled thighs, breathing deeply, he waited.

She couldn't believe that she actually said, "Why did you stop?" Trembling badly, all she could do was stare at his enticing mouth, her breathing as quick and uneven as his.

"The last thing I want to do is scare you."

She watched with widening eyes as he slowly unbuttoned his shirt, exposing the broad planes of his hair-roughened chest, and pulled the shirt free of his waistband. She had to force herself not to lean forward, not to inhale his male scent. He began to stroke his chest, his head leaning back, his eyes closed.

"What are you doing?"

"Remembering how much I enjoyed the feel of your soft hands on my chest. You used to caress me, starting at my neck." He matched action to his words as he smoothed over his dark skin. His voice deepened when he quietly said, "Your hands were so soft. Do you remember how you used your nails to tease my nipples? No matter how I begged you, baby, you wouldn't stop, not until I was aching for you. You knew just how to touch me." He released a throaty sigh.

Brynne closed her eyes, folding her arms protectively over her breasts.

His voice was velvety soft as he said, "Remember how you used to press your breasts against my chest? I loved the feel of your skin, soft as silk against mine. Your nipples were hard by then. It made me shake all over . . . just the feel of your breasts, of you. Do you remember, Brynne?"

"Yes," she whispered, trying to ignore the rapid beat of her heart and the unrelenting ache of her hard nipples. She suddenly felt the heat of desire deep inside. Her eyes were on his wide mouth, remembering the feel of the brush of his mustache against the engorged peak of her breast. "Why are you doing this?"

"Doing what, babe?"

"Tormenting me."

"Not tormenting. There is nothing wrong with remembering how good things were between us." He chuckled throatily. "We generated our own special brand of heat back then. Brown skin to brown skin. Your breasts were sensitive, and your dark brown nipples would darken until they looked like drops of bittersweet chocolate."

His voice deepened even more when he said, "Remember how you moaned as I licked your breasts? Oh, baby, I loved to take your sweet nipples into my mouth and lick them until they were pebbly hard, yet soft as velvet. You tasted so good. I couldn't make myself stop, not until you screamed my name. Do you remember, babe?"

She wanted to deny it, but she couldn't. She could only

nod her head as she watched his fingers move over his own chest.

He said huskily, "I enjoyed making you come by sucking your nipple."

Her hands were balled when she begged, "Devin . . . please stop."

"Stop what, babe?"

"I know what you're doing!" She was determined to ignore the way her aching nipples pressed against the confining lace of her bra. "You're trying to seduce me."

"Brynne, we're talking. I haven't touched you. I haven't even kissed you. But I will if that's what you want. Is it?"

"Don't!" Her voice betrayed her by its tremor.

"You're safe, baby. I'm not touching you, remember?"

She nodded, but her heart raced with awareness and excitement. It hadn't been so long since she'd felt this way that she couldn't recognize the sensations.

"I won't touch you, but you are free to touch me . . . any way you like. See, my hands are at my sides. I won't move them. If you want to feel my mouth on yours again, then take it. I won't stop you.

"Why would I? I've missed the feel and taste of your mouth on mine. I've also missed the feel of your tongue stroking mine." As he talked he slid down until his head rested against the back cushion, with legs stretched out in front of him, shoulders relaxed, and his hands remaining at his sides.

"I can't," she whispered, choking back tears.

"It's okay, baby. You don't have to do anything you don't want to do. If you like, you can always close your hands over mine. That way you can tell if I move."

"You won't move?"

"Not a muscle . . . I promise I won't do anything you don't want me to do. If you want my mouth . . . take it. If you want to caress my neck or my chest, then help yourself. I won't hurt you . . . not ever. You mean everything to me, babe. Don't you know that? It has always been you that I love . . . only you."

Even though her eyes were filled with doubts, nonetheless she moved over until she faced him. She looked into his eyes and said, "I'm ready. Are you?"

He nodded. She moved to encircle each of his wrists. Pressing her face against the side of his neck, Brynne inhaled deeply. She dropped her lids, concentrating on his clean male scent. It had been so very long since she felt safe enough to indulge her senses this way.

When she started to tremble, she reminded herself that she knew this man. If she could trust Devin to care for her child, then she could trust him not to take advantage of her. How could she have forgotten, even for a moment, that his caresses had always been warm and loving? A tear slipped beneath her lashes to roll down her cheek.

"What's wrong?" he asked against her temple.

"I'm fine. I was just indulging myself, enjoying your scent. Your skin is so hot. You always kept me warm, even on the coldest nights. We used to sleep in the nude. Do you remember, sweetheart?"

"Yes, you used to sleep on top of me."

She smiled as she pressed her lips against his neck. "You were wonderful, better than a feather mattress. I'm heavier than I was back then."

He teased, "A few well-placed pounds. All in the right places."

Brynne giggled, whispering in his ear, "Can I kiss you?"

"I'd like that."

"Thank you," she said before she kissed one lean cheek and his strong nose. She hesitated at his mouth. He let out a low moan when she pressed her lips against his. She sighed at the familiar, soft texture of his lips and the tickle of his mustache. She kissed him again and again. Gaining confidence, Brynne parted her lips a little more after each touch of her mouth against Devin's. "I missed this so much."

"Me too," he said as he breathed deeply. Yet he made no move to take control.

When she took his bottom lip into her mouth to suck, a

shudder shook his large frame. She took her time, but eventually she released his lip and then playfully nipped his top lip. She moaned his name as she traced the seams of his lips. She surprised them both when she tucked the tip of her tongue into the corner of his mouth to lave. He moaned heavily.

Longing for more, Brynne slid her tongue into his mouth, to explore his even white teeth, the fleshy inside of his mouth, and then finally she caressed his tongue with hers. Devin groaned huskily, but he didn't take over.

When she pulled back to catch her breath, she confessed, "You taste so good."

"So do you."

"As good as you remember?"

"Better." He smiled, his eyes closed as he relaxed against the sofa.

"We should stop," she said around a sigh as she kissed him yet again. "But I don't want to. Kiss me back, Devin. Kiss me . . . like you used to."

She didn't have to ask twice. He covered her lips with his own and pressed hungry kisses one after the other. Then he took her tongue into his mouth to caress, to stroke, and finally to savor. She had no idea that she cried out or that she pressed her breasts into his chest.

He was as out of breath as she was when he urged, "Unbutton your blouse, baby. Leave the bra on if you like, but please let me feel your breasts against my chest."

She cupped his jaw. "You won't—"

"I won't move my hands or my arms."

"What if you become—"

"Hard?"

Brynne nodded, biting her kiss-swollen bottom lip.

"I'm there now. If you move your hips closer you can feel it." Devin smiled at her. "Baby, you've felt my shaft before, but it's staying where it is, behind my zipper."

Nineteen

As Brynne rested her head on his shoulder, Devin made no move to encircle her in the warm shelter of his arms. What she'd been yearning for was to be held close and to feel safe. At the same time, she couldn't force from her mind the frightening feeling of being held down . . . powerless and vulnerable.

"What is it, babe? You're trembling."

"You don't want to know."

"If you've experienced it, the least I can do is listen." He kissed her temple. "Tell me."

She whispered against his throat, "He held me down. I was helpless, and I hated it. I couldn't move, Devin." Her eyes were suddenly brimming with tears.

"I'm so sorry, baby. Sorry I wasn't there to protect you." He kissed her lids, her damp cheeks.

"Because of it, I'm afraid to be held. I know it doesn't make sense, but what I craved the most is to be cradled by you."

"It doesn't have to make sense. Lean into me, Brynne, and wrap your arms around my neck, then just hold on to me. We'll pretend I'm holding you. Okay, baby?"

"Yes," she said around a sigh, and did just that, clinging to him. He said nothing, but she knew he felt her tears dampening his skin. "I missed being with you, sharing your life and you sharing mine. Devin, I missed that so much. When I first saw you at Ralph's, it took all my strength not to beg you to keep me safe. Instead I did what I had been doing for so long . . . I ran."

He kissed her hair. "I missed being with you like this. Missed you so much."

They were quiet for a time. It was Brynne who broke the silence when she whispered his name.

"Yes, love."

She took a deep, fortifying breath before she said, "I'm ready . . . ready for you to hold me. I want to feel your bare skin against mine, only with nothing between us."

He didn't move, didn't say anything for a while. Quietly he assured her, "You don't have to do this."

"I know," she said, yet she couldn't control the tremors in her hands as she fumbled with the buttons on her blouse. Freeing one button at a time, she tried to hurry before she lost her nerve, but her fingers refused to cooperate. After what felt like an eternity, she slid the last button through its buttonhole.

Although he was silent, she could hear his uneven breathing as he watched her pull back the pale blue silk and shrug the cloth off her shoulders. Her eyes never left him as she hesitated at the front clasp of her toffee-toned lace bra.

His voice was gruff when he said, "You are every bit as beautiful as I remembered."

"My breasts are larger from having Shanna. So is my backside."

"I noticed, but you won't hear any complaints out of me."

Brynne surprised them both by teasing, "Devin Prescott, I thought you were a leg man."

"No, I'm your man. I like every sweet inch of you, Brynne Armstrong."

"I have stretch marks on my stomach."

"I can't wait to kiss them. Even your belly button is sexy."

Brynne blushed when she whispered, "You never stopped there."

"You're right. I couldn't leave even an inch of your soft body untouched. I had to caress you with my lips and my tongue."

"Devin, what if I can't ever let you—"

"Shush, don't worry about that. Don't worry about anything. Right this moment, there is no one else that matters other than you and me, and our beautiful little girl upstairs."

Brynne nodded, then took a deep breath. "I'm ready."

"I'm all yours."

With panic rising inside her, she switched to a safer topic, "You must be tired of sitting so long without moving."

"I'm not tired of you. Let me feel your softness against my chest. I won't—"

"I know. You won't move unless I ask you to." She whispered nervously, "What if I want nothing between us? Not even a bra."

"Whatever . . . however you want it, baby."

With her eyes locked with his, she quickly released the clasp and peeled the bra away from her small yet full breasts before she lost her nerve. She pressed herself against him so fast, she doubted he'd caught more than a glimpse of her.

Burying her face against the base of his throat, Brynne inhaled his scent while concentrating on nothing more than breathing. She felt his tremor and let out a pent-up breath when he pressed kisses on her forehead, her brows, and her lowered lids. It was Brynne who lifted her face, unconsciously offering her lips to him. When he made no move to kiss her lips, she brushed against his, yet he still didn't take the initiative.

"Please . . . Devin."

Groaning deep in his throat, he caressed her soft lips

again and again. His mustache teased her skin before his firm lips lingered on hers. Yet he continued to hold back.

She moved to cup his nape in her small hands. "Please . . ." She moaned as she licked his lips.

His chest rose as he deepened the kiss, stroking her tongue with his. As the kiss continued, Brynne sighed, rubbing her breasts into the heat of his well-muscled chest, but it wasn't nearly enough.

"Hold me, sweetheart. I want to feel your arms around me," she begged.

Slowly he encircled her, pressing her close. They both sighed as she wrapped her arms trustingly around his neck.

"It has been so long . . . so long," she whimpered, her eyes closed as she focused on the solid beat of his heart. After a time, she admitted, "I'm sorry. I know I am being unfair to you . . . so selfish."

"You'll hear no complaints from me, baby. I'm where I want to be . . . with you in my arms." He pressed a series of kisses along her cheeks to the corners on either side of her mouth.

Tilting her head back so she could see his face, she confessed, "Yes . . . oh yes," an instant before she welcomed his wet, hungry kisses. When he ended the kiss, they were both trembling as they fought to catch their breath.

"You are so lovely. I never get tired of looking at you." He kissed her again before he said, "Your nipples are hard, baby. Do they ache?"

She blushed, unable to answer.

Devin trailed a string of kisses down her throat, lingering in the scented hollow. "Let me take that ache away."

Brynne nodded, unable to deny the yearning.

He didn't hesitate, but dropped his head to lick one plump breast. When she gasped, he stiffened. "What is it? Do you need me to stop?"

"Please . . . don't stop."

"Then why are you crying?" He wiped the moisture from her cheeks.

"I'm happy. I didn't think I'd ever be like this with you. I was afraid to even hope."

"Believe it," he breathed, then returned to lave the elongated tip of one breast. He repeatedly sponged the hard peak with the velvet heat of his tongue. He didn't stop until she begged for more. Devin didn't prolong her sweet agony. He began to suck her hard, brown nipple.

Eyes closed, Brynne cradled his head, holding him in place. Not wanting the pleasure to end, she was overwhelmed by the heat flowering deep inside. She called his name when he lifted his head, but before she could beg him not to stop, he devoured her soft mouth. While she struggled to collect her scattered wits, he moved to her other breast and began lavishing it with the same erotic attention. Lost in a sensuous haze, Brynne didn't hear their daughter's voice, but Devin did. He eased away.

"Please, don't—" she protested.

"Shanna is calling you."

Brynne blushed, trying to recover her equilibrium. Unable to meet his gaze, she slid off his lap, shoving her arms into the sleeves of her blouse while hurriedly fastening the buttons.

"Excuse me," she mumbled as she ran for the stairs. When she reached the landing, she called, "I'm coming," then hurried into her daughter's room.

"Mommy!" Shanna whimpered, rubbing her eyes with her balled fists, hugging her favorite teddy bear.

"I'm here, baby." Sitting down on the bed, Brynne smoothed her brow. "Why the tears, sweet pea?"

"I woke up and nobody was here. I got scared."

"Sh-sh. It's all right. You're in your new room in Daddy's house, remember?" Brynne kissed her damp cheeks.

Shanna nodded, snuggling against her.

"You okay, princess?" As Devin came around the other side of the bed, Brynne noticed he'd pulled on his shirt.

"Mmm-hmm. I got to go, Mommy."

"All right." Brynne pushed back the comforter. "Come on." She guided her into the bathroom.

Devin waited in the bedroom until they emerged. Brynne soon had Shanna tucked into bed.

Shanna clung to her hand. "Mommy, are you leaving? I don't want you to go."

"Sweet pea, Mommy can't stay. This is your special time with Daddy."

"Please, Mommy. Stay with me." Her large brown eyes filled with tears.

Devin volunteered, "You're more than welcome to stay over."

"Pl-e-e-a-se," Shanna begged.

"I'll stay, but you have to go to sleep, young lady. You have church in the morning with Daddy."

"You'll sleep with me?" Shanna persisted.

Brynne nodded. "Only for tonight."

They stayed until Shanna dropped back off to sleep. Moving quietly into the hall and closing the door, she said, somewhat embarrassed, "Are you sure it is not a problem?"

With a grin he said, "Absolutely. You're welcome to borrow a pair of my pajamas."

She laughed. "No thanks. I brought an overnight bag just in case she didn't settle down. It's in my trunk."

"I'll get it." He paused, then asked, "Are you coming back down?"

Flustered as she recalled what they had been doing when they were interrupted, she quickly said, "No, I don't want her to wake up alone. She's just a little nervous being in a new room." She squeezed his hand. "Please don't think she isn't happy here. It's just that—"

"I understand, babe. This place is new to her. I'll be right back. Your keys?"

"In my coat pocket." She stopped him again by placing her hand on his arm. Needing to know, she said, "Devin, I didn't mean for things to go so far. Are you angry because—"

He stroked a lean finger down her cheek. "I'm not anything but glad you're here. And you're welcome to sleep in any bed you like, including mine. Be right back."

Dealing with two equally powerful and conflicting emotions, Devin took care to close his bedroom door quietly behind him. Both Shanna and Brynne were asleep. After stripping, he walked into the connecting bath. His erection throbbed with every beat of his heart as he entered the multihead shower stall, closing the glass door behind him.

Turning on the water, he soaped his hands and used them to temporarily ease the relentless desire. It didn't take long to obtain the emotionless release that couldn't come close to soothing the yearning and pain in his heart.

It was the impotent rage that ate at him. There wasn't a damn thing he could say or do to alter the hell Brynne had managed to live through. Not only had the bastard raped her, but he had gotten away with it. None of the obstacles Devin had faced as he climbed to become one of the top quarterbacks in the NFL could compare to what his woman had faced alone. Yes, he'd dealt with racism when some didn't want to accept that hard work, talent, and skill were the reasons he was one of the highest paid quarterbacks in the league. That didn't even come close to what Brynne still struggled to deal with every single day.

And he had not been there for her. How could he live with it? What did that say about his manhood, that he'd gone on selfishly after she'd left, as if she meant nothing to him?

Feeling as if his legs were about to give out on him, he sank down onto the built-in marble bench, covering his face with his unsteady hands. The anguish he could no longer contain came in a rush of hot tears down his dark face.

It had been years since he allowed himself to cry, not since he had fully accepted that Brynne was gone and was not coming back. This devastation was even more intense because his woman had been hurt.

As he agonized over what she had suffered through no fault of her own, he hurt for her. Some sick son-of-a-bitch had forced himself into her body, taken what was hers alone. And because of him, she was frightened, terrified of men. Even a simple caress could cause her to quake with fear.

Her fear of being held had shown him as nothing else could just how deeply she'd been violated, both physically and emotionally. During the time they'd been a couple, he had never touched her in anger, yet she feared him as if he would take advantage of her vulnerability.

It was all he could do not to hold her against him where she would be safe from all possible harm. But he hadn't dared touch her, not unless she requested it. His large frame shook from rage as he cursed the lowlife dog. He wanted nothing more than to go after the bastard with his fists.

He'd tried but he couldn't get a name out of her. He'd been forced to stop when he realized that he was actually pressuring her. She deserved his support and his patience, not harassment. Yet he had no idea if he could do what she asked and let it go. His instinct told him to hire a private investigator and find her attacker, but he could only imagine her reaction if he did. He'd be lucky if she ever spoke to him again.

In all truth, he didn't trust himself with the coward. He had never thought he had it in him to take another's life, but he knew he had been wrong. He felt he was not above beating the bastard down and strangling the life out of him. Devin knew Brynne was right. He was not to be trusted with that information.

He closed his eyes, knowing they were damn lucky she'd not lost her life. The bastard could have given her HIV, which in some cases turned out to be a death sentence. It was a real blessing that her test results continued to be negative. There was no doubt in his mind that if her life ended, so would his. She was his world, as necessary to him as the air that filled his lungs.

It was a long time before his anguish subsided and he could turn off the shower. The water had long since cooled, but it didn't matter. Brynne and their daughter were what mattered. He vowed to find a way to make them a family or die in the attempt.

After drying off, he pulled on pajama bottoms, only because his daughter and Brynne were in the house, and then he climbed into his solitary California king–size bed. He closed his eyes, yet it was a long while before he could find solace in sleep.

Brynne moaned as Shanna raised one of her eyelids.

"Wake up, Mommy. Wake up."

"Why?" she answered tiredly.

"Daddy's making pancakes. He said to hurry up or he's gonna eat all of 'em. I want some." Shanna pulled on her arm. "Mommy, Daddy said—"

"I heard you." Brynne covered a yawn. "Come here, sweet pea. Give your old mommy a hug."

"Okay." Shanna complied and then insisted, "You gotta hurry. Daddy's big. He can eat a whole lot."

"I am coming," Brynne kissed her cheek. "Did you just wake up?"

Shanna shook her head. "I helped Daddy cook. Hurry, Mommy. My tummy is empty."

Brynne laughed. "Okay, okay. Tell your daddy I'll be there in five minutes."

"Yes, Mommy." Shanna, still in pajamas and bare feet, jumped down, and then asked, "How long?"

"Long enough for me to take a shower and dress. Go."

Shanna took off down the stairs.

The coffee was ready, and Shanna was seated at the kitchen table sipping hot chocolate and chatting non-stop while Devin flipped pancakes at the stove.

"Morning." Brynne smiled, taking the seat across from Shanna.

"Good morning, sleepyhead." Devin, dressed in a pair of

faded jeans and a white tee-shirt that followed the contours of his strong upper body, filled a mug with coffee. Before he handed over the hot drink, he leaned down and kissed Brynne's cheek. "I don't have to ask if you slept well."

Brynne teased, "Somebody's been talking."

"Not me, Mommy."

"Yes you, chatterbox." She eyed a heaping platter of breakfast sausage, pancakes, and fluffy scrambled eggs Devin placed in the center of the table. "Looks wonderful, Mr. Prescott. I forgot what a good cook you are. Your mama trained you well," she teased.

"Thank you, Ms. Armstrong." His dark eyes lingered on her lips as he sat down. "Shall I say grace?"

"Please." Brynne blushed, unable to meet his gaze.

The meal was filled with light banter. Afterward Brynne helped Shanna dress for church, while Devin also changed. When they joined him downstairs, Devin was dressed in a navy blue suit, pale blue shirt, and a navy and white striped tie.

"Do you like my dress, Daddy?" Shanna turned around for him, dancing from one patent leather–shoed foot to the other. She wore a pink and white striped dress with ruffled white ankle socks. Her curly brown hair was held off her face by a wide, pink velvet headband. Her pink coat and gloves matched her dress, and she carried a tiny white leather purse.

"Beautiful." He leaned down and kissed her cheek. "Wait until Granny sees your pretty dress."

Shanna nodded with an enthusiastic smile.

"You look very handsome," Brynne said as she straightened his tie, while trying to ignore the way her heart raced. It had been the same at breakfast. Her awareness of him as an attractive male scared her. Her instincts cautioned her to keep her distance.

"Thank you. Wish you were coming with us," he said as he held her coat for her. They walked out together.

"This is your time with Shanna. I'll see you two this evening." She hugged Shanna and then watched as Devin settled her in her car seat in the rear of his van.

Turning back to Brynne, he said, "You're welcome to have dinner with the family at my folks."

"No, thanks. My book club is coming over for a book discussion and for lunch. Enjoy your day." Brynne waved to Shanna and then took her overnight case from Devin. "Not too late, Devin. She has school in the morning."

"Six?" he called after her as she hurried toward her car.

"Fine." She waved. "Bye."

Twenty

The ladies in the Elegant Five Book Club had taken a break from their book discussion to enjoy the elaborate lunch Brynne had prepared in the dining room.

"Brynne, everything looks wonderful," Trenna said as she surveyed the buffet brimming with a variety of dishes, from baked seafood and cheese frittata, mixed green salad, spiral-sliced ham, hash browns, buttermilk biscuits, and three-tier coconut cake.

"It tastes better than it looks, which is more important." Laura grinned as she saluted Brynne with an upraised fork.

"Hear, hear," Vanessa agreed from her place at the dining room table.

"I second that," Maureen said as she sent Brynne a reassuring smile.

"Glad you ladies are enjoying it. It's not often I get to entertain without Shanna underfoot." Then Brynne blushed, "I didn't mean it like it sounded."

"Girl, please. We all know what you meant. I, for one, am enjoying a little peace without the kids," Vanessa laughed.

"I don't know how you two do it. Never having time to go out on a date."

"Laura, life is more than parties and men," Trenna scolded as she set her full plate beside Vanessa and took her seat. "Some of us take our responsibilities seriously."

Maureen laughed. "Unfortunately, social obligations aren't much different than working. I can't tell you how many nights I'd rather stay home with my feet up, a good book, and a bowl of popcorn."

"Not you too. Ladies, we are getting old fast. Approaching the dreaded thirties." Laura shook her head as she got up to help herself to a second helping of hash browns. "We have to do this now, before everything goes directly to the hips. These looks aren't going to last forever."

"Girl, you are so silly," Vanessa teased.

"Some of us are already over thirty and doing just fine, isn't that right, Trenna?" Maureen teased.

"That's right." Trenna laughed. "Brynne, this is a great idea. The five of us hardly ever find time to get together anymore. What happened to our once-a-month book sessions? We're lucky if we make it every other month."

"I'm with Trenna. We got to get serious about this. There are some darn good books out there," Vanessa said as she reached for her coffee cup.

It was Laura who said candidly, "I get the feeling that there is more going on than a book discussion and lunch. I still haven't gotten over the fact that Devin Prescott is Shanna's father. Girl, you know you can keep a secret. I couldn't have kept my mouth shut if a fine brother like that was my ex. Let us not forget rich."

"Me either," Trenna surprised everyone by agreeing. She shrugged off Maureen's and Vanessa's censoring looks. "Well, I'm only telling it like it is. When he comes into the nursery school to pick up Shanna, you should see the ladies eyeing that man. And most of them are married."

While the other ladies laughed, Brynne tried to conceal her embarrassment. Vanessa, Trenna, and Laura knew only a small part of the story.

"Am I the only one who hasn't met him?" Maureen asked.

"You don't watch football."

The five women were so different in temperament. They often joked it was a miracle that they'd maintained a friendship. Trenna and Brynne had been friends the longest. Vanessa entered their sisterhood when she started working part-time at Trenna's nursery school. Then when Brynne started working at the women's center, Laura and Maureen became part of the group. Their book club was a natural extention of their friendship.

Brynne exchanged a look with Maureen before she said, "I know we're only half through our book, but I need to talk to you. Laura is right. I have a bad habit of keeping things inside rather than sharing with the people I love." Brynne pushed away her barely touched plate.

"This sounds serious." Laura frowned.

Brynne could only nod. She didn't dare look at Maureen in case she'd lose her nerve.

"We're on your side, Brynne," Vanessa encouraged. "You've certainly been there for all of us, but especially me when I've felt overwhelmed."

"That's true." Maureen acknowledged, "I'm good at shutting people out when they get too close. But you weren't having it when you approached me about joining the book club. I've never regretted it."

Trenna put in, "Say what you have to say, girlfriend. We're not here to judge you."

Brynne forced a smile, determined not to get weepy. "I'm trying to do this without crying. I love you all. Our reading group has turned into so much more than enjoying books. It's a true sisterhood."

"Will you get on with it before I pull my hair out?" Laura teased.

"Take your time," Maureen advised.

Laura looked from one to the other with a frown. "You know, don't you?"

"Will you shut up and let the woman talk," Vanessa insisted.

"Yes, Laura. Maureen knows," Brynne confirmed. "She has been counseling me and I asked her not to tell anyone. If anyone is keeping secrets, it's me. This goes back to why I left St. Louis in the middle of a semester. My breakup with Devin wasn't the reason I left in the wee hours of the morning." She rushed to say, "I had been raped."

A gasp went through the room.

Laura said, "What?"

"Raped!" Vanessa cried out, while Trenna stared in horrified disbelief.

Brynne said, "Please, let me finish. Or I will never get it out." She rushed on, "It happened the last night Devin and I were together. We'd had a terrible fight. I turned down his proposal. Even though he wanted me to stay and talk it out, I refused and went back to my apartment alone. That's where it happened."

Vanessa, Trenna, and Laura stared at her in a stunned silence. Brynne couldn't bring herself to look at any of them, not if she wanted to finish what she'd started.

"Devin never knew. He had no idea why I left town." Brynne went on to tell them the details. "I did everything I was taught not to do. I was so ashamed that I had let him into my home. All I wanted to do was forget. I couldn't face Devin. It wasn't until later that I realized that I was pregnant."

Brynne paused for breath before she said, "I had no idea who fathered my baby. I did my best to bury the problem deep inside. It wasn't until Devin showed up that I faced the fact that he was my only hope of discovering if Shanna's father was the rapist or him. I asked him to take a paternity test."

She finally looked at her friends and realized there wasn't a dry eye at the table including Maureen's. She had no idea how it happened, but she was enveloped on all sides by her girlfriends, offering warm hugs and reassurances.

Laura said, "I'm so sorry, Brynne. When I think how often I badgered you about Shanna's father—" She broke off, unable to finish, her eyes brimming with tears.

"I should have known. I should have guessed," Trenna insisted, wiping at her own tears. "I knew something was wrong, but I was so worried about intruding on your privacy that I never pushed."

Vanessa sniffed as she squeezed Brynne's shoulder. "You poor baby. You've been carrying this horrible burden for so long. It breaks my heart that you had to suffer through this alone."

Touched by their support, Brynne smiled through her own tears. "Stop it, all of you. None of it is your fault. You didn't know because I was too much of a coward to face it."

"No, Brynne. You weren't a coward," Maureen insisted. "You did nothing wrong. That monster who raped you is the only one responsible."

Brynne wiped away her tears. "I can't thank you enough, Maureen, for all your help. I never could have come this far without you."

"I thought you guys were planning the annual fundraiser for the women's center." Laura's remark had all of them laughing. By mutual agreement they moved to the family room, their meal forgotten.

"Girl, how did you find the nerve to ask that man to take a paternity test? I just know I couldn't do it." Trenna shook her head in amazement.

"I wish I could have seen his face when you asked," Vanessa blurted out.

Everyone laughed, breaking the tension. Brynne was glad she was able to smile about it now. "Believe me when I say it wasn't pretty, especially when I couldn't tell him about the rape. For weeks Devin thought I had been two-timing him with another man. It was horrible."

"Oh no!" Laura gasped.

"Yes, if it hadn't been for Shanna, I couldn't have done it. She had been asking why she didn't have a daddy like the other kids in school. She wanted me to go find her one, even if it took going to the mall."

"The mall? Are you serious?" Trenna asked.

"Oh yes," Brynne smiled as she explained, and the ladies broke into giggles. When they settled down, Brynne went on to say. "After I ran into Devin at that party Laura dragged me to, I realized he was my only chance of learning the truth. It was certainly the hardest thing I've ever done. I can't tell you how relieved I was that Devin turned out to be my baby's father."

"Well, yeah," Laura said.

"That was a blessing," Vanessa insisted.

"That it was. Maureen helped me see that I had to tell Devin about the rape. I did try when I asked him to take the paternity test, but he didn't want to hear about me with some other man."

"That's understandable," Trenna said.

Laura demanded, "What about your attacker? Are you saying that he was never punished?"

"No. At this point it would be my word against his. I have no proof."

"That lowlife dog deserves to rot in somebody's jail," Trenna huffed.

Vanessa hissed, "I wonder how many other women he's hurt."

Brynne shook her head. "I have no way of knowing. I wish things had been different. I wish that I could have been stronger back then, but I wasn't. And I can't change it now."

"Don't even think about blaming yourself. You did the best you could at the time," Maureen reminded her. "And you suffered for years because of something that wasn't your fault. You're getting stronger every single day. And I, for one, am proud of you."

The others voiced their agreement. Brynne, touched by their love and support, smiled. "You know I love you all. And I'm sorry it took me so long to tell you about the rape."

"Forget that. What I want to know is, when is the wedding?" Laura asked.

That got the other ladies talking all at once. It was Trenna whose voice was loud enough to be heard over the others. "Hush! I want to hear her answer, because we all are going to be in this wedding."

Vanessa teased, "Looks like you got four bridesmaids whether you want them or not."

Brynne's brow was creased into a frown when she confessed, "There won't be a wedding."

"Before you tell us you don't have feelings for him, remember I have seen the man. And he is gorgeous." Laura laughed.

"I've seen him too. For once Laura is not exaggerating. Talk about tall, dark, and handsome! And a millionaire too." Trenna giggled as she fanned herself.

"Brynne, don't listen to them. There is no reason you have to rush into anything, especially marriage," Vanessa insisted.

Maureen was the only one who didn't offer an opinion, she waited for Brynne's response.

Laura persisted, "Vanessa, have you all forgotten, she was nearly engaged to the man?"

"Girl, who are you trying to fool? All you want is to be in the wedding and get another shot at Ralph Prescott." Trenna laughed.

"Ain't a thing wrong with that, if I do say so myself," Laura teased.

Vanessa sneered, "You're talking about Ralph the womanizer. What woman in her right mind would want that kind of heartache? Not me."

"I would." Laura volunteered. "The man is fine. Do you hear me?"

"Laura, I'm sure everyone in the neighborhood heard you." Maureen laughed.

"You don't even have a clue as to what it's like to do without, Maureen Sheppard. You come from money. It isn't noble to be poor. It's downright painful." Laura went on to say, "I for one am being honest enough to admit that it's just as easy to fall for a guy with money as it is to ignore one without it."

Maureen said, "It's not easy growing up, period. Money has nothing to do with love."

"Ladies, we've gotten way off track. This is about Brynne and her plans," Trenna reminded them, and then said to Brynne, "Well? Is there going to be a wedding?"

Brynne pressed shaking hands to her cheeks. She let out a sigh before she admitted, "Unfortunately, no. Besides the fact he has not come right out and asked me to marry him, there are other problems."

Trenna asked, "Did he ask indirectly?"

"Yes, but that doesn't mean—"

The ladies were off and running, willing to help with wedding plans.

Disgusted by the topic, Brynne shouted into the giggles and laughter. "Wait, one doggone minute! What he wants is a family. I just happen to be Shanna's mama."

Vanessa asked, "Do you love him?"

Maureen interrupted, "Brynne's right. Rushing into marriage won't solve a thing. It may cause more complications."

"This isn't a counseling session, Maureen," Trenna insisted. "All we have to do is look at her to know she still has feelings for the man. Do you think Shanna would be spending time with him and his family if she didn't trust him?"

"Well? Do you?" Vanessa persisted.

Reluctantly Brynne confessed, "Trenna is right. I do trust Devin. He's an excellent father, and she adores him. If anything, I have to stay on him not to spoil her rotten. The Prescotts have welcomed Shanna into their family with open arms. They all love her."

"That tells us exactly zero about your feelings for him," Laura said impatiently.

"Yes, but it takes more than love to get past being raped. I don't know if I can ever be a wife to him. And I'm not about to marry him with that hanging over our heads . . . not even for our daughter's sake."

"It takes time, Brynne," Maureen advised.

Vanessa assured, "If he loves you, he will give you the time you need."

The other three nodded their agreement.

Brynne sighed. "Enough! Let's get back to our book discussion."

It wasn't until after the kitchen was clean and her friends had gone home that Brynne wondered about Devin's feelings for her. Yes, he claimed he still loved her, but that didn't necessarily mean he could cope with her problem. The only thing that was clear was that he wanted them to be a family. Unfortunately, she couldn't find anything wrong with that.

Was she being selfish by not considering the possibility? Or was she only thinking about what was safer for her, rather than what it could mean to Shanna to grow up with both her parents under the same roof? Both she and Devin had grown up in two-parent homes. It had been also what she'd once dreamed of before the rape.

What about Devin? How long could he handle a sexless marriage? She shuddered, unable to even imagine him in such a sterile relationship. Despite what he said, he would never settle for less than a normal, healthy marriage. And she had to face the fact that there was no guarantee that she would one day be whole again. Devin deserved better.

"Well?" Devin leaned a broad shoulder against the mantel in Brynne's family room.

"Well what?" Brynne said as she made herself comfortable in an armchair. She was busy trying to appear calm, rather than show how nervous she was, now that Shanna wasn't there to run interference.

"Is she asleep?" His dark gaze moved over her soft features.

"Mmm-hmm. She finally ran out of steam." Brynne smiled. "She had a wonderful time with you and your family. All she could talk about was her daddy. And Granny and Grandpa. You're a good father, Devin. She loves you."

His gaze locked with hers for a long moment, then he grinned. "Thanks. That means a lot to me, coming from you."

Her eyes went wide when he crossed to her and effortlessly pulled her out of the armchair. Before she could protest, he sank onto the cushion with her on his lap.

"What do you think you're doing?"

"Getting comfortable. I'm comfortable. How about you?"

Her cheek rested against a broad shoulder. She sighed. "I don't know. Let me get back to you on that."

"Do that." He ran a caressing finger along her soft cheek, then traced her bottom lip. "How did your luncheon go with your girlfriends?"

"Book club. And it went fine, but I'm sure you're not interested in that."

"You're wrong. I'm interested in everything about you." Devin brushed his lips over her forehead. "So tell me about the meeting. What book did you discuss?"

Brynne could see by his expression that he was curious, not just making conversation. "We read *P.G. County* by Connie Briscoe, but we also talked about me and the recent changes in my life."

"Oh?"

"That's all you have to say?" She quirked a perfectly arched dark brown brow.

"Until I hear more. Did my name come into this conversation?" he asked with a knowing grin.

"You know it did. You are Shanna's dad."

"Hmm."

Brynne admitted, "The ladies were surprised that I had kept you a secret. You see, I never talked about you or what happened back in St. Louis. I kept it all inside. I wanted to forget . . . to pretend it didn't happen at all. It was easier that way." She relaxed against him when she saw the acceptance on his handsome features.

He kissed her temple. "You've moved past that in the last few weeks, haven't you?"

She nodded. "Finally I was able to tell my friends about the rape."

His eyes studied her for a time before he asked, "How did it go?"

"Much better than I expected. I've been dreading it. Maureen, my counselor, felt it was necessary to my recovery."

"Does knowing it's finally out in the open help?"

"I'm relieved. And I'm grateful. I have a wonderful group of friends."

Devin kissed her soft curls. "I'm proud of you, babe. It had to take a football field of courage to do what you did. I take it they were supportive?"

"Very much so."

Placing a finger beneath her chin, he tilted her head back until he could cover her mouth with his. His kiss was gentle. When she could catch her breath, she said somewhat breathlessly, "Devin, let me go. We shouldn't start anything we both know I can't finish."

"We," he emphasized the word, "don't know anything of the sort."

"Let me go."

"Baby, I'm not holding you down." His arms rested on the armrests. "Anytime you want to get up, please be my guest."

Realizing he was right, instead of getting up, she relaxed against his chest once more. "Sorry."

His voice was deep, almost gravelly when he said, "I admit it. I like holding you. I've been thinking . . . about us."

"Us?" She stiffened as she asked, "Aren't you taking a lot for granted?"

"Nope. The way I see it, we've already wasted years."

"Devin, I tried to be completely open with you. You know I can't sleep with you."

"You don't know what you can do, babe. You haven't tried, have you?"

"After what happened, I didn't want any man."

"You've been celibate since—"

"Yes!"

"Baby, I'm sorry I can't say the same. I started dating about six months after we broke up. It took me that long to accept it was really over. I slept around for a time. And then I stopped." He shocked her when he bluntly revealed, "It's been a year and a half since I've been inside a woman. Sex didn't mean anything. After what we shared, it was pointless. I didn't want anyone else."

She stared at him. "Why are you telling me this?"

"Because I don't want there to be any more secrets between us. I want all of it out there."

She found herself asking, "Did you use protection?"

He looked into her velvety soft brown eyes when he said, "I've never had unprotected sex with anyone, even with you. And I routinely have HIV tests. They've always been negative."

"I'm more at risk than you are," she said quietly.

"Not likely. It's been four years, and from what you told me your tests always come out negative."

She nodded, then, suddenly uncomfortable with the conversation, said, "Do we have to talk about this?"

He cradled her nape in his wide palm. "Yeah, we do. We've been apart for so long." He traced her full, lush lips. "Your mouth is as sexy as I remember. It's always driven me crazy. Brynne, I wanted to lock lips with you the moment I first laid eyes on you."

Her gaze went wide at the smoldering heat in the dark gray depths of his eyes. She felt his erection against her side. Before she could collect her scattered wits, Devin began to lower his head. The movement was slow, unhurried. He gave her time to stop him, yet she didn't. He caressed her lips with his own. Her heart began to pound with excitement and her unexpectedly heavy lids closed as he parted her lips. She whispered a protest, and Devin stopped.

Twenty-one

"We shouldn't. You're already..." She paused.

"I'm already what?"

"Aroused. I can feel your . . ."

He chuckled. "Erection? Glad you noticed."

"It's not funny."

"Yes, it is. It's certainly nothing for you to be concerned about." He kissed the tip of her nose. "I won't hurt you, baby . . . not ever. I was hard last night, yet I didn't lose control. Every time you're in my arms, my body prepares to make love to you. My penis is no threat to you, or what we feel for each other. I do my thinking with the head on my shoulders, babe."

Brynne blushed. "It's just that I . . ."

"What?"

"It makes me uneasy, knowing you want me that way," she said candidly.

"Nothing is going to happen that you don't want to happen. It didn't last night, did it?"

"No, but Devin . . ."

"And it won't tonight." He gave her a hard, quick kiss on

her soft lips. "Now that we've settled that, I have a suggestion. Let's go away. Just the two of us, spending time
alone . . . getting to know each other all over again. What
do you say about a long weekend? I know of a small country inn near Traverse City, right on Lake Michigan. It's too
late in the year for skiing, but the view is great. They also
have hiking and biking trails."

"What about Shanna?"

He laughed. "She has two doting grandparents who
can't wait to keep her for a weekend. She also has two uncles and an aunt who want to spoil her."

"But—"

"Please don't use our daughter as an excuse not to go. If
we're ever going to make it work, we both have to put forth
an effort. I believe what we once had is more than worth
another try. Don't you?"

As she worried her bottom lip, she wondered if they
were rushing things. And what about making it work? This
wasn't the first time he'd suggested a new beginning. Was
she strong enough to try?

"Brynne?"

"I don't know, Devin. This trip is kind of sudden, isn't it?"

"All I'm suggesting is a long weekend. Yes or no?"

She glared at him. "Why do I have to decide this very
minute?"

"You've got time. I'm flying to St. Louis on business in
the morning."

"That is sudden."

Devin kissed her temple. "Not really. I've been putting it
off because I didn't want to be away from my two sweet-
hearts. Let me up, babe. It's getting late, and you've got
work in the morning."

Embarrassed that she'd gotten so comfortable in his lap
that he'd been the one asking her to move, she quickly slid
off his hard, muscular thighs. "How long will you be away?"

"A couple of days, a week at most," he said as he came
to his feet, smoothing down his trousers.

Suddenly realizing that she was staring not only at his thighs but the outline of his sex, she turned so swiftly, she almost lost her balance.

"Brynne?"

"Yes?" She was forced to look at him.

"Kiss my little princess for me. I'll call." He rested a hand on a lean hip, unknowingly drawing her eyes to his taut midsection that gave way to formidable shoulders and powerful biceps. He still wore the silk shirt and trousers of the suit that he'd worn that morning which she suspected of having been custom-made for his long frame.

She managed to nod.

Devin slipped on his leather jacket that had been thrown over the end of the love seat. "You coming?"

"Of course."

He was a few steps behind her. He paused to kiss her cheek. "You have three, maybe four days to decide whether you want to go away with me next weekend. Bye."

It was after she locked up that she realized she was angry. She wanted to punch something. No, what she wanted was to punch Devin. How dare he casually suggest they go away together, and then just leave? He was acting as if he'd asked her to go out to a movie, for heaven's sake.

There was nothing casual about it. He was talking about several uninterrupted days of dealing with her fear of him. Why would she want to put herself in such an uncomfortable situation? He was either the most confident man on earth or the biggest optimist. At the moment she was leaning toward the latter. She'd spent years avoiding men and for good reason.

He knew she wasn't ready for the kind of intimacy he wanted. She could barely handle his kisses. Even when he'd done something as simple as hold her, she got panicky at the thought of being held down. It wasn't until he pointed out to her that she was free to get up any time she wanted that she was able to relax, more so than she ever believed possible.

She still couldn't get over the fact that she'd welcomed his caresses the other night. As long as she reminded herself that it had been Devin holding her, she was all right. She was able to relax because she knew deep inside he was a man of his word. Experience had taught her that he would never use his superior strength against a woman.

After meeting his parents, she understood why. Devin had been raised to respect women, and that respect started with his beloved mother and sister. He was a pro athlete, used to locker room language, yet he didn't normally swear around women. The times he'd forgotten himself were when he'd believed she had slept with another man and kept Shanna a secret. And then he learned she'd been raped. In all honesty, Brynne couldn't hold that against him.

Her friends had been right; she did trust Devin. The question was, did she trust him enough to spend several nights alone with him? No man could be expected to wait indefinitely for a woman's fears to disappear. Although Devin was a good man, he was no saint.

Shanna was not pleased when she realized that her father had gone away, and she would not be seeing him for several days. She whined and complained about every little thing. In short, she worked on Brynne's unsettled nerves.

It took a while before Brynne figured out that Shanna feared her dad wasn't coming back. Brynne tried to reassure her, but nothing seemed to work. It was his nightly telephone calls that eventually alleviated Shanna's fears.

Brynne didn't even try to fool herself into believing that Shanna was the only one looking forward to those calls. She knew better. Generally, he telephoned just before their daughter's bedtime. When it was Brynne's turn to talk, she couldn't find the words to tell him how much she missed him.

After dinner on Wednesday evening, Brynne laughed when Shanna beat her to the front door. She was in her daddy's arms as soon as Brynne got the door fully open.

Devin and Brynne exchanged a smile above their daughter's head while Shanna chattered nonstop, bringing him up to date on all her news. They didn't have a private word until after Shanna opened her present, a new doll, and took off to her room to find the drawings she'd made just for her dad.

Devin brushed a hand along Brynne's cheek. "How are you doing?"

"Good. As you can see, your daughter missed you." Brynne laughed.

"Yeah. The feeling was mutual. I got my hug from Shanna," he said a bit huskily, "What about you?"

She surprised herself when she wrapped her arms around his waist and squeezed. "I missed you. Did you get your business taken care of?"

He kissed her temple. "Yes, and I missed you, babe. I don't like being away from my two favorite ladies."

Before he could say more, Shanna came running into the family room and was brought up short by what she saw.

"Daddy, what are you doing to my mommy?"

"Giving her a hug and a kiss." He brushed his lips over Brynne's before he released her. Then, he squatted down until he was eye level with their daughter. "Is that okay with you?" He tickled her tummy.

Shanna giggled as she nodded so hard her ponytail bounced. "Look what I made!" She held up two drawings.

Brynne hadn't known she'd been holding her breath until her body forced her to breathe. She shouldn't have been surprised. It was the first time Shanna had ever seen her in a man's arms. Having Devin in their lives had brought about numerous adjustments, for both of them.

Devin didn't stay long. After Shanna was in bed and Brynne walked him to the door, he asked the question uppermost in her mind.

"Well?"

"What?"

Folding his arms over his chest, he said, "Don't play with me, lady. You know what I've been waiting for. Are you going away with me on Friday? Should I call my folks and arrange for Shanna to stay with them?"

"Yes and no," she teased, then quickly added, "I'm coming, and I've already talked to your mother. Your parents are looking forward to having Shanna."

Devin grinned. "Good. I'll make the arrangements."

Before he could ask for a hug, Brynne slid her arms up his chest and encircled his neck. She stretched up on tiptoes to press her lips ever so briefly against his, then she took a step back. "Bye."

"I still can't get over your daughter." Brynne laughed, determined to focus on the passing scenery rather than the man who handled the black Jaguar with casual ease.

Devin released a deep, throaty chuckle, "My daughter, huh?" as he momentarily took his eyes from Interstate 75 as they traveled north. The late-afternoon traffic was becoming crowded.

"Yes, she didn't even notice when we left. All she was interested in was playing with Kaleea, and playing video games with her uncle Wayne."

"Don't forget baking cookies with Granny. You're not worried about her, are you, babe?"

"Oh no." Brynne glanced at him. "I just hope your parents don't want us to come back and get her before the night is out. Three or four views of *The Lion King,* her current favorite, should do it."

They both laughed.

"They are tougher than that. After all, they put up with me and my brother and cousin through our teenaged years."

Brynne confessed, "I'm glad that Shanna is getting to know your family. It's wonderful that she is growing up as part of a large, loving family. It's better than the way I grew up, as an only child. Oh, don't get me wrong. I was happy. I had wonderful parents, but I always longed to have a brother or sister."

He laughed. "There were times when I would have gladly traded my brothers, sister, and cousin for some privacy."

Brynne smiled. "Really?"

"Really. As a kid, you get sick of sharing, but as an adult I realize how important it is to know someone always has your back. I admit, sometimes it feels as if somebody is always in your business, offering an opinion whether you want it or not."

"All I can say, from the outside looking in, it seems worth the sacrifices." She admitted quietly, "After my parents died, my family was gone. It really hit me at the funeral that I was alone in the world. The church was full of their friends and colleagues, but no aunts, uncles, or even a wayward cousin. Both my parents were only children and their parents had also passed."

He reached over and squeezed her hand. "I'm sorry you had to go through losing your parents alone. I wish I had known you then. We would have faced it together."

"Thank you." She was genuinely touched by the sincerity in his voice.

Changing the subject, he teased, "If you'd accepted my proposal, you'd have more family . . ."

"Devin, don't. Not this weekend. This is supposed to be a relaxing few days. You promised."

"I promised not to pressure you. That's all I promised."

She sighed. "You can be so pragmatic when you set your mind to something."

He teased. "What you mean is, I'm stubborn. I plan to ignore that comment."

"Why? It's the truth," she insisted. "Besides, you did not propose. What you did was suggest that Shanna, you, and I become a family."

"That was a proposal."

She shook her head. "It was a suggestion. Why are we even talking about this?"

"It isn't getting me anywhere," he grumbled.

"Nope. Give up?"

"No, babe. What I am is a man who goes after what he wants and doesn't stop until he gets it. If I hadn't been determined, I would never have made it into the pros."

"That's one of the things I've always admired about you. Shanna has a very good role model in you."

His voice was rich with emotion when he said, "Thank you. That means a lot."

Brynne returned her attention to the passing scenery; anything was better than staring at his striking profile or worrying about their sleeping arrangements. She'd purposely not asked, telling herself she would deal with it when the time came.

Although the roadway was clear and most of the snow had disappeared, the air was still brisk. The calendar proclaimed the change of season, but the brown countryside and bare-branched trees didn't yet display their spring bounty.

They were both dressed casually in jeans and sweaters. Hers was a pale pink cashmere cable knit, while his was a navy turtleneck. Both had shed their heavy outer jackets, and enjoyed warm air circulated from the heating system.

"Comfortable?"

"Mmm," she murmured.

"Remember to bring your bathing suit and hiking boots?"

"Yes. I doubt we'll need bathing suits."

"Indoor heated pools and hot tubs." He hesitated before he asked, "What's wrong, babe?"

She laughed, but it lacked humor. "Second guessing myself. I can't let it go. I keep asking myself how different everything would have been if only I'd stayed with you that night. Pointless, huh."

He took a hand off the steering column and reached for

her left hand resting in her lap. "Don't do this to yourself, Brynne. Hindsight is deceptive . . . a waste of time. Besides, you had no way of knowing what was waiting for you at home." He hesitated. "I've made my share of mistakes."

"Name one," she challenged.

"I should have come after you. I was wrong to leave things as they were between us for so long."

She turned to study his strong profile. "Why didn't you?"

"Ego. I couldn't get past the fact that you'd left me. What I did was brood, placing the blame on you and none on myself."

"It wasn't your fault. You did the best you could, under the circumstances. You had no way of knowing I'd been raped."

"Brynne, I knew I loved you. Love should have kept me at your side, no matter what. I failed you."

"No, Devin. You've conveniently forgotten you had an out-of-town game. You had to go away for a couple of days, and when you came back, I was gone."

"I should have come after you, then. I suspected you'd gone back to Detroit." He paused before he murmured in disgust, "I certainly had the means to track you down."

"Don't. Let's not play the blame game. It changes nothing. I've already wasted too many years doing just that, blaming myself."

Devin let out a frustrated groan, but he didn't force the issue. Instead he asked, "Are you hungry?"

"How could I be, with the sandwiches your mother packed for us? Besides being a nice lady, she is a great cook."

"That she is."

Devin stopped himself a number of times from asking her thoughts. He longed to tell her she had nothing to worry about from him. Nothing would happen that she didn't want to happen.

In all honesty, how could he reassure her when he was only flesh and blood? He had his limits. He would be lying if he didn't admit that he was on shaky ground. They had two nights ahead of them in the same suite with nothing between them but his willpower and her fears. Her fears didn't guarantee much beyond his frustration.

He swore beneath his breath. Whom was he trying to fool? He knew going in that there would be no assurances that she would ever be able to even sleep in the same bed with him without panicking. How he longed to be able to just hold her during the long nights.

Well, that wasn't entirely true. He was damn tired of cold showers or finding his own empty release so he could sleep at night. He wanted what they'd lost. He wanted his woman back.

He swallowed an impatient curse word. He had to stop thinking of his own selfish needs. This trip was a fresh start for the two of them. He had to prove to her that he was a man of his word. Time wasn't what was important. Regaining Brynne's trust and hopefully her love was all that mattered.

The resort, Shoreside Inn, was situated on the western arm of Traverse Bay overlooking the beach and lush gardens.

"Very nice," Brynne smiled as they pulled to a stop in the circular courtyard. "I bet it's fabulous in the summer months."

Devin saw the anxiety in her pretty brown eyes as the valet opened his door. He popped the trunk release before he came around to help her out.

He held her coat for her as he said, "We'll have to come back later in the year."

A bellman took their luggage while the doorman greeted them and ushered them inside to the reception desk. Devin was aware that Brynne was unusually quiet as they checked in and were shown to their suite on the top floor. After he tipped the bellman, Devin closed the door quietly behind them. He waited as she looked around the tastefully appointed sitting room rather than at him.

"What do you think?"

"It's beautiful." She had tossed her jacket on the back of an armchair, yet rubbed her hand up and down her cashmere-covered arms as if she were cold.

He crossed his arms over his chest. "Which bedroom would you prefer?"

Her smile looked forced when she said, "The blue one. You need the king-size bed, I don't."

Devin nodded, then picked up her garment bag and placed it on the padded bench at the foot of the queen-size bed in her room. Back in the sitting room, he asked, "Shall I call and make reservations for eight? Or do you need more time to get ready?"

"Eight is fine." She looked everywhere but at him.

Devin went over to her and took her hands into his. "I'll see you later. I'm going down to the gym for a quick run on the indoor track to work some of the kinks out."

"Okay."

Devin grabbed his own bag and walked into his room to change while trying not to be hurt by the look of sheer relief on her lovely face.

When it was time for dinner that evening, Brynne took a calming breath before she opened her bedroom door and walked into the sitting room. She nearly dropped her small black, beaded handbag when she spotted Devin standing by the French doors looking out at the private balcony and the dark beach.

She couldn't help but take note of the way his charcoal suit fit his large frame to perfection. The color seemed to intensify his eyes while the pale gray shirt and tie emphasized the smoothness of his dark skin. He was so attractive, no wonder women chased after him.

"You look good," she said with a smile, nervously licking suddenly dry lips.

He grinned. "Thank you, but you are the one who's

looking good. All I can say is wow! You're beautiful. I like the dress."

She blushed from the way his gaze moved from the soft curls framing her face, down to her bare throat, to the top swells of her breasts revealed by her form-fitting pink satin, spaghetti-strapped sheath, worn under a black, long-sleeved, knee-length, lace dress with a cinched-in waist and scallops edging the hem and neckline. Her small feet were encased in pink high heels with thin black leather straps that crossed over the toe and tied around her trim ankles. Her only jewelry was a pair of black pearl studs surrounded by diamonds and a single strand of black pearls, a gift from her parents.

"Here you go," he said as he draped the black cashmere shawl she carried over her shoulders. "Ready?"

She nodded, trying to ignoring the butterflies in her stomach as he guided her out of the suite and toward the elevator. His wide palm rested against the back of her waist as they rode down.

"Is the restaurant in the hotel?"

"In Traverse City."

"You know where you're going?" she loosened up enough to tease.

He chuckled. "Not exactly, but don't worry, we'll find it."

Brynne smiled, determined to relax and enjoy the evening. It was too late for her to be entertaining second thoughts.

The restaurant was located in the heart of the resort town. Marino's was elegant and sophisticated. The white linen–covered tables were candlelit and positioned around a circular floor-to-ceiling glass wall that overlooked the frolicking whitecaps of Traverse Bay.

They were seated in a somewhat secluded area of the dining room on midnight blue velvet upholstered chairs.

Brynne had been pleased that he had not been spotted by his fans seeking autographs. They would be able to enjoy the evening without interruption.

They started out the evening with champagne before dining on mixed green salad, topped with the house cream Italian dressing, twice-baked potatoes, lobsters stuffed with a seafood medley of crabmeat, shrimp, and scallops, followed by dessert of chocolate-dipped Florentine shortbread.

"Honey?" Devin prompted.

"I'm sorry. I was daydreaming. What did you say?" Brynne said.

"What do you think of the restaurant? The food?"

"Very nice." She smiled. "The food is excellent. Even though I miss Shanna, it's great to be able to have an adult conversation."

His eyes twinkled. "She is a joy, but she's also a handful." He reached out to play with her fingers. "Are you cold? Your hand is like ice."

"No, just a little nervous," she admitted candidly.

"Don't be. Nothing is going to happen that you don't want. Not that you need it, but there is a lock on your bedroom door, babe."

Brynne lowered her lashes, unsure of how to respond.

He surprised her when he said, "If you would be more comfortable, I can move to another room."

Twenty-two

⟞

"No, Devin. That's not necessary. It's not you . . . it's me." She forced a smile. "Besides, if we're apart, that defeats the purpose of this trip. I apologize. I shouldn't have said anything."

"Babe, you have nothing to be sorry about. I wish you could somehow forget all those worries you're carrying around and just enjoy yourself."

Gazing into his eyes, Brynne said, "You're such a special man, Devin. I know this has not been easy for you. Why do you bother? Why do you put up with me? There are so many women out there who aren't carrying around excess baggage."

He lifted her hand and carried it to his mustache-framed lips. He placed a tender kiss in the center of her palm. "I'm with you, which is where I want to be. How about you?"

"That's also true for me," she whispered, fighting back tears.

It was true. She didn't want to be anywhere else or with any other man. Devin had always been the one for her. How had she gotten so lucky? Despite her leaving him and keeping his child a secret, this wonderful man still cared for her. Just as she still cared for him.

The question for which she didn't have an answer was whether she would be able to show him how she felt about him. Could she sleep in his arms? Would she be able to go one step further and let him make love to her? Or would she freeze up with fear yet again?

She wouldn't be the only one hurt if their weekend together turned out badly. Somehow she had to find the courage to give them a fair shot at regaining what they'd lost.

"More champagne?" he asked, lifting the bottle from where it rested in the silver ice bucket.

"Yes, please."

After filling her champagne flute and his own, he raised his glass. "To us and a new beginning."

Brynne clicked her glass with his before she took a sip, while silently reciting to herself, *I can do this . . . I can do this,* again and again.

"Tired?"

"Yes. Sorry, I didn't mean to spoil our evening."

"You couldn't if you tried. It's been a long day."

Devin signaled their waiter for the check. He quickly took care of it with a credit card and then ushered her out. It wasn't until they waited for the car to be brought around that he was stopped by several sports fans wanting to get his autograph and to have a picture taken with him.

After they were in the car and under way, Devin said, "Sorry about that. It doesn't happen as much here in Michigan."

"Don't apologize. You have fans all over the country."

Brynne was fine until they entered their hotel suite, then suddenly her stomach felt as if it were in knots. She watched Devin walk over to the side table were a bar had been set up.

"Would you like a nightcap before you turn in? How about a brandy?" he asked. "It might help you relax."

"Can't fool you, huh? Yes, I'll take the brandy, but give me five minutes. I'd like to change into something more comfortable."

Devin came over to her, cupping her slender shoulders. "Babe, it's all right if you'd rather just go to bed. This isn't an endurance contest."

Brynne could see she'd shocked him when she slid her arms around his waist and rose up on tiptoe to brush her lips against the side of his neck, despite her jittery nerves. "Although I'm tired, I'm too keyed up to sleep. I'll be right back."

"Would you like to change into your bathing suit and try out the hot tub on the balcony?"

"Not tonight. I'll be back. While I'm gone, why don't you also change out of that suit into something comfortable? Then we can share a nightcap and just keep each other company until we get sleepy."

"Sounds like a plan."

Devin made use of the time to take an ice-cold shower. He was shivering when he dried off and pulled on a pair of well-worn jeans and his dress shirt. He didn't bother with more than a few buttons, rolling his sleeves up to his elbows. On bare feet, he returned to the sitting room and started the fire in the grate. He filled two squat tumblers with Hennessy before he made himself comfortable on the sofa, propping his feet up on the coffee table.

His relaxed pose was deceptive. He couldn't have been more anxious if his team was three points behind with less than a minute to go to get the job done. But he wasn't facing a line of three-hundred-plus-pound linebackers, just one petite woman who held his heart in the palms of her small hands.

Drumming his fingers on the armrest, he reminded himself that all he had to do was focus on her. Helping her maintain her frail sense of security was paramount. His own hunger wasn't the issue. He's been given a special gift. Time alone with the lady he loved without interruptions . . . just the two of them getting to know each other all over again. He didn't intend to blow it.

"Hi." She offered an anxious smile as she slowly entered the room.

"Cute PJs," he teased.

She laughed. "They are a birthday gift from your daughter. She picked them out by herself. My best friend, Vanessa, took her shopping. Shanna was very proud of her selection." Brynne absently smoothed the cardigan of the three-piece red silk pajama set covered in tiny white hearts. On her feet were matching ballerina-style slippers.

Brynne surprised him when she didn't take the love seat across from him but sank onto the sofa cushion beside him. Devin passed her the snifter of brandy.

"A toast?"

"Let's." He lifted his glass, waiting expectantly for her to do the honors.

"To us." She clinked her glass against his.

Stunned, he studied her, not taking the expected sip. He teased, "Okay, young lady. You want to tell me who you are and what you've done with Brynne?"

She laughed. "You forgot to drink."

Devin took a sip. "Now answer the question."

"What? You expected me to lock myself in my room, quaking with fear?" She shook her head. "No way. I'm tired of that. I've put my life on hold for far too many years. Enough already. I want what we had."

Although his heart raced, he forced himself to breathe evenly. He asked, "What brought this on?" while taking note of the fine tremor in her hand as she took another sip of liquid courage.

"Devin, I decided you were right. If I don't want my attacker to win, then I have to stop giving in to the fear. I don't want it to continue controlling my life."

"The sentiment is wonderful, but, baby, you're trembling. This weekend isn't a test. You don't have to prove anything to me."

She raised her chin. "I have to prove it to myself."

He closed his eyes, trying to contain his keen disappointment. "No, you don't. I accept you, just the way you are." Lifting his lids, he momentarily locked his eyes with hers, and then slowly rose to his feet. "I'll see you in the morning."

Brynne caught his arm. "Please, Devin, don't leave."

"I have to. You're not ready for intimacy. I meant it when I promised no pressure, babe."

"I'm ready." She slid her hand down his arm to clasp his large hand.

"Brynne, you're shaking."

"So what? I'm a little nervous . . . it's okay. Honey, stay with me. Let's talk awhile. Then we'll go to bed together." Her beautiful eyes were wide with a mixture of hope and dread.

He said nothing, clearly not convinced.

She stood, lifting a hand to caress his cheek. "Please, stop. Stop trying to push me away to protect me. The last person I need protection from is you."

He studied her for a long moment before he sat back down on one end of the sofa and retrieved his glass. "To us."

Brynne also sat down, feeling as if she'd won a major battle . . . but not the war. Devin had been right. She had a queasy stomach, and her hands and limbs were shaking, all testimony to a bad case of nerves. She assured herself the nerves didn't matter. For she knew that if she was to ever have anything that even resembled a normal life, she would have to take the risk. More than anything else, she wanted him back.

She peeked at him through her lashes. "Do you remember the night in Miami?"

He smiled, "Yeah. You flew down for the game. We went clubbing after the game."

"The hotel was right on the beach. And later we walked

barefoot in the sand." She studied him. "Remember how we made love . . ."

"I remember," he said softly, "but I still don't understand why you feel you have something—"

Rising to her knees, Brynne pressed her lips to the hollow at the base of his throat. "Don't go all serious on me."

Devin groaned. "Why do I feel like a lamb headed for slaughter?"

She giggled, her hands braced on his chest, "Relax . . . I promise it won't hurt a bit." Determined to ignore her tremors, she moved her lips over the skin exposed by his partially open shirt.

He said nothing, merely held still as her kisses warmed his dark brown skin while she stroked his chest. He released a throaty groan when she pressed her open mouth against his, licking his fleshy bottom lip. He deepened the kiss, easing her onto his lap.

Brynne was lost in his overwhelming heat as he covered her mouth with his. Then she moaned when his hot mustache-framed mouth slid down one side of her throat. As he tongued her pale brown skin, causing goose pimples to rise, she whimpered. He repeatedly caressed the other side of her throat. She didn't even think to protest when her cardigan slid down her arms. She wasn't thinking at all as she pressed her aching breasts against him, needing the firm pressure of his muscular chest. She moaned his name, wrapping her arms around his neck, kissing him again and again.

"Brynne . . ." He groaned her name, cupping her shoulders, holding her away from him. "Are you sure about this?"

She stared at him, unsure of everything, yet knowing she had to at least try if they were ever going to have any kind of happiness. Instead of answering, she reached for the hem of her lace-edged camisole. She heard him release a pent-up breath when the garment rose above her flat stomach and small waist. His hands were at his sides and he curled them into fists as the ripe curves of her small, lush breasts were revealed. She jerked the top over her head before she lost her nerve.

"You're so beautiful . . . as beautiful as you were that night on the beach," he said close to her ear as he tongued her small lobe. "I will never get tired of looking at you . . . never stopped wanting you, babe."

When he made no move to palm the sensitive peaks, she smoothed her hands over his fingers until they uncurled, then she took them and placed them against her softness. They both moaned when he cupped her.

"Touch me. I've missed the feel of your hands and your mouth on my breasts," Brynne candidly admitted.

Devin stared into her eyes. Evidently he found the confirmation he was looking for because he began to squeeze her cushiony softness, and then rubbed his thumbs over the hardening nipples. He worried them until they stood erect, dark and tempting like sweet drops of chocolate. When he took an elongated peak between his thumb and forefinger to gently tug, Brynne closed her eyes and threw back her head as pleasure rushed up and down her spine. She arched her back in a sweet offering that he didn't refuse.

She called his name when he took an aching crest into the heat of his mouth. Her cries increased in volume as he tantalized her. Leisurely, he licked the peak with the rough velvet of his tongue, before he applied suction that had her whimpering, trembling from the intense pleasure. Dazzling white hot flames of desire rose between her thighs and caused her to squeeze them tight while he turned his ministrations to the other nipple. The pleasure continued to build until it rushed over her in delicious waves as she reached a sharp, poignantly sweet climax.

Before Brynne could catch her breath or realize that their position had changed and she was indeed draped over the arm of the couch, Devin began to rain a series of wet kisses down to her stomach.

He tongued her navel while he slid her pajama bottoms

down her shapely hips and thighs until they pooled on the floor. Her first indication that he had no plans to stop at her belly button was when she felt his openmouthed kisses move from the underside of her belly into thick brown curls shielding her sex.

"You can't mean to—" she gasped, then was struggling for breath as he gently parted her plump, feminine folds.

Gently his large finger traced her damp folds as he huskily said, "Oh, but I do."

"But—"

"Tell me how it feels. Is it good, babe?"

She managed to nod her head as shivers of delight raced over her. As she fought to regain her equilibrium, he heated her softness several degrees more with first his warm breath, and then the sizzling hot wash of his tongue. She moaned, unable to hold back her surprise of the sheer enjoyment that seemed to spiral beyond her best efforts to hang on to her control.

She nearly screamed as he sponged her taut feminine pearl again and again. When Devin took the very heart of her feminine desire into his mouth to suckle, Brynne did scream, losing herself in a whirlwind of incomparable pleasure crested into a shattering climax. He didn't stop until her sobs of joy slowly subsided, and then he held her against his heart, moving a soothing hand over her back. She rested in his arms as her breathing gradually returned to normal.

Devin's voice was gruff with desire when he said, close to her ear, "You okay, baby?"

"I may never be okay again." She lifted her face until she could press kisses along his chest and in the scented hollow at the base of his throat. "I can't believe you did that. You didn't have to—"

"Yes, I needed to. I don't think you understand how much I've missed you, baby. And there is nothing that gives me more enjoyment than pleasuring you."

"But—"

He pressed his fingertips against her lips. "There is

nothing I want more than to be right here, loving you in any way you allow me to love you."

Brynne buried her face in the place where his neck and shoulder joined, luxuriating in his clean male scent. "Devin . . ." She was painfully aware that while she still tingled with satisfaction, she hadn't done a single thing to ease his needs. Feeling incredibly selfish, she whispered, "I haven't taken care of your—"

He brushed her lips with his. "Stop being so serious. We don't have to have all the answers tonight."

"It still doesn't change the fact that while—"

"The only fact I am interested in tonight is having you in my arms." He swept her up into his arms and carried her into her bedroom.

Brynne heart began to race as Devin placed her on the bed in the heavily shadowed room. The emotions that filled her mind had swiftly changed from desire to an over-whelming sense of fear. Her eyes went wide as he seemed to tower over her and began to open the few remaining buttons holding his shirt closed. He shrugged powerful shoulders, pushing the shirt off.

Lost in a panicky maze, she whimpered as the memories she'd tried to keep locked away in the back of her mind came rushing forward. It was no longer Devin's features she saw, but Connor's. The fear ballooned inside her chest, causing her heart to pound and her breath to quicken to uneven pants.

While he unsnapped his jeans, easing the zipper past his prominent erection, she stopped breathing altogether, as a piercing scream began building inside her head. As he pushed the garment down his hips, she scrambled to get as far away from him as she could, her petite frame shaking violently.

"No!"

Devin raised his head. He'd just stepped free of his jeans and immediately stilled. "What is it, baby? What's wrong?"

Brynne shook her head, her body curled into a protective ball while tears streamed down her drawn features. "Please . . . don't hurt me!"

He lifted his hands, palms raised as he whispered, "What is it? Why are you afraid of me? Baby, I won't hurt—"

As he moved to sit on the side of the bed, Brynne nearly fell off the opposite side in her effort to get as far away from him as possible. Devin quickly rose and took a step back as he yanked on his jeans and shirt.

"Please, Brynne. Tell me what I did wrong."

"Don't come any closer."

"I won't," he promised, then whispered urgently, "I'd never hurt you, baby. Never."

Tears streaked down her face as she hiccupped. "Just go . . . please."

He backed toward the open door. "I'm going. It's okay, baby. Everything is okay." He closed the door behind him.

Brynne had no idea how long she lay curled in a tight ball, sobbing. It was much later before she stopped shaking and was able to move. She reached for the lamp to flood the room with lights.

"It's not okay." Emotionally drained, she mumbled aloud, "It will never be okay."

Hot, scalding tears slipped from beneath her lids, soaking the pillow. How? How could she have mistaken Devin for her attacker? Devin was nothing like Connor. The two men didn't even look alike. But more than that, Devin was an honorable man.

Despite his superior physical conditioning, he had always touched her with gentle hands. His love for her had been in his eyes as he made unselfish love to her only moments before. She groaned in disgust at the way she'd repaid his thoughtfulness.

He must think she'd lost her mind, she decided as she recalled the way his eyes had said it all. They were filled with hurt and despair when he realized her fear had been directed at him.

How could she ever face him again? How? He had done nothing to earn her distrust. He'd brought her here in hopes of recapturing what they'd lost. And what had she done the very first time they were approaching true intimacy? She'd freaked out, totally losing it at the sight of his nudity.

It made no sense. Physically, Devin was much taller and more muscular, while Connor was five ten at the most and lean with whipcord strength. But it wasn't Devin she'd seen standing over her. It had been Connor's nude body. And the magnitude of her fear had been overwhelming. Suddenly she was back in her old apartment and it was happening all over again. She had begged Devin not to hurt her as if he were her rapist.

There was no question in her mind that she'd hurt him deeply. And she hated it. What was she going to do?

Exhausted, Brynne walked into the connecting bath to soak a washcloth with cold water. After wringing it out, she covered her swollen lids. She couldn't fix this with an apology. She'd ruined their weekend.

Was it even possible for her to feel whole again? Or was she facing years of therapy? How had she been so wrong? She had thought she was better because she'd faced her fears. She'd told Devin and her friends about the rape. What more was there?

Perhaps Maureen was right? Maybe by telling her therapy group she would finally be free of the past? And what if that wasn't enough? What then?

She couldn't expect Devin to wait for her to put her life back together again. It didn't matter what she wanted. He deserved better than a woman who panicked at the sight of his erection.

When she climbed into bed once more, sheer exhaustion claimed her. Despite her weariness, it was nearing dawn before she was able to sleep.

Twenty-three

From the time Brynne emerged from her bedroom late the next morning, she projected a false cheer that Devin went along with. His best efforts to ease her embarrassment failed miserably.

After sharing breakfast, they went hiking along the ski trails. It was late afternoon when they stopped to enjoy the view of Traverse Bay and eat the picnic lunch they carried in their backpacks.

"You haven't eaten more than a few bites," Devin said, fed up with pretending nothing was wrong. "You don't care for the food? Or is it the company?"

Brynne had been focusing on the view while picking at a loose thread on the border of the thermal blanket they used as a ground cover. She lifted her thick lashes as if it were an effort to meet his brooding gaze.

"The food is exceptional, just like the view and the company. You've gone to a lot of trouble to make this weekend special. Last night's dinner, today's hike and the picnic . . . all of it has been wonderful." Her eyes were troubled when she said in a whisper, "The problem is mine. I know I apologized this morning, but it doesn't feel as if it's enough. I want you to know, I'm truly sorry about the way I treated you. You deserve so—"

"Don't. Your apology wasn't necessary this morning. It's not necessary now." His voice was taut with frustration.

"But I was so unfair to you. The way I treated you, as if you were my attacker, was unforgivable." She shuddered from the painful memory. "Quite honestly, I don't understand why you're even speaking to me."

Devin fought his own volatile emotions, furious at the situation that hurt her so deeply and continued to cause her suffering, while also dealing with his own potent needs and raw hunger. It was his fault. He was the one who had expected too much, too soon. All his good intentions had flown out the window when he bared her sweet body.

"I want you to get that guilty look off your beautiful face. You were the one raped, remember. I was the one who forgot it. For that, I'm sorry." His hand was gentle when he reached out to caress her cheek.

She shook her head. Her dark eyes filled with tears that she hastily wiped away. "I still don't know what happened. I wanted you. I didn't panic until you put me down on the bed. I don't know if it was because the room was dark and you were standing over me in the nude. Or if—"

"Don't cry, baby. I rushed you. You just weren't ready for more. Please stop blaming yourself."

"I'm not, honestly. Honey, I freaked out last night. I sent you away when all you wanted from me was for me to be your lady, just like I was back in St. Louis. We both wanted what we lost back again."

"Brynne, it's okay, baby. We are okay. This we can handle."

"No, Devin. *We* weren't the problem." She jumped to her feet, her hands on her hips. "*I* was the only one who came apart."

"So? It's nothing that can't be fixed. We've got time. It

doesn't have to happen this weekend. And I do mean 'we.' There is nothing we can't handle together. It started for us in St. Louis, and it didn't end there." He angled his jaw upward as he watched her pace. "That's something I refuse to accept."

Brynne sank back down, smiling through a sheen of tears. "What have I ever done to deserve your love?"

"I could ask you the same thing. I'm not the one who has been to hell and back." He kissed the tip of her nose, then pulled back to study her.

"What makes you think I still love you?" she teased.

"You do," he said without hesitation. "If you didn't love me, you wouldn't have had Shanna. Nor would you have let me get as close as I did last night."

"But—"

"Last night you allowed me to remove every stitch of clothing from you and let me make love to you." He chuckled at her blush of embarrassment.

"As the kids used to say, we didn't go all the way."

He teased, "We came damn close."

"Close isn't good enough." She studied her hands as if they belonged to someone else. "You need a woman who can be just that . . . all woman."

He reached out to cradle her nape as he brushed her mouth with his. "I have what I need. I have you. We will work it out, babe. You'll see."

She leaned back against his chest and he wrapped his arms around her waist as they stared thoughtfully out at the rippling whitecaps. Despite the breeze coming off the bay, they were dressed warmly, and the sun was bright overhead.

When she shivered, he asked, "Cold?"

She shook her head. "You have no idea how much I want it to be true."

"All you have to do is believe . . . believe in us." He rested his chin on the top of her head. "Want to go dancing tonight? Show me if you still got the moves."

Brynne laughed. "Oh, I've got them. I don't know if we can say the same about you, old man."

"Old man!" he said in mock outrage. "We'll see who is an old man. If we're going dancing, we'd better start back. I doubt either one of us got much sleep last night."

"True. We should also call Shanna. I hope she is behaving herself."

"She, no doubt, is missing her mommy." He placed a lingering kiss on her temple and then began packing what remained of their meal. She caught his arm before he could rise.

"Let's make it more than dancing. Let's make a date for later. Me in your room after midnight?"

Devin's heart raced, and his sex began to swell from just the thought of spending the night with her in his arms. His eyes questioned hers before he firmly shook his head. "Not tonight. You're not ready, and we both know it. We're taking this slow, remember?"

"But Devin—"

"We're going out to eat and dance. Maybe if we're up to it, a jump into the hot tub. Later tonight, I'm sleeping in my room and you're sleeping in yours. In the morning we'll head back home to pick up our daughter."

"Haven't you forgotten something? The purpose of this weekend was to rekindle what we lost," she reminded him.

Devin finished clearing away their picnic as he fought the sexual needs that warred with his better judgment. He'd never let his penis do his thinking for him, and he wasn't about to start now.

His voice was deeper than normal when he said, "The purpose of the weekend was to spend some quality time together. We're getting to know each other all over again. No demands . . . no pressure on either one of us."

He swung the backpack onto his back. "Ready to go?"

"Yes," she snapped as she folded the blanket and stuffed it into her backpack. "Your mother should have named you Stubborn."

* * *

"I don't think I could eat another bite." Brynne shook her head as Devin held out a fork filled with decadent, chocolate mousse torte cake. "You eat it."

"Come on. You've haven't eaten enough today to keep a bird alive."

She giggled. "If I eat that, then you're going to have to roll me out of here." They had elected to eat dinner in the resort's four-star restaurant.

He grinned. "Then we're just going to have to work off this extraordinary meal on the dance floor." After signing the check, he rose to his feet and draped her cashmere shawl over her shoulders. Offering his arm, he escorted her out of the restaurant through the plush lobby, out the front double doors, and to the waiting car.

"Very smooth, Mr. Prescott. You had this all planned."

From his place behind the steering wheel, he grinned cockily. "You got that right." Once they were under way, he asked huskily, "Did I tell you how absolutely beautiful you are tonight?"

Brynne laughed. "You did, as you well know." She'd chosen a cream silk sheath dress, with long chiffon sleeves, that stopped above her knees. Diamonds sparkled in her ears, and thin gold bangles tingled on her left wrist. On her feet were bronze high heels. "Thank you again. I'm glad you noticed."

"I noticed. You take my breath away."

Brynne flushed with pleasure. They drove into town and pulled to a stop in front of the popular Purple Moon nightclub.

"I can't remember the last time I went dancing." She didn't ask, but she doubted he could say the same. It was disgraceful, the sheer number of women who followed pro athletes around, treating them as if the sun rose and set on their broad shoulders. She didn't want to speculate on how many women there had been since the two of them parted. She wasn't fooling herself. She knew Devin's masculine appeal. If he was alone, it was because he chose to be.

The club was filled to capacity while music poured through the sound system. The band played on the main floor. They threaded their way through the crowd to one of the small tables bordering the dance floor.

Brynne grabbed his hand before they were even seated when the band began playing an old favorite, Natalie Cole's "This Will Be (An Everlasting Love)." Devin chuckled, allowing her to lead him out on to the packed dance floor.

"You planned this, didn't you?" she said as they danced.

Leaning toward her to hear, he laughed. "As much as I would like to I can't take the credit."

Smiling, Brynne focused on nothing more than moving to the rhythmic beat. It was the song they had first danced to the night they'd met at a mutual friend's home. Even during the years they were apart, the song never failed to bring him to mind.

Devin said, close to her ear. "The singer is good but she can't touch Miss Natalie."

Brynne laughed, not missing a beat. As the band moved to the next upbeat song, she relaxed and concentrated on nothing more than enjoying herself. When the band switched to the slow, sexy rhythm of "Inseparable," Brynne found herself in Devin's arms. With her cheek on his chest, she closed her eyes and concentrated on following his lead.

When the song ended, he asked, "Enjoying yourself?"

"Very much, but I could use something to drink."

He nodded, clasping her hand. He led the way toward the crowded bar. She accepted the soft drink he handed her before they moved back toward their table. Devin's wide mouth seemed to be locked in a permanent grin as he sipped from his own bottled water.

"No alcohol?"

"Naw. I had enough wine at dinner. Can you believe this crowd? This must be the place." He quirked a brow. "Are you up to another go-round?"

"Are you?" she teased.

"Oh yeah."

They joined the crowd doing the hustle. When they returned to their table sometime later, they were both laughing and thirsty.

"Wow! You aren't even winded," she complained as she dropped into her chair. "I'm going to have to start running with you in the mornings."

Devin motioned to the waitress for a fresh round of drinks. "Want to start tomorrow at six before breakfast?"

Brynne quirked a perfectly arched brow. "Let me think about that. I might have spoken too hastily."

"Our daughter was game. She went running with me. Surely you can outdo a three-year-old?"

Brynne giggled. "Now that was downright nasty. You think I don't know her limit is about three blocks, and then she wants a piggyback ride?"

He chuckled. "Okay, I admit it. I did run with her on my back for a few miles, but she's a great coach. She kept urging me to go faster."

"I bet. She loves her daddy."

"And I love her."

"Thanks for tonight. I can't remember when I've had a better time."

He looked deep into her eyes. "Not even Miami?"

"Maybe." Brynne smiled at the sweet memory. She had flown in to surprise him. It was the night they made love for the first time.

"We're going to have to go back someday," he suggested.

She didn't dare admit how much she longed for the closeness they'd once taken for granted. It had been so long since they had shared true intimacy in both mind and body. Unaware that she was frowning, she wondered if it were still within the realm of possibility. As much as she dreaded another failure, her heart still yearned for what they'd lost.

Did she have the courage to try again tonight? What would he do if she came to him? Even though earlier he'd tried to discourage her, did she have the nerve to try?

"Something wrong, babe?"

"Not really. Do you think it's too cold outside to try out the hot tub on the balcony?"

"That's what makes it fun," he teased. "I'm game if you are."

She shook a finger at him. "I'm not making any promises."

Once they were in their suite, he quirked a brow. "Well? You game?"

"Absolutely. Meet you out on the balcony in five minutes. Don't laugh if I wear a sweat suit over my bathing suit." She could hear his deep, throaty chuckle as she went into her bedroom. She changed into the yellow one-piece swimsuit. She firmly pushed away thoughts of going to him later that night.

When she returned she wore the thick, white toweling robe that had the hotel's name embroidered on the pocket over her swimsuit.

As she walked out on the balcony, she noted that the soft lights rimming the hot tub were on and steam rose in the clear night air. Devin was already in the tub. He'd left his robe on a nearby lounge chair.

"How is it?"

"Cold," he teased, then shook his head. "No, it's great, but you can't hesitate. Take a deep breath and jump in." He held a hand out to her.

"I'm taking you at your word." Brynne was so busy giggling, she couldn't get her robe off fast enough. She caught his hand and he helped her in. Her teeth were chattering as she sank up to her chin in the blissfully hot water. "I don't believe I let you talk me into this."

"If nothing else, the view is exceptional. Champagne?"

"You're right about that. I'll share yours." She took a sip from his glass. "Thank you." Settling back against his side, she sighed. "It's a beautiful night."

He lifted a brow. "I would compliment you on your suit, but you were moving so fast, all I saw was a blur."

"You got that right."

They enjoyed a comfortable silence.

"You are not going to sleep on me, are you?"

"Almost."

"Should I carry you in?"

"No, but I think I'd better get out." Once she was in her robe, she glanced at him over her shoulder. She shivered, "You coming?"

"I'm right behind you." True to his word, he followed her inside.

"Thanks, Devin. I enjoyed myself tonight. All I need is a hot shower to get warm again."

He leaned down and kissed her cheek. "Glad you enjoyed it. Sleep well." With that he walked into his bedroom and closed the door quietly behind him.

Stunned, Brynne stood for a time staring at his door. Sighing heavily, she went into her own bedroom. Absently peeling off the wet bathing suit, she draped it over the heated towel bar. After she stepped into the tub and turned on the shower, she tried to decide what was best. He'd obviously decided not to push the issue. Which meant it was up to her to take the necessary steps to regain what they'd lost.

Could she go to him? It was what she wanted, but she also didn't want a repeat of last night's panic. How could she be sure it wouldn't happen again? Maybe she shouldn't be forcing the issue this way? Maybe she should wait until she was sure of herself? And exactly when would that be . . . the other side of never?

"No, no," she chimed as warm water rushed over her. "If I don't try, Connor wins. I can't let that happen. I won't let him control my life . . . not ever again," she mumbled aloud as she washed her hair. She cleaned her skin with her favorite gardenia-scented shower gel.

"I can do this." After drying off and perfuming her skin with lotion, she slipped into a yellow nightgown trimmed in lace. Seated at the vanity, she finished blow drying her hair. She attempted to style it, but was forced to stop because her hands were shaking so badly.

"Who am I trying to kid," she whispered. She was nowhere near ready to take him inside her body, no matter how badly she longed to show him what she felt for him.

Just the thought of sex had her stomach cramping with fear, and the memory of Connor forcing himself into her body came rushing back. Physically, Devin was much bigger than Connor, including the size of his male appendage.

Brynne shuddered when she realized what she had been thinking. She forced herself to take slow, calming breaths. This was about her and Devin and how they felt about each other. Nothing else. The one thing she knew without doubt was that Devin would never deliberately hurt her . . . not ever.

Pulling on the matching silk robe and belting it at her waist, Brynne hesitated in front of her closed bedroom door. Devin was right. They had all the time in the world. It didn't have to be all or nothing. There must be some middle ground . . . a compromise that would make them both feel as if they were moving closer rather than farther apart. All she had to do was figure out what it was.

She had no idea how long she stood there before she reached for the doorknob. Walking on bare feet, she crossed to his door. Hesitating only a moment, she quietly let herself inside.

The only light in the room came from the open drapes. Although the oversize bed was in shadow, Brynne had no trouble making out Devin's large, dark frame in the center of the bed.

He lay on his back, the comforter at the foot of the bed. His chest was bare, and the sheet stopped at his waist. He didn't stir as she approached the bed. Judging by his deep, even breathing, she knew he was asleep.

Twenty-four

≡

Devin wasn't sure what woke him, but the
familiar soft scent of his woman filled his lungs. It took him
a few moments to recognize that he was not dreaming, and
indeed it was Brynne's soft curls tickling the base of his
throat, her head resting on his left shoulder, her cushiony
soft breasts on his chest, her silk-covered mound and thighs
against the length of his thigh. His shaft began to thicken
and harden while his heart recognized what was his alone.

"Brynne," he said groggily, shifting his hips away from her
feminine allure. "What are you doing here? Are you okay?"

Her sigh warmed his throat. "I'm fine, and I'm not sure
why I am here, other than I want to be close to you."

The relief he felt gave way to caution as he felt her soft
tremors. He knew better than to get his hopes up, for keen
disappointment would follow. Yet despite his better judgment, his heart had picked up speed.

He was forced to clear his throat before he could say, "I
thought we agreed that it was best for now if we didn't rush
things. That you needed more time to adjust to me being
back in your life without pushing the lovemaking card."

"We did."

She said no more but pressed her soft mouth against the base of his throat, sending chills racing up and down his spine.

"Well?"

"Well, what?"

"Why are you in bed with me?" he demanded to know, unaware of the way he gently stroked the smooth line of her back.

She stiffened, tilting her head back until she could see his features. "If I'm making you uncomfortable, I'll leave. Just tell me."

"Uncomfortable" was too mild a word in his estimation. She was making him hot . . . aching, needy. There was no doubt that he was ready for what he wanted most and couldn't have. He ground his back molars before he eased his clenched jaw enough to say, "Give me a few minutes." He pulled back the sheet and then disappeared into the connecting bathroom.

Devin was glad he'd taken to wearing pajama bottoms. The last thing he needed was to send her into another panic attack. Despite what he'd told her that morning, he hadn't gotten past her reaction to his nudity.

After using the restroom and washing his hands, he dropped his pajamas and then walked into the shower stall to turn the cold water on full blast. He didn't stay in long, giving himself just enough time to cool off. After drying quickly and retrieving his pajamas, he hoped he had his libido under control.

She was right where he'd left her, in the center of his bed. He took a deep breath before crossing the room, to switch on the bedside lamp. He didn't join her in bed.

Covering her eyes at the sudden glare, she said, "We don't need that."

"Yeah, we do. Talk . . . make me understand what is going on with you. Don't tell me the world has changed direction in one night. I'm not buying it."

"I heard you in the shower. Why?"

He quirked a brow. "I needed to clear my head. Brynne, you're driving me nuts here. Will you please start explaining?"

Although she lay back against the pillows, he could tell her relaxed pose was deceptive. She was practically wringing her hands as she worried her plump bottom lip. "You know all of it."

"Humor me, okay? Tell me again."

Her troubled eyes met his. "This was the only way I could think of to show you that I'm serious. I want what you want. I want this weekend to be a new beginning for us. I know I'm not ready to take you inside my body, but I'm hopeful that you might let me sleep in your arms. Is that so wrong?"

Devin heard the plea for his understanding. This was obviously a test of her trust and faith in him. Walking over to the window, he looked out, seeing nothing. What he was doing was struggling with his own sexual desire.

In a sense, this was not even about him, but about her need to heal. He desperately wanted her to regain what she'd lost. She wanted to be whole as much as he wanted that for her.

Turning to face her, he saw her creased brow and troubled gaze. He went back to the bathroom, switched on the light, then turned off the bedside lamp. Then he climbed back into bed to pull her against him. Her head rested on his shoulder. He adjusted the sheet and comforter over them.

After a time, she whispered, "Nothing to say?"

"Nope." He closed his eyes, trying to ignore the beat of his pounding heart.

"But—"

"No doubts. We want the same thing. Together we will get it back."

After a time she said his name.

"Hmm?"

"Do you need the bathroom light on?"

He grinned. "I don't need it, but I thought you might."

"Not me." She got up and turned it off, and then nestled once more against him.

Devin concentrated on nothing more than keeping his breathing even and unhurried. When she shifted, he carefully angled his hips to keep his arousal away from her. Then she moved again, placing a silk covered thigh between his. It took all his resolve to suppress a heavy groan.

Forcing his thoughts away from the woman in his arms, he focused on his foundation and the goals he planned to implement in the coming year. He hoped to spend more time with the tenth grade students he'd promised to send through college if they graduated on time. A promise he'd made when they were in junior high school. So far only two students had dropped out. He could—

Brynne's soft sigh sliced into his thoughts as easily as a knife moving through creamy butter.

"Babe?" she whispered.

"Huh?"

"If this is too uncomfortable for you, please just tell me. You won't hurt my feelings. I can go back to my own bed."

"You don't make me uncomfortable . . . what you make me is aroused. I can handle that. What I can't handle is your being afraid of me."

"Devin—"

"Let me finish, babe. I'd rather face anything, even injury, than see that look of fear on your pretty face that I saw last night."

Brynne lifted a hand to caress his hair-roughened jaw. "I was never afraid of you. With you standing over me I saw your . . ."

"Erection?" he prompted.

She nodded and swallowed with difficulty before she said, "It reminded me of him."

"It's part of me, Brynne. I control my entire body, including my penis. The only time I can remember causing you any pain was the first time we made love. You were a virgin and that pain was something I couldn't help."

"I know all that."

"Do you? I think up here you know it." He touched her

forehead. "But deep inside, in your gut where that fear resides, you've forgotten what it was like to have me inside you."

"I remember, Devin."

"Do you?" He moved until his lips were close to her ear. "Tell me what you remember, babe."

"Devin," she gasped.

"There is no one to hear but me. If it's easier, then whisper it into my ear."

"Which time?"

"Any time . . . every time. The choice is yours."

She shifted until she was lying on her stomach, her chin propped on his shoulder.

He complained, "You're too far away."

She moved over. "Is that better?"

"Yeah. Which time?"

"The night we went out to celebrate your birthday. We had a romantic dinner and then went back to your place for a nightcap. Do you recall?"

"Maybe . . ."

"What do you mean, maybe?" She tugged playfully on his chin.

"Okay, okay. I remember. I'm just testing your memory. Go on. What about that night?"

"We were caught in the rain."

"More like a torrential downpour," he clarified. "The way I remember it, you were ticked long before we left the restaurant."

"With good reason. The nerve of that woman to plop her hips in your lap. I wanted to yank those braids out of her hair by the roots," she snapped.

He teased, "For a minute there I thought you might do just that."

"My mother raised me to be a lady. Not one bad word came out of my mouth, but that so-called fan got the message when I told her to get off my man while she could still walk."

"What you did was dump the pitcher of ice water over

her head and then sweetly suggest she cool off." He hooted with laughter. "Unfortunately, you soaked me as well."

"I did apologize to you. Besides, by the time we reached the car we were both drenched from the storm."

"Good thing it was a warm night."

"Not that warm. We had to get in the shower to warm up. It was the first time we showered together."

He smiled. "But not the last."

"No. We made love in the shower. We didn't even get out until the water ran cold."

"Exactly how do you make love in the shower?"

"You know."

"My memory is kind of fuzzy."

"We made love on that granite bench in your shower."

"Were you ready for me, babe?"

"Yes," she said, somewhat breathlessly. "You made sure of that." When he remained silent, she went on in a whisper, husky with emotion, "You caressed every inch of my body with soapy hands, and then you kissed every place you caressed. I felt as if a fire was burning deep inside, an overwhelming need for you. I wanted to take you inside my mouth and love you the way you loved me, but I was too embarrassed to try to please you that way."

"I never knew." His voice was thick with desire, inflamed by the mere thought.

"Even back then, I was selfish."

"You weren't selfish. You were inexperienced. There is a difference." He caressed her cheek. "And you gave me indescribable pleasure. I could not have taken your sweet mouth on my sex. I was too far gone, babe."

"You took me that way. You knelt on the floor of the shower—" She stopped, covering her face.

He finished. "—and gave you the sweet tonguing I had been longing to give you. You came apart in my arms."

Devin felt her tremor and wondered if the intimate memory had set an ache inside her, the way it had in him. He was so damn hard, he hurt. But not for all the money in the world would he trade places with any other man. Brynne was in bed with him, and that was what mattered.

"It didn't end with one climax. You were so hot, so wet, for me. I wanted you just as much. Do you remember there being any pain, babe?"

"No pain, just sheer, incredible pleasure," she confessed with a note of surprise. She admitted, "I'd forgotten."

"That's how it will be for us again. Every time we joined our bodies . . . pure bliss." As if he expected her to refute his claim, Devin ever so tenderly pressed his lips against hers. "Oh yes, baby. When you are ready, I'll prove it to you." Then he whispered close to her ear, "Am I not a man who keeps his word?"

"Always." Brynne kissed Devin in the sensitive place where his shoulder and neck joined. "I just hope you find it's worth the wait."

Without hesitation, he said, "It will be."

"I've been so unfair to you."

"Stop that. You're talking about my lady. Besides, I don't see it that way. Don't you know you're worth waiting for?"

"Devin, I'm a mess. I still haven't been able to tell my own story to the group of women I counsel. If I can't be honest with them, how can I be effective?"

"You are too hard on yourself, babe. Give yourself time. It's all going to work out. You will see." He nestled his face against her cheek. "Let's try to get some sleep. We need to leave after breakfast to miss the worst of the traffic."

She covered a yawn. "Back to the real world."

"Something like that," he said tiredly, just before he dropped off to sleep.

He didn't feel the brush of her lips against his or hear her whispered "I love you."

"Hungry?" She held out the bag of grapes toward him.

"No thanks." He didn't take his eyes off the road. "Can you believe this traffic?"

"It's your fault. If you had awakened me, instead of letting me sleep, we could have left earlier," Brynne didn't hesitate to remind him.

It was a surprisingly warm April day. The weather had held. No late snowstorms or even rain for that matter.

Devin grinned. "You needed the rest. You're not supposed to come back from vacation tired."

"Everyone's going to think we spent the entire weekend in bed, making love."

"Doesn't matter what anyone thinks. What matters is how we feel about each other."

Brynne didn't respond. She felt as if she'd been walking on eggshells all morning, trying not to say the wrong thing. She could only guess at his level of disappointment. If it was anything like her own, it was tremendous. She was fed up pretending that everything was okay, that they were okay. In her heart she accepted that nothing had changed, despite her best efforts. It was her fault the weekend had been a failure.

"What is it, babe? What's bothering you?"

"Can you stop at the next rest stop?" she asked in hopes of diverting his attention. "I had too much coffee, trying to wake up."

"Sure. There's one up ahead."

If only she could fix what was really wrong. Brynne jumped out as soon as he'd parked and raced for the building. Once she was inside the ladies' room she took her time. It wasn't until after she'd washed up, and was standing in front of the mirror fussing with her hair, that she admitted she was stalling for time.

"Coward," she mumbled aloud while putting the small brush and lipstick back into her leather tote bag. After settling in her seat with the seat belt fastened, she glanced over at Devin when he didn't start the motor. Finally she asked, "What?"

"You tell me. Something's on your mind."

Knowing it was pointless to argue with the man since he wasn't leaving until he was good and ready, Brynne said around a sigh, "There is no doubt where Shanna got her muleheadedness."

"She got a good measure of it from you, babe. If you want to get home before midnight, I'd start talking, if I were you." He drummed his fingers on the steering wheel.

Brynne, determined to ignore the play of firm muscle beneath his dark gray turtleneck sweater, unwittingly thrust out her lips in a pout. Devin laughed and leaned over to lightly brush her lips with his.

He said softly, "It can't be that bad."

"I know I disappointed you this weekend." She folded her arms beneath her breasts, unknowingly drawing his eyes to the plump curves beneath her black sweater. Like him, she had shed her heavy coat. "I disappointed myself."

"Brynne, what were you expecting?"

"Evidently a miracle," she snapped. "I wanted us back."

"We are back."

She shook her head vehemently. "It's not the same."

He cradled her chin until her eyes met his. "It's getting there. We still feel the same, don't we? I'm still in love with you."

Brynne's eyes filled with tears before she whispered, "Yes, I'm still in love with you. I never stopped." Blinking to clear her vision, she said impatiently, "We have a daughter, Devin. There's more at stake here than just the two of us."

"Then let's do what we should have done four years ago. Let's go ahead and get married, so we can move on with our lives."

She stared at him, not sure she'd heard correctly. "You can't be serious. How can you even consider saddling yourself with a woman who can't have sex with you?"

"It will happen . . . the sexual aspect, given time. I know exactly what I want, and that's you and Shanna."

"What you want is your daughter," she clarified.

"Yeah, I do. But I also want her mother. Shanna is a result of our love. You can't dispute that."

"No, I can't." She recalled the lovemaking that resulted in their daughter. "In fact, I'm not going to try. How happy do you think our little girl is going to be when her parents are fighting night after night like cats and dogs? Believe me, we will be fighting, if I don't give you any for the next twenty years. Devin, get real! You're a young, healthy, virile man. There is nothing wrong with your sex drive."

"I know that."

"Do you? Were you happy with the way things turned out this weekend?" Brynne's laugh held no humor. "I don't think so."

"Will any of us be any happier when I'm in St. Louis while you and Shanna are in Michigan? Or when Shanna is away from you for long weekends twice a month with me? I don't think so. Our little girl isn't going to like being apart from either one of us." He paused before he went on to say, "I'm not looking forward to going back and not being able to see you every day. Once the season starts, I will be on the road most weekends."

Brynne bowed her head. "I know."

"Then let's put an end to part of the problem. Let's get married and be a family. You and I can work the sex part out like any couple with problems . . . together." When she made no response, he said with frustration, "Do you think your parents didn't have problems? Or that mine don't? Of course they did. But both sets of parents stayed married, yours for over twenty years and mine over thirty. We've had excellent examples, babe."

"We were fortunate in our families. We both grew up in loving homes, but—"

He interrupted, "Do you want less for our baby girl?"

"Of course not," she said, her hands tightly clasped.

"Don't you want her to have a little brother or sister?"

She jerked her head around to glare at him. "For that to happen we have to have s-e-x. Something that didn't happen this weekend!"

He lifted one of her hands to his lips, placing a kiss on her knuckles. "It will happen."

"I have plenty of faith in you. It's me I have doubts about. I'm a mess."

"You're too hard on yourself. You slept in my arms last night. All you need is just a little faith that we can work it out. This isn't for our sakes only, but Shanna's as well. Think about it."

Devin started the car, backed out of the parking space, and headed for the crowded interstate. They were both quiet, both deep in thought. When they were approaching the Detroit exit, she whispered, "Are you sure this is what you want to do?"

"I'm sure," he said without hesitation.

Neither said more until he stopped the car in his parents' driveway, which was crowded with his siblings' cars. She touched his arm as he reached for the door handle.

Brynne had to clear her throat before she could speak. "Okay, let's get married. If you're absolutely sure and it's what you want."

Devin grinned, letting out a deep-throated chuckle. "I want you to be my wife." He leaned over to give her a kiss filled with tenderness. "You won't regret it, babe. You'll see."

All Brynne could do was pray that he was right. She was so afraid of being a disappointment to him that it was difficult to be hopeful.

He came around to open her door. When she slid out, he gave her a long hug. She clung to him for a moment. By the time they started toward the house, Shanna must have seen them from the kitchen window because she was out the back door, running toward them.

"Mommy! Daddy!" Shanna called at the top of her lungs. She threw herself at her mother, hugging her waist. Then she was boosted up by her father until she hung from one broad shoulder. She giggled as he tickled her.

Devin kissed her cheek. "Hey, princess. We missed you."

"I missed you too. Mommy, I didn't think you were ever going to come. Everybody is here."

Brynne and Devin exchanged a smile.

"Where is your jacket, young lady?" Brynne asked as she kissed her cheek. "It's not that warm out here."

"I forgot," she said, nestled beneath Devin's heavy jacket. "You took too long."

"Well, I guess we spent too much time trying to decide on a present for our little girl. Do you know where she is?" he teased.

"I'm here, Daddy!" Shanna shouted.

Devin chuckled as they approached the house.

"Couldn't wait, Mommy." She giggled. "Where is my present, Daddy?"

"You'll get it later," Devin promised as he held the door open for Brynne. The kitchen was filled with his family. "Hey. Looks like everyone is here."

"Sorry, Brynne," Donna said with a welcoming smile. "Shanna got away from me before I could get her coat on."

Brynne smiled, offering her hello to Anna and Kelli.

"We've been making cookies. Lots and lots of cookies. Didn't we, Granny?" Shanna insisted as Devin put her down.

"Oh yes," Donna laughed.

"You're in luck. We made more than cookies," Anna teased as she pulled a pot roast out of the oven. "How was the trip?"

"Great," Devin said, his hand laced with Brynne's. "Where are Dad and the fellows?"

"In the family room, watching the Pistons. Why?" Kelli asked, not even trying to hide her curiosity.

Devin kissed Brynne's temple. "We have news."

Twenty-five

Brynne's eyes flew to Devin. She resisted the urge to cover his mouth and tell him it was too soon. She settled for squeezing his hand, hard. She would have preferred to keep the news to themselves for a while, needing time to adjust.

"Is it what I think it is?" Donna's eyes filled with tears.

"Maybe," Devin teased.

"Mama, don't get excited. We don't know a thing yet." Anna warned, her dark gray eyes sparkling.

"You just hush and go get your father and the others. Quick!" Donna instructed, going over to Devin and Brynne. "Tell me!"

"No! Wait until I get back," Anna insisted before she ran out of the room.

"Son?"

Devin grinned. "I can't, Daddy's not here."

"And I can't wait. Tell me?"

Devin chuckled as he leaned down and whispered in his mother's ear.

"That's not fair. I can't hear a thing!" Kelli complained as she looked from Devin to Brynne.

Donna gasped, hugging her son. "You are! For real!"

"What's going on, son?" Lester asked, as he was followed by Ralph, Gavin, Wayne, Kyle, Wesley, and Anna.

Crying with happy tears, Donna screeched, "Devin and Brynne are going to get married!" She finally let go of Devin, only to hug Brynne. "I'm so happy for you two."

Everyone was talking at once. Brynne was passed around for hugs and kisses by the boisterous Prescotts. She certainly wasn't prepared for his family's wholehearted acceptance of her.

Shanna, not quite sure what was going on, tugged on her mother's hand. When Brynne dropped down to her level, she said in a loud whisper, "Are we getting married?"

"Yes."

Devin laughed at the excitement in his little girl's eyes. "Do you know what that means?"

She shrugged her small shoulders. He cupped her face when he explained. "Mommy and Daddy and you are going to be a family."

Frowning, she asked, "You will be my daddy all the time?"

"That's right. We're going to live together. Is that okay with you, princess?"

Shanna nodded, her ponytails bouncing. "Can I have a baby sister, like Kaleea?"

Brynne's gaze locked with Devin's before she said, "I'm not making any promises, but I sure hope so."

"This is great news. Ralph, break out the champagne," Lester urged as he slapped Devin on the back and gave Brynne a hug. "Devin is a good man, but if he starts acting up, just let me know. I'll straighten him out."

Brynne laughed. "I'll keep that in mind."

While Ralph went to get the champagne, Anna and Kelli went into the dining room and returned with the glasses. Everyone was talking at once when Ralph returned from the wine cellar with two bottles. He was soon filling glasses.

"What about us?" Wayne and Kyle complained.

"Yeah," Shanna added when she wasn't given a glass.

Laughing, Donna filled three champagne glasses with sparking apple juice.

With his arm around his wife, Wesley said, "Since I'm the oldest, I get to make the first toast. To Brynne and Devin. I hope you will be just as happy as Kelli and I have been."

"Here, here," Gavin echoed.

Brynne clinked her glass with Devin's before they sipped.

"My turn," Ralph called out. "To Brynne, Devin, and Shanna. May you always be as happy as you are today."

"Kiss! Kiss!" Anna laughed.

Much to everyone's delight, Devin leaned down and pressed his mouth to Brynne's.

Once all toasts had been made, Donna, Anna, and Kelli cornered Brynne and began questioning her about the wedding. No one would listen when Brynne explained nothing had been decided, including the date.

The men asked, "What about dinner?"

"Who cares about dinner? We have a wedding to plan," Kelli said excitedly.

"Mama, I'm hungry," Wayne groaned.

Donna laughed. "All right, but right after dinner, ladies, we talk."

Sunday dinner at the Prescotts', as usual, was noisy. Brynne was delighted at how comfortable Shanna was, giggling when one or more of her uncles teased her.

Donna leaned toward Brynne, whispering, "You doing okay?"

She smiled. "A bit overwhelmed. Everything is happening so fast."

Devin surprised her with a kiss, and she blushed.

"Uh-oh. None of that." Ralph grinned.

"Oh yes, plenty of that." Gavin laughed as he leaned over and kissed Anna.

Everyone laughed.

"I like the way you think," Wesley said, getting up to go over and kiss Kelli.

Kelli shook her finger at him. "Stop, there are impressionable young children here."

"Will you all stop? Some of us are trying to eat," Ralph joked.

"What's wrong, cuz?" Devin teased. "Getting nervous you might be next?"

Ralph scowled. "Not in this lifetime. Wayne and Kyle will be married before I will."

Both boys hooted with laughter.

"We'll see about that," Donna teased.

"If you knew what I know, you'd watch your step, son." Lester roared with laughter.

"The wedding has to be soon, if you two expect to get it done before the football season starts. Brynne, you're going to make a beautiful June bride." Anna smiled.

Brynne put down her fork when she realized her hands were shaking.

"June is less than two months away," Donna said excitedly. "That's doesn't give us much time."

"We can do it if we put our heads together." Kelli quizzed, "Well, you two. A June wedding?"

Devin took her hand into his. "What do you think, babe?"

Brynne's heart pounded with a mixture of excitement and fear. It was finally sinking in that she'd promised to be Devin's wife. It was something she'd once dreamed about and wanted more than anything else in the world. Her dark brown eyes stared into his dark gray ones. The solid strength and assurance that they would work out their problems was there.

His faith in her gave Brynne the courage to say, "June will be fine."

It was after Shanna was tucked in for the night that Brynne and Devin had an opportunity to talk privately.

"Are you okay?" he quizzed when she made herself comfortable on the cushion beside him on the sofa.

"My head is still spinning from all the wedding plans."

Devin chuckled. "Mama and the others got a bit carried away. The minute I made the announcement, the ladies were off and running. The Kentucky Derby has nothing on the Prescott women, and Kelli wasn't about to be left behind."

"Why did you make that announcement? I tried to stop you by squeezing your hand."

"I didn't realize. All I could think about was that you'd finally said yes." He asked, "Why did you want to wait?"

"It's not that. There wasn't enough time for me to get used to the idea." She was unaware of the frown creasing her forehead.

Devin smoothed a finger over her brow. "Babe, I didn't think you'd mind. I was so happy, it was natural for me to want to share our news with my family."

"I suppose," she murmured.

"How long did you need to get used to the idea?"

Brynne shrugged. "I'm sorry. I guess I'm just not used to being in the center of such a large family. Is it always like that?"

"What loud? Crazy?" At her nod, he laughed, "Yes, at times. It's part of being a family. We love each other, and that means no holding back. We share in each other's lives."

Confused, Brynne said, "But you have always been such a private person."

"I am, but I'm also a Prescott. Just as Shanna is, and you will be in two months. Is it so wrong that my mother, sister, and sister-in-law want to help you plan our wedding? They mean well."

Deciding to let the matter drop since there was no way she could win, Brynne said, "Nothing at all. June's just around the corner."

"Did you want a large wedding?"

"No, I'd like something small with only our close friends and family."

"Then what is it? I assumed you didn't want to spend months apart. Am I wrong?"

"No, Devin. That's not it. You living in St. Louis, with Shanna and me here, would be especially difficult on Shanna."

He frowned. "What's the problem? Have you changed your mind?"

"No!" Agitated, she jumped up and began moving restlessly around the room. "What makes you think I changed my mind?"

"I don't know, but something has you upset."

"Everything is happening too fast. My moving to St. Louis will mean I have to resign from my position at the women's center. We have to find a new school for Shanna. And what are we going to do about my house and your condo? I don't even know if they have a women's center in St. Louis. What am I going to do without a job?"

Devin came over to cup her slender shoulders. "None of this has to be decided tonight. We've got time . . . nothing but time. We can wait to get married if that's the problem. No pressure, okay."

Brynne rested her cheek against his chest, wrapping an arm around his waist. "No, we've waited long enough. If it hadn't been for me, we—"

"Don't," he interrupted. "The past is just that, in the past."

She nodded, then covered a sudden yawn. "Excuse me."

He brushed his mouth over her forehead. "It's been a long day. I'd better get out of here and let you get some rest. Come on, babe. Lock up behind me."

"Stay." She tightened her arms around him. "I want to sleep in your arms."

He eased back until he could study her features. "I'd like that too, but we have an impressionable young lady to consider. I can just hear her telling her teacher and Granny how Daddy slept in Mommy's bed."

Brynne giggled. "I can too. There's no such thing as a

secret with her around." Smoothing a hand over his chest, she said, "I'd like you to stay. That is, if you won't consider it a hardship, being together without . . . well, you know."

". . . without making love," he finished for her. "Don't get me wrong. There is nothing I would like more than to be with you. And I want to make love to you. As I told you last night, I control my penis, not the other way around." He kissed her temple. "Babe, I also don't want to pressure you into doing something you are clearly not ready for."

She smiled. "Hopefully, the more nights we spend together, we'll become comfortable with each other . . . like an old married couple."

He chuckled.

She didn't point out the obvious, that she was the one having the difficulty, not him. "We can set the clock, that way you will be out of here before Shanna wakes up."

"Brynne, are you sure this is what you want?"

"Absolutely." She desperately needed to get her life back. Spending their nights together was only the first, but important step toward regaining what they'd lost.

Brynne was stalling. After taking a bath and then creaming her skin with scented body cream, instead of going into the bedroom where Devin was waiting, she sat in front of her vanity staring at her reflection. She brushed her hair until her scalp complained, and then she sat wondering if the lace-trimmed camisole top of her dark green silk pajamas was too revealing.

"You need any help in there?" Devin called.

"I'll be right out."

That she was being silly was beside the point. She had promised to marry the man, for goodness' sake. She reached for perfume, but decided against using it. Taking a deep breath, Brynne hurried out before she could think of another excuse to delay.

"Hi. You look comfortable." Her queen-size bed looked

downright small with Devin in it. After turning off one of the bedside lamps, she paused.

Devin said nothing, merely pulled back the edge of the top sheet and down comforter. She released a small sigh of relief when she saw that, even though his broad chest was bare, he wore a pair of navy silk boxers.

"I'd better check on Shanna."

"I already did. She's asleep."

"Thanks. Would you like something to drink? Hot chocolate? A brandy?"

"Nothing for me." He patted the place beside him.

Brynne got into bed and smoothed the covers up to her chin. "I'm sorry. I guess you can see I'm a little nervous."

"Nothing is going to happen that you don't want to happen." He reached out and squeezed her hand and then released it.

"I know. Would you please turn out that lamp?"

"You sure?"

"Yes. The night light in the bathroom should be enough to keep us from bumping into the furniture." Brynne shut up, because she knew she was rambling.

Devin swung his legs over the side of the bed. Instead of reaching for the lamp, he retrieved his jeans from the nearby armchair.

"Where are you going?"

"Babe, it's late, and we're both tired. We can try this some other night."

"No, Devin. Please, stay."

He rested a hand on one lean hip. "I can feel your fear. I won't add to it."

"You're leaving when I want you to stay? I know I'm nervous, but it isn't as bad as Friday, even less than last night." She forced a smile. "See, I'm making progress. Please stay."

He looked into her eyes for a few moments, then reluctantly said, "If you're sure." At her nod, he turned off the lamp before he undressed and got back in bed.

Brynne listened to the sound of the house settling and his even breathing. Knowing he was close soothed her and she reached out to slip her hand in his. When his hold on her hand went slack and he sighed in his sleep, she granted herself the small liberty of sliding over until she could rest her head on his shoulder.

She held her breath when she felt him stir. He whispered her name in his sleep and slid his arm around her waist. She slowly released a breath. Although her lids felt heavy, she couldn't sleep. Yet she didn't consider leaving the warm haven of Devin's arms. Eventually she did drift off.

Brynne frowned when Devin whispered close to her ear. "It's after six, babe. I'd better go."

"So early," she complained, pressing her face against his sweater covered chest.

"Yeah, I'll see you tonight. Don't cook. I'll bring dinner. Okay?"

"Okay." She smiled when she felt his lips brush her cheek. "Bye."

They quickly settled into a routine of Devin spending the evenings and the nights beside Brynne. As one day slipped into the next, she accepted that she wanted him with them.

Brynne had just replaced the receiver, checking off another name from her list when she looked up at the knock on her open office door. She smiled, "You're early."

"No, you're late," Devin teased. He held up a large paper bag. "I thought this might happen so I brought lunch. Do you want to eat at the desk or the coffee table?"

"Coffee table. It's been crazy around here with the fund-raising dinner-dance week after next. Thanks for bringing lunch."

"My pleasure, babe. Besides, this way we won't have any interruptions." He flashed the grin that had her heart racing. Tossing his navy suede jacket over the armchair, he made himself comfortable on the small sofa and began unpacking the food.

"No interruptions here? I wish. What's up?"

His wide shoulders were covered by a dark green silk shirt, and he angled his long legs, covered by dark brown trousers, to one side of the low table.

"Is there something wrong with wanting to be alone with my beautiful fiancée?" he said as his dark gray eyes twinkled with laughter while he took in her black suit with a coral pinstripe, the straight skirt stopping above the knee with a flirty, ruffled hem.

"Not one thing, but you're making me curious." Her eyes sparkled as she watched him drape a napkin over her lap and then accepted the chopsticks and a carton of her personal favorite, shrimp fried rice. "Thank you. Smells wonderful." She took a bite. "Mmm. So what do you have? No, don't tell me. Let me guess, rice and pepper steak?"

"Yeah. Want some?"

"No, thanks. So tell me why you don't want to be interrupted."

"I'll tell you later. Eat and enjoy."

She leaned back against the cushions. "A girl could get used to this. You're spoiling me. Fixing dinner for me and Shanna almost every night and picking her up from school. Now this." She shook her head. "I can't take it. Just call me rotten."

He was so good to her. Everything he did made her feel so guilty because she hadn't been able to show how she felt about him. The guilt seemed to increase a bit more each day. She almost asked, many times, why he put up with her. She wouldn't be surprised if he woke up one morning and told her he'd had enough.

"There is nothing wrong with a man taking care of his lady. Believe me, things will be hectic once the football season starts." He held out egg rolls and chuckled when she took a big bite. "Good?"

She nodded as she chewed. "I didn't realize I was so hungry. I went back to sleep after you left this morning. Shanna woke me up, which meant we were late this morning. I didn't take time to eat more than a bite of toast. Don't worry. Shanna had banana and cereal for breakfast."

"I'm not worried. You've taken excellent care of my baby girl from day one."

Brynne beamed. "Thank you."

"I talked to Kelli. She and Wesley will be pleased to keep Shanna on the Saturday we're at the dinner-dance. In fact, they want her to spend the night."

"Are you sure they won't mind missing the affair, especially since your parents, Anna and Gavin, as well as Ralph and his date are planning to attend? I could ask Vanessa or Trenna to keep her."

"No need. Kelli and Wes seem to think it's a treat to get to spoil their niece. They have no idea she's a little giggle box."

Laughing, she said, "Shanna is going to be so excited. She absolutely adores Kaleea."

Brynne didn't dare reveal how much she hoped they could someday give Shanna a baby brother or sister. The way things were going, it seemed an impossibility.

"I've been thinking. I know how tough it will be for you to leave the women's center. You've worked hard to help your clients, and you're good at it."

"Going back to St. Louis will be an adjustment for all of us," she admitted.

"Not so much of an adjustment if you can continue your work. What do you think about starting a women's center in St. Louis?"

"What?"

"Unfortunately, I'm sure there is a need for the center. Babe, you know what needs to be done, and you know how to do it. Why not continue?"

"It would take a great deal of money to pull something like that off."

"Money won't be an issue. I can set you up the first year. And I'm sure I can help by drumming up some community support, and there's my team members. Perhaps we can get the Rams organization to pitch in?"

Incredulous, Brynne quizzed, "You'd do all that for me?"

"For you, babe, I'd do a hell of a lot more."

Brynne's eyes filled with tears. "Devin, I don't know what to say."

"Say yes."

"Yes!" Laughing, she launched herself into his arms. The kiss she gave him was filled with the warmth and love she had been unable to express. "You're a wonderful man. I do love you."

"I'm glad. I have something for you."

She pressed her hand against her pounding heart. "I don't know if I can stand any more good news."

Devin took Brynne's trembling hands into his. "Ready?"

"Stop stalling. Tell me what's going on before I pass out from nerves."

Devin got up, searched inside his jacket pocket, and pulled out a velvet box from a well-known jeweler. After placing the box in her lap, he reclaimed his seat. "I hope you like it."

"You didn't have to do this, babe. You already spent a small fortune on the first ring," she whispered unhappily, recalling that she refused to keep it and hurt him deeply. She hadn't expected another one.

"Open it." When she hesitated, he flipped open the lid. Nestled on a bed of satin was a pink diamond ring with three round stones, set in a platinum band.

"Oh, Devin."

"Do you like it?"

At a loss for words, she nodded.

"The first stone represents our past, when we first fell in love. The center and largest stone represents our present love that grows stronger each day, and the last stone is our future of everlasting love."

She blinked back tears as she whispered, "I love you so much."

"And I love you just as much." He brushed her lips with his.

"In St. Louis you gave me a pink diamond. Is one of these—" She stopped, not wanting to remind him of a sad time. "Don't answer that."

He smiled. "Yes, it's the first diamond. I had the jeweler reset it and add the others."

"I'm glad. Thank you, Devin." She slid her arms up and around his neck to press her lips against his in a lingering caress. "I love it. You have no idea how much it means to me that you kept that stone. I did want to marry you back then. I just couldn't. I'm sorry that—"

"Shush, love. I understand. At the time, even though I was hurt, I couldn't get rid of your ring. It has been in my safety deposit box all this time."

"Oh, honey."

When she pressed her lips to his once more, she sensed his hesitation. At the most inopportune times, she found herself almost desperately yearning for the closeness that they had once shared.

Although she knew he held back because he didn't want to scare her, nonetheless, she wished with all her heart that just once he'd give in just a little to the force of his need. He was so focused on not pressuring her that he ignored himself. Hoping to slip past his iron-clad control, she rained kisses along his strong jaw to the corner of his generous mouth. When her tongue slid past the seal of his full lips, they both shivered from the sweet contact.

There was a quick knock on the door before Laura peeked her head inside the room. "Oh! I'm sorry! I didn't realize—" She started backing out.

"Don't go." Devin rose to his feet. "I'm the one that should be leaving." He leaned down to brush his lips against Brynne's. "I'll see you later." He smiled at Laura "Good seeing you again. Laura, right?"

She nodded, clearly at a loss for words.

" 'Bye, ladies," Devin said with a wave.

Laura rushed on to say, "I'm so sorry, Brynne. I had no idea—"

"Will you hush and come on in here? I want to show you my ring." She held out her hand. "Well?"

Laura squealed and hugged Brynne.

Twenty-six

It was late when Brynne finished frosting the cupcakes for Shanna's nursery school class. She'd waited until Devin put their daughter to bed, knowing it would go much faster without Shanna's help. Now she was exhausted, wishing she hadn't turned down Devin's offer to clean up the kitchen.

As she walked quietly into her darkened bedroom, she didn't so much as glance toward the shadowed bed. She went into the connecting bath, unbuttoning her blouse as she moved. She slowed when she noted the room was lit by the night light and an array of candles surrounding the tub, with the flames flickering in their etched-glass containers.

Her head jerked toward the sound as she realized the shower was being turned off, and her eyes went wide as she watched the tall, powerfully built man drying off within the glass-walled shower stall. She tried but couldn't look away from his long, bare, brown frame. His back was to her.

She told herself that she had to get her feet moving before he saw her. Unfortunately, her feet weren't cooperating. She stood mesmerized by the sun yellow towel moving up long calves to the back of well-muscled thighs and over taut male buttocks. She watched his casual movements as he finished drying his back and then wrapped the towel around his trim waist. She still hadn't moved when he turned, opened the door, and walked out.

Brynne, blushing with embarrassment, said "I'm sorry. I thought you were asleep. I didn't realize . . ." Her voice trailed away.

"There is nothing to be sorry for." Devin paused in front of her, placed a kiss on the side of her throat that caused shivers of awareness to race up and down her spine, before he moved around her and turned the water on in the whirlpool tub. "Tired?"

She nodded, unable to sort out her thoughts. Her legs were trembling, and still she stood as if her feet were glued to the tile flooring.

"I'll be out of your way in a moment," he said as he went to the counter and switched on an electric razor. As he shaved, he told her about stopping by the high school and talking to his father's track team. When he finished, he rinsed out the sink, unhurriedly crossed over to the hamper, and placed his towel inside. He casually pulled on his dark blue pajama bottoms while reminding her about the tub, and then he quietly closed the bathroom door behind him.

Brynne had no idea how long she stood there, but she did manage to turn off the taps before flooding the floor. "Get used to it," she mumbled aloud as she undressed and got into the tub. Even with her eyes closed, she could recall every detail of Devin's gorgeous body. She whispered, "There ought to be a law against a man looking that good."

She frowned when she noticed that her nipples were hard and her breasts felt heavy. Unfortunately, they weren't the only parts of her affected by his nudity. She ached deep inside. It took her a few moments to recognize that there had not been any painful memories. Her head had been filled with thoughts of Devin . . . only him. Her hands weren't quite steady when she pulled on a burgundy silk slip gown after her bath. Even though she told herself she didn't need the protection of panties, she put them on anyway.

Brynne's heart was still pounding by the time she entered the bedroom. Devin lay on his back when she slid in beside him. For a time, she concentrated on listening to his deep, even breathing. She was aware of frowning as she nestled her head on his shoulder and her hand on his chest.

"Comfortable?" His deep throaty voice caused her to start.

She whispered, "I thought you were sleeping."

"Almost." He ran his hand absently up and down her bare arm. "You smell good."

"We need to talk." She released a pent-up breath before she said, "Honey, I can't stand it anymore. I've been feeling so selfish. How can you be happy with our arrangement?"

"I'm happy as long as I'm with you and our daughter." He kissed her temple.

Brynne snapped, "You know what I mean."

"We have an agreement," he reminded her as he continued to caress her arm.

"And you're not getting much from it."

Devin surprised her when he spanned her waist and pulled her up his chest until he could see her features. "What's wrong? Are you feeling neglected, babe?"

"You should be. There is nothing normal about what we're doing. Putting you through hell every night isn't my idea of a good time. I feel guilty."

"I'm not complaining."

"You should be," she persisted, tucking her face between the place where his head and shoulder joined.

He lowered his head while lifting her chin until he could gently stroke his mouth against hers. "Babe, tell me what you want and where you want it."

Brynne moaned, raining kisses on Devin's jaw, the corner of his mouth, before she licked his generous lips. When he made no move to deepen the kiss, she begged, "Kiss me, babe. Touch me."

She didn't have to ask twice. He kissed her the way she'd been longing to be kissed without realizing it. He nibbled on her top lip, and then sucked her bottom lip. Then he slipped his tongue inside her mouth, his tongue stroking hers. She whimpered, opening even more to his attention. As one kiss led to another, Brynne unwittingly rubbed the sensitive tips of her breasts against the firm muscles of Devin's chest.

He groaned, moving his open mouth down her throat. He tongued the sweetly scented hollow at the base of Brynne's throat. She shivered as Devin's open mouth moved lower, to the top swells of her breasts. She bit her bottom lip when she felt him tug her nightgown down past her waist, not stopping until she wore only a pair of bikini panties.

Before Brynne could think, let alone form a protest, Devin spanned her waist and raised her up until her breasts filled his vision. He licked one globe before he moved to do the same to the other. He laved every inch of her breast, ignoring her whimpers of pleasure. Only when she called out did he take the dark peak into his mouth to savor. He took his time, tonguing each sensitive nipple in turn before he began sucking in earnest.

Brynne was panting by the time Devin intensified the suction to what she longed for. Feeling a mounting tension and spiraling heat inside her womb, she began to call out his name. He took his time, causing the dazzling sensation to intensify and the ache to throb deep inside her feminine center.

Brynne sighed in relief when he parted her thighs and rhythmically squeezed her damp mound while he continued sucking her breast. Caught up in her pulsating need, she didn't even consider protesting when Devin peeled away her panties.

Whispering in her ear, he urged, "Open for me, babe."

She complied without hesitation, and then gasped when Devin told her to brace herself on her hands as he slid down her body until his hot mouth placed kisses on the tender flesh of her stomach, lingering at her navel before he moved into the brown curls covering her sex.

His voice was huskier than normal. "You are wet, baby . . . so wet . . . so ready for me."

He parted her plump feminine lips, opening her to the slow, mesmerizing strokes of his tongue. Eventually the searing heat intensified even more when he took her clitoris into the heat of his mouth to lave and then suckle. Devin didn't stop until Brynne reached a shatteringly sweet climax. Her entire body shook from the force of her release. Devin shifted until he was cradling her against his pounding heart as she quieted.

"Sweet. You're so sweet," he whispered, moving a caressing hand along her back down to her soft hips.

Brynne began stroking him from his broad, hair-covered chest to his trim waist. When her hand slid beneath the waistband of his pajamas, he caught and held it.

"Please, Devin. Let me. I can—"

He lifted her small hand to place a kiss in the palm. "Not tonight."

"But why? I can do this . . ." she faltered, unable to finish.

"You don't have to. Let's get some sleep." He kissed her forehead.

Brynne didn't voice her disappointment that he wouldn't even let her try. If only she could be sure that she wouldn't make a mess of it as she'd done in Traverse City, then she would have gone ahead despite his reluctance. Until she was sure of herself, she had no choice, but to keep quiet.

Slowly she was able to relax enough to sleep. She woke when she felt him ease out of the bed. He crossed to the bathroom and closed the door softly behind him. Her eyes filled when she heard the hiss of the shower. A crushing sense of failure and despair caused her to bite her bottom lip, holding back the sobs welling in her chest.

* * *

On Tuesday Brynne and Maureen were in Maureen's office seated at the conference table. They'd worked through their lunch, putting the last-minute touches on the preparation for the women's center fund-raising dinner-dance on Saturday night when Brynne revealed her intention to tell her own experience to her clients during the Thursday night group counseling session.

"Are you sure you're ready for this?" Maureen asked pointedly.

Brynne clasp and unclasped her hands as she said, "I have to."

"What happened to change your mind?"

"It doesn't matter. Just accept I know it's time."

"Brynne, there's more to this than 'it's time,' and we both know it."

"You've been urging me to do this for weeks. Don't tell me you've changed your mind?"

"No, but this is not about me. So answer the question. I thought things were going well for you." Maureen pushed aside the clipboard she'd used to jot down last-minute changes.

"They are and they aren't," Brynne hedged as she thought back on the past week.

Devin had been more than generous with his time and attention. He pleasured her almost every night, but when she suggested that she return the favor, he refused, preferring cold showers. The other night, when she'd gotten fed up and demanded to know why, he insisted that they had plenty of time and there was no need to rush into something she wasn't ready for.

"Try English," Maureen said. "That I understand."

"I want all of it behind me. I want to get on with my life." Brynne rushed on to say, "Talking to the women I've counseled just might be the last step toward that goal. I have to try and see if it will help. It certainly can't hurt."

"You're getting married in a few weeks. Is moving back to St. Louis what's upsetting you?"

Brynne blurted out, "What's upsetting me is not being able to pleasure my fiancé. How can we expect to move forward when I'm terrified of taking him inside my body?"

Maureen squeezed her hand. "You think talking to the group will change that?"

Blinking back tears, Brynne confessed, "I'm willing to take the risk. It certainly can't make things worse."

Maureen cautioned, "What if it doesn't turn out the way you've hoped? I'm not trying to discourage you, but I want you to consider more intense therapy as an option."

"I have no idea if this will work. The only thing I know for sure is I can't marry Devin unless I can be his wife in every sense of the word." She hesitated before she said, "Maureen, I need a favor. Can you make Thursday night's session? It would mean so much to me."

"Oh, honey, I can't promise because I have a meeting. But I promise to do my very best to get back before the session is over."

"Thank you." Brynne forced a smile, determined to hold back the tears that lately seemed to be so close to the surface.

Brynne's gaze moved yet again to the closed door. They were using the women's center conference room. Refreshments had been set out on the side table. The women had pushed back the table and were seated in a circle. Each was given an opportunity to share, but there was no pressure to actively participate. A few of the women had not yet been able to talk about their experiences. Yet they were encouraged to come each time.

Brynne knew firsthand that healing was not the same for everyone; more often than not, it took time. Their sessions often went quite late, depending on how much needed to be shared. They had started on Brynne's right and were slowly moving around the group. She was having trouble concentrating and was grateful for Candace Blackwood's calming presence.

Candace, like the other women, had been raped. She was a true survivor. Her rape had been particularly brutal and violent, yet she continued to participate in group discussion, even though she had successfully completed therapy a year ago. She also was a sought-after speaker and a frequent volunteer at the women's center.

Devin had noticed that something wasn't quite right with Brynne, yet she insisted she was just tired. She hadn't told him about her plan . . . not yet. What if she failed? Brynne's stomach was a knot of tension, but she swallowed a huge sigh of relief when Maureen slipped inside the conference room.

"Jeannie?" Brynne referred to the woman to her left. Brynne's heart pounded with dread when the woman vehemently shook her head as she tightly clasped her hands.

"I guess that's it for tonight," Candace said with a smile. The other women began talking among themselves as they started gathering their things.

"Not quite." Brynne was forced to clear her throat before she could go on, "Ladies, I know this is unusual, but I have something to share."

"Brynne, is this about your fancy society wedding? The one that, no doubt, none of us will be invited to attend," Regina Stubs said. She didn't even attempt to hide her bitterness and resentment.

Brynne had been counseling Regina a few weeks, and as of yet, she hadn't been able to reach the other woman. Brynne smiled, aware of the pain she heard in the other's voice. "No, Regina. This isn't about my wedding. And you are most certainly invited, just like all the other ladies here. No, this is personal. It's about me."

Brynne paused to put the clipboard with the legal pad she had been using to take notes under her chair. She folded her hands in her lap. "Ladies, this is Maureen Sheppard. Some of you know her as the director of the women's center, as well as my boss. Maureen is also my friend. She came tonight to support me."

Brynne stopped for a moment before she lifted her chin and then recited, "My name is Brynne Armstrong. And I am a rape survivor."

A prolonged silence followed the announcement. Brynne was forced to take a deep breath before she said, "Until recently, I haven't been able to face what happened or talk about it. I did all the things that a woman should never do."

Brynne told of her own painful experience. When she finished, she waited, anxious for their responses. She had no idea what to expect, but their support and genuine acceptance were nearly her undoing. She didn't even try to hold back the tears. Deep inside, she knew even her tears were okay, because she didn't have to be strong . . . didn't have to pretend that rape hadn't nearly destroyed her.

These women understood, as no one else could, exactly what had been taken away from her and what she faced day in and day out. They had all found the courage to live on despite it, because they were survivors. There was not a dry eye in the room as Brynne moved from one client to the next receiving their precious gifts of love, support, and acceptance.

"Congratulations! You did it!" Maureen grinned as she clasped Brynne's hands once the meeting had ended and they were alone. "Are you okay?"

"I'm not sure. I'm still shaking."

"It's done."

"Thank you for coming. I could not have done it without you."

Maureen shook her head. "You could, but I'm glad I made it in time."

Brynne hugged her anyway. "Thank you."

Together the two finished cleaning up and straightened the conference room. The janitorial service came in during the night.

After collecting her things Brynne linked her arm through Maureen's. "Let's get out of here."

Deciding to take the stairs, they were the last to leave the building. They paused in the well-lit parking lot, where a security guard was on duty. Maureen and her grandmother hadn't taken for granted the safety of the women who visited as well as that of the workers in the building.

"Thank you again." Brynne gave her a long hug. "I do so appreciate your support, your help, and your encouragement. You made this possible for me."

"No, darling. You did the hard work, but if you insist on thanking me, then you are more than welcome." Maureen laughed. "It went well, don't you think?"

Brynne nodded, blinking back tears. "Better than I could have imagined. Their acceptance and love was wonderful. I felt as if I'm no longer a victim. That finally I can hold my head up high." Her smile was a bit wobbly when she said, "It's almost over. I will know for sure by how well I can get on with my life."

Maureen kissed her cheek. "Go home. Get some rest. You're going to need it. Remember, only two more days until the dinner-dance." She looked worried as she asked, "Do you think anyone in this city is really going to pay a thousand dollars for a ticket? What were my grandmother and I thinking? What if no one comes?"

"You'll be there. I'll be there," Brynne reassured her friend. "Besides, no one would have the nerve to back out at the last minute and disappoint Mrs. Hale."

Maureen laughed. "My grandfather always said nobody could squeeze money out of a tightwad the way she can."

"I know that's right. See you in the morning." Brynne hurried to her SUV. She waved at Maureen inside her sleek red Mercedes as she drove out of the lot, heading for Interstate 94.

She was beginning to regret not telling Devin about her plans to speak to the group. She wanted him to be as proud of her as she was of herself. For so long she'd felt like a miserable coward. Restoring her confidence had been much harder than she had expected. Tonight was another step toward that goal.

As she took the exit to the Walter Reuther Expressway, she decided to wait and keep the news to herself a bit longer . . . just until she was absolutely certain she was ready to take the next step. She didn't want to disappoint Devin yet again.

She missed the intimacy they'd once shared and desperately wanted it back. She yearned to feel like a woman again, complete in every way. Soon, she promised herself, she would wake up with a huge smile on her face, knowing she had taken care of her man's needs. It would be better if she showed Devin that she was ready to make love to him by doing just that.

No more guilt and tears for her or cold showers for him. What better night to show him than the night of the dinner-dance? Shanna would be spending the night with Wesley and Kelli. And at the end of the evening, she and Devin would have the house to themselves.

Twenty-seven

*As their limousine moved through the late-*night traffic, Brynne couldn't stop smiling.

"We could not have wished for a better turnout, or for things to go smoother." Brynne gushed with excitement. "But then, how could it not be perfect? The food was fabulous, thanks to your sister's catering company, and the program went well. Maureen and her grandmother were thrilled by the turnout and the patrons' generosity. We made enough money to guarantee the women's center will be open next year."

She turned her head, touching her lips to Devin's. "Thank you, babe. Your fifty-thousand dollar donation and the matching funds you made in our daughter's name will be put to excellent use. It was a fabulous surprise."

Devin's dark gaze lingered on her red-tinted lips before he looked away. "You don't have to thank me. The Valerie Hale Sheppard Women's Crisis Center is doing remarkable work. I only have to look at you to see the benefits the center offers to the community."

"Nevertheless, the center is not your charity. You've given so generously to the Boys and Girls Clubs, plus you're sponsoring an entire class of youngsters' college fund. How can I even expect more?" Brynne didn't wait for his response but rushed on to say, "The Prescott family were more than generous with their checks. I still can't believe it. I'm so happy it went well and it is over."

Devin chuckled as he caressed the soft curls at her nape. "Have I told you how beautiful you are tonight?"

Brynne teased, "Yes, now stop changing the subject. I want to boast about you and your family."

"I'd rather talk about you and how good you look in that dress." He ran a finger along the sequined border of her black, strapless, floor-length silk gown. The matching sequin-covered belt emphasized her slim waist and womanly hips, while the split in the front showed off her shapely legs. Her small feet were prettily encased in black, sequin-covered four-inch heels. "Just looking at you makes my heart race."

"You are the one." Brynne smiled at him, lifting a small hand to smooth down the tiny row of onyx studs lining his pristine white silk shirt. His black custom-made tuxedo fit him to perfection.

As she fingered his black silk bow tie, she hoped he didn't detect her jittery nerves. She'd been anxious the entire day, and as the evening slipped away, her fear of failure accelerated. The dinner-dance had for a time been a powerful distraction, but now that they were headed home, her plans for what was left of the night suddenly seemed overly ambitious.

"You are very handsome tonight yourself, Devin Prescott. Every woman in the room had her eyes on you."

He quirked a brow. "I didn't notice."

"Good." She grinned.

He laughed as he fingered the cashmere of her black shawl that was lavishly embroidered with yellow and pink silk ribbon roses. "Are you warm enough?"

"With you beside me, I'm toasty."

Brynne glanced out at the passing scenery, taking note

that they were less than a mile away from her home. Her heart jumped. It was nearly time for the second part of the evening . . . the seduction. If only she knew how to go about it without his cooperation. Knowing him as well as she did, he was bound to need convincing.

Even though she had broken down and told him about her participation in the group sessions, he hadn't made the connection that it signaled a personal change for her. Or rather, she desperately hoped it would.

She had bought a sexy nightgown, but planned to start by inviting him to share her bath, and hoped they'd spend the rest of the night making love. As long as she didn't freeze at the sight of his erection, she was almost certain she could finish what she started.

Devin surprised her by asking, "What's bothering you, Brynne? Are you worried about Shanna spending the night away from home?"

She hurried to say, "No worries tonight."

She was unaware of the way she clasped her trembling fingers or worried her bottom lip. Her focus was on the limousine easing to a stop at the entrance to the gated community. In a moment, they'd be in her drive. She was thankful that he didn't pursue the matter, even though he didn't seem convinced.

Devin didn't wait for the driver to open the door, but stepped out and held a hand out to her. Once she was beside him, he tipped the driver and they walked hand-in-hand to her front door. Rather than fumble with the lock, she gave him her keys.

In the foyer, she asked, "Would you like something to drink?"

"Nothing for me."

She was moving toward the back of the house when he stopped her by cupping her shoulders. Then he kissed her soft nape.

"I probably should go. We both could use a full night's sleep."

Startled, she whirled around to face him. "Is that what you want?"

"No, but baby, we have to face facts. Neither of us has gotten much sleep the nights I've stayed over. I make you uncomfortable."

"That's not true."

"Unfortunately, it is. The last thing I want to do is put more pressure on you to do something you're clearly not ready to do. Don't worry about Shanna. I can pick her up in the morning."

"Devin, you're wrong." Brynne hoped he didn't hear the desperation in her voice.

He frowned as he rubbed a hand over his mustache. "Wrong about what, babe? The pressure I'm putting on you by sleeping beside you? I don't think so."

Frustrated, she said, "I want you to stay. This isn't how I planned it." Going into the family room where she'd left a light on, she absently threw her shawl and purse into one of the armchairs and turned to glare up at him. "Devin Prescott, you're not cooperating. It has to be to-night!"

"What are you talking about?" When she didn't answer, he folded his arms over his chest and said impatiently, "Why don't you come straight out with it?"

As calmly as she could manage, she took his hand to urge him over to the sofa. Once they were seated, rather than explaining, she nervously twisted her engagement ring.

"What is it, baby? What's got you so tied up in knots?" When she hesitated, he placed a finger beneath her chin so that he could see her eyes. "Are you having second thoughts about us?"

Gasping, she said, "Where did that come from? I've never even hinted at it. Stop putting words in my mouth."

He smoothed a gentle finger over her creased brow. "Something has placed a frown on that beautiful face. I'd like to know what."

Brynne slid her arms up around his neck until she was

cradling his nape. "Stay with me tonight. I want to sleep in your arms."

She urged his face down to hers. When their lips met, she released a sigh. When he would have pulled away, she parted her lips and licked his generous bottom lip. She sponged his top lip before returning to the bottom one to suckle. When he released a groan deep in his throat, she smiled before she slid her tongue over his.

Devin's hands tightened around her waist, and then he surprised her when he pulled away. There was a question in his nearly charcoal gray eyes as he studied her brown eyes.

"Talk to me. Tell me what's going on with you, babe."

Brynne smoothed a hand up his chest, undoing his tie. She forced a smile. "What? I need an invitation to kiss my own fiancé?"

He scowled, "No games. Tell me."

"Devin, I don't want to talk. We've done nothing but talk. What I want is to make love with you."

Brynne got up only to sit on his lap, her arms once more encircling his neck. She pressed soft kisses down his cheek to his throat while undoing the studs lining his shirt. She placed an openmouthed kiss at the base of his throat.

She whispered, "Make love with me."

Even though his voice was huskier than normal, his skepticism was apparent. "Brynne, I need to understand what brought about this sudden change."

She kissed his mouth, her tongue coaxing his until he returned her kisses. In fact he was the one deepening their kisses until he was hungrily stroking her tongue with his own. He moaned her name as he gathered her against his chest.

"Brynne . . ." he whispered into her ear. "Are you sure?"

"Yes, please just hurry." She kissed him again and again as her heart pounded with a combination of excitement and dread. She had to do it now, before she lost her nerve.

Devin cradled her against him, yet he hesitated. Not that she blamed him for doubting her. For weeks he'd ignored his own needs and concentrated on giving her the utmost pleasure. It was time . . . long past time she showed him what was in her heart.

"Babe . . ."

"I want you."

She gasped when he stood up with her in his arms. He carried her down the hall to her bedroom, which now had a new California king–size bed.

"Devin," she whispered when he freed her mouth.

He slowly released her legs, allowing her petite length to slide down his. Before she could formulate a response, his mouth moved down her silky, smooth pale brown throat, his hot tongue lingered in the fragrant hollow before he moved to tongue the sensitive spot behind her ear. She shivered in response. Because of the lamp she'd left on, she had no trouble making out his dark features.

"You are so sexy . . . so incredibly beautiful," he whispered throatily, unhooking the belt at her waist and then unzipping her dress, easing it down her shapely hips until it pooled on the carpet.

She was aware of the tremor in his hands as he smoothed them down her spine. Her limbs were far from steady as she stood in a black strapless bra, boy-cut lace panties, and sheer thigh-high, lace-edged stockings.

Pushing the jacket off his broad shoulders and down his well-muscled arms, she returned to undoing his shirt. The studs slowed her progress, but she didn't stop until he was bare to the waist.

He didn't question her urgency, her need to block out all else but his overwhelming masculinity. When his mouth once again covered hers, she was thrilled because he kissed her until all she could do was feel.

When Devin released her lips they were both breathless. Brynne didn't want to stop . . . not until it was done. She watched him remove his socks and shoes. His eyes went to hers as he opened and then unzipped his trousers. The trembling started, but she refused to take her eyes away from the blatant proof of his virility as he stepped out of his trousers. The hard ridge of his sex was outlined in his black silk boxers.

Moving to the bed, he pushed aside the down-filled comforter and top sheet and then sat on the side of the bed. His eyes caressed her as he waited for her. She couldn't move as her old fears returned. Then she focused on Devin's handsome features and saw his smile. His eyes were simmering with need, but they were also filled with tenderness, understanding, and undeniable love.

"Nothing is going to happen that you don't want to happen. I love you, Brynne Armstrong. I never stopped."

She nodded, rushing over to him. He pulled her between his thighs, against his flat stomach and deep chest. Her kiss was hot, almost urgent as she opened for the rough velvet heat of his tongue. Desire swirled around her, so much so that she wasn't aware of his removing her undergarments. She trembled as she felt his tongue travel down her neck to her breast. He leisurely licked the plump globe before he turned his focus to the engorged nipple.

Brynne's cries of escalating need didn't cause Devin to quicken his pace as he leisurely tongued her highly sensitive crest. When he took the hard peak into his mouth and sucked, she quivered while her knees buckled. If not for his strong arms, she would have collapsed in a heap at his feet.

"Sweet, so unbelievably sweet," he groaned an instant before he increased the suction, causing her to nearly scream his name.

Lost in a maze of sensuous sensation, as desire overshadowed all other considerations, she didn't realize she was cradling his head as if to keep him in place. When he finally lifted his head, she moaned a protest.

"Shush, babe. I'm a long way from finished."

He nestled her other plump breast before he took that tight peak into his mouth to lave and then suck. The intensity of his hot mouth caused her to tighten her inner muscles in delicious anticipation. He cupped her bottom, lifting her until she straddled his thighs. He sighed huskily as he moved his fingers through the dark brown curls covering her sex. Rhythmically, he squeezed her soft mound.

"Devin . . ." she called out when he parted the dew-slick folds, his tender ministrations causing her pleasure to spiral beyond control. She was a shivering mass of nerves by the time he slid a finger deep inside. She called out at the sweetness of his invasion, arching her back while yearning for more.

She was fast losing the small measure of resistance that remained, for all too soon he increased the suction on her breast while caressing her throbbing pearl of desire. The mesmerizing sensations soon had her climaxing. Feeling as if she were shattering into a million pieces of indescribable pleasure, Brynne nestled in Devin's arms until the tremors eased.

Lost in the sheer magic of the moment, she was unaware of his laying her on the bed or removing his boxers. Before she could collect her scattered wits, she was sharing sizzling hot, needy kisses.

"Was it good, babe?" he said into her ear as his kisses warmed her throat.

Unable to form a coherent thought, she rubbed her aching breasts into his firm-muscled chest and placed a series of kisses along his dark cheeks, down to his fragrant throat. Only when he begged for her mouth did she press her open mouth against his. One hungry kiss led to another and another. The hypnotizing whirl of desire was starting all over again, and soon she was caught in its magnetism.

Then she felt the blunt crest of his arousal moving against the damp folds of her sex . . . repeatedly he teased her until she whimpered, craving more. When he pulled back, she shook her head in protest, yet he resisted, withholding his male strength, his love.

His voice was raw with desire when he said, "I want you, baby. Do you want me . . . inside of you?"

Her thick lashes dropped as she gazed past the muscular planes of his hair-roughened chest, his concave stomach, the thicket of dark curls surrounding his erect shaft. His pulsating length rose hard and thick between their bodies. He tilted her chin until her eyes met his.

"I won't hurt you, Brynne," he said tenderly.

He was leaving the decision to her. For a time they looked into each other's eyes, their uneven breathing the only sound in the room. Her hands weren't steady when she caressed his shoulders, his rib cage, and his stomach.

She hesitated, but only for a moment as she took a deep breath before she moved her hand to touch the broad crown of his penis. He released a husky groan at the sweetness of the brief caress. Even though Brynne nodded, Devin made no move to join his body with hers. His eyes told her that he needed the words.

"I know, my love," she eventually said into his ear. "I know you won't hurt me. Yes, I want you . . . the way you want me. Please, Devin, do it now."

Doubt flickered across his strong, dark features. He reached inside the nightstand for a condom and quickly opened it and put it on. She took deep calming breaths, wanting to look away but refusing to give in to the underlying fear that had become so much a part of her since the fateful night that changed her life.

Devin lay on his back, his eyes studying hers. She waited, her breathing quick and uneven. Slowly he wrapped his hand around her neck to urge her mouth down to his. There was no mistake about his need as he kissed her hungrily.

They were both breathless with aching need when the kiss finally ended and he encircled her waist and lifted her over his hips. When he parted her dewy soft folds with the head of his shaft, she tensed. Slowly he rotated his hips, repeatedly caressing her soft opening while leaning forward until he could lave a pebble-hard nipple. Pleasure consumed her, leaving her numb to everything else and unable to concentrate on anything other than this special man. Quickly she reached yet another climax.

Before Brynne quieted Devin thrust upward, joining their bodies. By the time she realized that they were indeed one, she released a heartfelt sigh of relief and acceptance, unaware of the grateful tears that flowed from beneath her lashes. He ran a soothing hand up and down her back and small shoulders.

"Are you okay?" he whispered anxiously as he rested his forehead against hers, while holding himself motionless.

Brynne nodded. Listening to his ragged breathing, she could only imagine the effort it took for him to control his driving need. She sighed at the sweet kiss he placed on her closed lids.

"Open your eyes, baby. I don't want you to forget even for an instant that it's me inside you . . . loving you." He licked her bottom lip before he whispered, "Say it. Say my name."

With her eyes wide open, she said, "Devin . . . my love . . . my heart."

Then she gasped as he clasped her soft hips and began to withdraw, only to fill her tight sheath to the point of bursting yet again. As he repeated the process over and over again, the most exquisite sensations blinded her to all else.

"Yes, it's Devin," he growled while he worried the highly sensitive bud, the core of her feminine desires.

Panting, she tightened around him. "Hurry . . ." she urged, throwing her head back and arching her back. To her dismay, he slowed his movements.

Devin shook his head as he leaned back on his elbows, his lips tight, while he fought for control. "I'm yours, Brynne. Take what you need."

She rocked against him, tiny movements at first, but soon she braced her hands on his chest and pressed down in earnest, craving all his hard length. She moaned as the need inside her built to incredible proportions.

"Harder . . . Devin. I want it harder," she panted.

He used his strong pelvic muscles to give her the deep thrusts she yearned for while he worried her taut pearl. Sheer pleasure caused Brynne to scream his name as she reached a heart-stopping climax, her inner muscles squeezing him, milking him, and quickly sending him into a powerful, shuddering climax that culminated in a hoarse shout. He collapsed on the bed, pulling her close until her cheek rested on his shoulder. She luxuriated in his reassuring yet gentle embrace.

Devin was the first to speak as he smoothed Brynne's damp curls. "Are you all right, babe? I didn't hurt you, did I?"

Breathless, she grinned at him until she was able to say, "Not at all. You, my heart, made it wonderful . . . so special for me. Thank you." She pressed her lips against his.

Devin was also grinning. "No thanks necessary. I assure you the pleasure was mine."

He placed kisses across her forehead, down her cheeks to her kiss-swollen lips. His kisses were sweet, undemanding as he cupped her nape, his fingers in her hair. Brynne's eyes filled with tears as she moved to settle along his side.

"Why the tears? You said I didn't hurt you."

Twenty-eight

"You didn't. Devin, it's hard to explain."

"Try."

"I'm happy . . . overjoyed to finally be able to show how I feel about you."

Tightening his arm around her, he said throatily, "I love you, Brynne Armstrong . . . so much."

"I love you too. Every minute we spent apart, I loved you."

After kissing her tenderly, he confessed, "Even during those painful years, there has never been anyone else for me, only you. Believe me, I tried to get over you, but nothing worked. You were in my heart."

"Oh, Devin. I'm so thankful that you didn't give up on me. But I couldn't blame you if you had."

"I thought I gave up, but what I couldn't do was let go."

They shared a gentle kiss, relishing their closeness.

He was the first to stir. "Will you join me in the shower?"

She smiled. "I'd like that."

Devin disposed of the condom before he scooped her up and carried her into the bathroom. While he started the shower, she removed what was left of her makeup. As she gazed into the mirror, she noted that her eyes sparkled with happiness and her face was flushed with a combination of relief and excitement. For the first time in a very long time, she felt complete.

She could have danced with the joy of knowing that she'd given her man the ultimate pleasure. The residual feelings of guilt and selfishness had finally been laid to rest.

When she joined him, the shower was on full force. She pressed herself behind him, wrapped her arms around his waist, her cheek against his back. Warm water rushed over them from multi-showerheads. He turned, moving soapy hands down her back. He paused at her waist.

"Talk to me, babe. Tell me what caused the change."

She shook her head, taking the soap from him. "Not now. I don't want to talk about or even think of anything remotely serious for the rest of the night."

She soaped his neck, his shoulders, his chest and stomach, but she didn't stop there. Hoping he didn't feel her tremors, she moved soapy hands into the thick curls surrounding his sex and then traced the length of his throbbing shaft before moving to cradle the heavy sacs below.

Devin groaned from the sweetness of Brynne's caress. He released a pent-up breath when she moved her hands over his buttocks and then down his thighs, his hair-roughened calves, to his long narrow feet.

When she rose, he returned the favor by taking the soap and caressing her with large soapy hands. He started at her throat, over her shoulders and arms, squeezing her small yet incredibly soft, full breasts. He took his time, tugging her aching nipples between his thumb and forefinger, before he moved over her flat stomach into the dark curls surrounding her femininity. She shivered and whimpered when he parted her soft nether lips and slid a finger into the heat of her body.

It was Brynne's turn to cry out as he pleasured her. She was close to climaxing when he gave her a hard kiss and ducked out of the shower. Before she could question his disappearance, he was back, wearing a condom.

Sinking onto the built-in bench, Devin cupped her hips to guide her down onto his steel-hard sex. His kiss was white-hot with need before he dropped his head to lick the place where her neck and shoulder joined. His thrusts were hard, unrelenting, while Brynne clung to him, wrapping her arms and legs around him. There was nothing slow or easy about their loving, but hot and demanding. They soon reached completion, hers only seconds before his.

When they were back in bed, with her cradled against him, her cheek resting over his heart, he persisted, "Why tonight, Brynne? What changed?"

"Nothing and everything."

"What does that mean? Babe, please. I want to understand. Above all else, I don't want there to be any secrets between us."

"It's hard to explain. Maybe revealing to the ladies in my counseling group that I'd also been raped convinced me that I could take the next step toward healing. I don't know. All I knew was I could not go on the way I have, letting you make love to me again and again without giving you any sexual satisfaction. You think I didn't know how difficult it must have been for you, time and time again?"

"Brynne, it wasn't about me. I had to—"

"It was about you, my heart." She squeezed his waist. "I wanted you to know beyond doubt how much I appreciated you and your patience and understanding."

He pressed a kiss against her temple. "There's no need. You would have done the same, if the situation were reversed."

"Babe, I've made so many mistakes along the way. You suffered because of them."

"We both have made mistakes and suffered." He kissed her throat. "Do you have any idea how happy you made me tonight?"

Brynne laughed. "I have an idea. You've done the same

for me." She paused before she confessed, "But it isn't over."

"What do you mean? We're together, we have a beautiful daughter, and we're planning to be married. What more could we want?"

"I mean, it's not over for me . . . not yet."

He stiffened. "What are you saying? Are you ready to press charges against the bastard?"

"That's another one of my regrets. Because of my weakness, he has gone free." Her petite frame was taut with tension. Reluctantly she admitted, "Until recently, I've always thought of myself as his only victim. Now I'm beginning to wonder if there were others. I'm forced to live with a decision that seemed right for me at the time, but was wrong."

"Are you thinking about going after him now?"

"No. At this late date, it's his word against mine." She sighed tiredly. "I want it to be over. I want it behind me once and for all."

Devin gently uncurled her fingers in order to place a kiss in the center of each palm. "What can I do to help?"

She pressed her lips against his collarbone. "You've done that by being here for me. I have to do the rest for myself."

There was a prolonged silence before he asked, "What are you planning?"

"It won't be over for me, not until I've faced my attacker."

Devin pushed back the covers and rose to sit on the side of the bed. He switched on the light while he sat there, deep in thought.

When he turned back to her, he said, "Brynne, I don't like the sound of this. First of all, if you face him, you have no idea how it will affect you. And second, you aren't going anywhere near him, not without me. Understand?"

Blinking as her eyes adjusted to the light, Brynne could feel Devin's tension. It was raw, palpable. She scooted over until she could run a soothing hand up and down his arm.

"I wouldn't dream of it. If I do this, you, my heart, will be right beside me. We're a team."

He pulled her against his chest. "I know that's right." Sighing heavily, he said, "Now that we've got that straight, our next step is to find the bastard."

"I know where he is."

Devin stared at her, his brow wrinkled by a scowl. "How in the hell do you know that?"

"I hired a private investigator."

"And you kept this to yourself?"

"I hired a detective around the same time I asked you to take that paternity test. I thought that if he was Shanna's father, then I needed to know where he was for her sake. I can't express how relieved I was that he wasn't my baby's father. I thank my Heavenly Father every single day for that blessing."

"Why are you just telling me this?"

"Devin, please don't be angry. I'm telling you now because finally I feel as if I'm ready. I want it over. And for that to happen, I need to confront him. I can't marry you until it's behind me. All of it."

"What do you mean, you can't marry me? Are you looking for a reason not to marry me?"

"No, dear heart. Will you calm down?" Her eyes were bright from unshed tears when she said, "I'm in love with you. You have to believe that."

"I did, until you started talking about not marrying me. We've put our lives on hold for too damn long." He ran an unsteady hand over his hair. "I've tried to be understanding but, Brynne, even I have my limits. And breaking our engagement is it," he snarled.

She nearly shouted, "I'm not breaking our engagement."

"It sounded that way to me," he grated harshly.

"What I'm doing is trying to move forward. This isn't about us. It's about me. It's about me getting my life back." She moved until her cheek rested against his shoulder and then wrapped her arms around his waist. "Please, babe, be patient a little longer. Just a little longer. When it's all over, then we can focus on our new life together and our daughter." She rained kisses over his face, lingering on his mouth. "Tell me you understand. Please."

Reluctantly he murmured his agreement.

On Friday afternoon Devin and Brynne boarded a Lear jet bound for St. Louis. They sat side by side in plush leather armchairs. The jet was one of the fleet of private planes that Devin and his cousin, Ralph, had invested in several years back.

Devin was still smarting from the fact that he hadn't learned of their destination until the last minute, and then only because his pilot had to file a flight plan.

"You haven't said a word since we lifted off," he said tightly. "Why don't you come on out with it?"

"I don't know what you mean," Brynne said quietly.

He clenched his teeth, swallowing an angry retort. He hadn't been sleeping well. Instead of enjoying holding his woman through the nights, he lay awake wondering if they were a step away from disaster. He hadn't gotten beyond Brynne's declaration that she couldn't marry until she'd dealt with the past. Losing her once had ripped his heart out. The thought of it happening again was unacceptable.

It also bothered him that while everyone around them was excited about their upcoming wedding, Brynne didn't have much to say about it. He considered her self-absorption a real threat to their happiness.

This should have been a perfect time for them. She had finally been able to make love to him, able to take him inside her body. They both should be on top of the world, concentrating on the rekindling of their desire as their love for each other deepened. Instead their special night had ended in apprehension rather than jubilation, and the following days had been a repeat of that same pattern.

He suspected her total focus was on her upcoming confrontation with her attacker. If only he could solve the problem his way. He'd dearly love to go after the bastard with his fists.

When he asked to see the private investigator's report, she refused. She'd told him as little as possible about her attacker. She wouldn't even tell him the bastard's name. It hurt that she still didn't completely trust him.

Despite the inherent violence of his sport, Devin had never deliberately hurt another man. Yet in this case, he would be lying to himself if he didn't admit he couldn't vouch for the lowlife's safety. He wanted the bastard . . . he wanted him bad.

No matter how many times Devin reminded himself that this was not about him, he couldn't forget it had taken four pain-filled years for Brynne to tell him about the rape. Her lack of faith in his love had nearly destroyed them. What if history was repeating itself?

He wasn't making any bones about it. He was downright scared. There was a real possibility that seeing her attacker might cause her a major setback. Their entire future was at stake. Yet he couldn't, in good conscience, get in the way of what Brynne felt she needed to do in order to heal.

Now that they had started over, he would be damned if he would lose Brynne again. No way would he let her face the bastard without him. Whatever life brought their way, Devin was determined they'd face it together.

Brynne called his name twice before she regained his attention.

"Sorry. What were you saying?"

She slipped her hand into his. "Are you having second thoughts about us?"

He stiffened. "I'm not the one with doubts, babe. Can you make the same claim?" A muscle jumped in his jaw.

"I'm not having second thoughts. Or at least not about how I feel about you. You are my heart."

"Shouldn't that be all that truly matters? How we feel about each other? And our love for our daughter, of course?" He traced her perfectly arched brow.

She bit her bottom lip. "Absolutely. I thought you understood why I have to do this."

He placed a kiss in the center of a small palm. "I do. I just don't like it. Now, stop worrying. It's going to work out. Seeing this bastard again isn't going to be easy for you. But we'll get through this . . . together."

"You know I want you there with me, Devin, but there is one condition."

"Oh yeah." He quirked a black brow. "And what is that?"

"You have to promise me that you won't lose your temper. That you won't lay a hand on him."

Incredulous, he demanded, "You can't be serious?"

"But I am. Promise me."

"Hell no! I can't promise you that. Who knows what we might face with this lowlife? If he makes one move toward you or even says something I consider inappropriate to you, he's mine."

Devin shook from the effort to control the anger he'd been harboring since the instant he had heard of the rape. He longed to pace the confines of the plane, but due to turbulence the seat belt sign was still on.

Brynne persisted. "You have to give me your word."

"Why? You're not asking him to give you his word. And in my estimation, I'm a hell of a lot more trustworthy than that bastard will ever be."

"Devin, calm down. Not for a minute do I doubt you. You're a good and honorable man. Your character has never been in question." She sighed tiredly. "He is the one I don't trust. I don't want him to make you angry. What I dread most is putting you or your career at risk. That means no altercation."

Evidently frustrated by his brooding silence, she persisted, "All I want is to look him in the eye and tell him how I feel about what he did to me. I know he doesn't believe he violated me. I intend to disavow him of that notion."

Devin clenched his jaw so tight, his teeth ached. "He had no right to put his filthy hands on you. He knew you were mine and resented it."

"If you don't make me that promise, I can't let you come with me." She lifted her chin stubbornly.

He demanded, "You and who else is going to stop me?"

"This is not funny."

"Do I look amused?"

Brynne dropped her thick lashes momentarily, then she whispered, "You've worked very hard to get to where you are today. I don't want you to lose your temper and put yourself at risk. Nothing is worth that. Can you imagine the trouble you could get into if you were arrested for manhandling this guy? The repercussions would be disastrous."

"Brynne, don't you know you're more important to me than what I do out there on the football field?" He lifted her hand and brushed his lips over her small knuckles. "Will you stop worrying? You're right. This trip is for you. And if it eases your mind, I promise not to do anything to get in your way or keep you from doing what you need to do."

Brynne smiled, leaning back in the seat.

"Now tell me about him. Who is he? Why are you so sure he's still in St. Louis?"

"Connor Helm."

"Helm? Why do I recognize that name?"

"It could be because his father and grandfather both work for Rucker University. Dr. Robert Helm is the dean of economics. Dr. Alexander Helm is still the president of the university."

He frowned. "No wonder you didn't feel as if you could report the rape."

"I was afraid, too scared to tell anyone. Besides, I didn't think anyone would believe me. His family was highly respected and had too much influence in the St. Louis community. Plus I blamed myself for letting him into my apartment."

"Helm was in the wrong, not you, babe. Yes, you let him

in, but you didn't invite him into your bed. Helm did all that on his own." Deciding to change the subject, he asked, "What's he doing?"

"What else? He's following in his grandfather and father's footsteps. He's teaching at the university."

Devin hissed, "So he has gone on with his life as if nothing has happened, while you've lived every day in the past four years thinking you had that bastard's child."

"Please," she pleaded, "calm down."

"I'm fine." But he wasn't fine and they both knew it. "What else did you learn about this bastard?"

"He married a former beauty queen and daughter of a prominent businessman."

"I wonder how she will feel when she learns she's married to a rapist," Devin speculated.

"I'm not out to hurt her. I just want to face him so I can get my life back."

"I know, babe."

Brynne sighed. She reached into her black patent leather tote bag and handed him an envelope. "The investigator's report. I've told you most of it."

After he finished reading it, he slipped an arm around her and pressed his mouth against her temple. "It's going to all work out. Remember, together we can do anything."

Devin arranged for a limousine to be waiting for them when they touched down at the Lambert–St. Louis International Airport and to drop them off at his home in Ladue. Devin's large, six-bedroom, seven-bathroom home sat on four acres behind gated, security walls.

Since neither of them had much of an appetite, they decided to postpone dinner. Brynne was only willing to take time to freshen up before they faced the early evening rush-hour traffic. They made the eight-mile trip into the city in Devin's vintage gray Jaguar. Her mind wasn't on the passing scenery, but on what she was going to say to Connor.

Rucker University was located in the Midtown area not far from Edward Jones Dome, the stadium where the Rams played football on the River Front. Rucker was a small, private college that catered to prominent and wealthy African Americans around the country. The college was very proud of its humble beginnings, having been founded at the turn of the century by the former slave, Andrew Rucker, who became a wealthy, self-made, St. Louis real estate tycoon.

Taking the investigator's advice that she would have a better chance of seeing Connor without interruption at his home rather than his office on campus, Brynne stared nervously out the window as Devin searched for the correct address in the upscale neighborhood only a few blocks away from the university. The Helms' home was large and stately, set back from the street.

According to the investigator's report, the Helms were newlyweds, having been married less than six months. Mrs. Helm, daughter of a wealthy businessman, was from Atlanta. She didn't work outside their home and spent much of her time doing charity work. Connor Helm had obtained his doctorate and had his eye on heading the psychology department and eventually the university.

When Devin slowed the car to a stop in a wide drive, it was impossible to tell if anyone was home, since no cars were parked in the drive, but Brynne was relieved to note that the lights were on. Devin reached across the console and placed his hand over hers.

"Your hands are like ice." He rubbed them between his warm brown palms. "Better?"

"Yes," she managed to get out, along with a weak smile. "I wish this was over."

He said quietly, "There is no law that says we have to do this tonight. What if he isn't at home?"

"Then we wait until he gets home." Her chin jutted. "I'm not leaving St. Louis, until I've done all I came to do."

He kissed her cheek. "It's going to be okay, babe. Ready?"

She nodded. While Devin got out of the car and walked around to open her door, Brynne realized that her body wasn't cooperating. Her hands and legs were shaking, yet she managed to unclasp the seat belt and swing her legs out of the car. She was grateful for the hand he offered to steady her once she was on her feet.

Keeping her hand clasped protectively in his, he whispered close to her ear, "Helm won't touch you, not ever again. I promise, I won't let him near you."

"I know," she whispered back. "I'm ready."

They walked up the red brick pathway to the wide front door of the white colonial-style home.

"Let me handle this," she said as he pressed the doorbell.

He nodded. "Don't worry. I have your back."

Brynne tried to offer a reassuring smile, but the sound of approaching footsteps silenced her. The heavy inside door swung inward.

"May I help you?" an attractive brown-skinned woman asked from behind the glass storm door.

"Is this the Helm residence?" Brynne asked.

"Yes. May I help you?"

"Is Connor at home? My name is Brynne Armstrong and this is my fiancé. I'm an old friend of his."

"Yes, we were just finishing supper. Won't you come in." She opened the storm door, taking a step backward to allow them entrance into the wide foyer. Her gaze moved from Brynne to Devin. She smiled, "I bet you hear this all the time, but you look like that football—"

Offering his hand, he smiled. "Yes, I'm Devin Prescott."

She shook it, then laughed. "Forgive my manners. I'm Angelina Helm, Connor's wife. Please follow me."

They walked into an elegantly appointed living room. "Won't you have a seat? I'll get my husband."

"Thank you," Brynne murmured as she watched Mrs. Helm retrace her steps into the foyer and then down the long central hallway.

Both Brynne and Devin chose to remain standing. She

longed to go to him, seeking his reassurance, but knew if she did she would end up begging him to get her out of there. Only the need to put the past behind her and move forward kept her from bolting.

She didn't want to see Connor ever, didn't want to think of how he'd gone on with his life while hers had nearly fallen apart. For so long, only her determination to survive and care for her daughter had kept her going.

The rumble of voices and hurried heavy footsteps on the hardwood floor caused Brynne to lift her chin and square her slim shoulders.

Twenty-nine

Connor stopped abruptly at the entrance to the living room. A look of disbelief and anger were on his long, angular face. Like Devin, he wore his black natural cut close. His honey brown coloring was lighter than Devin's, and a short beard covered the acne scars of his youth. While Devin's chest and shoulders were muscled, Connor's chest and shoulders were narrow, and he stood a good four inches shorter than Devin.

"Hello, Connor," Brynne said stiffly. "I believe you know my fiancé, Devin Prescott."

The two men eyed each other. Connor was the first to look away. He cleared his throat before he said, "Brynne. When Angie said you were here, I couldn't believe it."

When he reached out a hand toward her, Brynne sent him a warning glare. "We won't be here long. I have a few things to say to you."

"Won't you please sit down." Angelina smiled. "Can I offer you something to drink? Coffee? Tea?"

"Thank you, but this isn't a social call," Brynne said tightly.

"Darling, if you'll excuse us, I'll show them into my

study." Connor hastily added, "I won't be long. A university matter we need to discuss."

Brynne interrupted, "Mrs. Helm, you are more than welcome to join our discussion. I have nothing to hide."

Connor quickly interjected, "My study is the first door on the left."

Devin ushered Brynne ahead of him down the hallway into the room.

"You okay?" Devin said, close to her ear.

Bynne managed a nod, but was shaking so badly that she didn't protest when he guided her over to one of the wingback chairs in front of the desk. Devin stood next to Brynne, resting a hand on her shoulder.

Neither spoke when Connor entered the room and closed the door behind him. He went to the chair behind the desk. He looked from one to the other before he sat down.

"Why are you here?" Connor directed his question to Brynne, but he hadn't taken his eyes off Devin, who had moved to lean back against the door and crossed his arms over his chest.

Brynne's laughter held no humor. "I would think you'd know. Surely it hasn't been so long that you've forgotten a detail like rape?"

"Now, wait one damn minute! I never raped you!"

"That is exactly what you did." Brynne's voice shook with fury. "You talked your way into my apartment and took what you wanted. You ignored my protest, ignored the way I fought you."

"That's not how I remember it." Connor's mouth was taut with tension. He moved to rise, but stopped at the look on Devin's face.

"Stay where you are and keep your hands where I can see them," Devin cautioned.

"What is this?" Connor demanded. "Why are you here? You had no right to talk your way past my wife with lies that we're old friends."

"What part didn't you understand, Helm? I would like

nothing better than to break you in half," Devin said with a harsh frown.

"Look, I don't know what either of you want, but I assure you, I've done nothing wrong. Brynne and I had consensual sex. I didn't rape anyone. If you've told anyone that, then you'll be facing a lawsuit."

"Go ahead," Devin urged. "I'd like nothing better than to meet you in a court of law."

Brynne angled her chin upward when she said, "I made three serious mistakes the night you raped me. The first was when I let you into my apartment because I thought you were my friend. I had no reason to doubt you when you asked to see my notes. My second mistake was not going to the hospital and the police. I let you get away with raping me because I was scared and because of your connection to the university president. The last mistake I made was in not calling Devin and letting him take care of your sorry behind. For almost—"

"I've heard enough!" Connor ran a hand over his hair. "You have no—"

Devin cut him off. "Let her finish."

Connor glared and his mouth tightened, but he was silent.

"Like I was saying, for four years I tried to forget what you did to me, pretending it never happened. Not anymore. I'm not afraid anymore. I'm not ashamed because of what you did to me. I know I did nothing wrong. Unfortunately, you can't say the same."

A muscle jumped in his cheek, his jaw taut. "If you don't leave, I'm calling the police. I don't have to listen to this," he swore nastily.

"Call the police. And I will call the news," Devin cut in. "All I have to do is mention my name. Wonder who will get here first?"

Scowling, Connor snapped at Brynne, "I don't know what you think you can accomplish four years after the fact."

"It's not too late for a civil suit, Helm," Devin said quietly, his voice edged with steel. "Believe me when I say it would give me pleasure to bury you in legal fees. I assure you, it could take years to sort it all out once I set my attorneys on the case. Shall we see whose reputation will stand up to the scrutiny? What will your bride think? Does she know you're a rapist?"

The knock on the door caused all three pairs of eyes to swing toward it. Devin was closest and he opened it without hesitation.

Angelina came in carrying a tray. "Coffee is ready. I also brought along some of the lemon pound cake our housekeeper made last night. It's very good."

"Let me take that for you," Devin offered and carried it over to the small table between the two visitor chairs. Then he moved to stand beside Brynne.

"Shall I pour?" Angelina smiled as she seated herself in the other chair. Her eyes went wide when she glanced at her husband and noted his tight features. "What's wrong, darling? Please don't tell me this is university business. Something has upset you."

Connor quickly rose, forcing a smile. "We'll talk later, sweetheart. Let me handle this. There is no need for you to stay and upset yourself."

"If this concerns you, sugar, it concerns me. We have no secrets."

Brynne exchanged a look with Devin before she said, "If I were married to you, Connor, I wouldn't appreciate your nasty little secret."

"But you aren't married to me," he bit out furiously.

Devin asked, "How long can you keep this hidden, Helm?"

"How many others are there?" Brynne asked. "Until recently, I thought I was the only woman you raped, but I've learned I was wrong. There have been several complaints against you that your father and grandfather have managed to keep hidden. It pays to come from an influential family."

"Rape? Others?" Angelina gasped in horror.

"She doesn't know what she's talking about." Connor jumped to his feet, his hands balled at his sides.

"You're mistaken. My husband never raped anyone. He isn't that kind of man. He knows how I feel about rape. He knows my sister was raped." Angelina shook her head vehemently.

Brynne said quietly, "I'm sorry about your sister, Mrs. Helm. Unfortunately, he is that kind of man. Connor and I met four years ago, while in graduate school at Rucker. We were friends, or at least I thought we were, until he forced himself on me."

"Shut the hell up! Angelina, she's lying."

Devin glared at the other man. "Watch your mouth, Helm."

Brynne slipped her hand into his, in hopes of calming him. "Why would I lie, Connor? What could I possibly gain from it?"

Angelina's beautiful features were drawn as she looked from one to the other. "Go ahead, Ms. Armstrong. Say what you came to say, so I can call you a liar to your face."

Brynne looked calmly at Angelina and began to recount the horrible details of that night.

"She is lying, Angie. Yes, we had sex that night, but I didn't rape her."

Brynne hissed, "You held me down and threatened me to keep me quiet. I would never have had sex with you. I was in love with Devin, and you knew it. I was also terrified of you, and you wouldn't leave. It took a butcher knife to finally get you out of my apartment.

"I believed you when you said that no one would take my word over yours, because of your family connections. I was so ashamed that I didn't report it. The next day when I saw you on campus, you threatened me, again. You told me that I'd better not tell Devin or anyone else for that matter, since it was your word against mine. I knew I couldn't stay, so I packed my things and left town in the middle of the night, like a criminal. It's taken me four years to come here and finally tell you how disgusting I think you are. You had no right to touch me . . . none."

"Darling, you can't believe her. She just said she didn't report it!" Connor turned to his wife.

"What about the report of the investigator, the one that Brynne hired to find you?" Devin said. "There have been others, a number of them. Your family has managed to pay people off to protect you."

Angelina shook her head. "It can't be true. All lies!"

Brynne said, "You're welcome to look at the report. I have it with me."

Connor snarled. "Hell, no!"

Brynne reached into her bag and handed over the document. "You can have it. I have another copy."

Furious, Connor said, "Haven't you said and done enough? Get the hell out of my house!"

Devin said, "You keep forgetting, you aren't the victim here."

"It's all lies, Angie. You can't mean to read that."

"Why shouldn't she read it?" Brynne asked. "If you're innocent, like you claim, then you have nothing to worry about."

Connor roared, "Shut the hell up, bitch! You got exactly what you deserved!"

Both women gasped at the verbal attack. They watched in stunned silence as in the blink of the eye, Devin crossed the room and slammed his fist into the other man's jaw. Connor went down like a house of cards.

"Who do you think you're talking to? If you have no respect for my woman, at least have a little for your own," Devin snarled.

Wiping the blood from his mouth, Connor didn't get up. "Call the police, Angie. You saw what he did!"

"I also heard what you said! You practically admitted it!" she cried, her eyes brimming with tears.

Connor demanded, "What? You can't believe that I raped her!"

His wife was crying so hard, she couldn't answer him.

"Get up, Helm. Face me like a man." Devin urged, his hands still balled into fists.

As he reached down to pull Connor up by his lapels, Brynne shouted, "No, Devin! Please, he isn't worth it."

"He deserved that and more," Devin growled. "He doesn't understand the word no when it comes from a woman. I'd love to help him understand that word with my fists. I won't hurt him much."

"Enough!" Brynne hurried to place herself between the two men. With both hands on Devin's chest, she stared up at him. "You're not helping the situation. I've said what I came to say. Devin, I want to leave now."

He took a deep breath before he nodded. "Okay. Let's go."

"Prescott, I warn you. You haven't heard the end of this," Connor snapped as he picked himself off the floor.

Devin said through his clenched teeth, "I sincerely hope not. Any time, Helm."

Brynne sent Connor a hard glare. "If you know what's good for you, you won't press charges against Devin. Believe me, if you do go after Devin, I won't hesitate to file a civil suit against you. I'm sure that won't be too difficult to convince the ladies mentioned in that report to join me. Unlike you, I have nothing to lose. You are less than a man. A snake is a step up for you."

Brynne turned on her heels, pausing only long enough to grab her bag. She walked out with Devin a few steps behind her. She could hear Angelina Helm's hysterical screams and sobs in the background.

Devin continued to send Brynne concerned glances as he took Interstate 55 toward Highway 40. Her face was turned away as she stared out the window, her small hands clenched in her lap. It wasn't until after his security gates closed behind them and he followed the drive to the front of the house that he realized she had been silently weeping.

Easing to a stop, he released his seat belt and then hers

to pull her into his arms. "It's all right, baby. I got you." Soothingly, he gently rocked her. "I won't let him near you . . . not ever again."

She shook her head because the words seemed to fail her.

"I've got you," he repeated.

He had no idea how long they sat that way. The car was lit only by the light coming from the dashboard and the outside lamps lining the long private drive. When she quieted somewhat, he pulled a packet of tissues from the glove compartment and mopped her damp cheeks.

"Blow," he instructed. After she complied, he asked, "Better?"

"Yes," she murmured. To his surprise, she started a fresh round of tears.

"Babe . . ."

She placed her hand over his lips, shaking her head. Eventually she looked up at him through spiky lashes, even managed a wobbly smile. "You don't understand. I'm fine. Finally, I am fine."

Not convinced, Devin said gruffly, "Brynne, you don't have to pretend for my sake. I can only imagine how difficult that confrontation was with Helm."

"I'm not pretending, my heart." She reached up and encircled his brown neck. "Don't you see? It's over. All of it. And I'm so happy."

Devin was not buying it. He started to shake his head, then stopped as he watched tears sparkle on her dark lashes. He kissed her brow. "Come on. Let's go inside."

Grabbing the keys, he came around to open her door, holding a hand out to her. With his arm around her waist, he guided her to the front door. Once they were inside he urged her down the spacious entry hall past the elegantly appointed formal living and dining rooms to the smaller, comfortable den. Switching on the lamps, he sat with her on the deep-cushioned leather sofa.

He motioned to the array of crystal decanters on a side table. "What do you need? Something to drink?"

Brynne shook her head. "Is your housekeeper here?

"No, Mrs. Kennedy comes in a couple times a week to check the place, clean, and keep the refrigerator stocked with the basics."

"Good. I want you all to myself." Caressing his dark brown cheek, Brynne surprised him by pressing one sweet kiss after another on his wide mouth. When she sponged his bottom lip with her velvety soft tongue, Devin automatically opened for her, moaning deeply, welcoming her sweet foray.

"Baby . . ." he eventually got out. Even though food was the last thing on his mind, he asked, "Aren't you hungry? We can go out if you like."

"Not hungry for food," she murmured as she deepened the kiss suckling his bottom lip. "Make love to me, Devin." Her small hands pushed off his leather jacket and then went to the base of his throat and began opening the buttons lining his shirt.

"What are you doing?"

"You know exactly what I'm doing." She licked the side of his throat as she moved her hands beneath his shirt to worry a flat nipple.

With his heart racing, breath quickening, he pulled away from her soft lips insisting, "We should talk about—"

"Why?" Brynne smiled at him an instant before she rose up on her knees so she could lave his earlobe, and then she took it into her mouth to suck.

Devin released a harsh groan as his body pulsed with desire and his shaft thickened, rising to the occasion, despite his struggle for control.

"Just because I was crying a few minutes ago doesn't mean I don't know what I want. It might not make any sense to you, but it makes perfect sense to me."

Thirty

≡

The heated strokes of Brynne's hot tongue on Devin's bare chest was driving him wild. When she licked a flat nipple, he nearly forgot his own name or why he felt the need to resist. Even though he was so hard he hurt, he had to make sure she was all right. He grasped her shoulders to hold her away from him.

"I need to understand what's going on with you, babe. Talk to me."

"Don't you know that nothing matters right this moment but you and me?" She struggled to pull his jacket and shirt from his wrists while he held her.

Studying her dark eyes, he tried to understand what he saw in their velvety brown depths. Even though he loved her with his whole heart, he wasn't about to let his sexual hunger cloud his judgment.

"Babe, why are you fighting me?"

"Is that what you think I'm doing?" he asked as he leaned back against the sofa, bracing his hands on his thighs.

"Yes! Now stop it!"

As Devin pulled off both his jacket and his shirt, his

eyes caressed her petite frame. Brynne slid forward until she locked her arms around his neck, placing kisses on his face, then lingering on his full lips. Devin smiled as he returned her sweet kisses. At first their lips merely touched playfully but soon began to cling, their kisses becoming deep and sensuous.

They were both breathless when she moved a caressing hand over his nipple. She worried each sensitive flat tip until they hardened, and he moaned huskily. Then she laved the small ebony disc until he shuddered, calling out her name. The sweetness of her wet caresses was driving him wild while shivers of desire raced along his nerve endings. He stopped breathing altogether when she moved lower to lick his concave, hard-muscled stomach.

She whispered, "Do you want me as much as I want you?"

"Do you doubt it?" he whispered back, trembling in response as his erection pulsed, hardening even more.

When he reached for her, she pushed his hands down to his sides and held them until he nodded his understanding, letting her take control of their lovemaking. He closed heavy lids, determined to ignore the demands of his body to finish what she started.

As time passed and she returned to her old self, his male instincts to take over surged. Rather than getting easier, it was harder than ever for him to yield to her needs and allow himself to simply relax and enjoy.

He didn't realize he was holding his breath until she was unsnapping his jeans and easing the zipper down over the prominent ridge of his aching sex. Her soft hands were nearly his undoing as she slid beneath the waistband of his briefs to rub the ultra sensitive head of his penis. He couldn't suppress a heavy groan at the sheer pleasure of her caress. It had been so long since she touched him intimately. He'd had no idea how badly he yearned for her soft touch until now.

When she moved over the length of his thick shaft, Devin closed his eyes, struggling to hang on to even a small measure of control. A husky groan rose from deep in his chest as he quivered.

Stopping, she said anxiously, "I'm doing this badly, aren't I?"

His voice thick with desire, he said, "There is no wrong way." He pushed his fingers into her soft curls, gently urging her mouth up to meet his. "It's not possible for me to want you more."

He took fierce, hungry kisses, and eventually his lips traveled down her neck, lingering at the place behind her ear. He took her earlobe into his mouth to suckle repeatedly. Then he dropped his head to the scented place between her breasts to lick her there, while quickly freeing her of her suit jacket and blouse. Then he unhooked the front clasp of her lacy bra.

Brynne gasped as he kissed and then laved a plump breast. Devin ignored his own driving need to bury himself inside her. He concentrated on giving her the utmost pleasure. He smiled when he heard her soft sigh, only then did he finally moved his attention to her other breast. He tongued the top swell to his satisfaction before he did the same to the lush under curve.

"Oh, Devin . . . please," Brynne begged.

"Tell me what you need," he urged as he inhaled her feminine scent. She smelled like flowers and woman . . . his woman.

She rubbed the aching peak of her breast against the seam of his mouth. "Take me into your mouth."

Devin, as eager as she was for the hot wash of his tongue over each hard nipple, took her into his mouth and applied an intense suction that soon had her whimpering with pleasure.

She felt so good, so right. He increased the suction even more. By the time he treated her other breast to the same sensuous attention, Brynne cried out, arching her back while squeezing her thighs together.

"Harder," she moaned, and then shivered with enjoyment when he accommodated her.

"Baby, do you want me . . . as much as I want you?" he whispered as he slid a hand beneath the hem of her long navy skirt to cup and then squeeze her lush behind. Impatient with the barrier of her clothing, Devin swiftly finished undressing her.

His breathing quickened even more when he caressed the satiny skin of her inner thighs. He felt her tremors in response. Moving his fingers through the soft cottony curls, he teased her wet folds before he parted them, to trace her soft opening, yet not going inside.

"Please . . ." she whimpered.

Entranced by her slick heat and the need in her voice, he whispered, "I intend to please you, baby. I want you wet, ready for me."

"I-I'm r-ready," she barely managed to get out.

"Mmm," he murmured as he returned to sucking her nipple while he fingered her soft entrance, teasing her before he began to slide a finger deep inside her tight sheath. He moved to caress her clitoris until she reached a quick, deliciously sweet climax.

He held her until she quieted, then rose to his feet and began removing his few remaining clothes. His gaze was on hers as he stood in the nude in front of her. He was pleased that she didn't divert her gaze from his jutting shaft.

Devin reached down and pulled her up against him. Smoothing his hands over the curve of her shoulders, down the slope of her back, he paused to caress her plump bottom, then squeezed her softness. He went on to caress her shapely thighs and calves. Dropping down to the carpet, Devin pressed his face against her stomach while he encircled her waist, supporting her trembling limbs.

Turning Brynne around until he could place tender kisses at the base of her spine, Devin kissed his way over her lush hips and down the backs of her legs. She was moaning his name when he parted her legs and kissed the soft skin of her inner thighs.

"Enough . . ."

"Your skin is like silk," he said throatily as he caught her against him when her knees gave out.

She was panting when he laid her on the thick carpet. She surprised him when she used her oh-so-soft hands to caress his firm-muscled thighs. She said, "No more teasing. I ache to have you deep inside."

Close to losing control, he had to know, "Are you sure? I'll try to understand after—" He stopped, not wanting any painful reminders.

"Yes . . . hurry."

He grabbed his jeans from the floor to search in the back pocket for a foil packet.

"Let me."

Pushing back his own doubts, he placed the condom in her palm. He groaned huskily as she smoothed it along his throbbing erection. He ached to be deep inside her, surrounded by her tight sheath.

"Now . . ." she urged as she parted her thighs for him.

His pulse raced as he relished her feminine beauty. Covering her body with his, his hands unsteady as he eased into her incredible heat, he knew he was too far gone for more intimate play . . . too damn needy. He paused, hoping to give her time to adjust to his size while giving himself time to gain some measure of control over his senses.

Brynne whispered, "All of you . . . I want every hard inch."

Devin closed his eyes. She was so wet, so unbelievably hot. He moaned as he lifted her legs to encircle his waist while he pressed forward, not stopping until he was lodged deep inside her tight sheath.

"Better?" he managed to ask.

"Oh yes," she whispered as she wrapped her arms around him, kissing his throat.

It took all his control to remain still and savor her sweetness. When she tightened her inner muscles, giving him the most exquisite caress along his throbbing shaft, he growled huskily. All too soon Devin pulled back, only to thrust forward again and again. He quickly established a mesmerizing rhythm that had Brynne clinging to him. As she rubbed her breasts into his chest, her womanly scent, combined with her sizzling heat, prove to be his undoing. He was close, so close to completion, but he needed her with him.

His voice was gruff with desire when he said close to her ear, "Come with me, babe."

Brynne shivered when Devin dropped his head to take her hard, aching nipple into the heat of his mouth. It was sweet but not enough to send her over the edge. He moved long fingers between their bodies to tantalize her even more by caressing her clitoris as he quickened his strokes.

Her entire body stiffened an instant before she screamed as she reached a heart-wrenching climax, her sweet body sent his into a mind-blowing release. They hung on to each other until the convulsions eased and their heart rates returned to normal.

Lifting himself, Devin rolled onto his back while holding Brynne at his side. "Are you all right? Did I scare you?"

She didn't say anything but lay with her eyes closed. Her pale brown cheeks were flushed, her lips were swollen from his kisses. She moved a soothing hand over his concave stomach, up his hair-roughened chest. Her eyes sparkled with tears.

She said, "I've never been better."

"Then why are you crying?" He didn't even try to hide his fear of her having some kind of setback. "You've worked so hard to find your way back, and you've been through so much. I'd hate if I—"

"Shush." She wiped her damp cheeks impatiently, pressing a kiss at the base of his throat. "I'm crying because I've never been happier. You didn't scare me, dear heart. How could you, when I know you would never do anything to hurt me? I know you love me. And nothing can change that."

Devin sighed heavily, allowing the fear to fade. He kissed her; the caress, although tender, was filled with his unshakable love.

"I'm glad . . . so glad we found each other again. I'm ashamed that because of my stupid pride, I let you go once. It won't ever happen again."

"I know, but you're wrong. You didn't let me go. I was the coward. I was the one who ran away from your love. All I thought about was me. Babe, I'm sorry I hurt you by not trusting you with the truth." She assured him, "It's a mistake I don't ever plan repeating. I'm yours for the duration. You're stuck with me and our little girl, Prescott."

He chuckled, stroking her soft curls. "Babe, how come you aren't ticked at me for punching Helm? You wanted me to keep my hands off him." Somberly, he said, "I tried, babe. I really did, but when he said what he did about you I lost it. The bastard deserved that punch and a lot worse for what he put you through."

Soothing him with a gentle caress to his hair-roughened cheek, she said, "I'm not angry. In fact, I'm glad you hit him. He had it coming." Pausing, she said, "I just didn't want you to get into trouble. I meant what I said to him. I will file a civil suit against him before I let him hurt you. His sterling reputation won't be worth two cents when I'm finished with his sorry behind."

Devin moved a large caressing hand down her spine. "That coward isn't going to the police. He has enough trouble on his hands dealing with his wife. Did you see the hurt on her face?"

"Yes, and I felt bad for her, because she clearly loves him. Do you think she believed me?"

"I don't know, but we certainly put some serious doubts in her mind. She doesn't seem like the type to quietly sit back and let a sexual predator control her life. His only hope is if he loves her enough to get help. His family can't protect him forever."

"I don't care what happens to him. I did what I needed to do for me. He no longer has any hold over me." Brynne looked into Devin's dark gray eyes when she asked, "You believe me, don't you, my heart?"

"Without a doubt."

They shared a long, tender kiss.

Devin said firmly, "If you decide you want to file a civil suit against him, I'm behind you all the way."

Brynne shook her head. "It's too late for that now, not unless the other women need my testimony. I'm not looking backward. I'm moving forward." She laughed when she heard his stomach growl. "I'd better feed you."

Devin grinned. "I've got all I need, right here in my arms."

"Me too." She sighed softly. "I promise to feed you in a moment, but first I need to ask you something."

"Anything," he said as he traced her plump bottom lip.

"I know I've made mistakes in the past, but never for a single second did I stop loving you."

He brushed her lips with his. "I know, babe."

"When I said I didn't want to get married, I meant not until I'd faced Connor. I had to be absolutely sure the past was behind me. That comment had nothing to do with how I feel about you. I love you, Devin Prescott, with all my heart. And I'd like nothing more than to be your wife."

"Brynne, I—"

She pressed her fingertips to his lips. "Let me finish. Devin, will you marry me as soon as possible? We can fly to Las Vegas and be husband and wife before dawn."

His voice was deep, filled with tenderness as he whispered her name. He covered her mouth with his. The kiss was filled with love and the unmistakable promise of a bright shared future.

"You have nothing to prove to me, Brynne Armstrong. I

know you love me. And I can't wait for you to wear my wedding band. But as much as I love you, I also value my hide." He laughed. "I know two ladies who wouldn't hesitate to go after me if we didn't have that big church wedding with all the family present—our little flower girl and your future mother-in-law."

Brynne joined in his laughter. "You've made your point. Shanna would never forgive us if she didn't get to wear her fancy dress and throw rose petals."

She placed a series of kisses on his jaw until he dropped his chin. Then she teased the corner of his mouth with her tongue. He moaned deep in his throat.

He lifted a brow. "Don't start something you can't finish."

"Oh, I can finish it," she bragged.

He chuckled, gathering her close. "Good."